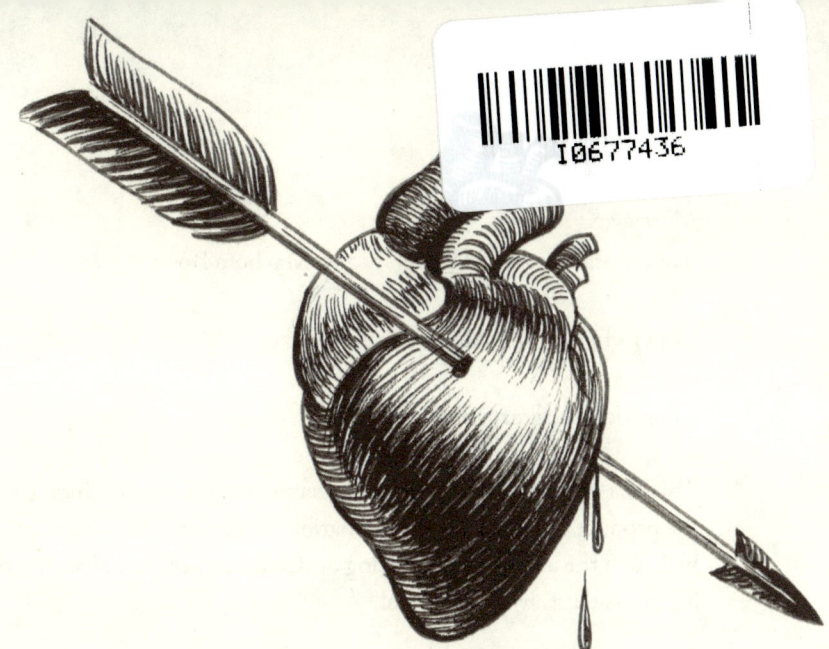

# MARRIAGE *is* MURDER

## SAWYER AND ROYCE:
## MATRIMONY AND MAYHEM
### BOOK 2

# AIMEE NICOLE WALKER

*Marriage is Murder*
Sawyer and Royce: Matrimony and Mayhem Book 2

Copyright © 2022 Aimee Nicole Walker

aimeenicolewalker@blogspot.com

Cover photo © Wander Aguiar—www.wanderaguiar.com

Cover design © Jay Aheer—www.simplydefinedart.com

Interior design and formatting provided by Stacey Ryan Blake of Champagne Book Design—www.champagnebookdesign.com

Editing provided by Susie Selva—www.susieselva.com

Proofreading provided by Lori Parks—lp.nerdproblems@gmail.com

"Then shall you know the wounds invisible that love's
keen arrows make."
—William Shakespeare, *As You Like It*

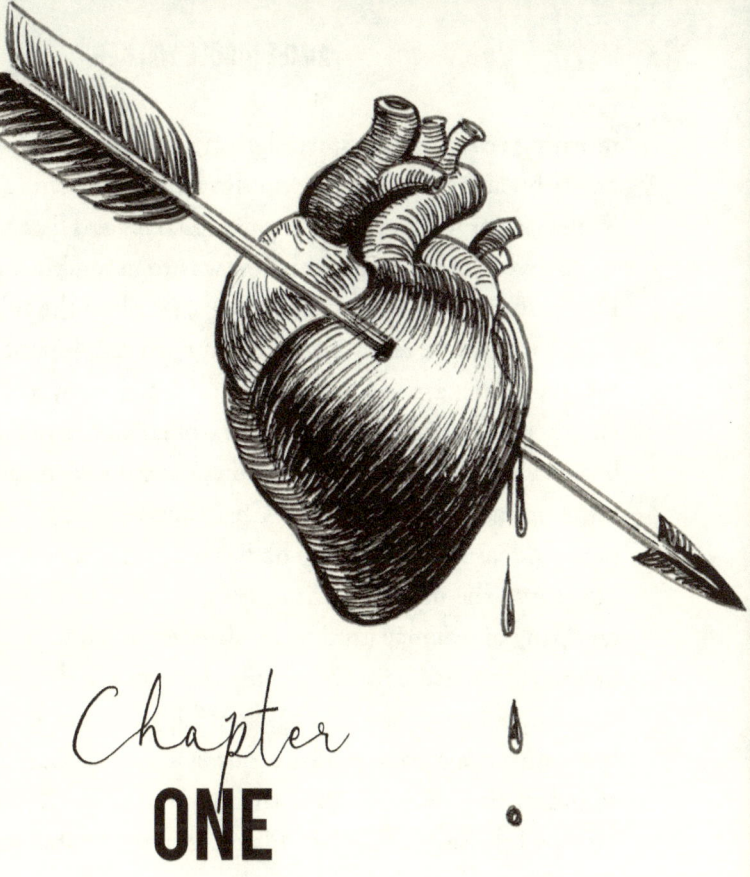

# Chapter
## ONE

"I HATE TO INTERRUPT A MASTER AT WORK…" SAWYER SAID hesitantly.

Royce responded with a grunt. "Almost there. Just trying to fit it in the hole. It requires finesse, not brute strength, you know." Another grunt echoed from behind the dryer and a savage curse quickly followed.

Sawyer bit back a chuckle as he stared down at the superb, jean-clad ass sticking up in the air. Royce had somehow managed to wedge himself under the laundry room sink to reach the back of the dryer. "You don't say," Sawyer remarked casually.

He glanced over at Bones, who sat on top of the washing machine looking mighty pissed Royce had moved his litter box from its usual spot to reattach the dryer hose to the exterior vent. The metal ring securing it had broken at some point, which Royce had discovered when he'd attempted to clean the vent with the new shop vac he'd purchased that morning on his weekly hardware store run. They had a Saturday morning routine that started with rambunctious sex, followed by a hearty breakfast, and ended with Royce finding some excuse to visit Sal's while Sawyer worked on newspaper puzzles and listened to audiobooks.

Royce's most recent mission was to assemble a tool kit for when Dru and the boys moved into their new place the following weekend. He'd come home from Sal's flushed with excitement because he'd put together a kickass toolbox *and* found a high-powered shop vac to rival all others. Royce enthusiastically extolled all the vacuum's features and boasted it had the strongest suction power on the market. He'd unboxed the shop vac like a little kid on Christmas morning. Sawyer had found it quite endearing until Royce had gazed at the chrome and red machine like it was the most beautiful thing in the world. He'd felt a momentary pang of jealousy until he recalled where he'd been in his audiobook before Royce had come bounding through the door with his new toy.

Royce had kissed him passionately before wheeling the assembled beast into the garage to test it out. Moments later, the loud whirring sound of the machine came through the door. Bones had darted for safety while Sawyer pushed Play to resume his book and returned his attention to his crossword puzzle.

Sawyer smiled when he'd read the next clue. *The absence of matter.* "Six letters. Gee, I wonder what it could be." He filled in the boxes with vacuum and moved on to the next clue.

"When was the last time you cleaned out the dryer vent?" Royce had asked Sawyer after he'd cleaned both vehicles.

Sawyer rolled his eyes toward the ceiling as if he were thinking hard about the answer.

Royce had laughed, seeing through Sawyer's antics, and said, "Doesn't matter. I'll take care of it now."

"We're supposed to meet my mom for lunch at the Hummingbird Café in an hour," Sawyer had reminded him.

"No problem."

Famous last words.

Noting the time constraint, Sawyer decided to assist Royce with the project, even though he could think of more exciting ways to burn off excess energy. Royce's mission started smoothly enough. He'd removed the exterior vent cover, the wire mesh guard, and stuck his vacuum hose inside the hole.

"Lint build-up is a huge fire hazard," Royce had said. But to his dismay, Sawyer's negligence hadn't resulted in their near death. His efforts didn't garner nearly enough lint to satisfy him, so they'd moved the project into the laundry room where Royce had discovered the vent hose had come loose. Dryer lint coated the wall behind the machine. "Whew, that was a close call," Royce said. "There's no telling how long it's been like this."

Forty minutes later, after much grunting and swearing, Royce was no closer to being ready for lunch.

"Aha! Nailed it."

"I'll call a press conference," Sawyer said dryly.

Warm laughter filled the small room. "Someone sounds a little jealous of my new toy."

Sawyer snorted. "Don't be ridiculous."

"Your mouth will always be my favorite thing that sucks," Royce said, then reached behind him. "Hand me the zip tie, please."

Sawyer gave him the plastic strip and continued staring at Royce's ass while he worked.

"There," Royce said a few seconds later. "That will hold until I can buy a new ring." When he stood up, the front of his shirt was covered in dust and dryer lint. "Pretty sure I've found the only place in this entire house you haven't cleaned within an inch of its life."

Sawyer hooked his finger in Royce's belt loop and pulled him close. "I'll correct the oversight going forward. Thanks for saving my life."

"I'll collect my reward when we get back," Royce said, pecking a quick kiss on Sawyer's lips.

Sawyer didn't go anywhere near the bedroom while Royce got ready so they wouldn't end up late. No one kept Evangeline O'Neal waiting.

"Is the Hummingbird Café that new restaurant that opened around Valentine's Day?" Royce asked once they were in the SUV and backing down the driveway.

"That was the weekend of the soft launch for friends, family, and investors to sample the menu and celebrate before the public grand opening," Sawyer said. "My mom and dad fall into the latter category and can't stop singing the café's praises."

They arrived at the restaurant with a few minutes to spare, but Sawyer spotted his mom's car in the lot already. The exterior of the building was red brick and glass with a classic black sign above the doorway. The big picture windows overlooking the sidewalk had a colorful garden etched in the glass. Flowers, butterflies, and hummingbirds adorned the bottom of the frame, trellises with blooming vines took up the sides, and a canopy of blossoms cascaded over the top.

Once inside, Sawyer scanned the crowded café but didn't see Evangeline. Perhaps they had additional seating elsewhere. A Black woman with short, curly hair, amber eyes, and an engaging smile stepped up to the hostess station. She wore a pink polo shirt with the café's logo and the name Rita embroidered on the front, dark jeans, and floral Chucks.

"Welcome to the Hummingbird Café," she said cheerfully. "Will it just be the two of you?"

"No, we're meeting my mother," Sawyer said, "but I don't see her."

"Evangeline?" Rita asked.

Sawyer smiled. "The one and only."

"We set her up in the garden out back. Follow me."

Sawyer admired the farmhouse-chic décor as they walked through the café. The aromas emanating from the kitchen made his stomach growl. He glanced over at Royce and caught him sniffing the air appreciatively.

"Is this your first visit with us?" Rita asked.

"It is," Royce replied, "but it won't be the last if the food tastes half as good as it smells."

Rita looked over her shoulder and said, "I promise the food tastes even better." She pushed open the door to the garden area before Royce could respond to her bold claim, and all their attention diverted to the splendor around them.

"Whoa," Sawyer whispered as he took in the setting.

The owners had divided the space into dozens of seating sections, each one surrounded by its own private garden to give it an air of intimacy. A red brick path wound throughout the minigardens, and a black wrought iron fence separated the eating area from a lush garden with dozens of hummingbird feeders hanging from the trees. Butterflies flitted around from flower to bush as a gentle breeze rustled the branches overhead.

"This is beautiful," Royce said. "Like stunning."

"Thank you," Rita said. "My husband, Ryan, is the master chef, but I'm the visionary when it comes to the design. We each know our strengths and work hard to stay out of the other's lane."

Rita stopped at a table in the far corner. Evangeline rose and greeted Sawyer and Royce with a hug and a kiss. She wore a pale pink sheath dress and nude heels that put her at nearly the same height as Royce and Sawyer. Evangeline's dark hair tumbled around her face in soft, romantic waves. She wore minimal makeup and a sheer lip tint, allowing her natural beauty to shine through. Evangeline formally introduced Rita to them and Sawyer never tired of hearing Royce referred to has his fiancé.

"It's lovely to meet you both," Rita said. "Matteo will be your server today, and he'll be right with you."

"Isn't this place something?" Evangeline asked. "It's all anyone is talking about right now."

"It's absolutely stunning," Royce said. "It's kind of how I envisioned our pool area, but I didn't get anywhere close to this kind of magic."

Evangeline looked up from her menu and patted his hand. "Don't sell yourself short, dear. You created an incredible oasis."

Leaning into Royce, Sawyer said, "It's my favorite part of our house."

"Yeah?" Royce asked.

"Definitely."

Sawyer gave the menu his full attention and was impressed by the variety of food offered. The café served traditional Southern classics one would expect to find in Georgia as well as fare from other regions, specifically New Orleans. "I can't remember the last time I had black-eyed peas and dirty rice," Sawyer said. "I can't decide if I want baby back ribs or fried chicken."

Royce looked over at him. "Not a salad today, huh?"

"Maybe as a starter."

5

Matteo arrived at the table with a basket of homemade biscuits and honey butter. He took their drink orders and left them alone to decide on food.

"I say we get a variety of things to share," Evangeline said. "I think the Hummingbird Café would be a wonderful choice to cater your wedding reception."

Royce glanced up from his menu and smiled. "She's wearing her wedding planner hat today."

When their engagement became official, Evangeline volunteered to plan and organize their special day. Neither of them had seen a reason why they should refuse. Jace and Holly had experienced nothing but trouble with the wedding planners they'd hired, and neither Royce nor Sawyer had the free time to do it themselves. Royce was still investigating homicides until his Explorer program was up and running. Sawyer split his duties between investigating cold cases and working with the *Sinister in Savannah* podcast team on an initiative to locate Savannah's missing people. The podcast's success and worldwide popularity was an investigative tool Sawyer couldn't pass up. Felix, Jonah, and Rocky had pitched the concept to him, and Mendoza had jumped all over the opportunity.

Evangeline planted her elbow on the table, leaned forward, and rested her chin in the palm of her hand. "You know, it would be nice if you would pick a wedding date so I can get going in earnest."

"Mom, we don't want to pull focus from Jace and Holly's wedding," Sawyer said. "They're getting married in two weeks. Why don't we wait until after their special day before we start planning ours?"

"He's getting cold feet," Royce said.

Neither Evangeline nor Sawyer acknowledged the ridiculous remark.

"I understand you don't want to tread all over Jace and Holly's wedding," Evangeline said. "And I agree. I hadn't planned on taking out an announcement in the paper or anything. I'm talking discreet inquiries on available venues. Two weeks might not seem like a lot of time to wait, but I assure you most venues have been booked for a solid year. This one," Evangeline said, patting Royce's hand, "said he wants to be married and honeymooned before the Explorer program officially kicks off in September. That gives me May through mid-August."

Sawyer and Royce exchanged a glance. "Okay," they said.

Evangeline clapped and pulled a notebook and pen from her handbag. "We're getting somewhere."

She launched into the different types of venues and the pros and cons of each. She probably would've talked for hours if Sawyer hadn't reached across the table and covered her hand.

"We don't want anything too formal," Sawyer said.

"Speak for yourself. I want a celebration to end all others to mark our special day," Royce said. He broke apart a biscuit and slathered honey butter on both pieces. Royce handed half to Sawyer before taking a bite of the other. Royce made appreciative noises as he chewed. "These are almost as good as Evangeline's."

She scoffed and waved him off. "I know damn well they're better than mine. No need to worry about my feelings."

Sawyer ignored his biscuit too long, so Royce snatched it and devoured it too. Sawyer reached over and wiped crumbs from the corner of his mouth. "Animal." His remark only received a shrug. Sawyer returned his attention to Evangeline, who seemed to be glowing exceptionally bright. He knew it was time to establish some ground rules for the wedding. "We want an intimate gathering with our family and closest friends."

"I think a ticker-tape parade would be nice," Royce said. "A marching band, perhaps."

Sawyer splayed his hand over Royce's face like a starfish and ignored his suggestions. "No churches. No riverboats. And nothing gimmicky."

Royce licked Sawyer's palm, and he snatched his hand back. "Don't listen to him. A horse-drawn carriage sounds pretty."

Sawyer laughed. "Okay, Cinderfella."

"Do you think they'd let me guide the horses?" Royce asked.

"No," Sawyer replied.

Evangeline bounced her gaze between them, smiling the entire time. "So, we want something informally formal, intimate yet grand, but not in a church or on a riverboat. You'd like a parade featuring the grooms in a horse-drawn carriage. Did I get it all?"

"Marching band," Royce said before he chomped into another buttered biscuit. Sawyer marveled at how Royce could eat whatever he wanted and never seemed to gain any weight, while Sawyer had to eat moderately and constantly exercise to maintain his physique.

Evangeline giggled and made another note.

Sawyer glanced up and saw a brawny lumberjack disguised as a chef making his way toward them. "Rita told me our biggest fan was dining with us today," the man said when he stopped at their table.

"And I brought my newest fan club recruits with me," Evangeline said, then introduced Sawyer and Royce to Ryan.

"You have a lovely restaurant," Royce said.

Ryan beamed with pride as he looked around. "Thank you. This part was my wife's vision."

"You should see it at night," Evangeline said. "There are hundreds of fairy lights tucked into the trees. It's like something out of a movie. Oh!" She fumbled in her purse and removed her cell phone. "I took pictures. I'm sure they won't do the real thing justice, but it will give you an idea. And the smell from the jasmine this summer will be phenomenal."

Evangeline showed them a picture of Sawyer's parents taken in the café garden, and the fairy lights did cast a warm, romantic glow. He thought the happiness radiating from his parents was even more beautiful than the twinkling lights.

Sawyer smiled and looked up at Ryan. "It's incredibly romantic."

"Ryan," Evangeline said. "Have you considered renting the outdoor space for special events? Say wedding receptions?"

"We've been talking about it but didn't want to bite off more than we can chew," Ryan replied.

Evangeline patted him on the shoulder. "I know two guinea pigs you could experiment on."

"Guinea pigs, Mom?" Sawyer asked in disbelief.

"Poor phrasing," she agreed. "I am adamantly opposed to testing anything on animals."

Sawyer leaned into Royce. "But your son and future son-in-law are fair game?"

Ryan chuckled. "When's the big day?"

"We're still hammering out that little detail," Evangeline replied. "I'm hoping to have a firm date soon."

"Tell you what," Ryan said, "let me know what you decide, and the garden is all yours. I'd be honored to host your reception here."

Matteo smiled as he approached, then looked at Ryan. "Chef, Oren needs you in the kitchen."

"Oren is my sous chef," Ryan replied. "I better get back in there. It was good to meet you both. I hope you enjoy your meals."

Once Ryan left, Matteo took their orders. They selected a wide variety of dishes, and Evangeline planned to mark down the ones they wanted to include for their reception meal. Before the plates came out, Royce's phone rang.

"No, no, no," he said when he saw the caller ID. He stood up and walked a few feet away.

Sawyer kept his eyes on Royce, noting the disappointment and resignation washing over his face as he listened to the call. Evangeline said something, but Sawyer didn't register her words. The call was brief, probably just long enough to give Royce an address and possibly a short description of what he was walking into but not much else.

Royce promptly returned to the table but didn't reclaim his seat. He leaned over and brushed a kiss on Evangeline's cheek. "Please forgive me," he said.

She patted his face. "There's nothing to forgive, honey. Be careful."

Royce nodded and walked around the table to cup Sawyer's face. "I'm damn sorry. Just a few more months, then these homicides will be someone else's problem." Royce leaned down and pressed a kiss to Sawyer's lips, lingering for several heartbeats. "I love you."

"I love you most."

Sawyer watched him walk away, hating the tension in Royce's frame.

"I read an article claiming we're on pace to have a record number of homicides this year," Evangeline said. "It's so sad."

"Tragic," Sawyer agreed.

"And the string of armed robberies plaguing the city is terrifying," his mom added. "They just brazenly stroll into small businesses in broad daylight while wearing masks and brandishing guns and walk right back out with all the cash in the store. Why haven't they been caught?"

It was the same question everyone had been asking—the citizens, the press, and especially the mayor who was up for reelection. Mendoza was under merciless scrutiny from the mayor and commissioner, which he rained down on Royce because he supervised the officers investigating the burglaries. The tension inside the precinct and around the city was swelling toward an ugly crescendo with every new robbery and each day that passed without an arrest. Sawyer's biggest concern was citizens taking the matter into their own hands. Up to that point, the gunmen had been solely focused on retrieving the cash from the safes and getting back out. No shots had been fired, and no one had been harmed. Sawyer had a bad feeling their luck wouldn't hold much longer.

"They choose smart locations," Sawyer said. "Easy access in and out. Places that do a lot of cash business but won't spend any of it toward the most basic security measures. It's not the same two guys each time based on witness descriptions of height and weight. We think there's between four to six people in the crew. Maybe more. They hide their faces beneath Spiderman or Deadpool masks to cover their eyes and mouths. They cover every inch of skin with black clothes, so witnesses can't see identifying details like tattoos or birth marks. They always wear gloves and don't leave behind forensic evidence we can use. Their voices are calm and modulated and never give anything away."

Evangeline shivered and rubbed her bare arms. "Sounds like the perfect crime."

"We'll catch them," Sawyer said. "I just hope innocent people don't get caught in the crosshairs before we do."

His mom trembled again. "Time to change the subject. How are things going with your new *Sinister in Savannah* partnership?"

Sawyer and the *Sinister* team recorded an episode twice a month featuring a missing Savannah native. They conducted interviews with the families and posted them to a dedicated website along with pictures and details of each case. They even set up a hotline to collect tips. The podcast's popularity had brought about a partnership with GeneMatch, the genealogy database used to catch a notorious serial killer who'd terrorized the West Coast for decades. They also worked closely with NamUs, the National Missing and Unidentified Persons System. Jonah and Avery, his boyfriend, developed software to generate age-enhanced photos of the missing people that exceeded the capabilities of all other tools available. *Sinister in Savannah* had also established a YouTube channel to reach a whole new demographic, and they'd received millions of views during the first month of their channel.

"We're still figuring things out along the way," Sawyer said, "but overall, I think it's going well. We haven't solved any of our cases yet, but it's just a matter of time."

"I'm proud of you, Sawyer."

"Thanks, Mom. That means a lot to me."

Sawyer glanced over and saw Matteo and Rita heading toward them with loaded trays. He explained Royce had been called into work, and Rita assured him they'd box up the leftovers so he could enjoy them later.

Sawyer and Evangeline devoured the delicious food, even if Royce's departure had sucked the joy out of their day the way Royce's new shop vac had pulled the lint from the dryer vent. Sawyer thought of Royce's giddy joy over his new toy and couldn't help but smile.

"Well," Evangeline said sometime later. "Everything was exquisite. How could we possibly narrow down the dishes to a few? People don't RSVP anymore. We'll go into the event not knowing who is coming or if they have allergies."

"I say we go buffet style with enough food to feed an army," Sawyer said. "We can always donate what we don't use."

"Deal." She jotted down a few notes, then turned to a clean page. "Now that we've gotten the wedding stuff started, I want to pivot to something that's been occupying my thoughts lately."

"Okay." Sawyer was sure he knew where the conversation was headed. His answer, however, was less certain.

Evangeline leaned forward and held his gaze. "Are you going to run for sheriff?"

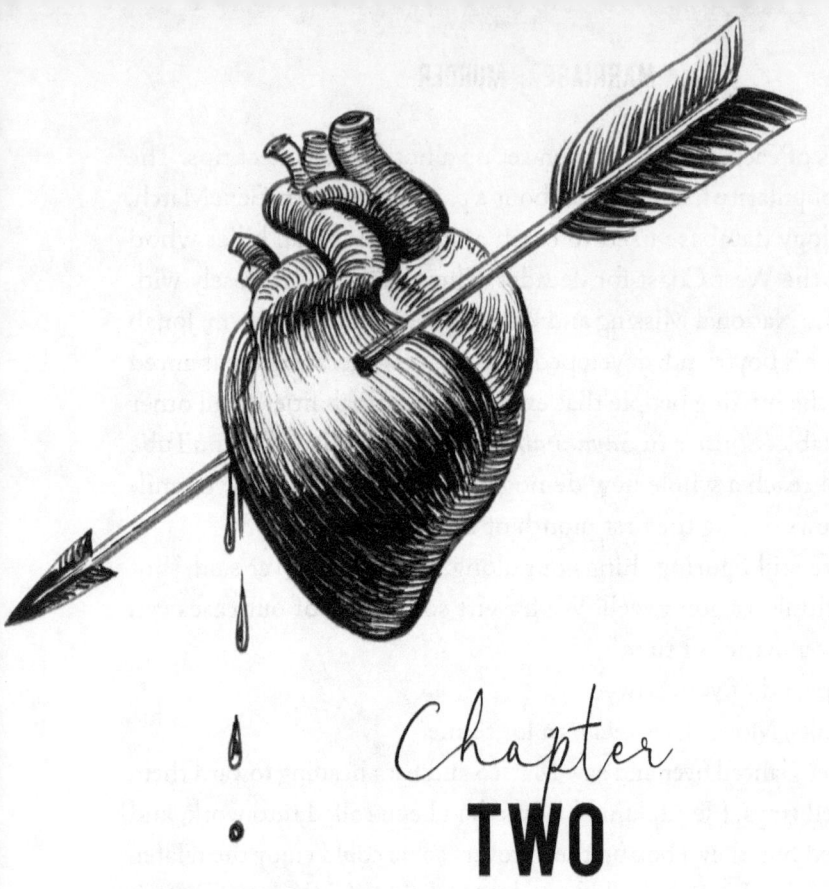

# Chapter
# TWO

**W**HEN ROYCE HAD PULLED UP TO THE PIRATE'S HOUSE restaurant, he figured he'd seen it all and that nothing could shock him at that point in his career. He'd gone through the usual steps of putting on his PPE, signing in at the scene, and chatting with the responding officers, Jennifer Wang and Sierra Knight, who happened to be two of his favorites. Something in their expressions had tipped Royce off that this crime scene was like no other he'd ever seen. His brows edged toward his hairline as they described arriving on location.

"Shot through the heart with an arrow?" Royce had asked when they'd finished.

Wang nodded. "He landed on the wedding cake."

"Smashed it to bits," Knight added. "Vanilla cake with strawberry filling."

Tara arrived before Royce could say anything further. She greeted the patrol officers and asked them to bring her up to speed. Royce noticed what looked like the top of a hickey peeking out from the collar of her shirt. He knew Tara and Candy had gone out a few times since he'd reintroduced them two months ago, but neither had mentioned the dates to him, and he didn't push. He really, really wanted to, though. As if sensing Royce's attention on her, Tara rolled her shoulders and adjusted her shirt before meeting his gaze with a quirked brow.

"Shot through the heart with an arrow?" she asked Royce.

"I had the same reaction. Does that make Cupid our prime suspect?"

"Or someone living out Bon Jovi lyrics," Tara replied. "Who discovered the body?"

"The cake designer," Knight replied. "She'd set up the wedding cake, then responded to an emergency on another job. When she came back to collect her payment, she found the guy collapsed onto her display. She and the others are out back waiting for you to interview them."

"Others?" Tara asked. "Who else is back there?"

Wang referred to her notes. "The catering staff hired to work the venue and the restaurant manager."

"Catering staff?" Royce asked. "Why would you rent a restaurant as a venue and not eat their food? Seems kind of rude."

Knight and Wang exchanged a glance before shrugging.

"If you don't need anything else," Wang said, "we'll join the officers canvassing the neighborhood."

"Let us know right away if you come up with a witness," Tara said.

"Will do," Knight replied.

They thanked the officers and headed into the section of the restaurant where the medical examiner, Dr. Fawkes, and the crime scene technicians were hard at work. Even though Wang and Knight had told them about the macabre scene, Royce was still caught off guard when he laid eyes on the middle-aged man sprawled on top of a table where a wedding cake had been set up. It was impossible to tell how many tiers the cake had once had, but based on the vanilla sponge and strawberry carnage, Royce would guess there'd been several.

Sure enough, there was an arrow sticking out of the victim's chest and a large circle of blood had pooled on his pale blue polo shirt and spread down to his khaki pants. The man had wrapped both hands around the arrow, probably in an attempt to pull it free, and maintained his grip in death. Blood also trickled from his slack mouth. Wide-set blue eyes a shade darker than his shirt stared sightlessly at the ceiling. The victim's hair was mostly blond with some graying at the temples. He'd meticulously styled the strands and lacquered them into place. The cut reminded Royce of his sister's old Ken doll, minus the matted cake and icing.

Dr. Fawkes looked up from her examination and nodded. "We meet again, Sergeant Locke and Detective South."

"Ma'am," Tara replied with a polite nod.

"No offense, Doc, but I'm seeing you more often than I'd like," Royce told her.

She smiled, but it didn't lessen the weariness in her gaze. "Likewise."

Royce studied the body again. "Who do we have here?" A young lady on Fawkes's crew handed him an evidence bag with a wallet in it. "Thanks," he said, reaching inside it with his gloved hand. "Leonard Fellows," Royce said, then read off his address for Tara to jot down.

"I'll get a warrant to search his home," Tara said as Royce looked through the wallet.

He found the usual cards—bank, credit, health insurance, and business. The latter ranged from florists to bakers and dressmakers to clergy members. Not the typical business cards Royce found in a man's wallet. The last card in the stack explained the unusual collection.

"Leonard goes by Leo," Royce said. "And he owns Cupid's Arrow. They plan weddings." Royce hoped like hell Leo Fellows wasn't one of the planners Jace had fired. He'd hate for his big brother to be a suspect in a murder investigation two weeks before his wedding. Royce raised his head and met his partner's inscrutable expression. "Their company slogan is 'Our aim is true.'" Royce turned the card around to show Tara the logo in the upper left corner, an arrow through a red heart.

They both looked over at the prone man.

"'Curiouser and curiouser,'" Tara said.

Royce narrowed his eyes at the reference to Bailey's favorite bedtime story. He would've mentioned it, but the medical examiner's conversation commandeered his thoughts. Fawkes and crew started discussing ways to extract the arrow before transportation. They'd removed Leo's hands from the shaft and were now debating how to move forward.

"We can't take him out of here with the arrow sticking out," Fawkes said. "I can't cut it out of him because it would destroy physical evidence. I could clip the shaft at the body and leave the broadhead buried in his chest for now."

Royce, who knew zilch about arrows, had nothing to contribute to the conversation.

"The arrowhead screws into the carbon shaft," Tara interjected. "May I?"

"By all means," Dr. Fawkes said, gesturing for Tara to take a crack at it.

Tara carefully stepped up to the body and inspected the point of impact. "The arrowhead has penetrated deeply enough that it won't come out without causing massive damage to the surrounding tissue." She gripped the shaft close to the body and began to twist it. Moments later, the empty shaft came free. "Here you go."

A technician moved forward with an evidence bag to collect it. Once sealed, Tara continued to study the arrow.

She looked up at Royce, but whatever she'd been about to say died on her lips. "What?" she asked instead.

"Who are you?" Royce asked.

Tara shrugged. "I spent a lot of time with my grandpop as a little girl and learned how to shoot several types of bows. I even participated in archery competitions. We didn't use broadheads, though. Those are reserved for hunting."

"You hunt?" Royce asked.

"I have in the past, but I don't any longer."

He thought of his little buttercup. "Bailey's favorite Disney movie is *Bambi*," Royce said.

"I've met her hamsters, Thumper and Flower."

Royce smiled. "Sawyer and I bought her those for her birthday. She has strong opinions about the person who killed *Bambi's* mother."

"Point taken."

15

Narrowing his eyes, Royce asked, "Are you a good shot? The skill could come in handy if the zombie apocalypse occurs."

Tara's mouth quivered, but she didn't smile. "I'll do in a pinch," she replied blithely.

They'd gleaned the victim's name, address, and cause of death, so Royce and Tara got out of the way to let the medical examiner and the crime lab work. They headed out the back of the restaurant and found a small gathering clustered together at a picnic table. All heads swiveled in their direction as they approached.

Royce made quick introductions. "Who found Mr. Fellows?"

A petite brunette raised her hand. "I'm Kylie Grimshaw." She wore a pale yellow t-shirt with a white Cakes by Kylie logo and white pants that stopped well short of her ankle. Royce couldn't remember what they were called, but Evangeline had a pair in every color and often wore them with a wedgie sandal or whatever it was called. Kylie wore a pair of pristine white slip-on canvas sneakers.

"Mind if we talk over there?" Royce asked, tipping his head to a space a few feet away.

"Of course." She stood up slowly and paused as if assessing the ability of her legs to support her weight. Kylie inhaled deeply and took a shaky step toward Royce.

"You okay?" he asked.

She nodded jerkily and took another step. This one was steadier than the first. By the time she reached Royce and Tara, she'd stopped trembling.

"I'm very sorry for what you've witnessed today, Ms. Grimshaw," Royce said. "It must've been a terrible shock."

"You could say that."

"Did you know Mr. Fellows well?" Tara asked.

Kylie shook her head. "I'd never met him before today. I've always worked with Sally."

"Who's Sally?" Royce asked.

Kylie toyed with the collar of her t-shirt and stared off into space. "Sally Collins. She owns Cupid's Arrow."

"Mr. Fellows has a card claiming he's the owner of the business," Royce said.

"Um, co-owners, I guess," Kylie added. "You'll need Sally's phone number. Someone will need to alert the bride and groom that they'll need to find a different reception site."

Royce made a note of the number Kylie read off from her phone and encouraged her to continue.

"I arrived before…" She looked at Royce blankly.

"Mr. Fellows," he supplied.

"Yes, Mr. Fellows. I arrived before him to set up the cake." Kylie paused, took a shaky breath, and pressed on. "Only the restaurant manager was on site. The caterer and his staff hadn't arrived yet. I got to work right away and had the cake fully set up but still no Mr. Fellows. Sally had phoned me earlier this week and explained her grandmother had fallen and broken her hip and she wanted to be with her after surgery. Sally told me her partner was filling in and would bring the payment for the cake. I waited, and I waited, and I waited some more. I took a call from one of my employees who was having issues on another site, so I decided to head there and help her out. She called me back when I was halfway there and said the situation was resolved, so I came back here to see if Mr. Fellows had arrived with my check."

"How long were you gone?" Royce asked.

Kylie scrunched up her brow. "Fifteen minutes. Twenty, maybe."

"Mind if I check your call log?" Tara asked. "It's important we be as accurate as possible since Leo was killed in that window."

"Of course." Kylie pulled out her phone and showed Tara her log. "This is when Cecily called me, and here is where I called 911."

Tara opened her portfolio and jotted the times down. That's when Royce noticed the rainbow and unicorn stickers adorning the front of her portfolio. He knew exactly where they'd come from since he'd bought them for Bailey at the store the previous week. Tara did the manual calculations and said, "The first call came in at twelve ten and the call to 911 was fifteen minutes and thirty-seven seconds later."

"And the catering crew arrived in that window also?" Royce asked.

Kylie worked her bottom lip for a few seconds before responding.

"I assume so, but I can't say for sure. They could've entered the restaurant through the kitchen while I was installing the cake. I had my earbuds in and wasn't paying attention." The statement reminded him of Sawyer, and he nearly smiled before remembering where he was.

"Did you notice anything out of the ordinary when you were coming and going either time?" Tara asked. "Someone loitering or out of place?"

"No," Kylie replied. "Mr. Fellows running behind schedule was the only thing out of the ordinary. That's so unusual for an event planner. They are sticklers for punctuality."

Royce jotted the detail down, collected her contact information, and asked her to stick around a little longer in case they had follow-up questions. Then they moved on to the catering crew and the restaurant manager. They interviewed everyone separately but collected nearly the same answer, which meant it was either rehearsed or simply the truth. The catering staff claimed they entered through the kitchen as Kylie suggested and had just taken a smoke break when they heard the cake designer's blood-curdling screams. Royce could tell by the smell rolling off their clothes what kind of smoke break they'd had. The only variance in their stories was their arrival time at The Pirate's House, which ranged from eleven thirty to eleven fifty. None of them had seen anyone lurking around the back of the restaurant where the kitchen was located.

Royce and Tara spoke to Delia, the restaurant manager, next. She'd claimed to be in the kitchen the entire morning and only left when she stepped outside to join the catering crew for a smoke break. They walked her through the possible entrances the killer could've used, but she kept nixing their suggestions. The side entrances were locked, and the back door opened off the kitchen.

"There's no way we missed seeing someone carrying a bow and arrow through there, which leaves the front door and the hidden tunnel beneath the restaurant," Delia said.

"It could've been a folding survival bow," Tara said. "Those fit in a backpack. The arrow shaft I removed from the victim was shorter than a standard arrow and fits the theory."

Royce never knew such a thing existed. He'd been imagining

something big and cumbersome. "I still have to think our person is smart enough to avoid the main entrance on a busy spring afternoon. That leaves the tunnel. I've heard of the underground system under the city, but I've never been down inside them."

They collected the catering staff's contact information and released them along with Kylie Grimshaw. Royce turned to Delia with a grim smile. "Can you show me the tunnel access?"

"Sure. You're going to need good flashlights."

Tara made a quick trip to her car and returned with two powerful lights. Delia led them to a musty-smelling storage room lined with metal racks. A paneled section of the wall swung open to reveal a staircase.

Royce aimed the flashlight down and saw footprints in the dust on the steps.

"How often does anyone in the restaurant come down here?" Royce asked.

"Never," Delia replied. "It's forbidden. I wouldn't trust those rickety steps with a toddler's weight on them."

"Someone's been here," he said. "Those look like recent impressions. The tread looks more like a boot than a tennis shoe."

"Do we follow it down?" Tara asked.

"I can't allow that without discussing it with the owner," Delia said.

Royce shook his head. "I don't want to disturb the evidence." He squatted down and snapped several pictures of the prints, and they all stepped back. "Where does the tunnel come out?"

"Down by the river," Delia said. "Want me to show you?"

"Can you just tell us? We need as little disturbance as possible to preserve any evidence," Royce explained. Then he snagged a CSI tech and asked them to carefully process the storage room and the footprint in the dust.

Delia told them which way to go, and Royce, Tara, and two techs carefully made their way to the river looking for any signs of recent travel. They hit the jackpot in the muddy riverbank.

"These prints look just like the one on the steps," Tara said, pointing to the depressions that disappeared once the assailant reached the grass line. "I bet he was parked nearby. Walked to and from the tunnel on foot."

The techs set up to make casts of the prints for future comparison. Royce and Tara stepped out of their way.

"His transportation could've been anything," Tara added after a pause. "Bike, motorcycle, car…"

Royce crossed his arms over his chest. "We have another dilemma."

"Which is?" Tara asked.

"Regulations require us to notify next of kin, but a wedding party is planning to descend on this spot to celebrate their nuptials."

Tara nodded. "I'll call his business partner on our way to Leo's house. Maybe this Sally Collins can pull off a miracle to save the wedding from being ruined."

"Deal."

They left Tara's car at the crime scene and climbed into Royce's SUV. Tara's chat with Sally Collins was brief. The business partner gasped and shrieked "What?" so loud Royce heard her, even though she wasn't on speakerphone. Tara asked her a series of questions and jotted down the answers in her portfolio.

"We'll need to interview everyone on your staff," Tara said. "And we'd like access to Mr. Fellows's voice and email messages. When can you make them available?" Tara listened for a moment and said, "Tomorrow morning is fine. Does nine work?" Tara then pivoted to asking about Leo's next of kin. After she disconnected, Tara snickered and looked over at Royce.

"You'll never guess who Leo is married to," she said.

Royce chuckled. "What do I get if I guess right? One of those unicorn stickers?" He glanced over and caught Tara smiling down at the cheerful art on the otherwise dull black leather of her portfolio.

Tara jerked her head in his direction and narrowed her eyes. "You'll be jealous when she gives me one of the new scratch-n-sniff stickers I bought her."

"She better save the pizza ones for me," Royce replied.

"Let's see how good you are at guessing, and I'll see what I can arrange with my little princess."

Royce couldn't tell if Tara was even aware she'd claimed Bailey for herself, but the revelation turned his insides to goo. "I'm going to go with…Mrs. Fellows," Royce said.

Tara snorted. "Nope. Leo Fellows is married to none other than Grace Huxley."

"The wrecking ball?" he asked. "So the wedding planner is—was—married to the most prominent divorce attorney in Savannah?"

"I've heard men's testicles retract whenever she draws near," Tara said.

"This family profits on planning the marriages and dissolving them. They get the money coming and going."

"According to Sally Collins, Leo and Grace were in the middle of a divorce."

Royce narrowed his eyes. "Well, isn't that interesting?"

The address on Leo's license was located two streets over from Royce and Sawyer's house in Baker's Crossing. The properties and lawns were twice as big in this section of their zip code. Leo's home was a sprawling gray ranch with a wraparound porch and white trim. A woman was kneeling in front of one of the massive flower beds filled with colorful azaleas and camellias. She glanced up as they approached. Her gloved hands stilled, and her eyes widened in alarm.

Grace Huxley was nearly unrecognizable in her sweatpants, faded t-shirt, sun visor, and flip-flops. The dirt smudge on her cheek seemed especially out of character, but there was no mistaking her cunning eyes. He'd seen them hundreds of times on billboards and in print ads and commercials.

"I'm Sergeant Locke, and this is Detective South."

"Oh god," she said, staggering to her feet. "Is it Sam? Has something happened to my son?"

"No, ma'am," Royce said.

She clutched her chest and closed her eyes. Tension melted from her face, but her relaxed state didn't last long. She reopened her eyes and searched their expressions. "Oh, this can't be good."

"Are you Grace Huxley?" Tara asked. The woman nodded jerkily. "And you're married to Leonard Fellows." Her eyes widened once more, but she nodded. "We're separated, but yes, we're still married."

"I'm sorry to inform you that your husband was the victim of a homicide this afternoon," Royce said.

Grace staggered back a few steps, and Tara reached out to steady her.

"Ma'am, maybe we should sit down to continue this conversation," Tara suggested.

"Yes, of course," Grace said. "Forgive my poor manners." The attorney visibly pulled herself together. Her posture became more rigid, and her face became an expressionless mask. "Let's go inside."

Grace led them through the front door to a living room with cathedral ceilings and thick wood beams stained to match the gleaming floors below. She gestured to an arrangement of white leather furniture, then asked, "Can I get either of you something to drink?"

Royce and Tara declined her offer and sat together on the couch while Grace eased herself into the club chair across from them. She kicked off her flip-flops and tucked her feet beneath her. A large bouquet sat in the middle of the coffee table between them and beside it was a crystal dish filled with colorful candies.

"Leo's dead?" she asked. But before they answered, she spoke again. "How? Where?"

"We're not releasing many details right now, ma'am," Royce said. "I can say that Mr. Fellows was working at one of his firm's events."

"Oh, yes. The wedding planning." Grace sighed and stared off into space for several moments. Her gaze softened, and Royce assumed her eyes had lost focus as she traversed her private thoughts. But she blinked and zeroed in on Royce and Tara again with her wide blue eyes. "I had suspected he'd been in the midst of a midlife crisis before he left his previous employer, but I was certain of it when he decided to buy into that Cupid's Arrow nonsense."

"So, this was a new business endeavor for Mr. Fellows?" Royce asked.

Grace nodded. "One day, he was working as chief operating officer for Abbot and Marsh, a global logistics company he'd helped build from scratch, and the next, he's announcing a new venture."

"How long ago was this?" Tara asked.

"Seven months." Grace snorted. "It was a complete shock. Wedding planning? He's not prone to sentimentality or romance."

"What do you attribute the leap to?" Tara asked.

Grace lifted her hand and rubbed her index and middle fingers over her thumb. "Money, of course. Wedding planning is a huge racket. Do you have any idea how much money these people charge to make phone calls and arrange appointments?"

Royce figured the job was more complicated than her description, but he wasn't about to say anything that would make her clam up.

"Thousands and thousands of dollars per client," Grace said before they could answer.

"Savannah is known for destination weddings," Tara remarked. "Isn't there a lot of competition?"

"Naturally, but Leo loved the thrill of the hunt."

"Mr. Fellows hunted?" Royce asked.

"Heavens no. Leo trekking through the woods to stalk an animal?" Grace snorted at the mere idea. "I was using a metaphor, Sergeant. He wasn't into hobbies. He kayaked on occasion until he got hit in the head with a paddle when teaching our son. Leo lost his tooth and had to get an implant. I think he gave it up completely after that. I encouraged him to try something else like golf, but he wasn't interested. Work was his one true passion. Closing deals and beating the competition was his lifeblood. I didn't understand his decision to buy into the business, but he seemed energized about making it into the most successful wedding planning company in Savannah. I think it reminded him of the early days at Abbot & Marsh."

"Who did he buy his half of the business from?" Tara asked.

"Jennifer Ludwig."

"How did they meet?" Royce asked.

"I have no idea." Grace sighed deeply. "Oh, Leo. What have you gotten yourself into?"

"You mentioned your separation from Mr. Fellows," Royce said. "Was it amicable?"

"Not exactly," she replied. "Separating thirty years of joint property and finances is complicated."

"When did you separate?" Tara asked.

"Six months ago. I was furious that Leo invested *our* money into that business without consulting me. I'm an attorney who specializes in divorces, and my husband buys a wedding planning business? I don't want to be the punchline of someone's joke." Grace sighed heavily. "Our marriage was already over by that point. Hell, it had been over for more than twenty years. Our son, Sam, was old enough to understand that some relationships just don't work out, and I was tired of existing in a loveless marriage."

"Was Mr. Fellows upset?" Royce asked.

"Not in the least," Grace replied. "Leo's displeasure turned to fury when my attorney filed an injunction to freeze our joint assets and investments. I refused to back down. Leo wasn't investing another dime of my money or any assets I had rights to in that dumb business venture of his."

Royce couldn't blame her one bit. He asked her to account for her morning up until they arrived at her home.

"Gardening club," Grace replied without blinking. "We had our annual awards ceremony this morning followed by a catered lunch. We have thirty members, and some even brought guests, so there are plenty of people who can vouch for me. I felt motivated and started working on my flowers."

Royce looked up from his notes. "Do you know anyone who'd want to harm your husband?"

The widow snorted. "Leo was aloof and robotic. He could grate on your last nerve like a grain of sand under your fingernail, but murder? I simply cannot imagine him stirring up the kind of passion that would provoke someone to kill him."

*Ouch.* "So, that's a no?" Royce asked.

"It's a hell no, Sergeant."

"Okay," Royce said, "tell me who you think had the most to gain from his death."

Grace paused for a moment before replying. "I do, but I didn't kill him. That leaves his new business partner and Larry."

"Who's Larry?" Royce asked.

"Leo's twin brother. They're freakishly identical except for their personalities and dominant sides. Larry is sweet and left-handed. Leo is callous and right-handed."

"And what's his gain?" Tara asked.

"Leo and Larry have very wealthy parents. Their mother passed a few years back and a decent chunk of their inheritance has already been paid out, but the bulk of it remains in a trust until their father, Albert, passes away. With Leo gone, I assume Larry will inherit everything."

That was a motive they couldn't afford to overlook.

"Can we get an address for Larry?" Tara asked.

"Sure, let me go get my address book. I have Leo's new address in there too." She stood up but didn't walk away. "Larry won't be home. He spends his weekends at his place on St. Simons Island. Will you please allow me to break the news to him?"

"Of course," Royce replied.

"I'll need to revise that warrant," Tara remarked when they were alone again.

"Twins, killer Cupid, and a midlife crisis," Royce said. "I feel like we've fallen through Alice's rabbit hole." He leaned forward to take a piece of candy, but Tara grabbed his wrist.

"Better not eat or drink anything, then."

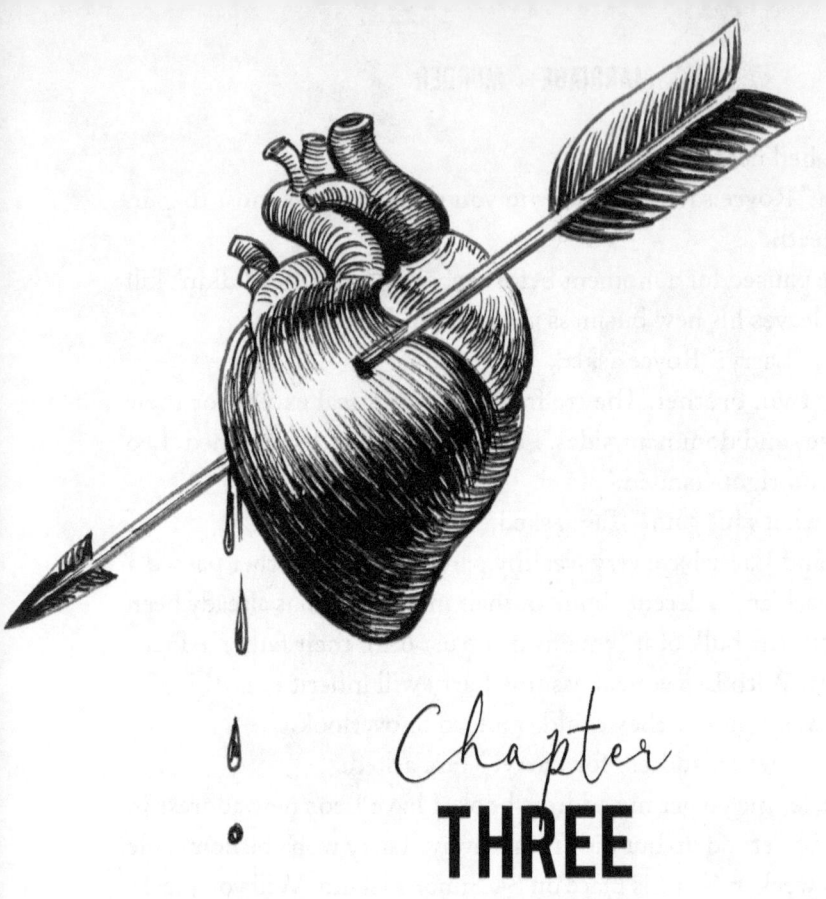

# Chapter
# THREE

**S**AWYER'S SKIN FELT CONSTRICTED AND ITCHY AS HE PACED THE living room. He wished he could blame it on a food allergy, but this was different. No rash of hives would break out all over his skin. Sawyer's contagion spread much deeper than the surface, pumping through his veins and seeping into his muscles and bones. His changes would be on a molecular level, his metamorphosis—

Sawyer cut off his thought with a snort. A superhero he was not and never would be.

*Meow.*

Sawyer glanced up to where Bones stretched out on the highest perch of his tree. The damn thing was so big Royce had anchored it to the wall in several places. His man had loved having to bust out his drill to assemble the tree and his stud finder to make sure he was securing it properly. Sawyer had a stud for Royce to find and something he could drill. Lord, it sounded like he was writing a porn script. He chuckled.

*Meow.*

Sawyer walked over to his beautiful boy and scratched his chin. "I put the scary vacuum away, Bones."

He'd been too worked up by the conversation his mother had instigated at the end of the meal and again when she'd dropped him off at home. He'd had to do something to work it off and decided to try out Royce's newest toy, cleaning under the bed and between the couch cushions with the long, thin attachment.

Bones assessed him coolly, still unsure if he would forgive Sawyer for disrupting his peaceful bird watching with the loud machine. The big beast couldn't resist Sawyer's charms for long and soon began purring loudly, moving his head to help Sawyer's fingers find the right spot. Sawyer felt his tension fade and chastised himself for getting so worked up in the first place. Evangeline had simply asked him if he'd planned to run for sheriff.

"I don't know," he'd answered honestly.

"Do you want to talk about it?" He'd only heard concern in her voice, not pressure.

"Nope." He'd thought that would be the end of it, but Sawyer should've known better.

Evangeline had just waited until she'd pulled into his driveway before trying a different approach. "What's holding you back from making a decision?" He wasn't ready to delve too deeply into the subject, but he'd had to give her something.

"The biggest concern is lack of privacy," Sawyer admitted. It felt like someone had opened a valve and released a little pressure, so he shared a little more. "Everything I do and everyone I love would be under a microscope."

Evangeline had arched a dark brow and peered at him with a mixture of humor and concern. "And you don't think we'll hold up under the scrutiny?"

Sawyer scrubbed a hand over his face. "That's not what I meant." But who or what was he trying to protect? His loved ones or his pride? He'd looked down at his left hand. The diamonds in his platinum engagement band glittered in the sunlight, sparking pure joy in his soul.

The ring and all the promises it entailed were the future he wanted to focus on, not some misguided revenge plot. "I'm not sure our county is ready for a gay sheriff," he'd said. "And I'm not going to pretend to be someone I'm not."

"There's only one way to find out," Evangeline had responded. "I can put together an exploratory committee and get a feel for what the constituents think about you."

Sawyer hadn't said yes or no. He'd smiled at his mother and said, "Planning a wedding and a potential campaign is too much for anyone, even you."

"Bet me," she'd said.

Sawyer hadn't accepted her challenge, but he hadn't rejected it either. He'd leaned over, kissed Evangeline's cheek, and told her he loved her. Hours later, Sawyer still wasn't sure if what he'd said, or hadn't said, constituted consent for his mother to set up the exploratory committee, and the uncertainty was wreaking havoc on his nervous system. He'd tried meditation, an audiobook, and cleaning, and he still didn't feel better. He could've called his mom and cleared the air, but he didn't do that either. A part of him felt like running for sheriff was the only way he could atone for running from his problem years ago. He wanted to make things right, but at what cost?

*Meow.*

Sawyer lifted Bones off the perch and cradled him against his chest. His cat rubbed his head against Sawyer's scruffy chin and purred harder. Sawyer walked over to the couch and sprawled on it, shifting his attention to scratching the beast's ears. Bones stretched out on top of him and continued to purr until Sawyer's blood pressure dropped and peace enveloped him.

Sawyer scratched both ears, and Bones closed his eyes. "Who's my best boy?"

Eventually, Sawyer drifted off to sleep. When he woke, Bones had returned to his high perch to resume watching his birds. Sawyer turned on the television but couldn't find an interesting documentary, so he settled for an old western. The heroine was hanging laundry on the line and pretending not to notice the gunslinger gazing at her. The scene reminded him of Royce's quest to fix the dryer before it caused a fire. Sawyer was pretty sure he'd stared just as lustily at Royce's ass as the cowboy was doing with the lovely hotel owner. If Royce had the dryer vent ring thingy, he could swap out the temporary fix, and they could live out the handyman porn images that had flittered across Sawyer's mind earlier.

With a solid plan he could get behind, he vacated the couch and retrieved his car keys. Sawyer whistled as he entered Royce's favorite store a few minutes later.

Sal stood behind the counter drinking a cup of coffee, and it smelled as strong as the brew Royce favored. The older man toasted him with his mug before taking a sip.

"Fancy seeing you here," Sal said. "Did Royce forget something on his list this morning?"

"No." Sawyer told him about Royce testing out his new shop vac as soon as he got home.

Sal cackled and slapped the counter. "I love that kid."

"Makes two of us," Sawyer replied. "So I'm here to buy a ring."

Sal smiled and nodded his head toward Sawyer's left hand. "We don't sell that kind of hardware here."

Royce chuckled. "I've already custom ordered Royce's wedding ring." The tungsten band with meteorite inlay was due to arrive at the jeweler soon. "I'm here to buy the kind that secures the dryer hose to the exterior vent."

"Ah," Sal said. "One dryer vent clamp coming right up."

"You can tell me the aisle number, and I'll get it," Sawyer offered.

The older man shook his head and set his coffee cup down on the counter. "I need to move around to loosen up my stiff joints. Too much standing or sitting makes my arthritis worse. Be back in a jiffy."

While Sawyer waited, he looked around the store Royce loved so much. He could easily picture his man working the counter and bullshitting with customers. Sawyer also had no issues imagining the two of them getting up to stockroom hijinks after hours.

What the hell was up with his superhyped sex drive all of a sudden?

Handyman porn and stockroom hijinks? His sexual peak was supposed to be twenty years in the past, but his libido hadn't gotten the memo.

"Excuse me," a soft, feminine voice said from behind him. Sawyer whirled around to find a pregnant woman holding a can of paint in each hand. She wore a light blue Baby on Board t-shirt, a pair of white shorts, and battered sneakers. Her light brown hair had been braided and slung over one shoulder. She had the greenest eyes Sawyer had ever seen. "Mind if I set these on the counter? They're a little heavy."

Her remark spurred Sawyer into action. "Please forgive me." Instead of moving aside, he stepped forward and eased the heavy cans from her hands, then set them on the counter for her.

She shook her head and smiled ruefully. "I should've grabbed a cart. I know better. George back in the paint department offered to get me one or help me to the front counter, but I'm too stubborn for my own good." She heaved a weighted sigh, placed her hands on her hips, and stretched her back.

"Looks like you're getting ready for a big event," Sawyer said.

The woman giggled. "Do you mean childbirth or painting the nursery?"

Sawyer laughed too. "Um, both."

She extended her hand. "I'm Courtney, by the way."

Sawyer shook it and introduced himself.

"I know," she said with a rueful smile. "We've never met, but we have a mutual friend in the sheriff's department."

Sawyer searched his brain for any mention of a pregnant friend of a friend, but he couldn't come up with anything until he recalled Charlie crashing his promotion celebration at Joe's. His former partner had told Sawyer about witnessing a tryst between Sheriff Wheeler and a female deputy who later became pregnant. Charlie had claimed Wheeler was trying to run her off the way he had Sawyer. Charlie had also admitted to being Felix's confidential source for the reporter's scathing newspaper articles on the sheriff's department. What had Charlie said about Sawyer to Courtney and why? The simple joy he'd felt from being in Royce's favorite place dimmed.

The expression on his face must've betrayed his inner turmoil because Courtney's easy-going smile collapsed. Sawyer didn't know this woman—didn't owe her anything—but he still wanted to relieve the worry creasing her brow. Heart now in his throat, Sawyer was unable to speak. What would he say? Luckily, Sal returned and spared him from continuing what was sure to be a very awkward conversation.

"I don't know why, but these things only come in multipacks," Sal said as he rounded the counter. He held up a plastic package with two dryer vent clamps in it. "Is that okay?"

"Sure," Sawyer said, finding his voice. "They look kind of flimsy, so it will be good to have a backup. Royce will store it in the ginormous toolbox he has in the garage."

Sal chuckled. "Pretty sure that boy is the sole reason I've stayed in business all these years." He scanned the bar code on the plastic wrapper and started to give Sawyer a total when the automatic front doors whooshed open. Sal turned his head to greet the customer and froze. All the color leached from the man's face. Sensing danger, Sawyer snapped his head to the right and saw two figures dressed in black clothes and wearing Deadpool masks. They held guns in front of them and quickly advanced on the counter. One was about six feet tall, and the other was a few inches shorter. Both were lean, bordering on an unhealthy kind of skinny.

"Everybody get down," the shorter man yelled. His voice was firm without a hint of a quiver, but these guys were old pros at this by now. "Facedown on the ground. Toss your cell phones away and put your hands out in front of you where I can see them." Something about him was familiar, so Sawyer froze and didn't immediately respond until the man aimed the gun at his face. "No one needs to be a hero. We just want the money. Down on the fucking ground."

Sawyer removed his phone from his pocket and tossed it down in front of him. Behind him, Courtney started to sob. Sawyer glanced over his shoulder to make sure she was okay. She swayed on shaky legs, and he forgot about their awkward introduction and his own safety. He turned and reached a hand to her. She snagged it like he was her lifeline, and he helped her get down.

"Easy now," Sawyer said gently.

Once she was in position, Sawyer lay down and put his hands on the floor above his head and pressed his forehead to the cold tile.

"Not you, old man," the taller gunman yelled. "Where's the safe?"

"I-in my office in the b-back," Sal stammered.

"You and I are going to the vault," the burglar told him. "Let's move it."

"Okay, okay," Sal said nervously. "Please don't hurt anyone."

"Check for other employees and customers," the shorter guy called after them.

Sawyer tilted his head just enough so he could see the gunman's black biker boots in his periphery. Moments later, a third person joined Sawyer and Courtney on the ground. He assumed it was the guy working the paint counter.

"Where's your cell phone," the shorter gunman demanded of the newcomer.

"My p-p-pocket," the guy said.

"Toss it out in front of you. No one try to be a fucking hero, and you'll all go home in one piece." The gunman walked over to Courtney's cell phone and stomped on it until it cracked. He repeated the process with the other two on the ground.

"C-can I please lie on my s-side?" Courtney asked. "This position hurts."

"Shut your mouth and quit bitching," the gunman snarled, but Sawyer saw his boots moving toward a display of lawn chair cushions. A moment later, a floral pillow came into view when the gunman dropped it on the floor. "Push that under you."

Courtney cried as she reached out and awkwardly positioned the cushion under her swollen belly. The black boots came closer as the gunman stood over Sawyer.

"Well, what do we have here?" the man asked. Sawyer had no idea what he was talking about until the gunman added, "He must love you a lot." *He.* How could this man know Sawyer was in a relationship with a man? The gunman laughed, and the sick feeling of familiarity returned. And then he knew. Sawyer was so shocked that the gunman nearly succeeded in removing the ring from his finger. Rage surged through Sawyer, and he made a fist before the man could take it off.

The gunman pressed the cold metal barrel of his gun against Sawyer's head. "Give me the ring, or I'll shoot you."

Sawyer bit his tongue to keep from telling Benton Locke to go fuck himself.

The sound of running feet reached his ears, followed by the taller gunman yelling, "I got it. Let's get out of here."

Benton didn't budge. He shoved the gun harder against Sawyer's head and stomped his booted foot on top of Sawyer's hand. The pain was excruciating, but Sawyer somehow maintained his fist.

"What the hell's wrong with you?" the taller burglar said. "Let's go."

Beside him, Courtney screamed, "My water just broke!"

"I'm outta here," the smarter gunman said.

"Fuck," Benton cursed and withdrew the gun from Sawyer's head. "This ain't over."

Benton raced after his buddy. Sawyer leaped to his feet and ran to the sliding glass door. He turned off the automatic sensor and locked the door before sprinting back to the people still lying on the ground.

"Sal," Sawyer yelled toward the back of the store. "Are you okay?"

"Yeah," the older man called out.

Sawyer went to the phone behind the counter and dialed 911. He identified himself to the operator and explained the situation, stressing that the gunmen had left the premises. "One of the hostages is in labor."

"Help is on the way," she said calmly.

Sal came shuffling up to the front, and Sawyer passed him the phone so he could help Courtney. George was kneeling beside her, holding her hand. The fluid on the ground was free of blood, which he took as a good sign.

"It's going to be okay, honey," the older man said.

"Hey," Sawyer said, dropping to his knees by Courtney. "Are you having any labor pains?"

"My back has been hurting all day. I think those might've been contractions."

"An ambulance is on the way," Sawyer assured her. "It's been a long time since I did training on helping women in labor, but I remember the basics."

"How'd my life get so screwed up?" Courtney asked in a shaky voice.

"Well, I'm sure a man is at the center of it."

Her green eyes filled with tears, and she erupted into laughter. "You can say that again."

Sawyer picked out the wailing sirens over the rush of blood in his ears. "I think the cavalry is here. I'm going to go check."

"No," Courtney said, snagging his wrist. "Please don't leave me."

Sawyer nodded and looked over at George. "Will you go let the police in? Keep your hands up and in front of you so they can see them at all times. Don't make any sudden moves or reach for anything until they're certain you're safe."

"Okay," George said and slowly rose on shaking legs.

"My employee is unlocking the door," Sal told the 911 operator. "Make sure they don't shoot him by mistake. No one mixes paint like George."

Sal's employee released a bark of dry laughter. "That remark's gonna cost you, Sal."

"I'll let you have an extra day off next week," Sal replied.

George unlocked the door and stayed put with his hands up. Four officers rushed in with guns out and searched the rest of the store. Once they were sure it was safe, they radioed for the EMTs to enter.

They gently placed Courtney on the gurney as Sal, Sawyer, and George watched. Courtney looked at Sawyer with pleading green eyes.

"Can he please come to the hospital with me?" she asked one of the officers.

"Sergeant Key needs to give a statement," the patrolman replied.

"Let me ride to the hospital with Courtney. Have dispatch send Ashcroft and Chen there to meet me. They're the detectives leading the robbery investigations. They can take my statement there."

The officers looked uncertain until Courtney cried out in pain.

"We need to get going," one of the EMTs said.

"Okay, okay," the officer said. "We'll let Chen and Ashcroft know you're at the hospital."

"Thanks." Sawyer followed the gurney out to the ambulance.

The trip was short and loud. Sawyer worried Courtney would break every bone in his right hand. It reminded him of the vicious stomp he'd taken to his left, and he examined it closer. A few of the knuckles looked swollen and red, and the damn thing throbbed like a son of a bitch, but the damage could've been worse.

Sawyer went up to labor and delivery with Courtney, and they got her settled into a suite and hooked up to monitors. The nurses were calm and kind, assuring her the baby's heartbeat looked nice and steady. They mistook Sawyer for the baby's father and went about assessing Courtney's labor progression.

Sawyer quickly turned his back to give her privacy, which made Courtney laugh and explain their relationship—or lack thereof. Sawyer recalled the pregnant deputy in Charlie's story was married. If Courtney was the same person, where was her husband?

"He's just helping me out. Can I call my mom?" she asked, gesturing to the phone on the bedside table.

"Sure, honey," the nurse replied. "I'm going to go call your doctor and let her know you're here. You're almost five centimeters dilated, so you're halfway there. I'll be back in a bit to check on you."

Sawyer stayed with Courtney until her mom arrived, then he went in search of Ashcroft and Chen. He expected to find them in the waiting room and was surprised when the only people he saw were family members of expectant mothers. Sawyer reached for his phone automatically and remembered it had been smashed. He approached the nurses' station, introduced himself, and explained the dilemma. She smiled, made a few calls, and tracked Chen and Ashcroft down.

They arrived in labor and delivery a few minutes later, but they weren't alone. Royce muscled everyone out of his way to get to Sawyer, cupping his face and turning it this way and that way before scanning his body.

"They told me you were injured in an armed robbery," Royce said, his voice thick and heavy.

Sawyer looked at Ashcroft and Chen. "Why the hell did you tell him that?"

"Because they told us you were one of the hostages in the armed robbery and went to the hospital in an ambulance," Chen said. "We went to the ER, and you weren't there. We checked in the surgery unit, and you weren't there either. I never would've guessed labor and delivery."

"Piss-poor communication from the responding officers," Ashcroft grumbled. He slapped Royce on the shoulder. "Sorry for the heart attack, buddy."

Royce pulled Sawyer into his arm and held him tight. "Are you okay?"

"Yeah," Sawyer said. He pulled back and looked down at his left hand. "Could probably use some ice."

"I'll go get you some," Chen said.

"What happened to your hand?" Royce asked.

"And why are they treating you in L&D?" Ashcroft inquired.

Sawyer forced his gaze away from Royce's gray eyes and looked over at Ashcroft. "I'll explain everything, but do you mind if I have a private word with Royce first?"

"No problem," Ashcroft said and pointed to a cluster of empty seats. "I'll just be over there."

Royce placed his hand at the small of Sawyer's back and guided him out of the unit and around the corner to a darkened alcove. Royce embraced Sawyer and kissed him before Sawyer had a chance to speak. Sawyer leaned into Royce, fear licking at his conscience and making him shiver. He hadn't been around Benton much. What if he was wrong? Then he remembered the laughter and the gunman's determination to take the ring Royce had given him. He knew he wasn't wrong, but he found no comfort in the knowledge.

Sawyer pulled back and told Royce what had happened. His gray eyes narrowed when Sawyer repeated the part where the gunman had remarked, "He must love you a lot."

"You should've let the ring go," Royce said. "I would've bought you another one. No scrap of metal is worth your life."

Sawyer took a shaky breath. "You're missing the point." He repeated what the gunman said, emphasizing the pronoun.

Royce cocked his head to the side. "It's someone you know."

Swallowing down his fear, Sawyer said, "It's someone you know too."

Royce's expression hardened before he closed his eyes. For a minute, Sawyer feared the love of his life would reject him.

"Maybe I'm wrong," Sawyer said quickly. "I haven't been around him much."

Royce's eyes snapped open, and the expression was cold and distant. Sawyer hadn't seen this version of Royce since their first day working together. He braced himself for the worst, and maybe something in his expression gave his inner turmoil away. Royce took a deep breath and pressed his forehead to Sawyer's.

"It was Benton, wasn't it?"

"I'm pretty sure. I'm going off the laugh, the familiarity of his voice, and his knowledge that a man had put the ring on my finger. But I could be wrong. My sexual orientation isn't a secret."

Royce wrapped both arms around Sawyer and held him tightly. "I'll end him."

They were still embracing when Chen and Ashcroft rounded the corner. Chen carried a bag of ice, and Ashcroft held a paper cup of dark sludge masquerading as coffee.

"Ready to give your statement?" the latter asked.

Sawyer searched Royce's gaze. His recognition wasn't much to go on. Could he testify in court that Benton Locke had held a gun to his head? No. All he could say was that the voice sounded like Benton's.

Royce nodded and pressed a quick kiss to his lips. "This could be the break they need."

Sawyer started at the beginning and told them everything, listing each detail and observation. Ashcroft and Chen shifted their gaze to Royce when Sawyer revealed who he believed the shorter gunman to be.

"We can't bring him in on that alone," Ashcroft said.

"No," Chen replied, "but it gives us a solid lead to follow. Up until now, we've been chasing our tails. These guys have always been a few steps ahead of us." He looked at Royce. "I'm sorry, man."

"You don't have anything to be sorry about," Royce said. "Do your job. Bring these fuckers down."

"Any idea who Benton's associates might be?" Ashcroft asked.

Royce released a heavy sigh. "I haven't talked to my brother in three years, unless you count him jeering at me from a moving vehicle. I'm not sure who he's running with now." A stern expression crossed his face. "Bet I could find out, though."

"Huh-uh," Chen said. "You need to stay clear of this and let us do our jobs. You don't want any of this to blow back on you, Ro. There's already a wild theory circulating that at least a few of the crew are cops."

Sawyer held his breath while waiting for Royce to reply. He wasn't the kind of person who stood on the sidelines. After a long pause, Royce relented with a stiff nod.

"You're right. I shouldn't be the officer supervising the investigations either. I'll talk to Mendoza about the situation on Monday."

"How about you do it now?" their chief said.

They all turned to see Mendoza approaching, and he wasn't alone. Abe Beecham, the chief's best friend and Bryan County Sheriff, strolled alongside him. The men were dressed in casual t-shirts and jeans and could've come from anywhere. For the first time since Royce suggested it, Sawyer detected the hint of something more between the two men.

"What are you doing here, Chief?" Sawyer asked.

"Dispatch told me one of my officers was rushed to the hospital after an armed robbery at a hardware store. I've been all over this place looking for a wounded officer. I'm relieved no one is hurt, but I'm damned curious what Royce wants to tell me on Monday."

"And why are you up here in labor and delivery?" Abe asked.

Royce, Chen, and Ashcroft took Mendoza aside, and Sawyer filled Abe in on the incident. The brawny sheriff glanced over at Royce.

"I sympathize," Abe said. "I come from a long line of losers. Best thing I ever did was move to Georgia after my military career ended to get away from them. No one would've elected me sheriff in my hometown after the trouble my family caused."

Sawyer was dying to know more but didn't push. He expected Royce to resume his homicide investigation, but his fiancé wasn't hearing it.

"I know where I'm needed."

"I'm fine," Sawyer assured him once they were in the SUV heading home.

"Well, I'm not," Royce replied. "What were you even doing at Sal's?"

"I went to get a dryer vent clamp so we could live out the handyman porn fantasy I had earlier today."

Royce braked at a stop sign and looked over with a smirk. "Yeah?"

"Uh-huh. Then I thought about all the trouble we could get into in the stockroom someday when we own the hardware store."

Royce chuckled as he brought Sawyer's swollen hand to his lips and kissed it.

When they got inside the house, sex was suddenly the last thing on Sawyer's mind. The memory of having a gun pressed to his head came rushing back. One squeeze of the trigger and he would've been snuffed out. Erased from this earth.

Sensing his mood, Royce slid his arms around his waist from behind and rested his chin on Sawyer's shoulder.

"Hey, are you hungry?" Sawyer asked. "You didn't get a chance to eat lunch and probably haven't stopped since you left the restaurant. We have a ton of leftovers."

"I don't want food."

Sawyer snorted. "Since when?" He tried to turn around, but Royce tightened his embrace.

"I don't want to see that look of fear in your eyes ever again," Royce said, his voice as firm as the hold he had on Sawyer's body and heart.

Sawyer was momentarily confused. Royce hadn't been at the store during the robbery, and no one had mentioned security cameras. He managed to turn in the circle of Royce's arms and look into his gray eyes.

"What do you mean?" he asked.

Royce caressed Sawyer's cheek with the back of his hand. "There was this look of fear in your eyes right before you told me your suspicions about Benton. It was like you thought the truth might break us, but, baby, I chose you. And I will always choose you."

Holy fuck, this man. No one could unravel Sawyer so quickly. And Royce wasn't finished taking him apart. He lifted Sawyer's sore hand and rubbed his thumb over the red knuckles.

"Don't you ever pull a stunt like that again," Royce said, kissing Sawyer's hand. "Ever."

"It wasn't a conscious decision," Sawyer replied. "It was instinct."

Royce backed him up against the counter and gripped his jaw. "I need to hear the words."

"I promise." Sawyer pressed a kiss to Royce's firm lips. "I need one from you too."

"Name it."

"Stay far away from this investigation. Let Ashcroft and Chen do their jobs."

Royce inhaled sharply, his nostrils flaring. Then he exhaled and nodded.

"I need to hear the words," Sawyer said, mimicking him from moments before.

Royce's beautiful mouth curved into a wry grin. "I promise."

They sealed their vow with a long, languid kiss. Afterward, Royce pulled back and smiled at him.

"I'm ready for food now," he said.

"And there's my guy."

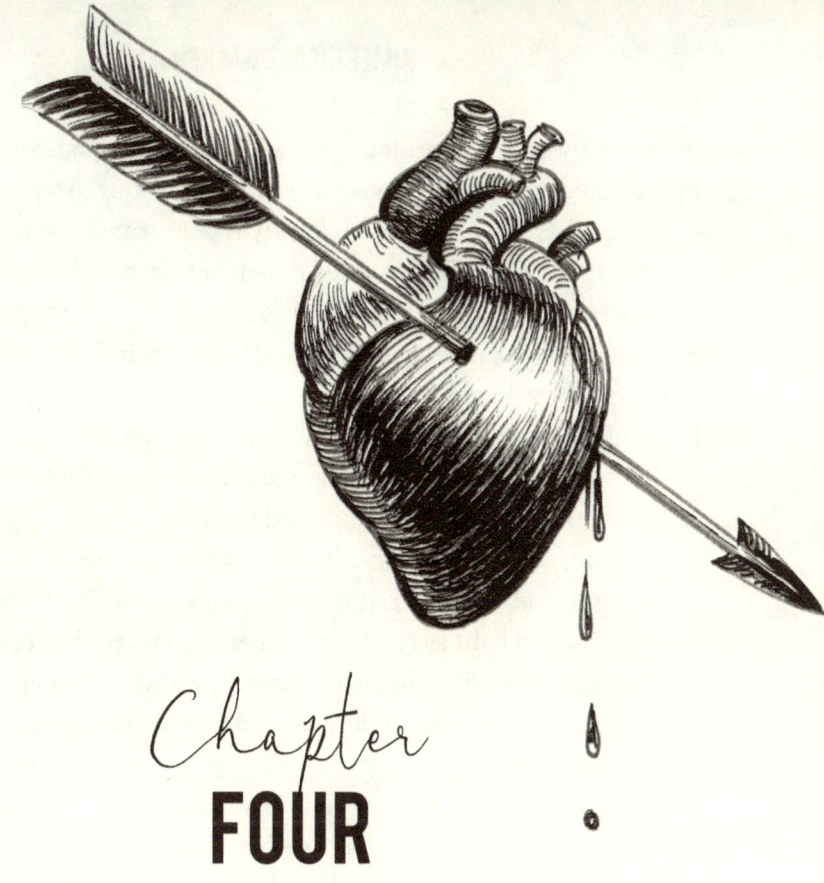

*Chapter*

# FOUR

**S**LEEP HAD RANGED FROM FITFUL TO NONEXISTENT AS ROYCE'S overactive brain replayed the events at the hardware store. In one vivid dream, Sawyer's voice had narrated the scene just as he had at the hospital, but Royce's brain hadn't been happy with the account. Like a director, his subconscious cut and reframed the narrative until the imagery playing behind his eyelids had morphed into a Quentin Tarantino movie. The somewhat calm scenario Sawyer had described turned into a blood bath where the hero died an awful death instead of escaping unscathed. This wasn't just any villain either. It was the little brother he'd loved so much.

Memories of an innocent boy smiling and laughing at Royce's antics intermingled with the man Benton had become. He knew drugs had played a big part, but Royce wasn't giving him a pass. His brother had held a gun to Sawyer's head for fuck's sake. If Benton had pulled the trigger—as he had in the dream—Royce's life would've ended too.

Royce had woken to burning lungs and tears streaming down his face. He'd sucked in air and furiously wiped the moisture away.

*He's okay. He's okay. He's okay.* Royce repeated the mantra, and eventually, his racing heart settled down, but sleep had still eluded him for the rest of the night. He'd promised Sawyer he wouldn't get involved, but that didn't mean he couldn't make a list of possible associates. While it was true Royce and Benton had lost touch, he could name the guys Benton had been friends with before his drug addiction had driven a wedge between them. He'd make the list and pass it off to Chen and Ashcroft, then dust off his hands and walk away.

Royce had lain awake for hours, holding Sawyer in his arms and watching the sunlight filter into their room and shift with each hour. A ribbon of warm light slashed across their bed where Royce's legs were tangled with Sawyer's. He forced himself to think of something more positive, and his brain naturally landed on the handyman porn remarks Sawyer had made.

Royce closed his eyes and let his vivid imagination run wild. He pictured himself up on a ladder, but instead of changing a lighting fixture, he held on to the top rung for dear life while Sawyer spread his ass cheeks and rimmed him. Then Sawyer would fumble around in Royce's tool belt until he found the lube Royce just happened to keep handy. With his jeans tangled around his work boots, Royce wouldn't be able to spread his legs too far, which would make Sawyer's penetration even more delicious and dirty. The man in his arms yawned, arched his back, and pressed his ass against Royce's erection at the same time fantasy Royce cried out from swift, deep penetration.

Sleepy laughter rumbled through Sawyer, and Royce felt an electric zing in his balls. Or maybe the shockwaves came from Sawyer pushing back harder against his cock.

"Getting started without me?" Sawyer's voice was heavy with sleep and desire.

Royce slid both hands up Sawyer's torso. He used one to cover Sawyer's neck and the other to toy with his nipples. "It's all your fault."

Sawyer laughed again. "Always is. What did I do this time?"

Royce trailed his fingers from Sawyer's nipples down to circle his navel and lower again to his happy trail and pubic hair. His knuckles brushed against the leaking head of Sawyer's dick. "It was all that talk about handyman porn. I've been awake for a while and figured dirty thoughts of you were safer than the other kind." He didn't need to explain what he meant.

"I'm okay, baby," Sawyer said huskily. "Besides horny as hell now. Tell me about this fantasy."

"Hand me the lube first."

Sawyer eased forward to retrieve the bottle from his bedside table. He handed it to Royce over his shoulder and settled back into Royce's embrace. "You were saying?"

Royce shoved the blankets down their bodies and drizzled lube over his middle finger. "Where should I begin?" he asked. Then he pressed his slick finger against Sawyer's rim, circling it to wet and entice. Sawyer moaned and lifted his top, bent leg higher, and Royce said, "Here feels like a good spot."

He slid his right arm under Sawyer's neck and bent his arm to hold him in place. Royce sank his teeth into Sawyer's shoulder and chuckled when his man bucked in his embrace. Royce began retelling the vivid fantasy Sawyer had interrupted while easing his finger inside Sawyer's tight channel, drawing out his pleasure and groans.

Sawyer lifted his bent leg higher until his knee nearly touched his chest. Yoga for the win. Sawyer's flexibility distracted Royce from his storytelling.

"I don't remember where I was," he said.

"Knuckle deep in my ass," Sawyer reminded him.

Royce pushed the pad of his finger against Sawyer's prostate.

"Fuck me," Sawyer groaned.

Royce forced a playful sigh through his lips. "Fuck you or tell you a story? Which is it?"

"Both." Sawyer arched his back. "I'm greedy."

Royce eased his finger out and pushed back in, eliciting a shaky breath and more cursing from his man. "So greedy."

Royce decided to prolong the torture by starting his story over from the beginning.

"And you said, 'My, what big tools you have,'" Royce whispered in Sawyer's ear.

Sawyer snorted. "Yeah, yeah, and then you proceeded to demonstrate what you can do with them. Give me your cock already."

"So greedy," Royce repeated, pegging his prostate once more.

Sawyer wiggled his hips. "We've already established that."

"You want me to skip right past the part where you yanked down my pants and shoved your face between my ass cheeks."

Sawyer moaned. "Okay, maybe I want to hear that part."

"While I was on the ladder," Royce added, "you did me dirty. My boots were tangled up in my pant legs, and I couldn't spread my legs very far, but you still managed to drive your dick deep into me."

Sawyer stilled. "Please tell me I didn't use WD-40 for lube."

Royce chuckled. "Now, why didn't I think of that? I love the way it smells. But I just happened to have a bottle of lube in my tool belt."

"I bet you did," Sawyer said. "A guy never knows when he'll need an emergency fuck."

Royce eased his finger from Sawyer's tight clench and fumbled around on the bed with his left hand until he located the lube again. He drizzled the slickness over his cock before tossing the bottle aside. Royce shifted a little lower in bed and aligned his cock to Sawyer's pucker. This was their lazy Sunday sex position, and he knew the perfect angle to drive his man wild—deep enough to arouse but too shallow to get him off.

"Put me on my knees and fuck me," Sawyer demanded.

Royce wrapped one arm around Sawyer's chest, gripped his thigh with the other, and rolled to his back so Sawyer lay on his chest. If he was frustrated by the first position, he would lose his cool over this one. Royce planted his feet on the bed and thrust his hips upward, driving as deep into Sawyer's ass as the angle allowed.

"Damn you," Sawyer snarled.

Royce looked down his fiancé's tanned and toned torso to watch Sawyer's dick dribble all over his stomach. With each thrust home, more precum leaked from the slit.

"Look how badly you want me," Royce whispered in his ear.

Sawyer reached down to stroke himself, but Royce swatted his hand away and changed the tempo to short thrusts.

"I swear, I'm gonna—" Sawyer's words died and were replaced with a lusty moan when Royce twisted his nipples with just the right amount of pressure. Royce couldn't see Sawyer's face, but he knew damn well his beautiful brown eyes had rolled back in his head.

"Whatcha gonna do, baby?" Royce asked. "Come so hard your vision goes black?" Royce trailed his fingers down Sawyer's torso, noting the sheen of sweat coating his skin as his man wiggled and squirmed to get deeper penetration. Royce slid his fingers into the short curls at the base of his cock and tugged. "Tell me what you're going to do."

Sawyer kicked his legs out and jackknifed up into a reverse cowboy position. With one deft move, he outmaneuvered Royce, who watched the play of muscles in Sawyer's back as he rose and fell on Royce's cock.

"I'm going to wreck you," Sawyer said and set out to do just that.

Royce was no match for Sawyer's flexibility and grace, and the tormentor became ensnared in the trap of his own making. Sawyer used his powerful legs to ride Royce's cock like it had been made for him and him alone. A mirror hung above the dresser across from the bed, but Sawyer's strong back blocked Royce from seeing the expression on Sawyer's face. He craned his neck to look around Sawyer and was glad he did. Sawyer braced himself with one hand on Royce's thigh and used the other to jerk himself off. Sawyer's head fell back, his eyes drooped closed, and his mouth went slack. Pleasure built and coiled until Royce thought he'd implode. His balls tightened against his body in warning.

"Sexiest fucker I've ever seen," Royce said.

Sawyer's eyes snapped open, their gazes met in the mirror, and they came together. Sawyer rode Royce's dick until the last drops were spent, then he gently eased off and crashed to the bed beside Royce.

"Good morning," Sawyer said breathlessly.

"It is now," Royce said, rolling over and spooning up behind Sawyer. "Just another minute."

Sawyer snorted but did not attempt to move. "What time do you need to meet Tara?" Royce had told him about the murder the previous night after Tara had texted a final update.

"She's picking me up at eight to catch me up before we meet with Leo's business partner and the staff at Cupid's Arrow. Hopefully, the warrants to search Leo's home and business are signed and ready to go. The partner seemed willing to help yesterday but could've changed her mind after the shock wore off."

"What do you expect to find at his office?" Sawyer asked.

"According to Leo's wife, the business partner has a strong motive for wanting Leo dead. And I'm sure there's no shortage of pissed-off clients."

"Hmmm," Sawyer said, doing a full body stretch any cat would envy. "What's that mean?"

"Just thinking of our favorite groomzilla and hoping he's not one of Leo's angry clients."

Royce's heart sank. Jace was on his fifth wedding planner, and he didn't have anything nice to say about any of them. With the wedding only two weeks away, Royce figured he'd stick it out with the current organizer. "Did he mention any of the planners to you by name?" he asked Sawyer.

"Nope. He called them all assholes and assigned them a number. I'm pretty sure Asshole One and Asshole Three were women, though."

Royce scrubbed a hand over his face. "In one weekend, both my brothers might end up as suspects in major crimes."

Sawyer rolled over and faced him. "Even if you do find some scathing email from Jace, we both know he didn't shoot an arrow into Leo Fellows's chest." When Royce didn't agree with him right away, Sawyer tweaked his nipple. "Don't we?"

Royce flinched and knocked his hand away. "The Jace we know now isn't capable of doing that, no." The brother who'd come home from the war broken and bruised, though? Royce might've believed that man capable of murdering the wedding planner. Had the stress from the wedding triggered—

"Fuck!" Royce yelled when Sawyer tweaked his nipple again.

"Go take a shower while I feed the cat and start breakfast."

"Or you could join me in the shower, and we'll feed the cat and make breakfast together."

Sawyer eyed him speculatively. "We only have an hour before Tara arrives."

Royce leaned forward and nipped Sawyer's bottom lip. "Plenty of time."

"Western omelet or scrambled eggs with peppers, onions, and cheese?" Royce asked once they'd showered, dressed, and fed the beast.

Sawyer retrieved the orange juice from the refrigerator and set it on the counter. "Um, scrambled sounds good."

They worked together to prepare a simple breakfast of eggs and toast.

"What's on your agenda today?" Royce asked as he stacked their plates in the dishwasher.

"I'm not sure," Sawyer replied. "I'm probably going to swing by the hospital to see how Courtney and her baby are doing. I wish I'd thought to give her my phone number." He shook his head ruefully when he recalled they didn't have phones. "I'll go to the cellular store when they open to buy a new phone, then I'll swing by the hospital to see Courtney. I want to check on Sal to see how he's doing today."

They'd talked to him the previous evening, and he'd seemed okay, but it was a good idea to check for delayed trauma.

"You better swing by your parents' house first thing. I bet your dad has had his hands full keeping Evangeline at home after you talked to her. Probably had to tie her to the bed or something."

"Gross," Sawyer said.

"I didn't mean it like that, but don't think for a second those two aren't familiar with a little slap and tickle."

Sawyer covered his ears and groaned.

The doorbell rang, and Royce went to answer it. He expected to find Tara at the door, but it was Evangeline instead. She was still wearing her pink satin pajamas and slippers. A white headband pulled her long hair back from her face. The woman wasn't wearing an ounce of makeup, and somehow she looked younger. She'd recently starred in an ad campaign for antiwrinkle cream. Royce would've joked that the shit was some kind of miracle cure, but Evangeline had a wild look in her eyes.

"Where is my son?" she asked tersely.

"He's in the kitchen. Not a single hair out of place."

Evangeline took a deep, shaky breath and kissed Royce's cheek. "Good, because I'm going to murder him for almost getting murdered."

Royce started to follow her but saw Tara's sporty sedan pull into the driveway. He held up a finger to let her know he'd be right there and followed his future mother-in-law. They should've encouraged her to come over the previous evening to see for herself that Sawyer was okay. Baron might've had to hoist her over his shoulder to get her out the door again, but Royce was certain his future father-in-law wouldn't mind. He stood by his slap and tickle comment. When Royce reached the kitchen, Evangeline was already in Sawyer's arms, sobbing against his shoulder. Sawyer's expression read *help me*, but Royce pointed to his watch, then the front door.

"I'm sorry I didn't call you as soon as I woke up," Sawyer said. "I wasn't thinking clearly, and Royce distracted me with sex."

Royce's mouth fell open in shock as Sawyer threw him under the bus. He mouthed "This is war" to Sawyer and retrieved his travel mug. By the time he reached the door, Royce heard Evangeline giggling and knew they'd be okay.

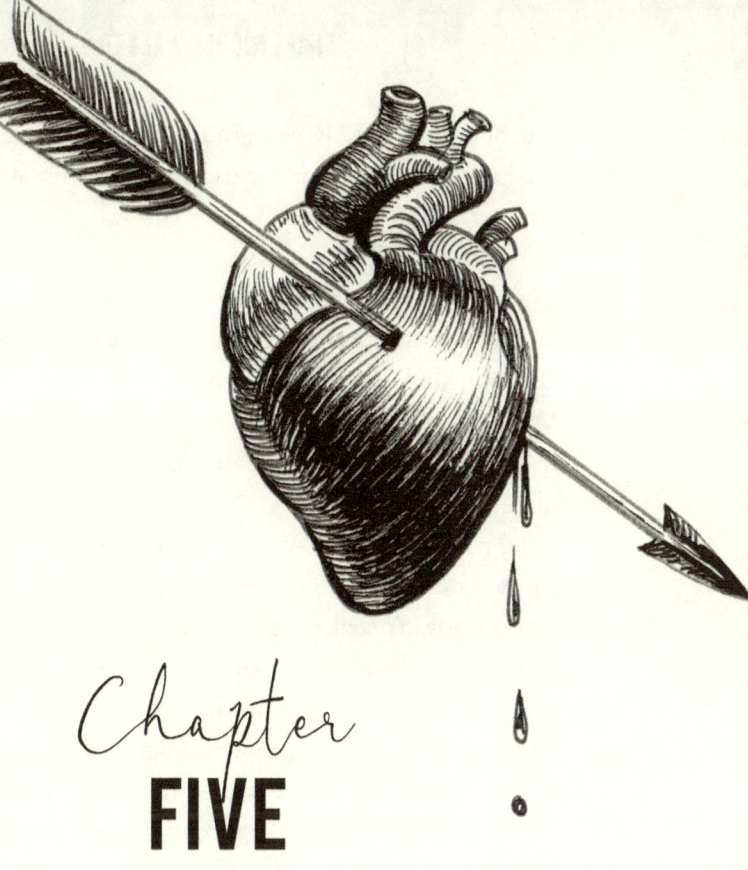

*Chapter*
# FIVE

"**M**ORNING, PARTNER," ROYCE SAID AS HE SLID INTO THE passenger seat of Tara's low-slung rocket. He'd become so used to sitting up high that it felt like he was riding on a skateboard.

"Did I just see Sawyer's mom enter your house in her pjs?" Tara asked as she backed out of the driveway.

"Yep. He talked to Evangeline last night and assured her he was fine, but I'm guessing she read about the incident in the morning paper and needed more assurances."

"The story is everywhere," Tara said. "News, radio, and paper. They're really leaning into that hero label for Sawyer."

Royce stifled a groan but couldn't keep the irritation from his voice. "That's just great."

Tara glanced over. "It pisses you off that people think Sawyer is a hero?"

"No, of course not," Royce groused. "But I do wonder if the press is just making a big fuss or if my fiancé has downplayed his role in the burglary."

"Why?"

Good question, and more nightmare fodder to keep him awake at night. "So I know if I should be mad at Sawyer," Royce finally said.

Tara chuckled and shook her head.

"What now?" Royce asked.

"Why waste the energy of negative emotion? Why not just be grateful he's alive?"

"Oh, I'm ecstatic the love of my life survived the robbery," Royce said. "I just want to make sure he stays alive."

"Sawyer doesn't strike me as a careless person," Tara said.

And up until last night, Royce would've agreed. Well, there was the incident when Sawyer had disobeyed a direct order and entered the church where Royce was squaring off against an arsonist and a puritanical priest. Sawyer had nearly died in that fire because he'd refused to let Royce face them alone. Yesterday, Sawyer refused to give up the engagement ring Royce had given him. The common denominator in both scenarios was Sawyer's love for Royce. It was fierce, all-consuming, and possibly deadly.

"Ro," Tara said, interrupting his thoughts. "What's really eating you?"

He took a deep breath and ran a hand through his hair. "They'll turn on him like rabid animals."

"Who? The press?" Tara asked.

"Yeah. Right now, Sawyer is back to being their golden boy, but what happens when they find out my brother is part of the robbery crew? And it will happen. It's only a matter of time before a gunman or a hostage gets a jumpy trigger finger. Bloodshed will ensue, and lips will loosen. The press and citizens are already questioning why the department hasn't made a single arrest in any of the robberies so far. When Benton's involvement comes to light, everyone will assume I helped cover up his crimes."

"Nope," Tara said.

Ignoring her dismissal, Royce continued, "And everyone close to me will get caught up in the explosion. That includes you."

"This again?" Tara's vainly concealed irritation made him smile. "We discussed the situation last night when I brought you up to speed on the Cupid case. I'm not worried about the potential repercussions, and I don't want a new partner. You'll have to work harder to get rid of me. And don't sell yourself short, Ro. Yeah, some people will raise hell over your brother being involved in the crew, but most will judge you based on your character and deeds. You're going to come out of this okay."

Royce wanted to believe Tara was right. More for Sawyer than himself. The one thing that struck Royce about the situation was that not a single person had questioned Sawyer's judgment. Not Royce, not anyone at the department, and not even Jace or Dru when Royce had called them last night. He needed his brother and sister to be aware in case Benton tried to involve them somehow. Royce wasn't worried so much about Jace and Holly, but Dru and the boys were in a vulnerable spot until they moved out. It was only a matter of time before the heat got to Benton.

Royce expected Dru to resist the notion that their baby brother was that far gone, but she'd only shown concern for Sawyer. That was the greatest testament to the bridge they'd been building over the past two months. It also reminded Royce of the trust Sawyer instilled in people. He had a real chance at winning the election if he chose to run for sheriff. A ruined opportunity was the last thing Royce wanted, but the negative press from being associated with the Locke family could do just that. Hell, Abe had pretty much said the same thing when discussing his own situation with Sawyer. He'd had to move away to pursue a career in law enforcement.

His phone buzzed with a text from Chen. *We've already checked the guys on your list. Sketchy AF but seem clean for these robberies. I'll dig deeper.*

Royce blew out a frustrated breath. "Damn it."

"Problem?" Tara asked.

"I sent Chen a list of Benton's past associates when Bones commandeered Sawyer's attention this morning." He'd slipped his little partner in crime a chunk of his toast under the table for his efforts. "Nothing panned out."

"Yet," Tara stressed. "I have faith in our unit. It will happen."

*The sooner the better for everyone involved.*

Royce forced his attention to their latest investigation because that's where he needed to spend his energy. "Any updates on the warrants for Leo's residence, car, and Cupid's Arrow?"

"Signed, sealed, and delivered this morning," Tara replied. "I had his car towed to our lot last night, and the crime scene team will go over it today. The cyber team has his cell phone and will try to unlock it. Oh, I grabbed his key ring too. It's in the glove box."

"Nice work. You're on fire this morning."

"I credit the fluffiest blueberry pancakes I've ever had."

Those just happened to be Candy's specialty. She made them from scratch every Sunday and had mastered a texture and height Royce had never been able to duplicate. He also knew damn well his godchildren adored those pancakes. Was Tara trying to provoke Royce into thumping his chest over the kids, or was it her subtle way of letting Royce know she and Candy were serious about each other? As if the stickers and *Alice in Wonderland* references hadn't clued him in.

"They're a particular favorite of mine too," Royce said.

Then he opened Tara's glove compartment and pulled out the evidence bag containing a keychain. He removed the keys and examined them closely, looking for signs of a storage unit or something else they'd need a warrant to search. Leo had a Honda keyless fob, several door keys, and two smaller ones. He gestured to the latter and said, "Wonder what these go to?"

"Let's hope we find out easily."

Cupid's Arrow was in a new strip mall with a large chain grocery store anchoring one end and an auto parts store on the other. One of the vast windows featured a silhouette of a cherub etched into the glass. He'd drawn back his bow but hadn't let the arrow fly. Beneath Cupid was their slogan: Our aim is true! The other window featured the business's name in large, elegant script. Below it, their phone number and website appeared in a much smaller and boring font.

The parking lot in front of the business was empty, but Royce figured the employees parked in the back. As they approached the door, Royce noted a diverse group of people standing in the center of the space. All of them were dressed casually, and the business hours on the door stated they were closed on Sunday. He assumed those gathered inside were the employees Sally had promised to make available for interviews.

A blonde woman, who appeared to be in her late forties or early fifties, stood in the middle and was doing most of the talking. The group of twentysomethings gathered around her was so focused on the conversation, they hadn't noticed the two detectives approaching. Royce figured the blonde lady in the middle was Sally Collins, but what was she saying to hold their attention? Royce was glad they'd proceeded with the warrant because he had a feeling Sally had changed her mind about helping them out.

Tara tried the door, but it was locked. She lifted her hand to knock, but Royce stopped her.

"Let's just watch them interact for a moment. I want to get a feel for the group dynamic."

The blonde woman swept her arm out as if to gesture to the office, and that's when she saw Tara and Royce on the other side of the glass. Her mouth fell open, and she blinked a few times before she collected herself and crossed the room to unlock the door and open it.

She plastered a professional smile on her face and said, "Detectives Locke and South? I'm Sally Collins."

Tara extended her hand. "I'm Detective South, and this is my partner, Sergeant Locke."

"Ma'am," Royce said when he shook her hand.

Sally stepped back and gestured for them to step inside, then she locked the door again behind them. "May I introduce you to my staff?"

"Please do," Royce said.

Sally made introductions. Stella, a Black woman with purple braids and killer cheekbones, was introduced as Leo's assistant. She was the first one they'd want to talk to after their interview with Sally. Next, they met John, a ginger with green eyes and freckles who Sally introduced as her savior instead of an assistant. The guy didn't blush or wave her off. He smiled wryly and nodded.

"And these are our wedding consultants, Joy, Billy, and Simone."

Joy was a petite Asian woman with several delicate butterfly tattoos spanning her right forearm. Billy was also Asian and had eyes the color of expensive whiskey. Simone was Latina and her smile was as sunny as the yellow shirt she wore.

"Where do you want to start?" Sally asked after Royce and Tara shook everyone's hands.

"Drinks?" Stella suggested. "What can I get you?"

"It's a little early for me," Royce teased.

Stella smiled. "Water? Coffee?"

They both accepted water, and Royce looked around the large room while they waited. The long rear wall was covered in a wedding-themed mural. The artist had painted a white picket fence with a flower-covered arbor in the center. In front were two mannequins, one in a tuxedo and another in a wedding dress, while Cupid observed from the mural with a smug smile on his face. The mannequins were jarring, and he gave the weird tableau a double take. A row of chairs faced the painted wall and each one was a different style. Royce was grateful they hadn't filled the seats with a bunch of creepy mannequins. Off to the side, an elegantly appointed table was set up for a mock reception. There was a large bookshelf teeming with fabric sample books that reminded Royce of the ones Julian the tailor had pulled out during their tuxedo fitting. Royce knew from Jace's ramblings that a person could customize every aspect of their wedding. He briefly wondered what Sawyer thought about running off to Vegas with him, even though Evangeline would kill them deader than dead if they did.

Opposite the mock wedding was a portioned area with a cubicle providing four workspaces. Royce figured the door Stella had disappeared through led to the executive offices and possibly a breakroom or kitchenette.

"Why don't I go ahead and show you to my office so we can get started," Sally suggested.

"Certainly," Tara replied.

Sally led them through the door Stella had used, and she met them on the other side. The assistant smiled and handed them the water bottles.

"Chat with you soon," Stella said.

Sally's office was an elegantly appointed space with a desk and shelving unit made from light wood and polished to a shine. An ivory velvet couch and matching chairs sat opposite her desk, and Sally settled on the sofa while Tara and Royce took the club chairs facing her.

Sally smiled, crossed her jean-clad legs, and folded her hands on her knees. Everything about her posture spoke of ease and comfort in their presence, which wasn't the vibe Royce had gotten when they'd first walked up to the door.

"How are you holding up?" Royce asked. "I'm sure the news of Leo's death came as an awful shock to you."

Her eyes widened like she hadn't expected him to inquire about her frame of mind. Sally inhaled deeply and released a slow breath. "It was shocking. It still is if I'm being honest. I didn't know Leo very well, but still. Killed at one of our venues? I never would've guessed that in a million years."

"What kind of death had you envisioned for Mr. Fellows?" Tara asked.

Sally placed both hands over her heart and stared at them with wide eyes. "None. I never imagined Leo dead at all."

"You said you didn't know him well, but how long have you known him?" Royce asked.

"Seven months," Sally replied without hesitation.

"That answer came quick," Tara remarked.

Sally smiled indulgently. "It's when Leo bought out my former partner's share in the business."

Royce jotted down her reply before meeting her gaze once more. "You'd never met Leo before the purchase? He didn't come in and interview the staff?"

"Nope," Sally said.

"Why'd your former partner want out of the business?" Tara asked.

Sally tipped her head to the side. "I guess I should direct you to

Jennifer for answers to those questions, but I guess there's no harm in repeating what she told me."

"Jennifer is your former partner?" Royce clarified.

Sally nodded. "Jennifer Ludwig. She'd experienced some health concerns with blood pressure, cholesterol, and blood sugar. Jennifer worked with her doctor and a nutritionist to change her lifestyle. She'd lost a ton of weight, but some of her numbers didn't improve. Her doctor suggested stress was the culprit and encouraged her to make even bigger changes." A hint of bitterness had crept into Sally's voice.

"Let me guess," he said, "Ms. Ludwig didn't tell you about these changes until after she made them?"

Sally nodded. "I'd been naïve about going into business with her and hadn't hired a lawyer to protect my interests. Jennifer owned fifty-one percent of the business and could sell her interests to anyone at any time. And she did. One Friday evening, she wished me a happy weekend and headed out. The following Monday, she brought Leo around and introduced us to the new controlling partner in Cupid's Arrow."

Royce grimaced. "Ouch. That had to sting."

"More than a little," Sally replied.

"Why not allow you to buy her half?" Tara asked.

Sally averted her face but not before Royce saw a telltale blush creeping across her cheeks. "Jennifer knew my financial position wouldn't allow me to buy her out, so she didn't ask. I guess she wanted to spare my feelings."

"Do you know how or when Jennifer met Leo?" Tara asked.

Sally lifted her head once more. Embarrassment still tinged her cheeks but less severely. "No, I'm afraid not. You'll have to ask Jennifer about that."

"Fair enough," Tara replied. "Can you provide us with her contact information?"

Sally removed her cell phone from her pocket and provided Jennifer's phone number and home address. "She travels a lot, so she might not be home. This business is stressful, and I do hope Jennifer is enjoying her early retirement." Sally's words, spoken in dulcet tones, said one thing, but the hard look in her eyes expressed something else entirely.

"When we spoke with Leo's wife, she implied the wedding planning business came out of nowhere. Is that also your impression?"

Sally snorted. "Oh, yes. Leo is—was—a bit, well…robotic. I doubt he had a whimsical or romantic bone in his body. Leo was more comfortable handling the operational aspects of the business. He'd helped build a global shipping conglomerate out of thin air. If I'd heard that once, I'd heard it a thousand times."

"Would it be unusual for Leo to be at wedding venues, then?" Royce consulted his notes from the previous day. "The cake artist mentioned Leo was filling in for you."

"Yes, my grandmother fell and broke her hip last week and had surgery. Leo offered to work my events for me this weekend so I could visit her." Sally took a deep breath. "He was an odd duck sometimes but seemed to place a high value on family."

"I wish your grandmother a swift recovery," Royce said.

"Thank you, Sergeant."

"So, who knew Leo would be working and where?" Tara asked.

Sally tilted her head to the side. "Everyone on our staff, the clients involved, and anyone Leo might've told." She narrowed her eyes. "Surely you don't think one of us killed him."

"We don't know what to think," Tara admitted. "We're just putting preliminary information together. Can you tell us if any clients were particularly upset with Leo?"

She puffed out her cheeks and exhaled. "To be honest, Leo was just the kind of person who got under your skin. He wasn't mean or cruel, just annoying. But still. Killing him? That's so…extreme."

They continued questioning her about Leo, but it quickly became clear Sally didn't know much beyond their business dealings.

"He was married to the best divorce attorney in town, and they have a son," Sally remarked. "I can't remember the boy's name and couldn't tell you his age. I don't know anything else about Leo."

"Anything about his previous employer?" Tara asked.

"Nope."

"Or his twin brother?" Royce asked.

Sally's eyes widened. "There's seriously two of them?"

"Yes, ma'am."

If Leo placed a high value on family, then why hadn't Sally known he had a twin? Royce new some people preferred to keep their personal and professional lives separate, and maybe Leo had just taken that to a more extreme level.

They'd run through their initial questions for Sally, though he anticipated he'd have more later. "Well, I guess we'll start interviewing the rest of the staff, starting with Stella, then we'll look at his computer and listen to any saved voicemail messages."

Sally bit her bottom lip, and Royce braced himself for a reversal. "About that," Sally began. "I talked to my attorney out of an abundance of caution." She smiled wryly at them. "You see, I learned my lesson about leaping before I look. My attorney said I should insist you present a warrant first. I don't want to make this harder on anyone, but I have to look out for my best interests."

"No problem," Royce said.

Sally sighed. "Oh, I'm so glad you understand."

"We understand perfectly," Tara said as she opened her portfolio with the glittery unicorn and rainbow stickers and deftly removed the signed warrant. The smile melted from Sally's face when Tara extended it to her. "Here you go."

Sally accepted the folded document and snapped it open.

Royce and Tara rose to their feet, but she remained seated.

"We'll start with the staff interviews," Tara said. "That will give you enough time to phone your lawyer for advice or have them present."

Sally folded the document and set it on the couch beside her, then looked at Tara. "That won't be necessary. We'll fully cooperate."

They set up the staff interviews in the sitting area of the showroom. Stella didn't have much to say about Leo other than she viewed him in a mostly positive light. She claimed Leo was professional if not a little mechanical and standoffish at times. She claimed to know nothing about his personal life. Just when Royce was ready to chalk their interview up as a loss, Stella let it slip that Leo was always grateful for the team's effort and never lost his temper.

"As opposed to?" Royce prodded.

Stella grimaced. "I really shouldn't say."

"Oh, but you should," Tara told her.

"Miss Ludwig, the previous owner," Stella whispered. "I was her assistant before Leo came. She might've been more knowledgeable about weddings, but Leo was easier to work for."

"You said she had a temper?"

"Oh, mercy me," Stella said, fanning herself. "She wasn't violent or anything, but she had a nasty habit of raising her voice and taking her frustrations out on the messenger. I got anxious whenever I had to deliver bad news."

John, Sally's assistant, was tighter lipped, claiming not to have any opinion on Leo—personally or professionally. "I didn't have much interaction with him here, and Leo wasn't the kind of guy to chat you up at the water cooler." The latter remark rang true, but the part about John not forming an opinion about Leo? Bullshit. It was human nature to do so and was usually done on a subconscious level. Rather than call John out on it, Royce recorded the observation in his notes.

The first two wedding consultants, Joy and Simone, pretty much mirrored what Sally and Stella had said about Leo. They didn't volunteer any new information, but Royce had high hopes for Billy, who looked very uncomfortable when he sat down with them. The guy kept glancing over his shoulder as if he expected to see something or someone behind him.

"What was Miss Collins talking about before we arrived?" Tara asked. Royce knew she'd picked up on Billy's tense vibe and got straight down to business.

Billy swallowed hard, and Royce knew her aim was true. "We just had our typical staff meeting," he replied.

Royce bounced his pen off his legal pad. "You're not usually open on Sundays, though."

"Yes, that's right, but I was referring more to the tone of her pep talk instead of the day of the week. She's just trying to keep up morale."

Royce noted his distant stare and frown. "Billy," he said, snagging the man's attention. "Your demeanor indicates the chat didn't work. Want to tell us what's bothering you?"

Billy took a deep breath and vented his frustrations. He said the first thing Leo had done after coming on board was change their pay structure.

"Oh, that's usually not a good thing," Tara remarked.

"Right?" Billy asked. "And we didn't think Leo's suggestion would be any different."

"What did he change?" Tara asked.

"How we were paid. Initially, Leo had planned to change the consultants from salary to commission. Of course, we balked. I mean, our salaries weren't huge, but it was guaranteed income. Leo kept saying the sky was the limit with the commissions. The more business we brought in, the more we'd get paid. It was too big a change with too little warning."

"What happened?" Royce asked.

"Leo came back with a new proposal to ease us into the new pay scale. He'd start us off with a small base salary but pay us commission on the business we brought in. The commission percentage was smaller since he was giving us a base salary, but Leo said it would allow us to see how much money we could potentially earn. He offered a yearlong trial run."

"How'd the experiment work out?" Tara asked.

"Beyond our wildest dreams," Billy admitted. "I made more in the first four months than I did all of last year."

"Impressive," Royce said.

"Simone, Joy, and I had planned to tell Leo we were ready to transition to a full-commission salary."

Royce tilted his head and considered that. "If you were making more money, were the owners making less?" Billy hadn't known the answer to the question. Royce glanced across the expanse of the showroom and caught Sally watching them. She stiffened and busied herself looking through a book on the shelf. Royce returned his attention to Billy. "What did Sally think about the changes?"

"Which ones?" Billy asked.

"We've been discussing your compensation," Royce replied. "Have there been other changes?"

Billy worried his bottom lip with his teeth. Sensing Royce's scrutiny, he released his abused flesh. "Leo came in and changed everything. Look at this place. It's gaudy as hell with that mural and those mannequins. Sally had an eye twitch for a solid week after the installation. We cheered her up by posing Jack and Jill in new….um, positions each morning before she arrived. Anyway, I'm not sure who brought in the leather harness and strap-on, but we had a field day with that one."

Royce's mouth tilted up. "You named them?"

Billy shrugged.

"Please tell me you have pictures," Tara said.

Billy cast another furtive glance over his shoulder, then pulled out his phone. He scrolled through his album, then laughed when he found what he was looking for. He turned the phone around so Tara and Royce could see it. The wedding clothes had been scattered all around the makeshift altar. Someone had dressed Jack in nothing but a black leather harness and bent him over a chair. Jill stood behind him, wearing nothing but a strap-on.

Billy tucked his phone away. "There've been tea parties and everything."

"Wow," Royce said. "Sounds like elaborate staging. Wasn't it time-consuming to create the scenes and take them down before Leo arrived at the office?"

"Nah, he worked remotely a lot. I just don't think his heart was in the job, you know?" Billy sighed. "I'm going to miss Jack and Jill."

"The mannequins are out of here, huh?" Tara asked.

"Honestly, I'm shocked Sally hasn't tossed them into the dumpster already," he replied. "She's already called a contract—" He stopped suddenly, and snapped his mouth shut. Billy bounced widened eyes between Royce and Tara.

"It's okay," Royce said. "We need to know the truth of how things were going around here. Tacky taste or not, Leo Fellows didn't deserve to die."

"You're right, of course," Billy said. "Sally is proceeding with plans to restore our office to its former elegance."

"And the pay scale?" Tara asked. "How'd Sally react to those changes?"

"She supported our efforts to keep our original salaries. She and Leo even had an argument about it." A hesitant expression washed over his features, and Royce figured they'd have to prompt him again, but Billy continued on his own. "We thought she was looking out for us, but when we started making more money, Sally reminded us that commission work was feast or famine. We told her we were willing to take the risk, and it was obvious she didn't like us taking Leo's side. She didn't say anything directly to us, but she gave us the cold shoulder for a few days. Right before you got here, she said we were going back to our old pay scale immediately."

Royce wondered if the now savvier Sally had reworked the partnership with Leo. Had they written up legal documents to protect their interests if something happened to the other partner? Would those arrangements include life insurance policies? People have certainly killed for less. Royce jotted down a note to ask Sally later. "One last thing," he said. "You mentioned that Leo's heart didn't seem to be in the wedding planning business. So, why do you think he invested in Cupid's Arrow?"

"Money," Billy said. "It's a lucrative business if you play your cards right. Anything else?"

"That's all for now," Royce said. "Thank you for your time."

"No problem."

Sally started in their direction as soon as Billy stood up. Royce watched their body language as they passed by each other. While Sally kept her head facing forward, her gaze briefly strayed toward the younger man. Billy's head never moved, and he didn't alter his posture, so it was impossible to tell if the two made eye contact. And if so, what had it meant?

Sally's smile was cool when she reached Royce and Tara. "I'll show you to Leo's office now."

"Thank you," Royce said.

Leo's office was utilitarian at best. Dark, boring furniture chosen for function over fashion. A desk and matching filing cabinet, a floor lamp, a leather executive chair, and two visitor chairs were the only things in the space. Before he met Sawyer, Royce probably wouldn't have noticed the lack of personality. He wouldn't have thought the room could use some plants, an area rug, and artwork.

Royce turned and smiled at Sally, who hovered in the doorway. "We'll let you know if we have any questions," he said.

Sally nodded jerkily and left them to it.

The shelves were bare except for one framed photo of a blond teenage boy in a soccer uniform. No fabric books, no pictures of different china patterns, no mini kiosk of venue pamphlets. Nothing.

Tara turned to face Royce and put her hands on her hips. "We saw more character in the bail bondsman's office last week. What prospective couple would sign on with this company after seeing this office?"

"Well, it sounds like Leo didn't work with the clients very often," Royce replied as he looked around the room. He crossed to the filing cabinet and opened the top drawer. It was empty. And so were the second, third, and fourth drawers. "No client files or business ledgers. Nothing."

Tara sat down in Leo's chair and started looking through his desk. The middle drawer had a few pens, highlighters, and paper clips, but that was it. The drawers on the right were as empty as the filing cabinet. She looked up at Royce.

"What the fuck is this?" Tara asked. "Either someone emptied this office before we got here, or Leo's involvement is nothing more than a front."

"A front that got him killed?" Royce asked. "Let's see if we can find anything on his computer. It isn't unheard of for a company to go paperless and keep digital records."

Tara wiggled the mouse, and the screen came alive. "It's not password protected, so that should make it easier." She clicked on the internet browser and looked at the history. The only thing Leo accessed was his Gmail account for the business. Tara clicked on it, and Leo's inbox popped up. "There's certainly plenty of activity here," she said.

"Do you want to confiscate the computer or download all the files to a flash drive?"

"Depends on what he's stored on it and whether we need our tech team to check for deleted or hidden content."

Tara clicked around in several places and shook her head. "It appears clean. There are no saved files. I checked his trash and didn't find any deleted documents. He could've emptied the trash, so we could take it back and have our people go through it."

"Let's go through some emails first to see if anything suspicious pops up."

Forty minutes later, the only thing they'd found were emails from pissed-off clients and vendors—many that Leo hadn't acknowledged at all. His outgoing correspondence was all productivity reports and earning statements for Joy, Billy, and Simone.

"These statements look like something generated from QuickBooks. My brother uses it for his landscaping business."

"Where's the software to run the program?" Royce said.

"Not on this computer."

Royce rubbed a hand over his jaw. "We'll confiscate the computer for evidence, and I'll get a warrant for the financial records. Let's listen to the voicemail."

Tara looked at the phone on the far-left corner of the desk. "The system is similar to the one we have at the station. We'll need his password or an override."

"I'll go get Sally," Royce said.

Royce located her in her office down the hall. She was typing furiously on her phone until Royce knocked on the doorframe. She glanced up at him with a serene expression on her face.

"Yes, Sergeant?"

"I need either Leo's voicemail password or an override."

Sally removed a pen from her desk and wrote a series of numbers on a sticky note and handed it to him. "I don't know his password, but this override should get you into his messages."

"Thanks."

"I hate to be rude, but do you have any idea how much longer you'll be?" Sally asked. She held up her phone. "I have a birthday party to attend in a bit."

"We'll make sure you don't miss it."

Royce returned to Leo's office and handed the code to Tara. She typed it in and hit Play on her recorder. The first half dozen saved messages were more of the same complaints from his email, but they hit the jackpot on the final voicemail message.

"Leo," a woman said shrilly. "It's Jennifer. Your six months is up, and your first payment is now three weeks late. I don't care if your big payday hasn't happened yet. You owe me money. Call me right away, or you'll be sorry."

Tara stopped the recording and grinned up at him. "Sounds like a threat."

"That was from Friday?" Royce asked.

"Just before five o'clock. It's a saved message, which means Leo listened to it."

Royce narrowed his eyes. "Someone did. Might not have been Leo. Will you write up an evidence receipt for the computer while I go ask Sally a few more questions?"

"Sure."

Once again, Sally was typing away on her phone.

"I have a few follow-up questions for you," Royce said.

"Okay."

"We just listened to a message from Jennifer, and she claimed Leo was late with a payment. Know anything about it?"

"No, sir," Sally replied. "I haven't talked to Jennifer since she abruptly left the business."

Royce couldn't blame her. "She also mentioned Leo was supposed to come into some kind of big payday."

"Wow. Um, I couldn't tell you anything about that."

"Leo didn't mention anything in passing?" Royce asked

Sally shook her head. "No. If I were to guess, though, I'd say the money was coming from a divorce settlement."

Tara entered the office a moment later and handed the evidence receipt to Sally. "We're confiscating the computer and will return it as soon as our tech team has finished with it."

Sally accepted the form and nodded. "Anything else?"

"Did you and Leo have a formal plan in place in case one of you died?" Royce asked.

Sally narrowed her eyes. "Are you sure I don't need my lawyer?"

"No, I'm not sure," he replied. "Cops will say you don't need a lawyer if you don't have anything to hide. Lawyers will say to never speak to the police without an attorney present. That's your decision to make. If you'd like to call your attorney, we'll wait."

Sally checked her watch and sighed. "I don't have anything to hide, so don't make me regret this."

"I'll do my best," Royce said.

"Yes, Leo and I formed a legitimate partnership that included life insurance policies and a formal plan for the business if one of us were to die. I learned from my mistake with Jennifer."

Royce's pulse kicked into a jaunty trot. "And are you the beneficiary on the life insurance policy?"

"Nope. Leo's policy will pay off his debt to Jennifer. Any extra would pay out to a secondary beneficiary, but I don't know who that is. I assume his son or a custodian acting on his behalf."

"And ownership of Cupid's Arrow?" Royce asked.

Sally notched her chin higher. "I've become the sole owner with Leo's passing. I know that sounds like a powerful motive, but I didn't kill him."

"May we have a copy of your agreement with Leo and any documents or addenda that go with it?" Tara asked.

Sally tilted her head slightly to the right. "Not until I discuss it with my attorney first."

Royce held her gaze for a few moments. "Fair enough. Thanks for your assistance. We'll be in touch if we have additional questions."

Sally nodded, and they left after stopping by Leo's office to take his computer. John shot to his feet when he saw them coming and opened the door for Royce.

"Where to next, partner?" Tara asked once he stowed the computer in her trunk.

"Let's check out Leo's house."

The address Grace Huxley had provided was for a small bungalow in a middle-class neighborhood. It was as stark and nondescript as Leo's office. Not a flower bed or shrub anywhere.

"This is sure a step down from the house Leo shared with his family," Tara quipped.

"Maybe he's not the kind of person who wants, needs, or notices creature comforts."

They retrieved evidence boxes and bags from Tara's trunk then headed to the front door. Royce removed Leo's keychain from his pocket and found the right key on his first try.

"I should've confirmed which of these keys open the doors at Cupid's Arrow."

"His office didn't look like he was there enough to need one," Tara remarked.

The interior of the bungalow was as sparse as the exterior. The living room furniture amounted to a folding lawn chair, a TV tray, and an enormous flat screen affixed to the wall.

Tara gestured to the television and said, "Is it all men? Why does anyone need a TV that big? You can see up the actor's nostrils on this bad boy."

Leo's dining room was empty as were the kitchen cabinets and refrigerator. A quick look in his trash revealed numerous takeout containers. Searching the rest of the kitchen revealed a canister of instant coffee but no creamer or sugar and a single mug. No plates. No silverware.

"Broke or frugal?" Royce asked.

"I had more shit as a college freshman," Tara said. "This feels like a person who's given up."

"Maybe. But why? Sure, his marriage failed, but Grace claims the spark had burned out a long time ago for them both. And seven months isn't long enough to deem his business a wash. And what about this mysterious payday? Sounds like an incredible incentive to live."

Tara blew out a breath. "The source of the payout might just be the solution to this homicide."

The bedroom consisted of a neatly made double bed with a dull-gray duvet cover. Leo's dresser held shirts, socks, underwear, and pants. A few suits hung in his closet, but he mostly owned khaki pants and polo shirts. All his clothing was in drab tones or neutrals. Not a pink polo in sight. And no storage containers, no accordion files with papers, and no secret porn stash. They moved on to the spare bedroom that served as Leo's home office—the only room that showed any sign of life. It was jammed full of office furniture and unpacked boxes. Royce had to turn sideways and scoot between the objects to get to his desk. He handed a laptop to Tara, who turned it on while Royce turned his attention to the desk's contents. He quickly discovered the drawers were locked, so he fished out Leo's keys and tested one of the small ones.

"Bingo," he said. "Hand me a box."

Tara set down the laptop and handed one over. Royce filled it to the brim with file folders, ledgers, and flash drives. They wouldn't know if any of it was vital until they looked through it.

The laptop pinged a few times, and Tara growled.

Royce glanced up. "No luck?"

She shook her head. "This one is password protected."

"Bag it, and we'll have our tech team try to crack it."

The same key that unlocked the desk worked in the lock on the filing cabinet. Royce removed a few more files and ledgers and placed them in the evidence box.

"I think that's it," he said after he emptied the last drawer.

The property didn't have a garage, but it did have a small shed at the back. The second little key worked in the padlock.

"I bet Jimmy Hoffa is in there," Tara said.

Royce snickered and opened the door to reveal a push mower and gas can.

Royce relocked the shed, and the pair headed back to Tara's car and stowed the evidence in her trunk with Leo's work computer.

"Let's see if Larry's back yet," Royce said.

A white sedan was parked in front of the garage. Royce and Tara walked up to the front porch and rang the bell. The door swung open, and Larry Fellows greeted them with red, watery eyes. He looked as if he'd been crying hard. Royce was grateful for Grace's heads up, or he would've thought he was looking at Leo.

"Larry Fellows?" Royce asked.

"Yes," he replied, stepping aside and gesturing for them to come in. "You must be the detectives Gracie told me about."

Tara introduced herself and Royce, and they followed Larry into the living room where three cats meowed and wound themselves around his legs. Larry sat on a sofa, and the felines jumped onto his lap. The most persistent cat was white with black spots that looked like ink splotches. The feline looked over at Royce and meowed loudly. The mark between his ears almost looked like a heart.

"Romeo," Larry scolded the cat. "Don't be rude."

An orange tabby purred loudly and body checked Romeo out of the way. "Be a good girl, Ginger."

A fluffy black feline with one green eye and one blue watched the newcomers suspiciously, twitching his half tail in irritation. Larry called the black cat Hijinks and ran a hand over its sleek fur.

"Your cats look happy to see you," Royce remarked.

"They act like I've been gone for a month instead of a few days," Larry said. He placed all three cats on the floor and gently shooed them away. He turned his attention to Royce and Tara. "Can I get you something to drink?"

They declined and got right into the interview, starting with the last time he'd spoken to his brother.

"It was yesterday morning," Larry said, then paused to wipe his eyes. "I think around ten fifteen."

"Did he seem agitated or upset?" Tara asked.

"Not at all. We were just discussing some issues regarding our elderly father's care."

"Can you think of anyone who'd want to harm Leo?" Royce asked.

"Not a single soul. I know he and Gracie's divorce had gotten pretty contentious, but she's not the type to kill a man." He sighed and shook his head. "It's a shame their marriage failed. After all these years, they suddenly couldn't make it work? Then again, I've never been married, so what do I know?"

They took Larry through all the recent and seemingly sudden changes in Leo's life, looking for clues as to who might've wanted him dead. Like with Grace, Leo's sudden interest in wedding planning had come as a big surprise. Larry claimed he wasn't familiar with Jennifer Ludwig and had no idea how the two had met or what their financial arrangement had been.

"There's a rumor that your brother was about to come into some money," Tara said. "Do you know anything about that?"

Larry took a deep breath and averted his gaze for a few seconds. "Our father isn't in good health, and we stand to inherit quite a bit of money. The sum would've been larger if my brother had his way."

"Meaning?" Royce asked.

"My brother wanted to move Dad to a less expensive nursing facility because the current one costs over ten thousand dollars per month."

Royce let out a whistle. "That's a lot of money."

"It is, but my parents earned the money and set some aside for this very reason. Neither Leo nor I have paid one cent for his care."

"Would you say your brother is money centric?" Royce asked.

Larry tilted his head and considered the question. Royce could see the war raging in the older man's eyes.

"If we're to get justice for your brother, we need you to be honest," Royce said.

"Yes," Larry finally said. "Leo could be avaricious and selfish." His chin wobbled, and he pressed a tissue to his nose. "He was flawed like everyone else, but most of our flaws don't drive people to kill us." Larry shook his head. "I'm afraid I don't have answers for you, Detectives."

After a few more questions, Royce and Tara wrapped up the interview and thanked him for his time.

"So far we have a short list of people with an ax to grind with Leo," Royce said once they were back in her car. "I'd really like to chat with Jennifer Ludwig about her voicemail message on Friday."

Tara nodded. "Let's hope Jennifer and the files we removed from Leo's house offer some answers."

Royce had an unsettling feeling they'd only begun to scratch the surface on this one. He had exactly one week to settle this case before his vacation started. He'd vowed to be on hand as Jace's brother and best man to ensure he and Holly had the perfect wedding. That promise was now added motivation to solve Leo's murder.

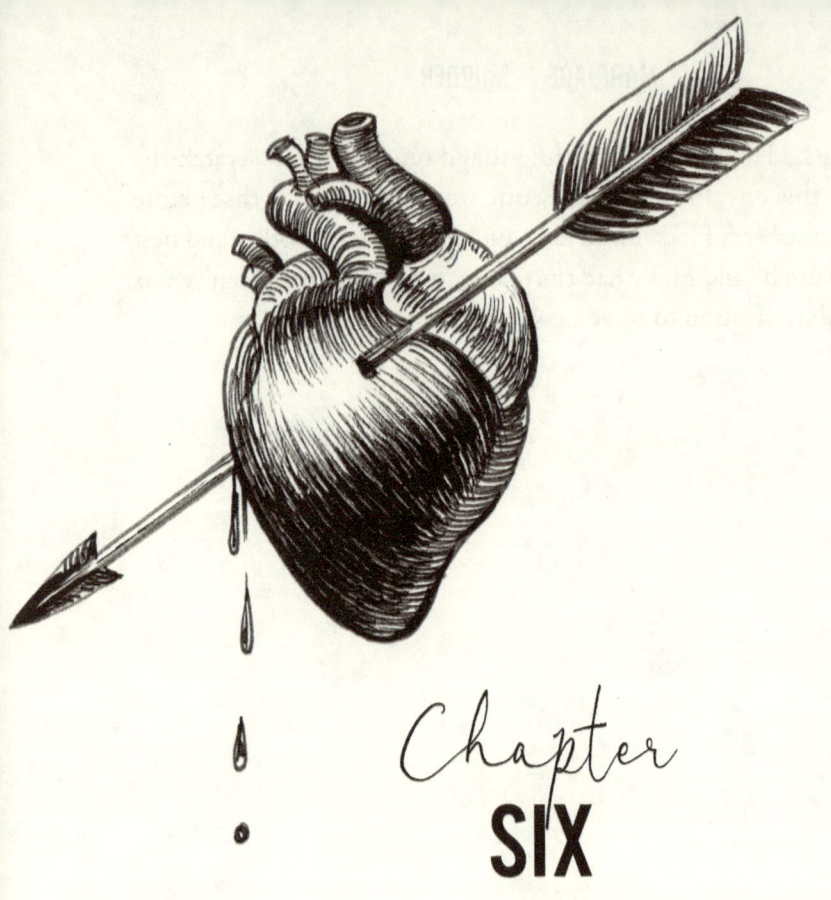

*Chapter*
## SIX

**H**OLLY EYED THE BOX OF DONUTS IN THE CENTER OF THE conference table, then glared at Sawyer.

"Monday morning debriefings require donuts and strong coffee," he said. "Sherry Rigby sends her best."

"Literally," Topher said, reaching into the box and helping himself to a powdered donut. "I don't even care if my pants get tight or I get powdered sugar all over my shirt."

"You don't have to fit into a wedding dress in two weeks either," Holly countered.

"I'll bring in carrots next time," Sawyer said.

Holly narrowed her eyes. "And I'll sharpen one and shank you with it."

Sawyer bit his lip to keep from laughing at her vehement response. He remembered how stressful the final weeks before a wedding were, but he didn't dare tell her she was worrying about nothing.

Holly heaved a weighted sigh and reached for a donut with chocolate icing and sprinkles. "Fuck it. Jace will still want me if I show up in a burlap sack."

"Too true," Sawyer said, recalling the light in Jace's eyes every time he looked at Holly. It didn't matter what they were doing or what she wore. The man was crazy about her. Sawyer experienced the Locke brand of devotion daily and knew just how lucky he and Holly were.

Holly chomped into her donut and closed her eyes, savoring the first bite. Sawyer waited for the rapture to settle before calling their weekly meeting to order, then he told them about the next missing person case he would work on with the *Sinister in Savannah* team and his fresh look at a cold counterfeit money case.

"What about you, Hols?" Sawyer asked.

She detailed her investigation into unsolved bank robberies from the late 2000s.

Topher dusted the powdered sugar off his shirt and sipped his coffee. "Do you think our recent rash of burglaries is connected?" he asked Holly.

"The current assailants have chosen smaller payouts from corner markets and stores that don't have security cameras. If the old players are involved, they would've brought in some new blood."

Holly glanced at Sawyer, and he recalled the conversation they'd had about Benton on Sunday. She'd known Royce was in the field and had come over to hang out with Sawyer. When he'd first woken up, he'd been distracted by Royce's lovemaking and then by his mother's visit. Memories of the previous night had creeped in once he was alone, and he'd found himself dwelling on what would've happened if Benton had pulled the trigger. He'd gone about his business replacing his phone, visiting Courtney and baby Aiden, and checking up on Sal, but he hadn't stopped reliving the feeling of cold metal pressed to his head.

He'd needed someone to talk to besides Royce and his mom. Evangeline would've wrapped herself around him and never left, and Royce would've felt torn between his duty to his job and to Sawyer. Holly appeared on his doorstep like an answer to a prayer, and he was grateful for her friendship. She let him get everything off his chest—the incident itself and the aftermath of realizing the person pressing a gun to his head was Benton Locke.

"He used to be such a good kid," Holly had said tearfully. She'd taken a long, shaky breath, then added, "Between the drugs and his crimes, this can only end one way." The somberness in her voice led him to believe she meant the morgue.

Sawyer wasn't willing to give up so easily. Even though Benton had held a gun to his head, he didn't want Royce's baby brother to die from an overdose or in a police shootout.

"What about you, Toph?" Sawyer asked, getting his mind back on track. "Any luck on the home invasion case?"

It was the most recent of all the cold cases they'd reviewed—only five years old—but it had a host of problems. No one witnessed the home invasion that resulted in an elderly woman's death. The intruder hadn't left any physical evidence behind, and none of the stolen goods had ended up at local pawn shops. The case had gone cold quickly and stayed that way. Topher was doing his best to thaw it out, but his frustrations were evident in his expression and voice as he recapped his investigation.

"Solving cold cases is a long game that requires patience and determination," Sawyer said. "I can't say we got lucky with the Magnolia Murders because a fourth young lady lost her life." But the harsh reality was, without Rachel Morgan's death, they might not have ever solved the original three homicides. "We're not going to close them all, but we can give it our best shot. Keep digging and see what turns up."

After their weekly debriefing ended, Sawyer headed to his office. He'd just sat down when his cell phone rang. It was Felix.

"No comment," Sawyer said in lieu of a traditional greeting.

Felix chuckled. "Oh, come on. Not even a short interview or statement for your old pal?"

"Fine." Sawyer drew out a suspenseful silence and said, "Do you have your pen handy?"

"Yep," Felix replied eagerly. "Let me have it."

Sawyer bit back the chuckle and first retort that came to mind. "I have no comment." He spoke slowly and enunciated carefully.

"You're such a dick," Felix said. "Where's the hero who solved the Magnolia Murders and rescued a pregnant deputy from a gunman?"

"I am no one's hero."

It was a phrase Sawyer had uttered when the first reporter had managed to track him down on Sunday, and he'd repeated it when another cornered him outside the hospital after visiting Courtney and Aiden. He'd keep on saying it until the press refocused their attention elsewhere.

"That's not the story Courtney Capshaw told me," Felix countered.

Sawyer almost caved and asked about Felix's conversation with her. Had Courtney mentioned their mutual friend in the sheriff's department to the news-thirsty reporter? Charlie Price was Sawyer's only friend, if you could call him that, leftover from his CCSD days. Who else could she have been referencing?

"I figured you'd be jumping all over your return to golden boy status," Felix said, jarring Sawyer from his thoughts.

He didn't bother suppressing a groan. "Fuck you, Felix. You were the one who came up with that awful name to begin with, and I hate it." Unless Royce said it, then the words took on an entirely different meaning.

"I used it one time," Felix countered. "I used regular font and lowercase letters. No bold print. No underlines. No italics. I never meant for it to become a moniker you would despise me for."

"That's the reason you think I despise you?" Sawyer asked. "We've been down this road before."

Felix chuckled warmly. "And we keep traveling it, so methinks the subject isn't water under the bridge."

Sawyer's stomach churned and bile rocketed upward. He reached for his coffee to wash it back down, fighting acid with acid. "That's not on you," Sawyer finally said. "This is my personal demon, and I don't mean to keep taking it out on you."

"Want to talk about it?" Felix asked.

"Are you recording this call?"

A scoffing sound came through the phone. "Reporter Felix is taking a break. You're talking to your friend now."

"Still doesn't answer my question," Sawyer said.

"No," Felix said. "I am not recording this call."

Sawyer drummed his fingers against his desk. On the one hand, confiding in Felix could be the worst decision he ever made, but on the other, he needed an objective voice in his ear. Sawyer loved Evangeline and Royce more than life, but they were the president and vice president of his fan club. And maybe he wasn't being fair, but he suspected their opinions were slightly skewed.

"Evangeline wants to put together an exploratory committee to see what the public thinks of me running for sheriff."

"Ah," Felix said. "Are you giving it serious consideration?"

Sawyer nodded, then realized Felix couldn't see him. "I am."

"Do you want my opinion?" Felix asked.

Sawyer braced himself. "God help me, but I do."

"We'll start with the pros," Felix said. "You'd make a brilliant sheriff, and the county would be lucky to have someone like you at the helm. I think the public views you favorably and doesn't care who you love."

"And the cons?" Sawyer asked.

"You hate politics and loathe having your privacy exploited even more. A gay candidate will be more heavily scrutinized than a straight one, and the intensity will only grow if you win. The sheriff's job is more about managing personnel, and I honestly think it would be a waste of your brainpower at this point in your life. You'd get bored quickly and miss the thrill of investigation. I say give it another decade or two before you pursue that kind of position. The people of Chatham County are better off with you solving crimes others can't or won't."

"What about taking down Wheeler?" Sawyer asked.

"That's not your job, buddy. It wasn't then. It isn't now. And there's the crux of the problem, isn't it? You feel like you didn't do enough when you had a chance to run him out."

Sawyer rubbed his chest where the pressure was building. "Maybe."

"That's not a good enough reason to turn your life upside down now. There will be more opportunities and other people who can expose Wheeler as the son of a bitch we know him to be."

Sawyer pictured Courtney as she was yesterday, her face flushed as she cradled Aiden. Who would look out for them? If his suspicion was true and Charlie's speculation was accurate, Wheeler was Aiden's father. Hostile didn't begin to describe the environment Wheeler would create for Courtney when she returned to work. Hell was more like it.

"Sawyer, you still there?" Felix asked.

"Yeah, I'm just thinking about what you said."

"And feeling amazed by how right I am?"

Sawyer chuckled. "Something like that." Then he changed the subject. "Did you receive the information on Andrea Dodd I sent to your assistant for our next missing person feature?"

*Sinister in Savannah* had gotten so big so fast, and the guys had hired an agent, a publicist, and a personal assistant to oversee daily operations while they pursued their other careers. They'd even rented an office and converted one room into a recording studio.

"I did," Felix said. "I saw that her mom, Beverly, was recently diagnosed with terminal cancer. I hope we're able to get answers for her. Rocky has already started digging, and Jonah is working on the age progression images. Are we still on for the interview with her family this week?"

"Yeah."

"Hey, Sawyer," Felix said. "Stay golden."

"Fuck off," he grumbled and disconnected without saying goodbye when Felix's laughter erupted in his ear.

He opened Andrea Dodd's file and reviewed the pitifully small amount of information inside. The detective assigned to work the missing person case in 1987 had seemed too willing to label her a runaway and move on. The whole point of their project's platform was to make people care about the missing, and it was hard to do when they had such little information to go on. Andrea Dodd, if alive, would be fifty-one years old. For the public to care about reuniting her with her family, Sawyer needed to take Andrea from a one-dimensional photo to a real person. He needed to know who her friends were and what had been happening in her life before she'd disappeared. None of that was in her file. He hoped the family interview portion of the show piqued their audience's interest.

When his phone rang, he suspected Royce was checking to see what his plans were for lunch. A glance at the screen showed it was Cassandra Moniteau, his GeneMatch consultant. Sawyer's pulse leaped when he considered the ramifications of her call. He took a sip of water, cleared his throat, and answered.

"Sergeant Key," he said.

"Good morning, Sergeant. It's Cassandra with GeneMatch. How are you?"

He could tell by the tone of her voice that she was calling with bad news. It was the same soft pitch people had used at Vic's funeral to ask how he was holding up. He'd wanted to say, "My husband has been dead for less than a week. How the hell do you think I'm doing?" But he'd simply smiled and told them he was hanging in there.

Sawyer tilted his head and stretched his neck. "Oh, damn," he said. "Just rip the bandage off, Cassandra."

"We've made a positive ID on one of the DNA profiles you sent us last month."

They'd profiled Jessie Walters, a sixteen-year-old boy who'd gone missing in 1985, and Deandra Schultz, a seventeen-year-old girl who'd disappeared in 2002. Which family was he about to devastate? "Jessie or Deandra?"

"Jessie," Cassandra said softly.

Sawyer pictured Alice Walters as he'd last seen her. In her mid-seventies, Alice's quest to find out what had happened to her son kept her active and sharp. Fuck. Would the truth take away her purpose for living?

"Where did you find him?" Sawyer asked.

"Chicago. Allegations were recently made that the police department and the crime lab they used back then had misidentified victims or improperly assigned them to a serial killer who'd been convicted of targeting gay men. If the John Doe was assumed homosexual, they'd allegedly assigned the victim to Denny Lee Matthews, dubbed the Boystown Killer, and dusted off their hands. The justice department became involved, and now CPD is retesting all the DNA of Denny Lee Matthews's alleged victims. I can't attest to anyone's motives, but I do know Jessie Walters's DNA sample was with the other Boystown victims."

Sawyer rubbed a hand over his face. "Christ."

"I'm sorry, Sergeant Key," Cassandra said. "I really wish I had better news for you."

"I just hope this doesn't kill his mother."

"I've got the contact number for the new detective assigned to Jessie's investigation. His name is Rio Santiago, and he works cold cases like you. Seems like a nice guy who's committed to getting justice, especially for the potentially misidentified Boystown victims."

Sawyer jotted down Santiago's number and called him. He wanted as much preliminary information about what had happened to Jessie before calling Jack and Alice, and he needed to act fast. The last thing he wanted was for them to find out from a news outlet.

Santiago answered on the second ring and seemed eager to assist Sawyer.

"There's no kind way to say this," the Chicago detective said somberly. "Jessie Walters was sexually assaulted, bludgeoned to death, and placed in a dumpster. The perp attempted to set the bin on fire to destroy evidence, but a pop-up storm doused the flames. Attempting to hide evidence with fire wasn't part of Denny Lee Matthews's typical MO, and from where I sit, there's no connection between Matthews and Jessie Walters."

"Other than the investigating officer deciding Jessie was gay, right?" Sawyer asked.

Santiago blew out a frustrated breath. "Walters was wearing a mesh crop top, leather shorts, and eyeliner. So, yes, they assumed he was gay and therefore must be one of Matthews's victims. It's not right, and I'll do everything I can to find the real killer, but I don't have much to go on."

"I have a suggestion," Sawyer said, then told Santiago about his project with *Sinister in Savannah*. "We could do a follow-up and have you on the show. It could potentially lead you to someone who knew Jessie."

"That's an excellent idea," Santiago said. "I'm game, but I need to clear it with my supervisor first."

"No problem." Sawyer could only imagine the kind of hell storm the department was under—deserved or not. "Just give me a call when you get an answer."

"Will do," Santiago said. "In the meantime, I'm going to send you everything I have on Jessie Walters's homicide. Feel free to share my contact information with his family, and please pass along my condolences."

Sawyer thanked Santiago again and they disconnected. The email came within five minutes, and Sawyer forced himself to open the link and review every document available. The photos were brutal and brought tears to his eyes. No one deserved to end up in a dumpster like trash. He pulled himself together and dialed Jack and Alice's home number. Alice answered on the third ring. Her voice brightened when she realized Sawyer was calling.

"You have an update for us?"

"Yes, ma'am," he said, knowing he too was guilty of using the funeral voice. "Is Mr. Walters home. I'd like to come by to see you."

There was a hitch in Alice's breath. "Yes," she whispered. "We're both here."

"May I come over now?"

She started crying softly. "Yes, please."

Jack Walters answered the door. His white hair looked even thinner than the last time they'd spoken, and his shoulders stooped even more. He extended a frail hand to Sawyer, and Sawyer shook it. "Sergeant Key," he said, his voice reduced to a hoarse whisper.

They'd shown Sawyer home videos when they first met. Jack had once been a robust man with a booming voice. He was now a husk of his former self, and Sawyer was convinced grief played a more prominent role in his decline rather than age alone.

"Hello, sir."

"Come on into the kitchen. Alice is setting out coffee and cookies. I told her she shouldn't fuss because this wasn't a social call."

"Sometimes it just feels good to be busy," Sawyer said.

Jack nodded and sighed. "Yes, I know that's true."

Alice tried her best to put on a brave face and muster a smile. Sawyer took one look at her tear-soaked cheeks and hugged her. It just seemed like the right thing to do. She pulled back and dabbed at her eyes with a tissue.

"I'll get makeup all over your shirt," she said.

"I'm not worried about that."

Sawyer pulled out a chair and sat down, and the older couple did the same. He went through the phone calls with GeneMatch and Detective Santiago as gently as he could, but he didn't lie or hold anything back. He didn't want them finding out from anyone other than him, and once this update hit the media, he was sure reporters would be calling and knocking at their front door.

He paused a few times to let the couple cry and console each other.

"I should pull myself together," Alice kept saying. "I'm sure you have other things to do."

"This is where I need to be right now. Take all the time you need."

Once he finished, Sawyer provided them with Detective Santiago's contact information. "He seems genuinely invested in Jessie's case. I think his resources are spread thin, but I'm going to do everything in my power to get justice for your son."

Alice dabbed at her eyes and sniffled. She met her husband's gaze across the table and reached for his hands. "I think we always knew our Jessie was different."

Tears spilled down Jack's cheeks. "But we didn't know how to handle it. I was afraid for my son, not disappointed. I should've done more to show him. Why didn't I? How could I let him think running away was his only option?"

Sawyer had no way of knowing what their homelife had been like with Jessie or how their worry manifested. It often looked like disappointment and intolerance. But he saw how much they loved their son and regretted whatever role they had played in his decision to run, and Sawyer wanted to comfort them.

"I'm not sure you're being fair to yourselves," he said. "I was in my early teens when I realized I was gay. My parents had championed LGBTQ+ rights long before I was born, but I still kept my secret from them because I struggled to accept the truth about myself. I've learned that many in the community have the same internal battle. Fear is a powerful thing. Jessie might not have feared your reactions, but he could have worried what your acceptance would cost you. He could've been thinking about what your family, friends, or church members would've said behind your backs or worried they would publicly shun you. I know those thoughts ran through my mind."

*And you know a little something about running away too,* a tiny voice said.

Alice reached over and squeezed Sawyer's hand. "Thank you. At least now we can bring our Jessie home."

"We'll find solace in that," Jack added.

When it was time for him to leave, Alice insisted he take some of her oatmeal chocolate chip cookies with him. Sawyer didn't resist and stress ate them on his way back to the precinct. He started to phone Felix with an update, but a call from Royce came through first.

"Free for lunch?" Royce asked him.

"What did you have in mind?"

"You, me, your office, and a locked door."

"Be there in five minutes," Sawyer said.

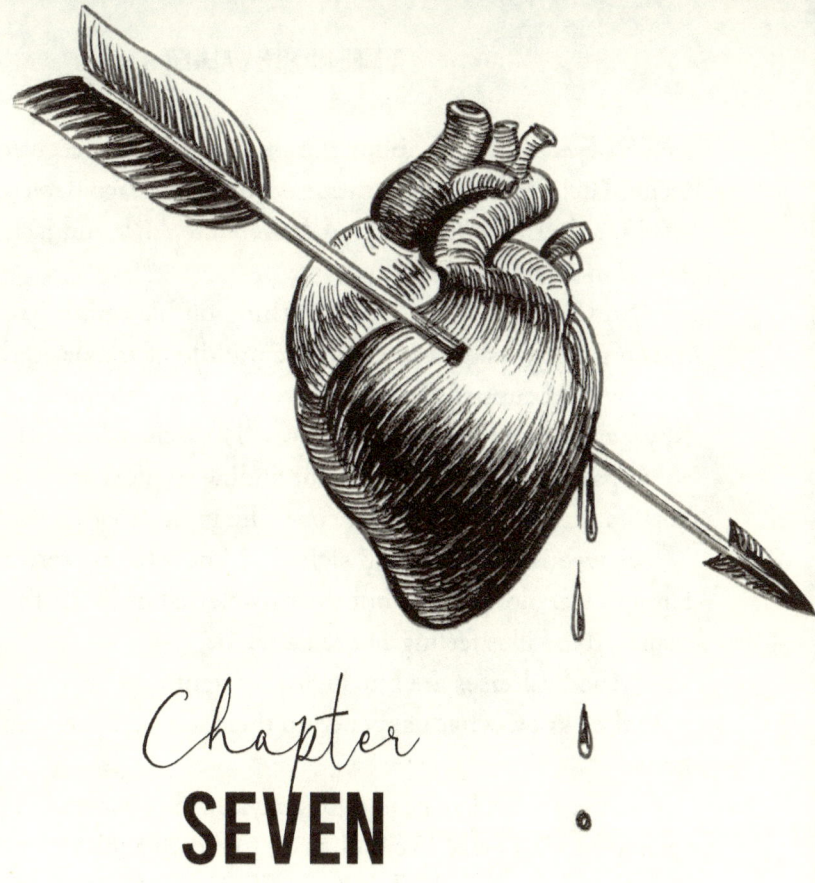

# Chapter
# SEVEN

ROYCE HAD PROACTIVELY SWUNG BY BYTES AND BREW ON HIS way back to the station. If Sawyer hadn't been available, he would've placed his soup and sandwich in the refrigerator for him to reheat later. He'd also swung by the Explorer training rooms and his office and was impressed with the renovation progress. Soon, he and Sawyer would have two locking doors to choose from for private lunches. It also meant the classrooms would be filled with kids who looked to Royce as a role model. Funny how the mere thought of it no longer lanced terror straight through his heart.

Neither Holly nor Topher were at their desks, so Royce went straight to Sawyer's office to unpack the bag. He'd just set Sawyer's broccoli cheddar soup on the desk when his favorite nightmare slayer walked into the room. One look at Sawyer's brooding, dark expression and Royce knew something was up.

"What happened?" he asked.

Sawyer told him about the phone call he'd received from the GeneMatch rep, the conversation with the Chicago detective, and the resulting death notification he'd delivered to Alice and Jack Walters.

"I'm sorry," Royce said.

Suddenly, food was the last thing on his mind. Royce pushed the containers aside and sat in the middle of the desk, then leaned forward and cupped Sawyer's face. His man propped his elbows on Royce's thighs and met him halfway. Their closed-mouth kiss wasn't about passion or lust; it was about finding comfort and relief from the horrors of their jobs with someone who understood.

Sawyer drew back and sighed. "I knew happy results for these families were long shots, but the tiny eternal optimist this job hasn't managed to kill is feeling a little battered."

"The Walterses are hurting badly right now," Royce said, "but at least they know what happened to their son, and they can bring him home."

"That's what I've been telling myself," Sawyer said. "I just got off the phone with Felix. We both want to record a follow-up special and do what we can to help the Chicago PD solve Jessie's murder. I'm just waiting to hear back from Detective Santiago about his participation."

"Better to turn the hurt and disappointment into something positive," Royce said.

"Well, I ate my weight in oatmeal cookies on the way back here."

Royce grimaced and Sawyer laughed at his aversion to oatmeal.

"They had chocolate chips instead of raisins," Sawyer explained.

"Still no dice."

Sawyer looked at the food on the desk. "So, this really is a lunch date?"

They'd joked about doing more than kissing in Sawyer's office but hadn't crossed that line yet. That didn't stop the fantasies from rolling through Royce's mind like a raunchy porn flick.

Sawyer bit his bottom lip and inhaled sharply. "Don't look at me like that unless you mean it."

"Oh, I always mean it," Royce replied. "I just know better than to cross certain lines."

Sawyer squinted and tipped his head back. "Since when?"

"Since the day I decided to be the man you deserve."

"Fuck, I love you," Sawyer said.

"I love you most." Royce leaned forward and pressed a quick kiss to Sawyer's lips. "But I'm not going to bend you over this desk and fuck you."

Sawyer snapped his fingers. "Damn it. Well, I guess you can feed me and tell me about the latest developments in your investigation."

Royce groaned and slid off Sawyer's desk, then walked around and dropped into one of the visitor's chairs.

"That bad, huh?" Sawyer asked.

"It's just frustrating. We keep hearing Leo was expecting to come into a sizable chunk of change, but the source of said elusive windfall varies based on who's telling the story. And we found no clue about it in Leo's confiscated files. Most were just joint financial documents with Grace Huxley, and none of them were recent. I have a feeling the current stuff is on his personal computer, but it's password protected. Our cyber techs are working on that. We found some flash drives too, but they contained thousands of family pictures, dating back to black-and-white photos taken long before Leo and Larry were born. Someone took the time to scan them all onto flash drives." Which gave some credence to Sally's assertion that Leo prized family.

"I bet the originals are in a safe deposit box at a bank," Sawyer said.

"We're putting together warrants for his financial institutions, so we'll soon find out."

Sawyer scrunched up his brow, and Royce could practically hear his gears grinding. "Where'd this idea of a financial windfall even come from?" he asked.

"The first person to mention it was Jennifer Ludwig," Royce replied. "She sold her shares of Cupid's Arrow to Leo, giving an industry novice controlling shares over her longtime partner, Sally Collins."

Sawyer pulled the lid off his soup and pushed a spoon into the creamy broth. Royce wished he'd picked the cheesy broccoli over vegetable beef. Seeing Royce's intense stare, Sawyer shoved the soup across the desk and reached for the other container, even though he had no idea what was inside. The gesture made Royce's chest tighten but in a good way. Sawyer picked up a wedge of his turkey club sandwich and placed it on Royce's open wrapper, then he helped himself to half of Royce's Reuben, and opened the lid on the vegetable soup.

"What happens to Leo's share of the business now that he's dead?" Sawyer asked before spooning up a bite.

Royce swallowed a bite of turkey club before answering. "According to Sally, she's now the sole owner of Cupid's Arrow. And one of her consultants claimed she's already made plans to renovate the space." Royce explained the terms of the agreement as Sally had recited them. "We asked to see a copy, but she wanted to speak to her attorney first." Royce and Tara decided to give Sally a little longer before they circled back to her.

"I would seek legal counsel too if I were her," Sawyer said. "What did Ludwig say when you interviewed her?"

"She's on vacation in the Bahamas, but we spoke to her over the phone this morning. She said she'd have her attorney send the agreement she had with Leo if we don't find a copy in his records. I asked her to send it anyway to make sure it matches whatever we do find."

"So she has a solid alibi?"

"Yeah," Royce said. "Jennifer has been there for over a week and has tons of receipts to prove it. I confirmed her hotel stay and car rental. Sally was also out of town. Either one of them could have hired someone to kill Leo, though."

"What did Ludwig say about the source of the money Leo was expecting?" Sawyer asked.

Royce shrugged and took a bite of the soup Sawyer had traded. "She claims she didn't ask. The source didn't matter to her."

"How'd she and Leo meet?"

Royce dropped his pickle spear onto Sawyer's sandwich wrapper. He only liked pickles when sliced thin, battered, and fried, but Sawyer loved them in all variations. Royce forgot the question when Sawyer lifted the spear to his mouth. He wrapped his lips around the pickle and sucked the juice from one end. Sawyer made everything look sexy, and eating was no exception.

"You're telegraphing your dirty thoughts again," Sawyer quipped, then *crunch*ed through the spear.

Royce forced his gaze away from Sawyer's mouth and met his twinkling eyes. "What did you ask me?"

"I wanted to know how Jennifer Ludwig and Leo met."

"Rotary Club," Royce said, sounding breathless.

"What are some other theories about the money?" Sawyer asked. They both knew it would be one hell of a motivator.

"Sally Collins, the partner, assumed the money would come from his pending divorce settlement. Leo's twin brother, Larry, speculated his brother was banking on their dad dying so he could get his hands on an inheritance."

"Cold," Sawyer said.

"Right?" But it didn't jive with someone who valued family, so Royce wasn't convinced. "I circled back to Grace Huxley and asked her about the divorce settlement. She claimed there was none. In fact, Leo stood to lose money in their divorce, not gain it."

"Where does she think the money was coming from?" Sawyer asked.

"She's doubtful there was an influx of cash coming at all. She did say at one point Leo was contemplating a lawsuit against Abbot & Marsh for wrongful termination."

"Is that the place he worked before buying into the wedding planning business?"

Royce lifted the Reuben to his mouth but paused. "Leo Fellows didn't just work at Abbot & Marsh. He was the chief operating officer and one of the founders." He sank his teeth into the sandwich and savored the different textures and flavors.

"I think it's odd you eat sauerkraut but don't like pickles."

Royce shrugged. "I like what I like."

"So the divorce settlement is the only one you can rule out right now," Sawyer said. "Grace Huxley has to know lying to you would only come back to haunt her. It's possible Leo's influx of cash was from something illegal too."

"True. I'm hoping Leo's phone activity will reveal something. We should get the records soon. We're waiting on a judge to sign off on the warrant for Leo's personal and business financial accounts. Hopefully, we'll find some deposits to trace."

"Follow the money," Sawyer said.

Sawyer's phone vibrated, and he checked the screen. He tapped his phone, then smiled at whatever came up.

"Is that a YouTube notification from some hot-for-cop fan making thirsty remarks on your last *Sinister in Savannah* feature?"

Sawyer looked up at him with a puzzled expression. "Huh?"

Royce chuckled. Of course Sawyer hadn't bothered to read the comments on the videos. Unfortunately, Royce revealed that he had. "You're popular with the true-crime enthusiasts. People want you to arrest them."

Sawyer scrunched up his face. "What for?"

"Anything and everything," Royce told him.

Sawyer snorted and shook his head. Then he turned his phone around and revealed a photo of a newborn baby. "Just a picture of Aiden. Courtney's mom got her a temporary phone until the replacement arrives from her carrier."

"Cute little guy," Royce said. "I got home so late last night we didn't have a chance to talk about your visit with Courtney. I see it went well if you've given your phone number to the newest member of the Sawyer Key Fan Club."

Sawyer looked up and grimaced. "I might've also volunteered us to paint Aiden's nursery this weekend. She'd been buying paint to do the job herself when the robbery went down." Sawyer averted his gaze and absently stirred his soup.

"Out with it," Royce said.

Sawyer met his gaze. "I'm pretty sure Courtney was the deputy who had an affair with Wheeler." He told Royce about her mutual friend remark.

"Of all the people for you to run into," Royce said. "That's quite a coincidence."

Sawyer scowled. "I don't believe in them."

Royce knew as much, but he needed Sawyer to admit it out loud. He'd been imprisoned by indecision for a few months, and it was taking a toll on him. "I think the universe is telling you something."

Sawyer took a deep breath. "That I should run for sheriff?"

"Maybe, but it's not the only potential message, GB. You've been blaming yourself for the situation Courtney is in, but you don't even know if she's the deputy in question. If it is Courtney, you were there to help her out during a crisis. You should consider the score settled."

"Until the next time Wheeler fucks someone over." Sawyer pressed. "Then I'll have to relive this turmoil all over again." He shook his head. "I need a more permanent solution."

Royce studied Sawyer's expression. If he were passionate about the idea of running for sheriff, energy would be coursing through his body like static. The dour expression tugging his sexy lips into a frown looked more suited to a funeral. And that's when Royce truly understood the root of Sawyer's problem. If he ran for sheriff, it would be the death of the private oasis they'd built together. There was no such thing as privacy in politics. Even if Sawyer won—and Royce believed he would if the Locke affiliation didn't clobber his chances—Sawyer would be under constant scrutiny. The gay sheriff taking down his homophobic predecessor would make national headlines. Some people loved that kind of attention, but it would kill something beautiful inside Sawyer. Royce could speak his concerns out loud, and Sawyer would listen, but it would be better if Sawyer came to the conclusion on his own.

Giving Sawyer an alternative option to consider was something he could do, though. "We could come up with other ways to take Wheeler down."

Sawyer's lips quirked into a wry smile. "I'm not really a superhero, although I wouldn't mind roleplaying that with you naked."

Royce was nearly distracted from his train of thought, but he managed to steer himself back on course. Chocolate brown eyes glittered with smug pride, so Royce's temporary derailment must've shown on his face.

Sawyer took a deep breath and said, "I think my problem is more deeply rooted than I realized."

"Of course it is."

Sawyer smiled wryly and shook his head. "You're just going to let me parse this out piece by piece like some personal quest?"

Royce chuckled, then leaned across the desk to kiss him. "I'll be right beside you the entire way."

Sawyer checked his watch and glanced up at him. "How much time do you have?"

"Until Tara gets back from lunch or I have a break in my case." Royce tilted his head to the side and studied Sawyer. "What did you have in mind?"

"Come closer and I'll tell you."

Royce rose to his feet. Sawyer shoved their food to the far end of the desk and scooted his chair back so Royce could resume his perch in the middle. Royce snagged Sawyer by the tie and pulled him closer. "Here I am," he said.

Sawyer chose to express his intentions with actions, not words. He rose to his feet, cupped Royce's face, and pressed their mouths together in a devastating kiss. Sawyer kept it mostly chaste with only the barest hint of tongue here and there. The scent of Sawyer's body wash tickled his senses and stirred something else a little farther south.

Royce pulled back and stared into Sawyer's eyes. "What's this scent called again?"

"Juniper and sea salt."

"Delicious," Royce said. When he leaned forward for more kisses, he had every intention of delving deeper into his fiancé's mouth. He'd almost reached his target when Sawyer's phone rang. "Ignore it."

Sawyer inhaled a long shaky breath and released it slowly. "Can't. It could be Courtney needing a ride home." Sawyer pulled his phone out and checked the display. "Nope. It's Evangeline." He accepted the call and greeted his mother warmly.

Royce could hear her, even though Sawyer hadn't put the call on speaker.

Sawyer laughed. "Mom, slow down. You're talking too fast, and I only made out three or four words from that entire spiel. How much coffee did you drink today?" He listened as she repeated herself. His gaze met Royce's, and something delicious and dreamy sparked in their depths. "Let me put you on speaker. Royce is with me right now." He punched the button and held the phone between them.

"Hello, boys," Evangeline said. "I have exciting news to share. I found the most amazing venue for your wedding ceremony, and they've had a cancellation for July thirtieth. Would you be able to pop over for a few minutes for a tour? I don't dare let the event coordinator out of my sight. She might get a call from someone else."

"We'll take it," Royce said.

Evangeline snorted. "You don't even know where the venue is."

"Doesn't matter," Royce replied. "I'd settle for a pit of snakes."

Sawyer scowled at him. "Speak for yourself."

"They wouldn't be poisonous," Royce countered.

Sawyer shook his head. "No damn snakes."

"As if that would ever be an option, Sawyer," Evangeline said. "Are you guys sure July thirtieth isn't too soon?"

"Is it too soon for our wedding planner, though?" Royce asked.

Evangeline snorted and called out, "Denise, put us down for the thirtieth."

"Yes, Ms. O'Neal. I'd be happy to," came the reply.

Butterflies took flight in the pit of Royce's stomach, matching the joy dancing in Sawyer's glittering gaze. They were indeed doing this, and nothing in Royce's life had felt so right.

"Guess I better start making calls," Evangeline said. "We now have a wedding date and venues for the ceremony and reception. Picking out food with Ryan and Rita will be a snap. We'll need to choose a cake designer, which might be a problem. They're all probably booked months in advance."

"Sherry Rigby," Royce and Sawyer said at the same time.

Evangeline gasped. "That's a wonderful idea. Why didn't I think of her? I know she makes amazing pastries, cookies, and cupcakes, but I wonder if she makes wedding cakes."

"I'd be fine with a pretty cupcake display and a pastry buffet," Sawyer said.

Royce grinned. "Suits us better than a fancy cake that shoots flames ten feet in the air."

"That was not an option," Evangeline said.

Royce laughed. "Chocolate waterfall?"

"Gross," she hissed. "I have a photographer in mind. Her vision is pure artistry, and she's trying to get her business off the ground. Printing invitations is child's play now."

"Group text," Sawyer suggested. "Or a Facebook event invite."

Evangeline snorted, then giggled. "I can't with you. Which leaves us with tuxedos or suits as the only other big consideration. Oh, and a DJ."

"I'll create a playlist," Sawyer said. "We'll hook it up to a Bluetooth speaker."

Royce laughed. "And one of your audiobooks will start playing. Probably during some sexy times."

"Oh god," Evangeline said. "I'll handle the DJ right away."

"I'm picking up my tuxedo for Jace's wedding soon," Royce said. "They were able to accommodate us on short notice. Sawyer can come with me when I pick mine up, and we'll schedule fittings."

Evangeline sighed. "Perfect. You guys still didn't ask where the ceremony will take place."

"Doesn't matter," Royce and Sawyer said at the same time.

They laughed, and Royce kissed Sawyer's smile. "We'll see it on the invitation," he said.

"Fine," Evangeline said. "I won't keep you any longer. I know you have work to do. Love you."

"Love you too," Royce and Sawyer said. They told her goodbye, disconnected the call, and stared into each other's eyes.

"We're really doing this," Sawyer said excitedly.

"Hell yeah, we are."

Just as Royce moved in for another kiss, his phone pinged with an incoming text. He checked his phone and saw it was a message from Tara.

*Have Leo's phone records.*

Royce looked back up and found Sawyer smiling at him.

"Go catch your killer Cupid," Sawyer said.

Royce kissed him fast and hard. "Do not steal Courtney's baby."

Sawyer laughed. "He's cute, though, right?"

"Yeah, but let's approach parenthood in a way that doesn't involve us breaking the law."

"Fine," Sawyer agreed.

After another quick kiss, Royce left Sawyer and headed up to the MCU's bullpen where Tara waited for him. Something was off about her appearance, and he had a sneaky suspicion her lunch hadn't been as PG as his was with Sawyer. Her hair was perfectly styled and nothing about her face gave her away. No puffy lips or lipstick stains on her collar. So what was it? That's when he noticed her shirt wasn't buttoned properly. Royce couldn't fight back the laughter rumbling through him.

"What are you laughing at?" Tara asked.

Royce pointed to her shirt. "Manage to get in some boxing practice over lunch?"

Tara's mouth quirked up. "Something like that." She handed him a printout of phone records and said, "I'm going to the locker room to fix my shirt. See if you can't close this case while I'm gone."

Royce flopped down in his chair. The first thing he did was look at the incoming and outgoing calls on the morning Leo died. Just as Larry had said, Leo had called him at ten fifteen. Larry was wrong about being the last person to speak to his brother, though. Leo had placed a call to a local cell phone number right before eleven o'clock, which lasted for over ten minutes. Too long to be a message but too short to be a deep conversation. Was it long enough to entice someone to kill Leo? And who? A pissed-off client, vendor, or competitor?

"One way to find out," Royce said. He picked up his desk phone and dialed the number since it would come up as unknown on someone's caller ID. After four rings, a voicemail message picked up.

"Hello, you've reached Glen Bishop, CFO for Abbot & Marsh. Please leave your name and number—"

Royce hung up the phone and smiled like the Cheshire Cat when Tara strode into the bullpen. "Guess who Leo called last?"

After a few guesses, Tara glared at Royce. "Just fucking tell me already."

"Glen Bishop, the CFO for Abbot & Marsh. The company is one potential source for Leo's large payout. And their CFO is the last person he spoke to. That's two dots we've connected."

"It's time we pay them a visit," Tara said. "See if we can connect a few more."

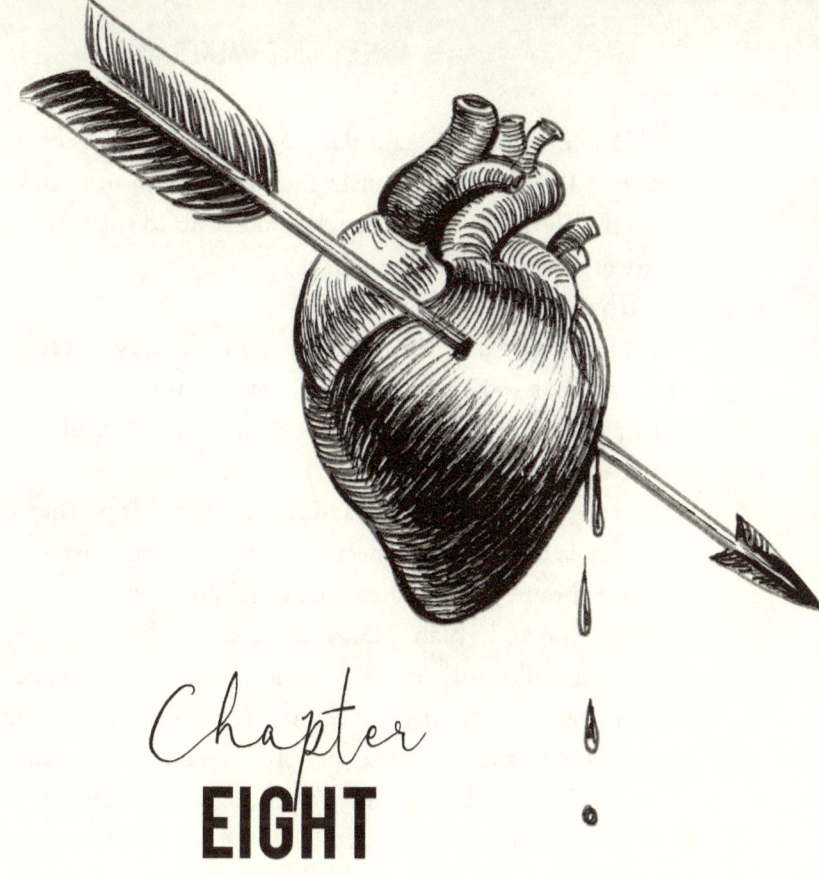

# Chapter
# EIGHT

EVERY SURFACE IN THE LOBBY OF ABBOT & MARSH'S FIVE-STORY
building was polished to a shine. The marble, wood, chrome, and
glass sparkled with vitality, which was in direct contrast to the
shark-eyed woman at the reception desk. Her name tag read Ms. Lively,
but Royce had seen more animation in Leo Fellows's dead stare on
Saturday afternoon.

"Can I help you?" Ms. Lively asked, her voice dull and devoid of
emotion.

"We're here to see Glen Bishop," Tara said while Royce pondered
who'd taken a shop vac to the receptionist's soul.

Ms. Lively looked from Royce to Tara without blinking her ice-
blue eyes. "Do you have an appointment?" Still no inflection.

Royce showed her his badge. "I'm Sergeant Locke with the
Savannah Police Department, and this is Detective South. It's impera-
tive we speak to Mr. Bishop."

"One minute," she said flatly and picked up a receiver. "Calista, Savannah PD is here to see Mr. Bishop." After a second, she hung up and said, "Elevators are to the left. Take it up to the fifth floor. Calista will meet you there."

"Thank you," Tara said.

"Have a nice day." Ms. Lively's robotic delivery of a typically cheerful phrase was so jarring that Royce stared at her even after Tara had walked away. She didn't blink. She didn't smile. Nothing.

"Let's go, Locke."

Royce tore himself away and caught up to his partner at the elevator bank. "Is this what corporate America does to a person? I seriously think we should go back there and check for a pulse."

Tara snorted. "Nah. That's the look of a woman who's been told she should smile more too many times. Like, I'm talking her entire life. She can trace it as far back as Sunday school and family gatherings as a kid. It would start with the nice church lady or an overzealous aunt or uncle. 'Smile and look pretty,' they'd say. The habit would continue with her teachers in elementary school. It wouldn't be enough that she got excellent grades. In high school, some dickhead Casanova would tell her she'd be so much prettier if she smiled. Oh, and he could be the one to put a smile on her face. Ugh. The pattern would continue at every job. Her evaluations would speak of her glowing job performance but would recommend she be more personable and approachable. And can you imagine the jokes she's heard with the last name Lively?"

Guilt heated Royce's face. "Sounds like you're talking from experience."

"Let's just say I learned to fake a lot of shit as a queer kid. It made me miserable. One day, I decided I wouldn't fake another damn thing for another damn person. I'll smile when I fucking want to and not a second before." Tara savagely pushed the button for the fifth floor and crossed her arms over her chest.

"I really like you," Royce said.

Tara looked at him and quirked a brow. "Even though you think I'm stealing your best girl and her kids?"

Royce smiled. "They have plenty of love to go around." And they did. There was nothing more he wanted than for Candy to find real happiness with a partner who would worship her beyond their dying breath and be a good parent to Marc, Daniel, and Bailey. It wasn't too much to ask for. "And I can tell you really care about them."

Tara didn't verbalize a response, but her dazzling smile told him everything he needed to know.

When the elevators opened on the top floor, a brunette dressed head to toe in severe black greeted them. Her clothes were drab and somber, but her smile was warm and engaging. She introduced herself as Calista and shook their hands.

"Right this way," she said, then led them down a corridor at a brisk pace. "Mr. Bishop is in the middle of an important phone call. I'll show you to the conference room, and he'll join you as soon as he's finished." She opened a door and flipped on a light switch. "Here we are," Calista said. "Can I get either of you something to drink while you wait? Coffee, tea, water, or soda?"

Royce and Tara declined and sat down in two of the ten leather executive chairs positioned around the long, narrow table. A console for conference calls sat in the center, and a tablet was placed in front of each chair for video chats.

"Do you think he was on a call before we arrived, or is he stalling for time?" Royce asked.

Tara shrugged. "Could go either way. I'd imagine the CFO of a global logistics company spends a lot of time on the phone. Then again, he might be phoning his lawyer or stalling for time."

"Or putting his alibi together," Royce suggested.

"That too," Tara said. She set her portfolio down and Royce noticed a few more stickers. He recognized Daniel's contribution from the superheroes now decorating the black leather.

"I see you've charmed Candy's two youngest kids." Marc would be the hardest to impress. He was Marcus's firstborn and his namesake. The boy hadn't slept properly for months after his dad died. Daniel had been too young to truly understand, and Bailey had been an infant. Tara was the first person Candy had dated in the three years since Marcus's death. "How's Marc?"

Tara met his curious gaze with a soft smile. "He wants me to teach him how to box."

The idea warmed Royce's heart. "What does his mother say about that?"

Tara's smile turned dreamy. "Candy first made sure he didn't want to learn for the wrong reasons. She talked to him about bullying people and starting fights. Then she worried he was the one getting bullied and wanted to defend himself." Tara chuckled. "Marc told her he just wanted to learn because it's badass. That sparked a conversation about language, and afterward, I got the green light. I gave him an old punching bag and taught him some basic moves. They're great kids." Tara's eyes glazed over with an emotion she didn't verbalize, but she didn't need to. He recognized someone who'd been gobsmacked by love.

Before Royce could comment further, a trio of dour-faced men entered the boardroom. Two of them looked to be in their midfifties and wore suits. The first guy through the door was stockily built with sandy brown hair going gray at the temples. He wore a black three-piece suit and a red tie. The man behind him wore a navy-blue suit with a white shirt open at the throat and no tie. He was the tallest of the three, probably an inch or two over six feet. It was always hard to judge someone's height when sitting down. He sported a severe combover, which only made his gray hair look thinner. The last man to shuffle in appeared to be two decades older. He had thick, impeccably styled white hair and bushy white eyebrows. He was dressed for golf in a polo shirt, khakis, and a visor and smelled like sunscreen.

Royce pegged the first two as the CEO and CFO, but who was Arnold Palmer bringing up the rear? Had they yanked their attorney off the course?

The guy in the black suit extended his hand and said, "I'm Bart Alexander, CEO of Abbot & Marsh." After an aggressive handshake, he gestured to the blue-suited man standing beside him. "This is Glen Bishop, our CFO." They shook hands. "And this is Archie Hayes, our board chairman." So not their attorney.

Royce and Tara shook hands with Archie, then the trio sat down across from them.

Bart folded his hands on the table while the other two kept theirs out of sight. "What can we do for you?" Bart asked.

They'd only asked to speak to Glen Bishop but ended up landing the CEO and chairman too. Because they had nothing to hide or because they had everything to lose? Rather than inquire about Leo's unexpected windfall, Royce decided to take advantage of their willingness to speak. But after only a few minutes of asking the most basic background questions about their company, it became apparent why Bart was present. He barely let the other two men get a word in edgewise.

"Why are you asking questions you can find the answers to on the internet?" Bart asked.

Royce held his gaze. "Because I don't want the watered-down, PR-approved answers. I simply want the truth."

"But what does Abbot & Marsh have to do with Leo's death? We're all deeply shocked and saddened by his passing, but he hasn't worked here for eight months."

"But you've known him for decades," Tara countered. "Part of solving someone's murder is finding out who they were and who might want to harm them."

Bart scowled at her. "Which prompted you to run right over here?"

"Sir," Royce said patiently. "Mr. Fellows died two days ago. I'd hardly say we rushed right over."

"Get on with it, Sergeant," Bart snarled. "We have deals to close."

Royce bristled at his tone but kept his cool. "Why did Leo leave Abbot & Marsh?"

"What does that have to do with anything?" Glen asked. The CFO might've been bigger in stature, but Bart had the dominant personality. How did Leo fit in?

"It's none of your business," Bart said smugly. "And don't you need a warrant?"

Royce held his gaze. He would not be intimidated by this blowhard bully. "I assure you, Mr. Alexander, everything to do with Leo Fellows is very much our business."

"We'd only need a warrant to search the premises," Tara explained. "We're only here to learn what we can about Leo Fellows and his frame of mind at the time of his death. He'd made such drastic changes in the past year. He quit your company and—"

"He didn't quit. We fired him," Archie Hayes said, his voice gruff but firm.

"Archie, don't," Bart said.

The chairman turned his head to look down the table at Bart. "It's the truth. We didn't break any rules, and we don't have anything to hide. We should cooperate with the police and try to keep our company name out of the coverage." Archie returned his attention to Royce and Tara once more.

"Why did you terminate his employment?" Tara asked.

"As chief operating officer, Leo was in charge of daily operations. When profits fell, performances faltered, and morale had plummeted for three consecutive quarters, the board decided we needed new leadership. Removing Leo from his position was a unanimous decision."

Bart nodded. "A wise one."

"Brutal," Royce said.

"Not at all," Archie countered. "We offered Leo a handsome severance package."

"How handsome?" Tara asked.

"We're not at liberty to disclose that information per the legal agreement all parties signed," Bart replied. Another document they needed to track down.

"For crying out loud, Bart," Archie said. "Leo has been murdered, and these detectives are trying to bring his killer to justice." He shook his head and added, "Leo's package included a lump sum financial settlement and continuation of his employee benefits for three years."

Was Abbot & Marsh the source of the payout Leo kept referring to?

"When was Leo supposed to receive his lump sum?" Royce asked.

The three men exchanged a confused glance.

"He received it a few weeks after he left," Archie said.

Royce jotted that down. "When was Leo's employment terminated?"

The chairman scrunched up his forehead, and his eyebrows looked like fuzzy caterpillars about to square off. "Eight months ago." A month before buying Jennifer Ludwig's half of Cupid's Arrow.

"Look," Bart said, "I know I've come off strong here, but I'm just protective of the company I built from nothing."

"We," Glen said softly.

"*We*, what?" Bart asked him.

Glen turned his head and met Bart's gaze head-on. A flush crept up his neck and mottled his cheeks. "*We* built this company from nothing."

Bart patted Glen on the back. "That's what I mean," he said before aiming his steely gaze at Royce. "We are very sorry for Grace and Sam, but we can't be of any help to you. None of us has even spoken to Leo since his last day at Abbot & Marsh."

Royce slid his gaze to Glen once more, and the CFO averted his eyes but not before Royce saw his cheeks turn a darker shade.

"Leo's phone records tell a different story," Tara said.

"That's preposterous," Bart blustered. "None of us—" His protest died when he turned to look at Glen Bishop. "Glen?" Bart stared hard enough to bore holes into Bishop's head.

Hearing his name must've shaken Glen from his reverie. He darted a glance at Bart before locking eyes with Royce. "Leo only left a voice-mail message."

"What did he want?" Bart asked tersely.

Glen shrugged but didn't look at him. "He just said he wanted to speak to me. I never called him back."

"Mr. Bishop," Royce began slowly, "you have to know that Leo's phone records included the duration of the call. Would you like to change your answer?"

Glen kept his eyes locked on Royce, but Bart focused on Glen. The longer the CEO stared at his CFO, the redder his face became. Glen was the opposite. The color leached out of his face like someone was draining the life from his body.

"How long?" Bart asked without looking away.

"Ten minutes and forty-two seconds," Tara replied. "Too long for a voicemail message, but even if it weren't, you'd surely know the purpose for his call after ten minutes."

"You're the last known person to speak to Leo before he died," Royce said. "We need to know what you talked about, Mr. Bishop."

The CFO squared his shoulders, and color seeped back into his face. "I'd like to consult with my attorney before I continue this interview."

Royce removed a business card from his portfolio and slid it across the table. He held Glen's gaze as he and Tara stood up. "Don't keep me waiting long, Mr. Bishop. The longer you drag this out, the more likely it is the press will get a hold of Leo's connection to your company." Royce looked at the chairman. "I think Leo's murder would affect Abbot & Marsh's bottom line far worse than he ever could have alive."

The white-haired man bristled, and his bushy eyebrows performed a mating dance. "Are you threatening me, Sergeant?"

Royce rapped his knuckles against the table. "I look forward to your call, Mr. Bishop."

Once they were in the elevator headed down to the lobby, Tara said, "What I wouldn't give to be a fly in that room right now. I thought the top of Bart Alexander's head was going to blow off or steam was going to shoot out his ears."

Royce snorted. "You've been watching too many cartoons with the kids."

Tara chuckled. "I finally realized why people have them."

"Kids?" Royce asked.

Tara nodded. "Yeah. They keep you young, they love without prejudice, and they make your heart swell with emotions you never knew existed." She rubbed her chest as if experiencing the sensation right then. She chuckled and shook her head like she was laughing at a private joke only she knew. "Anyway, that dynamic is interesting. Something wacky is going on there, but I'm not sure how we're going to find out what."

"Let's track down Leo's executive assistant," Royce said. "He or she probably knew Leo as well as or even better than Grace."

"We could ask Ms. Lively at the front desk."

Royce chuckled at the suggestion. "We won't be getting any information out of her. Remember how Leo kept Jennifer Ludwig's former assistant?"

"Yeah."

"What do you want to bet Abbot & Marsh's new COO inherited Leo's assistant. Think about it. Having someone familiar with the position would make the transition smoother."

"How will we find out who that was?" Tara asked as they stepped out of the elevator on the first floor.

"Grace Huxley."

Once they exited the building, Royce retrieved his phone, consulted his notes, and dialed her number. He expected to have to leave a message for Grace, but the receptionist put him on hold. Grace picked up after a few minutes.

"What can I do for you, Sergeant?" she asked.

"I forgot to ask you the name of Leo's assistant at Abbot & Marsh."

"Marcie McKnight," Grace replied without hesitation. "She sent me the prettiest flower arrangement today. Such a lovely young lady."

Royce confirmed the spelling of her name and said, "Would you happen to have a contact number for her?"

Tara peered down at his notepad, then typed rapidly on her phone.

"I don't, but you could call Abbot & Marsh and ask for her. She stayed on after Leo left."

"I'll do that." But he wouldn't. Marcie wouldn't speak to them freely at the office. "Thank you for your time."

"Before you go," Grace said. "I just wanted to let you know Larry will be making all the final arrangements for Leo and settling his affairs. He asked me this morning how soon we could expect the medical examiner to release Leo to the funeral home. Do you know when that might happen?"

"It depends on how busy the ME's office is, so there's no set time. I wouldn't think she'll be much longer."

"I understand," Grace said.

"Would you like me to call her and ask? I don't mind."

"No, Sergeant, but thank you. Larry can call her office if he's worried about it."

"Just let me know if you change your mind," he said.

They exchanged goodbyes, and Royce disconnected the call. He turned to look at Tara, who held up her phone so he could see her screen. She'd found Marcie McKnight's Facebook profile. In the photo, she wore a black tank top, a tiny pair of black shorts, and pink ballet slippers. She'd been photographed midleap. One long leg stretched out in front of her and the other behind her. Marcie's arms were lifted gracefully in the air, and her head was tilted back, sending waves of red hair cascading down her back. She wore a rapturous look on her face as if she and the music she danced to had become one. With her eyes closed, Royce couldn't tell the color of her irises, but he guessed they were blue or green.

"I don't know jack about ballet, but it looks like she got good height on her leap," he said. His Bailey buttercup had recently started dance classes, and he wondered if she'd ever love it as much as Marcie obviously did.

"While you were chatting with Grace, I scanned her profile. Guess who teaches ballet at Bailey's studio?" Tara asked.

"You've seen my buttercup dance?"

Tara giggled, slapped a hand over her mouth, and nodded. Royce didn't know his partner could make that sound.

"What's so funny?"

Tara uncovered her mouth and smiled. "Imagine Fred Flintstone trying to do ballet."

Royce thought of Bailey's chubby feet and laughed. "I need video next time."

"You got it."

"Does she enjoy it?" Royce asked.

"There are cookies and punch after each class, so yeah, your buttercup is a big fan of ballet night."

Royce laughed warmly. "That's my girl."

"I scrolled down through her pictures, and there were dozens of photos of Marcie working with students of all ages. I have an idea." Tara hit a button on her phone, then lifted it to her ear. "Yes, hello," she said when someone answered. "My friend's daughter takes ballet lessons at your studio, and my little girl has expressed interest in starting dance. I'm not sure if she's just obsessed with the tutu and ballet slippers or if she really wants to take a class. Would it be possible for us to come in and observe before we commit?" Tara's smile indicated she received the answer she wanted. "My friend highly recommends Marcie. Can you tell me what nights she teaches?" Tara's grin stretched wider, and she gave Royce a thumbs-up. "Thank you so much. You've been very helpful."

"Well?" Royce asked.

Tara's eyes glittered with excitement. "Her next class is tonight at six. I bet she heads over directly after leaving the office. I say we ambush her in the parking lot of the studio because her guard will be down."

"Ambush her?"

Tara snorted. "Shut up and drive."

"I'm going to make a follow-up call about the warrant for Leo's financial records when we get back to the office," Royce said. "You know what the key will be to solving this case?"

"Following the money," Tara said.

Royce entertained her with his "Show me the money" impression from *Jerry Maguire*.

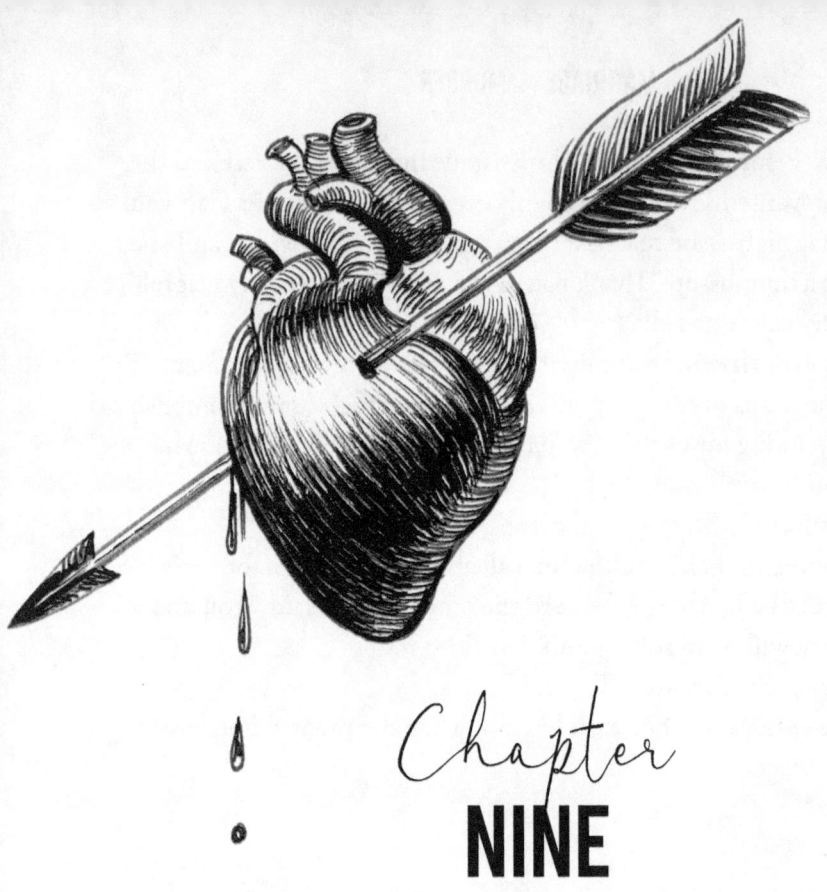

## Chapter
# NINE

"**S**ECOND HOUSE ON THE LEFT," COURTNEY SAID SOFTLY. "IT'S not much, but it's a start."

Sawyer slowed, flipped on his signal, and turned into the driveway of a small blue house with white shutters. The siding was faded, and the paint on the trim had started to chip, but the property was tidy, and it had a cute trellis arch around the front door where green vines had begun their climb. The driveway was uneven and had a sizable pothole near the street. Sawyer had been driving more cautiously than usual but still hit it harder than he wanted to with the passengers he had on board. Courtney's little donut pillow thingy would only absorb so much shock.

Sawyer winced as he stopped in front of the carport. "Sorry."

"That should be my line," Courtney said.

Sawyer shifted his car into park and looked at her. "Why?"

Courtney looked at him, her face pale and expression grim. "The nurse who discharged us assumed you were my husband and Aiden's father. She even said Aiden looked like you. It was pretty uncomfortable."

Sawyer couldn't help but wonder about Courtney's marital status again or worry about who she'd lean on over the next few weeks. Here he was, a virtual stranger, bringing her home from the hospital. Courtney had explained Aidan was three weeks early so her mother had gone into work to rearrange her leave time. What happened if she couldn't get it approved? She couldn't stay there by herself.

"Not for me," Sawyer replied. "I mean, I was making ridiculous cooing noises and telling Aiden he was the prettiest baby ever when she walked in. I was wearing a ring on my left hand and was there to take you home. It wasn't much of a leap, yeah? The nurse didn't mean any harm, and she was apologetic after you told her I was just a friend." Sawyer studied her wan face. "Have you been worrying about that this entire time?"

Courtney nodded. "I've just found you, and I don't want someone's assumptions to run you off." Then her chin wobbled, and her eyes filled with tears. "Ugh. Stupid hormones."

"Hey," Sawyer said softly. "The only place I'm going is inside your house to set up the little man's crib while the two of you nap."

Tears spilled down her cheeks. "I don't deserve your friendship. I'm an awful person."

"You let me be the judge of that," Sawyer said. "Come on. Let's get you inside and as comfortable as possible."

Courtney snorted. "Pretty sure that ship has sailed. There's no way in hell my body will ever return to normal after childbirth."

"Said every mama who's delivered a child." Sawyer smiled at her. "Stay put while I come around to help you out."

Courtney's chin wobbled again, and more tears spilled down her face when she nodded.

Sawyer helped her out of the car, then retrieved Aiden's car seat, his diaper bag, and Courtney's overnight bag and purse. He was weighed down like a pack mule but refused Courtney's offer to carry something.

"The nurse said you can't hold anything heavier than Aiden right now. She didn't mean inside his carrier."

Courtney rifled through her purse and pulled out a set of keys. "I'm wondering what kind of a mess I left the place in."

"I couldn't care less," Sawyer said. He looked down at the newborn in his carrier. "What about you, Aiden?" The sleeping baby scrunched up his precious face. "He doesn't care either."

Courtney's home was spotless except for a box of Cheez-Its sitting on the counter and a mug on the coffee table. The plaid furniture was outdated but still in excellent condition. Courtney had added some throw pillows and an accent rug in complementing colors.

"It's a real pigsty," Sawyer teased.

Courtney chuckled. "I'm a bit of a neat freak."

Sawyer set the bags down and gently placed Aiden's carrier on the coffee table. He smiled at Courtney and pointed to himself. "Kindred spirits. Are you hungry? Do you want me to make you something to eat before I start on the crib?"

Courtney yawned and shook her head. "I just want to nap while Aiden is sleeping. I have a bassinette set up in my room, so I think we'll just head in there. Aiden's bedroom is the only one on the right side of the hallway."

She gingerly crossed the room and eased her son from his carrier, then pressed a kiss to his forehead. "I never knew it was possible to love someone this much."

Sawyer's heart squeezed in his chest. His mind had drifted off several times since he'd arrived at the hospital, and he'd fantasized about experiencing the joys of bringing a baby home with Royce. Oh, the looks they'd share, and the hours they'd spend just staring at their son or daughter. Baby fever had held Sawyer in its clutches the moment Kelsey's little girl was born and hadn't let up since. The call to fatherhood just grew louder with every precious newborn he met.

"He's a miracle," Sawyer said to Courtney. "Do you need any help getting settled?"

"Nah." She lifted her head and met Sawyer's gaze. "In case you're not here when I wake up, I just want to say thank you."

"You're welcome, and I'll still be here after your nap."

She gave him another watery smile before shuffling down the

hallway. After he heard her bedroom door shut, Sawyer headed out to his car to retrieve the toolbox he'd grabbed from home and the paint and supplies he'd picked up at Sal's on his way to the hospital. Courtney's small SUV was still in the parking lot, and he assured Sal it would get moved as soon as possible.

"I'm not worried about that," Sal had said. "How're mom and baby doing?"

"They're doing great. How about you?"

The older man smiled. "Your fella has called me every day and asked the same thing. I'm doing okay. Guess I'm made from tougher stuff than I realized. I'll have a security system installed as soon as a technician can get out here. The only businesses getting robbed are ones without cameras and alarms. I'm getting too old for this bullshit, but I want to retire on my terms."

Sawyer had been thrilled to see his fighting spirit and said, "The security system is a great idea, but I don't think there's an ideal age to have a gun aimed at your head."

"I suppose not," Sal had said. "Do you think the gunmen will get caught?"

"Yeah, Sal, I do. All it takes is a single mistake. We find one, and they'll sing like canaries for a deal." It was only a matter of time before SPD located Benton, and Sawyer didn't doubt the lengths Royce's little brother would go to save his neck.

Sawyer carried the supplies, paint, and tools into the house and down the hall to Aiden's nursery. Courtney had already filled in nail holes and prepped the drywall. He debated if he should paint first, then set up the crib. It wouldn't take him long to paint, even if it needed two coats. He might even be able to surprise Courtney, who had no idea he'd retrieved her paint. But the one thing he hadn't grabbed was a ladder. Her ceilings weren't very high, so even a step ladder would work. He checked her utility room but didn't find one. Courtney didn't have a garage, but she did have a small shed in the backyard. The only thing he found there was a push mower and gardening tools.

Sawyer headed back inside and decided to assemble the crib first.

He pulled out his phone and sent a quick text to Royce. *How late will you be tonight?*

Royce's response was fast. *Interview at six, then I should be home afterward unless something breaks. Miss me?*

*Always,* Sawyer replied. *Could you bring a ladder over to Courtney's after you finish? I'd like to paint Aiden's room.*

*Sure. Text me her address. I'll bring dinner with me and help you paint. Is she doing okay?*

Sawyer thought about Courtney's high emotions. *As good as can be expected of a new mama. I love you.*

*Love you most,* Royce replied.

Sawyer tucked his phone away and got started on the crib. The only directions included in the box were in French. Sawyer had studied the language in high school and college, but it felt like a million years ago. He could translate enough words and use the pictures provided to figure it out. Sawyer was halfway through the build when he heard a car pull up outside. The visitor could've stopped at a neighbor's house, but he peeked through the blinds to be sure. The last thing he wanted was for someone to wake Courtney and Aiden by knocking on the door or ringing the bell.

Scratch that. The last thing he wanted was to confront Josiah Wheeler at Courtney's house, but that's who was parked in her driveway. Sawyer hoped the man would drive off when he realized Courtney's vehicle wasn't there and hissed out a string of curses when the sheriff pushed the driver's side door open and climbed out of his pickup with a large bouquet. He shut the door and checked his reflection in the window, smiling because he liked what he saw.

Sawyer knew he needed to act fast yet remained frozen in place as every argument he'd ever had with the corrupt son of a bitch—real and imagined—played through his head like a video montage. Sawyer seethed with every step the asshole took toward Courtney's front door. He'd taken the high road when leaving CCSD, but he wasn't better off for it. Courtney sure as hell wasn't either.

The seeds of discontent sown into his soul were becoming thorny vines that would twine, tangle, and cut until his soul was bloody and unrecognizable if Sawyer didn't act fast. If running for sheriff wasn't the answer, he'd need to find another way to rid the county of Wheeler. Anxiety pulsed through Sawyer, but he channeled Royce's fearlessness as he hurriedly made his way to Courtney's front door.

Wheeler froze when Sawyer stepped out onto the front porch and closed the door behind him. The older man narrowed his green eyes and seemed at a loss for words. Sawyer had thought the sheriff was quite handsome when they first met, but it didn't take Wheeler long to betray the ugliness at his core. Sawyer knew the sheriff was pushing sixty, but he looked closer to forty. He worked out a lot and liked to show off his physique with tight clothes, including his sheriff's uniform. He'd dressed casually for this visit in painted-on jeans, a skin-tight Braves tee, a pair of scuffed cowboy boots, and a white Stetson.

"What the hell are you doing here?" Wheeler asked.

Sawyer crossed his arms over his chest. "I was just about to ask you the same thing. I wasn't aware the sheriff made house calls to deliver flowers to his deputies and meet their newborns. Is this something new, or is it a campaign publicity stunt? Can we expect camera crews to arrive? Or are you moonlighting as a delivery boy?"

"Still see you're an arrogant little prick," Wheeler snarled.

"Nothing little about my prick," Sawyer said, knowing a dick reference from a gay man would rattle him. "Still see you're buying your clothes in the junior's department."

Wheeler's big body tensed. His nostrils flared, and he balled both hands into fists. "I should fuck you up once and for all," Wheeler said.

Sawyer tilted his head and studied his nemesis. "Is that what your anger is really about? Unrequited lust? Pissed because you're not my type. Most homophobes are closet cases, but I still never pegged you as one." Sawyer grinned sheepishly at the verb he'd used. The pun hadn't been deliberate, but the flush of anger on Wheeler's face delighted Sawyer.

"I said *fuck you up*. I didn't say anything about fucking you. Disgusting."

Sawyer held open his arms. "Here I am. Take your best shot."

"You'd just cry to every media outlet or go after me with one of your mommy or daddy's attorneys." Wheeler smiled, revealing perfect white teeth. "How'd that work out for you last time?"

Sawyer thought of all that had transpired since leaving the sheriff's department, and a genuine smile spread across his face. "Damn good." Wheeler shouldn't expect a thank you from him anytime soon, but if the jerk wanted to hold his breath…

"You better not be using Courtney in your vendetta against me," Wheeler said. "You'll regret it."

Sawyer was at a crossroads, and though he didn't know the correct path forward for him, he wasn't about to back down from this son of a bitch. He also knew his journey didn't include throwing Courtney and Aiden to the wolves—or wolf in this case. Sawyer and Courtney hadn't discussed her relationship with Wheeler, though the conversation would need to happen sooner rather than later. Regardless of the outcome, he wouldn't want her to come to any harm.

"Personal vendetta?" Sawyer asked. Channeling Royce, he held up a finger. "I don't have a clue what you're talking about." He held up a second finger. "I don't care enough about you to find out." He rotated his hand and dropped his index finger so only his middle one stood up. "And I think you should leave. Courtney and her baby are resting."

Wheeler took a step toward him, so Sawyer advanced two. Surprise registered in the older man's eyes because he'd expected Sawyer to back down.

"Would you like me to pass along your flowers?" Sawyer asked.

Wheeler's lips curled into an ugly sneer. "Get bent, Key."

"Planning on it," Sawyer replied and added a flirty wink.

"Fucking nasty queers." Wheeler pivoted on his heels and headed to his truck.

Sawyer stood there like a silent sentinel until the sheriff backed down the driveway and sped off, his truck belching a plume of black diesel exhaust in its wake. Sawyer shook his head in disgust before heading back inside to finish the crib. Courtney was standing just inside the door, and her unexpected presence made him jump.

"I want to be you when I grow up," Courtney said.

His pulse was already racing from his confrontation with Wheeler, but now it felt like his heart leaped into his throat. "You scared the hell out of me," he whispered.

She slapped a hand to her mouth and giggled. Then she dropped her hand to her stomach. "Don't make me laugh. Too soon."

"Hey, it's not my fault you find my misery hilarious."

Courtney gripped his bicep. "What did you do there at the end? Blow him a kiss or shoot him a wink?"

Sawyer grinned. "Wink."

Courtney started to giggle but clutched her stomach again. "Feels like my uterus is going to fall out of my vagina."

Sawyer grimaced and looked around the room until he found her donut pillow. "You need to sit down. I'm sure gravity isn't your best friend right now." He helped her settle on the couch, then squatted down in front of her. "Can I make you something to eat?"

"You've done so much already. You helped me stay calm during the robbery, stuck by me at the hospital until my mom arrived, brought us home, and chased away the boogeyman."

"Please don't call a press conference," Sawyer teased. "My fiancé works hard to keep me humble. You'll mess up his efforts." Courtney waved him off and rolled her eyes. "Are you hungry?" he asked.

"Yeah," she said softly.

Sawyer rose to his feet and headed into the kitchen. Courtney's pantry and refrigerator were fully stocked, so he gave her several options to choose from. She settled on a grilled cheese sandwich and tomato soup.

She dunked her sandwich triangle into the soup and took a bite. "Why does food always taste better when someone else makes it?"

"It just does."

"What's your guy like?" Courtney asked.

"Royce is quite a character." And just saying his name made Sawyer smile. "You'll get to meet him later. He's bringing a ladder over for me."

"Why?"

"I stopped by the hardware store and picked up your paint. Sal saved it for you. I thought to grab some painting supplies but forgot about needing a ladder. Royce will bring one over, and we'll paint the room for you."

Courtney set her grilled cheese down and burst into tears. "You're so sweet."

"I'm an asshole. Just ask Royce when he gets here."

Courtney only cried harder. "I've made such a mess of my life."

Sawyer retrieved the tissue box from the end table and held it out to her. Courtney pulled out two tissues and blew her nose.

"Charlie told you about my affair with Sheriff Wheeler, didn't he?" Courtney asked.

"He told me the sheriff had an affair with a female deputy and had started treating her cruelly once she became pregnant. He never mentioned you by name. If you hadn't referenced a mutual friend at the hardware store, I never would've connected the dots."

"Why are you helping me?" Courtney asked. "You should be repulsed I was intimate with someone who mistreated you."

Sawyer released a slow breath. "And maybe you should be furious I didn't fight harder to have Wheeler resign. If I had, you wouldn't have met him."

Courtney shook her head. "I've known him for at least twenty years."

Sawyer scowled. "How old are you?"

She chuckled and wiped her nose. "Twenty-six. Josiah Wheeler is a family friend. More like a friend of a family friend, but he's been on the periphery since I was a kid. My relationship with him had nothing to do with you, so put that notion right out of your head."

Sawyer sagged back against the couch, feeling relieved she wasn't a casualty of his cowardice.

"And if not for that jerk," Courtney said, "I wouldn't have Aiden. I regret so many things, but never my precious baby."

"Never," Sawyer agreed. "What are you going to do?"

Courtney picked up her sandwich and dunked it again. "I'm going to eat this yummy food. The rest will click into place once I've had time to heal. I don't need to know the answer right this minute, but I have some big decisions to make when I'm in a healthier headspace. Right now, I'm just so angry at myself for being stupid. I thought I was smarter than the rest of the fools who fell for Josiah's chameleon act."

Sawyer tipped his head to the side. "Chameleon act?"

Courtney took a few bites of soup before answering. "He has a nose for sniffing out vulnerable women and a knack for becoming exactly what they need."

"And you were vulnerable?" Sawyer asked.

Courtney nodded. "I was so lonely. Hank, my estranged husband, is a long-haul trucker. He was gone for weeks and sometimes months at a time. It seemed like he volunteered for jobs that kept him away the longest. When Hank was home, he wanted to hang out with his buddies. We were high school sweethearts, and I'd never been with anyone besides him. Hank's actions felt like rejection to me, but that's no excuse for my behavior." Courtney sighed heavily. "Anyway, Josiah saw the cracks and exploited my weaknesses. He started out by showering me with attention and performing little acts of kindness that felt huge to me. Our affair evolved from there. When I discovered my pregnancy, Hank had been away for eight weeks, and we hadn't been intimate in over four months. Hank moved out and filed for a divorce once I came clean about the affair and resulting pregnancy."

"Was he unkind?" Sawyer asked.

Courtney smiled sadly and shook her head. "He seemed relieved."

Sawyer wasn't sure what to say to that. "Does the rest of your family know who Aiden's father is?"

She spooned a few bites of soup before answering. "Just my mom. Everyone else knows I had an affair, but they don't know who I cheated on Hank with. My brothers, uncles, and cousins are so protective. If they found out, they would form a posse and go after Josiah." She scrunched up her face into a scowl. "Did that jackass bring me flowers, or were my eyes playing tricks on me?"

"No, he brought you flowers."

She snorted. "Wheeler's just trying to suck up to me so I'll keep my mouth shut."

"You think he's worried about his wife finding out?"

Courtney rolled her eyes. "Do you know Shelly Wheeler?"

"I know she's Savannah's most successful real estate agent, but we've never personally met." She'd never attended any of the sheriff department's functions during Sawyer's tenure there.

"They hate each other, so she doesn't care about his affairs, and they are legion," Courtney said. "The things I'd witnessed and overheard over the years would make your hair curl." Her lips trembled but she pulled herself together. "Which is why I should've known better. How could I have been so stupid to think I was special? When he left here, I promise you he took those flowers to his latest conquest. It's the constituents he's worried about. His pride couldn't handle losing an election."

Sawyer started to respond, but the front door opened, and Courtney's mom, Kathy, came in carrying grocery bags in one hand and dragging a suitcase behind her with the other. He stood up and offered to help, but she waved him off.

"This is everything I brought," Kathy said.

Courtney set her bowl of soup on the table. "Were you able to switch around your leave time?"

Kathy sat on the couch beside her daughter and put an arm around her. "Yes, but I had to throw the biggest hissy fit you ever saw."

"So that's who I learned it from," Courtney teased.

"You better hope Aiden doesn't take after us." Kathy looked from Sawyer to Courtney. "Did I barge in and interrupt something?"

"No, Mom. Sawyer was just keeping me company while I ate the food he cooked for me. Josiah stopped by with flowers."

"Bastard," Kathy hissed.

Sawyer decided to give the women privacy to talk. He stood up and said, "I'll go finish putting the crib together."

"What did Josiah say to you?" he heard Kathy say as he disappeared down the hall.

"Nothing," Courtney replied. "Sawyer ran him off."

The house was small, so bits and pieces of their conversation penetrated his consciousness as he turned the instructions this way and that to figure out the steps.

"The son of a bitch better not think he'll get off without paying child support." She snickered. "I don't think he was thinking about anything when he was getting off."

"Mom," Courtney admonished.

Kathy laughed. "Oh, now you're the blushing virgin. It's not too late to turn your Uncle Louie on him. He has pigs, and they don't leave behind any evidence."

Sawyer bit back a laugh. He liked Kathy a lot.

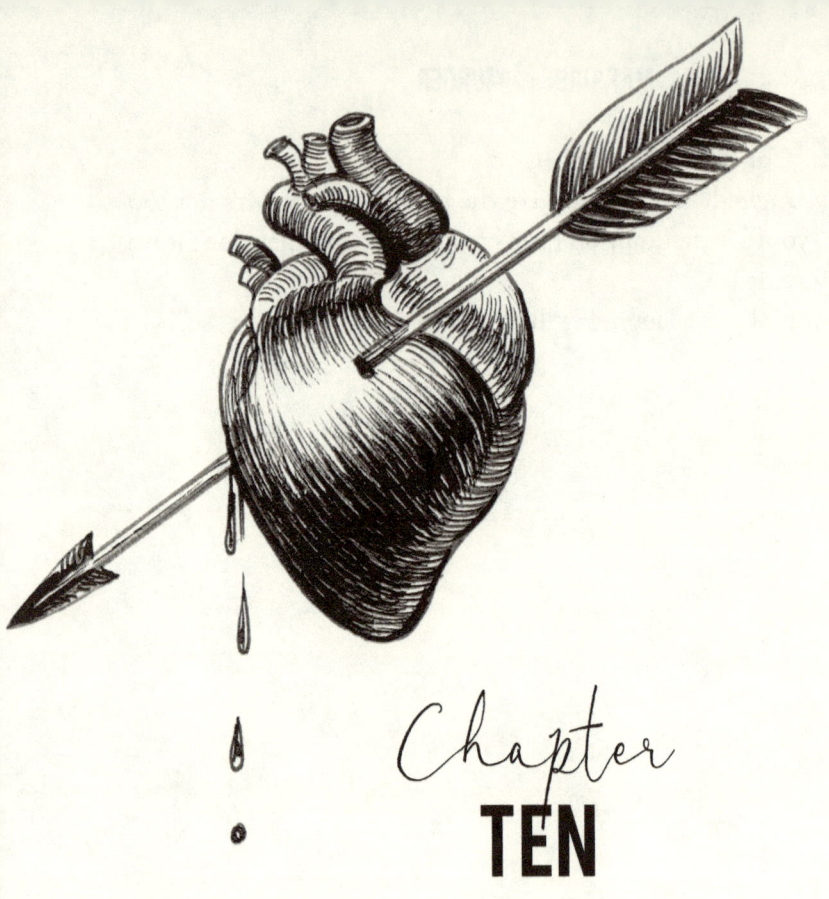

# Chapter
# TEN

ROYCE'S PHONE VIBRATED WITH A MESSAGE FROM SAWYER.
Everyone *wants Chinese.*

*Who's everyone?* He wrote back.

Sawyer told him about Kathy's arrival, promising Royce would
adore her. He followed that up with a photo of a white crib, which had
been made up with baby zoo animal bedding. In the background, he
could see where Sawyer had started paint prep by cutting in baseboards
and corners with the palest blue paint Royce had ever seen. Someday
soon, they'd be putting rooms together for their children. The realiza-
tion nearly knocked the breath from his lungs.

"You okay?" Tara asked.

Royce forced himself to look at her. "Yeah, I'm great."

Tara cocked her head to the side and studied him. "You sure? You've
got a funny expression on your face, and you were rubbing your chest."

"Sawyer sent me a picture of the crib he built for his new friend.

I'm going over to help as soon as we wrap up this interview." Unless Marcie McKnight gave them information that broke the case wide open.

Royce looked back at his phone and tapped out a response. *Nice! Text me what everyone wants.* Sawyer sent him a thumbs-up emoji.

"And you don't like painting?" Tara asked.

Royce looked at his partner. "Huh?"

"I'm just trying to figure out the source of your stress."

He smiled. "Longing, not stress."

Tara pursed her lips and nodded.

"What's that face?" Royce demanded.

"I've worked with both you and Key for three years now."

"Yeah, so?"

Tara chuckled. "You don't think I know what longing looks like on you?"

Royce heaved a sigh. "Well, maybe there's a little fear mixed in. We have…" He paused to search for the right word.

"Baby fever," Tara supplied.

"Yeah, I guess that's it. Scares the shit out of me."

Tara frowned. "Why? You and Sawyer will make wonderful fathers. And maybe you'll stop resenting the time I spend with the Wilkeses."

"I don't resent you," Royce argued. He turned his head and stared out the window until his vision lost focus. "Well, maybe a little. The Locke DNA is filled with liars, cheats, and criminals. I have no business—"

"Hey," Tara said abruptly. "I hate to interrupt a string of ridiculous bullshit, but Marcie just pulled in."

Royce blinked to clear his vision, and sure enough, Marcie McKnight was getting out of a sensible Honda. "Let's go. And a string of ridiculous bullshit?" Royce asked once they cleared the car.

"I don't care who your parents are, Ro. You're going to be an amazing father. Maybe save the fretting for something legitimate."

Royce playfully staggered like she'd hit him with a one-two punch. "Go easy on me, champ."

Marcie McKnight stepped out of her car and hoisted a large canvas bag over her shoulder. She wore a pale pink leotard with a matching skirt over it and a pair of flip-flops. She'd coiled her long hair into a loose bun on top of her head.

"Ms. McKnight, may we have a word?" Tara said firmly once Marcie had stepped out of her car.

The redhead flinched and placed a hand over her stomach. "Oh my gosh. You startled me." She bounced her gaze between Royce and Tara, settling on Royce. Her pretty bow mouth curved upward into a welcoming smile but collapsed when she saw the badge he wore on a chain around his neck. "Is there a problem?"

"Forgive my partner," Royce said. "She's usually a paragon of tact and grace."

Tara threw him a quick look that promised retribution. "I apologize, ma'am," Tara said to Marcie. "Can we have a few minutes of your time? We need to ask you a few questions about Leo Fellows."

Marcie's eyes widened. They were amber, not blue or green. "Leo?" She glanced at her watch, then scanned the parking lot. "I have a class starting soon. Could you give me your number and I'll call you afterward?"

"This is important," Royce said. "I spoke to Grace Huxley just a short while ago about Leo's time at Abbot & Marsh, and she said you'd be the best person to talk to about Leo's employment there. She spoke so highly of you and said Leo wouldn't have been able to function without you."

Marcie offered a thin smile. "I know Grace has a reputation for being a bulldog, but she's always been so sweet to me."

"She loved your flowers," Royce added. "They brightened her day."

With that remark, Marcie's hesitation dissolved, and she aimed a megawatt smile at Royce. "I'm so glad. I was so shocked and saddened to hear someone had killed Leo. How can I help?"

"Well, for starters, did Leo have any enemies?" Royce asked.

Marcie bit her lower lip and briefly averted her gaze. "I haven't talked to Leo since he left Abbot & Marsh, so I don't know."

"Fair enough," Tara said. "But what about during his time working there?"

Her eyes widened, and her shoulders inched up a notch. "Surely, you don't think someone from Abbot & Marsh killed him. No." Marcie shook her head. "I can't believe that."

"We're just working to form an accurate picture of what was happening in Leo's life and the key players involved. Over the past seven or so months, Mr. Fellows made some pretty drastic changes."

Marcie's shoulders relaxed and she nodded. "Yeah, the wedding planning thing came out of nowhere." She chuckled dryly. "I adored working for Leo, but he was the least romantic guy I knew. The things he'd buy Grace for Christmas, her birthday, and their anniversary were so dry and uninspiring. I volunteered to help him out once, but he declined." Marcie briefly closed her eyes and shook her head. "Leo told me his gifts might suck, but at least Grace knew they came from him."

"He wasn't wrong," Royce said.

Marcie smiled. "No, I guess not."

"Were you surprised when Leo and Grace separated?" Tara asked.

"Yes and no. I had never met two people who were more different than Leo and Grace. She's all fiery passion, and he's…um." Marcie paused to grimace. "A bit cool and indifferent. But they seemed to make it work, you know?"

He did know a little something about combining opposite personalities, though no one would describe Royce or Sawyer as cool or indifferent. "What was Leo like as an employer?"

"That's where he excelled. Leo was never going to shake a pair of pompoms like a cheerleader, but he was never going to scream at the people working for him when a volatile situation arose. He gave credit where it was due. When things didn't go well, he sat people down and calmly explained what went wrong and how they could fix it. Working for Leo was a breath of fresh air." A stern expression washed over her face. "Others in the C-suite could've learned a lot from his example."

"C-suite?" Royce asked.

"It's what they call the people in CEO, CFO, and COO positions," Tara explained. "Are you referring to a certain situation or particular person, Ms. McKnight?"

"Call me Marcie, please," she said, then looked nervously around her as if she expected Glen and Bart to burst out of the bushes.

"We won't be able to solve Leo's murder if people aren't forthright," Royce said.

Marcie raked her bottom lip with her pearly white teeth. She finally nodded and said, "Okay." Royce wasn't sure if she was talking to herself or them. "Have you spoken to anyone at Abbot & Marsh?"

"Somewhat," Tara said, then gave a summary of the scene from the conference room.

Marcie blew out a breath. "There was a whole lot of volatility toward the end of his time at Abbot & Marsh. At first, I chalked it up to typical business stuff, you know? Competition is fierce, and the pressure to do more never eases up. But then I caught the tail end of an argument between Glen Bishop and Leo."

"Glen is the CFO," Royce confirmed.

Marcie nodded. "Glen was accusing Leo of some sort of betrayal at the top of his lungs. Glen had exposed a temper under duress before, but this felt different. It seemed…personal."

"Do you recall what Glen said to Leo?" Tara asked.

Marcie took a deep breath and exhaled. "Glen said, 'I trusted you, Leo, and you stabbed me in the back. I can't stand to even look at you now.' Then he slammed out of Leo's office, nearly knocking me over in the process."

"Did you talk to Leo about it?" Royce asked.

"No. I decided not to approach him after the confrontation. Leo came out of his office a few minutes later looking pale and sallow. He gave me a lame excuse and left. Two days later, the entire corporation received an internal memo that Leo Fellows had been terminated and Justin Jones would be replacing him as COO."

Royce looked up from his notes. "What's Justin like?"

Marcie sigh. "The ultimate yes-man. I wanted to leave out of loyalty to Leo, but he talked me out of it. He said good-paying jobs like mine were hard to find. I'd established myself as a go-to person and wouldn't like starting over at the bottom of another corporation. He was right about that."

"So you spoke to Leo after he left?" Tara asked.

"Just that once." A few cars pulled into the parking lot, and Marcie forced a smile to her lips and waved at the arrivals. "Talking to the cops outside the studio is probably bad for business."

"We can talk later," Royce offered.

She met his gaze, and he saw a spark of interest there, but a little girl in a white tutu called out to her, and she smiled and waved as she walked by. Marcie turned her full attention to Royce once more. "Honestly, I don't know anything else. Leo danced around the subject of his termination, and you can bet I asked. He simply told me it would be water under the bridge, and he was looking forward to a new venture." Marcie smiled and shook her head. "Wedding planning. Who'd have guessed it? Anyway, Leo stopped responding to my messages and didn't return my calls. I took the hint. I sure hope you figure out who killed him."

"We'll give it our best shot," Royce said.

After they walked away, Tara nudged him with her elbow. "Let's just hope our aim is true."

"You're every bit the asshole my last partner was," Royce teased.

Tara laughed and patted her chest. "I'll own that."

"I'm going to give Glen Bishop until ten o'clock tomorrow morning. If he doesn't call one of us to finish his interview, I'm going to put the terrible in Terrible Tuesday."

"Looking forward to it," Tara said. Once inside the car, she looked over at Royce. "Can I ask you a personal question?"

"Sure."

"Has Sawyer ever struggled with your bisexuality?" Tara asked.

Royce had been about to start the car, but he dropped his hand instead. "Not that he's ever expressed." He thought back over their relationship, looking for signs Sawyer had struggled or harbored fears over Royce's attraction to women. He'd never betrayed those feelings if they existed. Royce witnessed the fear Sawyer had of losing him, even though his fiancé thought he'd hidden it well. "And I don't think it's ever been an issue for him. I've had sex with women in the past, and yes, I enjoyed it, but I've only ever loved one person, and that's Sawyer. I make sure he damn well knows it. I don't leave things to chance, and we don't play guessing games. My past experiences are immaterial to him. Why do you ask?"

Tara turned her head and stared out the windshield. "A lot of gay people struggle with it. They think, 'why would this person stick with me and put up with rejection and bullshit if they don't have to.'"

"Are you one of those gay people who struggle with it?" Royce asked gently.

Tara took a deep breath. "I'm falling so fucking hard, Ro. Every instinct for self-preservation is screaming at me to erect my shields, but then Candy smiles at me or cuddles into me, and it's all I can do to remember how to breathe." She looked over at Royce, and he saw the helplessness in her pale blue eyes. He'd been there and done that, lost the battle, and embraced the scars. "Candy has never dated a woman before me. I don't want to be an experiment."

More kids arrived and Royce was pleased to see a few little boys among them. He watched their joyful interactions as he let Tara's words settle. Royce's first instinct was to get defensive, but he could understand where Tara was coming from.

"Regardless of gender or orientation, isn't all dating an experiment? You go on dates, you get tangled in the sheets, you meet friends and family, and you look for common ground to build something on. Sometimes it works. Sometimes it doesn't. That's dating. Even if you and Candy Cane don't work out, it doesn't mean you were nothing but an experiment to her. I've known my girl for a very long time, and there isn't a cruel bone in her body. If she's said or done something to hurt you, she'd want to know so she could fix it."

Tara shook her head. "It's nothing she said or did."

"Then what triggered the urge to raise the shields?" Royce asked, knowing there had to be a reason.

"We went to art night at the elementary school last week. Candy was swarmed by several other moms, and she introduced me as her girlfriend. None of the women said anything, but you could see the surprise written all over their faces and hear their gears grinding. Once they got past their shock, they were very polite and welcoming to me."

"But?"

Tara sighed.

"Oh, that's a weighty one, champ," Royce said.

Tara narrowed her eyes. "Is champ my new nickname now?"

"Probably, unless it offends you."

"Nah," Tara said.

"Quit stalling and tell the rest of the story about the mean moms at art night."

"They weren't mean, but I felt their eyes on us the entire night. There were a few occasions when I caught them staring at us and whispering."

"Human nature," Royce said. "Was Candy bothered by it?" A wry smile curved one side of Tara's face. "So, no, she wasn't."

Tara shook her head. "Until the next time when someone says something directly to her."

Royce laughed and crossed his arms over his chest. "I sure as hell hope you capture her response on video. No one should ever mistake Candy's kind heart for weakness. It's her superpower."

"Why would she choose me when she can date some dude and avoid the extra scrutiny?" Tara asked.

"Come on. You know we don't choose who we love."

"Love, huh?" Tara asked. "I don't even know what that looks like."

"Don't you?"

Tara looked out the windshield again and sat quietly for a moment.

"Tell me what you admire most about Candy," Royce said.

"God, where do I start?" Then Tara began naming all Candy's attributes, ranging from her personality to her profession and her flawless beauty to her skills as a parent.

"Don't forget her cooking," Royce said. When Tara didn't respond right away, he glanced at her and saw a dopey smile. "What?"

"I never thought I'd want to be a mom," Tara said. "I guess I never allowed myself to believe it would ever be in the cards for me." She looked at Royce. "I fucking love those kids, man."

It was so much easier for Tara to admit her feelings for Marc, Daniel, and Bailey than it was for their mom. Royce understood it and read the truth in Tara's earnest gaze.

"Then you don't let some busybody moms or dads from the school push you away. You're the champ."

Tara nodded. "I'm the champ," she whispered.

"Weak. I'm going to need you to say it louder and mean it."

Narrowing her eyes, Tara said. "Are we doing the *Jerry Maguire* thing again?"

Royce laughed. "If that's what it takes. Let's hear it. Loud and proud."

His phone rang just when Tara opened her mouth to admit she was the champ or tell Royce to fuck off. He saw it was Rocky Jacobs, private detective slash podcaster slash pain in his ass. "This should be interesting," he told Tara and accepted the call. "How's it going, trouble?"

"You'll be singing an entirely different tune after you hear what I have to say," Rocky replied.

Royce snorted. "Doubtful. What's up?"

"I want to talk to you about Leo Fellows. I wouldn't normally disclose details from one of my investigations, but someone murdered the man, and I feel morally obligated to share what I know."

Royce felt his eyebrows arching toward his hairline. "Wow. I am impressed. Where are you?"

"My office."

"We'll be right there," Royce said before disconnecting the call.

"What's up?" Tara asked.

Royce shifted his SUV into drive, then told Tara what Rocky had said.

"This sounds promising. Do you think it has something to do with the accusation Glen lobbed at Leo?"

"I think we can save our energy from overspeculating since we're only a few minutes from Rocky's office."

The private detective met them in the lobby, and Royce introduced Tara and Rocky. They shook hands, and Rocky showed them to his office where a blue file lay in the center of his desk. He rested his hands on top of the file and pinned Royce with a somber expression.

"Reputation is everything in my line of work," he said. "If it gets out that I showed you the contents of this file, I may not have a business for much longer."

Anticipation coursed through him, but Royce tempered it by giving

Rocky the assurance he needed. "I'll do everything I can to leave your name out of the investigation. You have my word."

Rocky took a deep breath and opened the file. He removed a photo and slid it across his desk to them. Royce immediately recognized Leo Fellows, but the woman he was kissing wasn't his wife.

"Well, well, well," Tara said. "Who's the lady?"

"Her name is Nancy Bishop, and she's married to—"

"Glen Bishop," Royce and Tara said at the same time.

"Yep. Glen hired me about nine months ago to prove his wife was having an affair. It didn't take me long. Bishop has a lot of interests and hobbies, and they take him away from their house several nights a week. Glen would pull away from home, and Leo would drive up five or ten minutes later and let himself in using a side door on the garage."

"Are you certain her visitor was Leo Fellows?" Royce asked. "He has an identical twin named Larry."

Rocky glowered at him for a few seconds, but Royce thought it was a valid question. "This isn't my first rodeo. Of course I'm sure."

"Did your investigation result in a divorce?" Royce asked.

"Not that I'm aware of," Rocky said. "Truth is, I gave Mr. Bishop the proof he needed and dusted off my hands."

"What kind of hobbies is Glen Bishop into?" Tara asked.

Rocky leaned back in his chair and steepled his fingers together. "He serves on the chamber of commerce, a few historical societies, and is an avid hunter."

Royce and Tara exchanged a knowing glance, one that Rocky's shrewd blue eyes didn't miss.

"You know, I've yet to hear how Leo Fellows was murdered," he said.

"I can't reveal that," Royce replied.

Rocky chuckled. "I scratched your back." He reached his left hand over his right shoulder, stretched to reach a spot on his back, then dropped his hand in his lap. "Mine itches, but I can't reach it."

"Fine," Royce said, "but you cannot breathe a word of this to anyone, especially not to Felix."

Rocky crossed his heart and aimed an angelic smile at him.

Royce rolled his eyes, not falling for his act for even a second. But

Rocky had done them a solid favor, so he would return it. But just once. "He was shot through the heart with an arrow."

"He must've given love a bad name," Rocky quipped and started playing air guitar.

Royce slid the photo back across the desk and stood up. "And that's our cue to leave."

Tara laughed all the way to the car. "I like him."

"Give him a chance, and he'll change your mind," Royce said.

"Now what?"

Royce thought for a second. They couldn't drive straight to Glen's house with the accusation. Bishop would know exactly where the information had come from. They could try speaking to Nancy Bishop, but what would they give as a reason? Patience is what they needed.

"You're going to go have dinner with your girl and her little darlings. I will take Chinese takeout to our ever-growing extended family and help Sawyer paint a nursery. We'll give Glen Bishop until ten o'clock tomorrow morning to call us on his own."

"And if we don't hear from him?" Tara asked.

"The gloves come off, champ, and we give a whole new meaning to Terrible Tuesday."

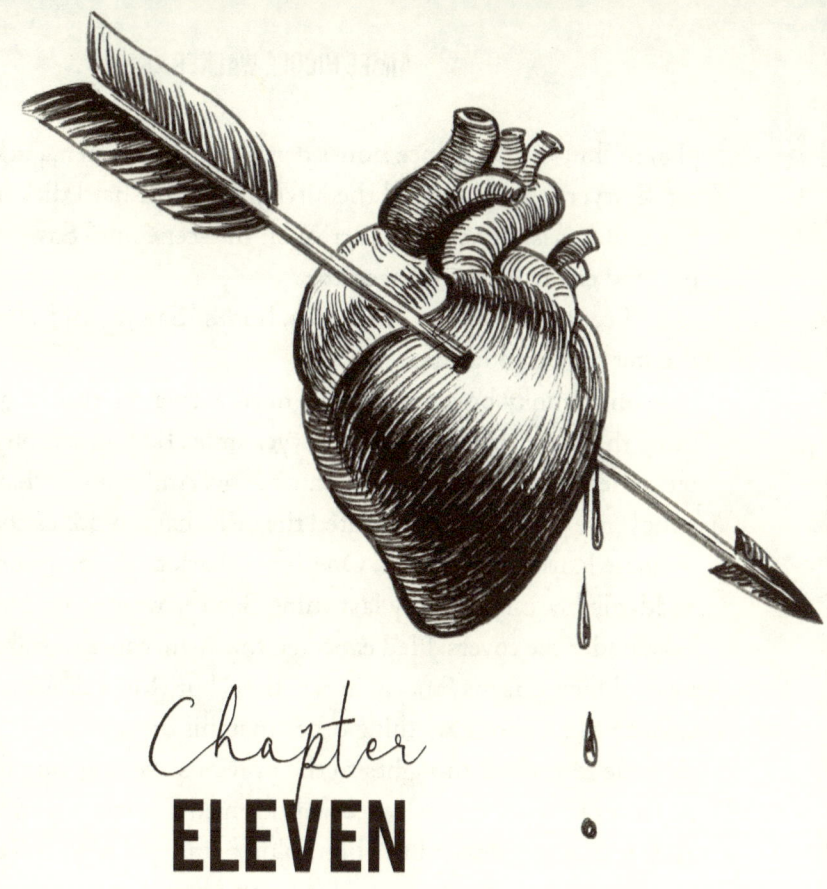

*Chapter*
# ELEVEN

**S**AWYER JERKED TO CONSCIOUSNESS IN THE MIDDLE OF THE MOST delicious dream. He'd been living out his favorite fantasy where he slid beneath the covers and woke Royce with his mouth and tongue. Dream Royce had been about to come when Sawyer found himself staring at their bedroom ceiling, fully awake with a throbbing erection.

*No. No. No. Why?*

Feeling a disturbance in the force, Sawyer turned his head and saw Bones sitting on the edge of his nightstand. His big, bushy tail, suspiciously close to Sawyer's face, swished in annoyance. So Bones was responsible for yanking him out of his explicit fantasy. Sawyer decided he wouldn't give in to the beast's demands for food and rolled over onto his side. That's when Bones bit his ear.

Sawyer threw back the covers and pointed at the door. Smelling a trick, Bones didn't budge from the nightstand. There went his genius plan to shut the door once Bones darted for the kitchen. *Fucking genius cat.* Sawyer headed toward the kitchen, his still-hard dick jutting out like a compass. Bones didn't arrive on the scene until Sawyer removed his food can from the refrigerator.

"I could've used the extra sleep, Bones," Sawyer said as he plopped the wet food into his dish.

His chunky boy attacked his meal with a mixture of growls and purrs that never failed to make Sawyer smile. Bones was still a feral kitten at heart, even after years of pampering. And just like that, Sawyer's annoyance withered. He updated the task chart so Bones couldn't manipulate Royce with his lies. On his way back to the bedroom, exercise suddenly became the very last thing Sawyer wanted to do, so he slid back under the covers. He'd expected the disturbance to wake Royce so he could live out his fantasy in real time, but Royce didn't stir. Sawyer tried to think about anything other than his dick.

He forced his thoughts to the previous evening, but all he could think about was the way Royce had charmed Courtney, Kathy, and baby Aiden. Sawyer recalled the light blue paint splatters in Royce's hair, the soy sauce on his shirt, and his laughing gray eyes. Royce had never looked more beautiful to him. Sawyer had planned to demonstrate his affection when they got home, but they'd pivoted to a discussion about Royce's investigation, and the moment passed. He'd planned to recapture it once they got into bed and turned on the television, but Sawyer fell asleep almost immediately.

Instead of easing the ache between his legs, his trip down memory lane only made his urges stronger. Sawyer lazily stroked his chest while reliving his fantasy until he could no longer ignore the pressure in his groin. As much as he wanted to slide beneath the blankets and lick Royce's cock until he became hard, there was an ick factor he couldn't ignore. Sleeping people couldn't consent. So Sawyer did the only thing he could. Channeling Bones, he reached over and knocked a heavy book onto their hardwood floor where it landed with a huge *BANG!*

Royce jerked upright and looked around the room for the threat. Then his gaze landed on Sawyer, who smiled innocently.

"Good morning," he said.

Royce scowled and ran a hand through his tousled blond hair. He heaved a sigh and rolled his eyes. "If you wanted to wake me up with your mouth on my cock, you should've done it. Christ. What the hell was that noise? Sounded like a cannon."

"I accidentally knocked my book onto the floor," Sawyer replied.

Royce licked his bottom lip, and Sawyer couldn't tear his eyes off the movement. "The same way Bones knocks shit off any surface when he feels he's being ignored or starved?"

"Bones and I are both deeply hurt by your accusations."

Royce tried so hard to hang on to his annoyance, but he must've seen the longing in Sawyer's early morning gaze because he eased back down and nestled beneath the covers. "Come and get me."

Sawyer snorted. "You're too eager now, and I think the mood has passed."

Royce snaked a hand over and wrapped it around Sawyer's hard-on. "Baby, you're in a bad way." He retracted his hand and licked the precum off his palm. "Better get beneath the covers. That look in your eyes and the taste of you on my tongue. Mmmm, I won't stay soft long."

Sawyer darted beneath the covers and positioned himself between Royce's legs. "Less slutty," he said.

Royce chuckled and closed his legs a little. "Just your hot breath on my skin is giving me a chub."

Sawyer loved how the darkness heightened his other senses. Royce's crisp leg hair tickled his palms and made them tingle. Sawyer closed his eyes and trailed his nose along Royce's pelvis, drawing his musky, rich scent in deep. His man smelled like carnal promises he couldn't wait to devour. He slowly licked Royce's cock, loving the way it jumped under his tongue. Royce's groan trembled through his entire body, making Sawyer aware of his strong thighs bracketing his ribcage. The soft sheets beneath Sawyer teased his erect nipples and provided delicious friction for his cock. If he wasn't careful, he'd rub one out much too soon.

Sawyer parted his lips and drew Royce's cock into his mouth, pressing his nose into the tight curls at the base. He breathed deeply, noticing his intoxicating scent grew stronger with arousal. Sawyer swirled his tongue around the root of Royce's shaft, loving the way his dick thickened and filled his mouth. Sawyer eased back, teasing the sensitive crown, then swallowed him back down again. On the second pass, Royce was at half-mast, and on the third, his dick was fully erect and ringing Sawyer's tonsils like a dinner bell.

Royce growled and tensed, his breath hissing between his teeth. "You suck me so damn good."

Sawyer imagined what Royce looked like above the blankets and wondered where his hands were. Tucked under his head to resist reaching under the blankets and taking over, or was he playing with his nipples? One tucked and one toying? The imagery had Sawyer rubbing his dick against the mattress as Royce's erection dribbled onto his tongue.

Alternating between licking and sucking, Sawyer quickly made Royce a quivering, snarling mess.

"Quit toying with me and put me out of my misery," Royce demanded.

Sawyer swirled his tongue and captured another pearl of precum off his crown. "Yeah, you're suffering. Poor baby." Sawyer let Royce's dick slip from his mouth to suck his balls one at a time.

Royce reached a hand beneath the covers and fisted Sawyer's hair. "Suck me off, asshole."

Sawyer hummed and switched his attention to Royce's taint, licking and sucking his way toward Royce's pucker but stopping just shy of the target.

"Fuck, I'm going to blow," Royce said when Sawyer repeated the pattern, starting with a tongue swipe up the length of his cock to capture a new pearl and ending with the merest brush of his tongue over Royce's pucker.

"If you come on the sheets, you have to wash them," Sawyer said before sinking his teeth into Royce's thigh.

"I want to come in your mouth. Now."

Sawyer chuckled and complied, sucking Royce's cock down to the root once more. Royce grunted, tightened his fist in Sawyer's hair, and arched his body. He came hard and loud, alternating between high praise for Sawyer's wicked mouth and cursing his devious brain.

Sawyer crawled up his body, clearing the covers and not stopping until he straddled Royce's face. He gripped his cock and smeared his precum on Royce's lips. "I'm not done yet."

Royce licked away the sticky essence and closed one eye. "You're too eager now, and I think the mood has passed." Royce smiled, and Sawyer took advantage, pushing the head of his dick inside Royce's hot mouth.

He closed his eyes and bucked his hips forward. Royce tightened his lips around his shaft and applied the perfect amount of pressure to drive him wild. After a few thrusts, Royce pulled free and said, "Less slutty."

Sawyer's entire body trembled with the need to come, and he pushed inside Royce's mouth again. "Quit toying with me and put me out of my misery."

Royce chuckled, and it reverberated up Sawyer's shaft and made his balls draw tighter against his body. With their gazes locked, Sawyer slowly worked his dick in and out of Royce's wet, hot clench.

"Fuck, I'm going to blow," Sawyer warned. Euphoria pumped through his veins as he fucked Royce's mouth. He pulled back at the last moment, spurting his release all over Royce's lips, chin, and neck. Smiling down at his handiwork, Sawyer said, "Clean up in aisle three," and flopped down on his back beside Royce.

Royce glared at him. "Oh, I see how it is."

Without warning, Royce rolled onto his side and pushed his head between the curve of Sawyer's neck and shoulder, rubbing his face and smearing the cum all over Sawyer's skin. Then he captured Sawyer's mouth in a hungry, passionate kiss.

"Covered in your cum is my favorite way to start the day," Royce said.

They lay there in a tangle of arms and legs, panting into the otherwise quiet morning. Sawyer's alarm clock went off, sounding incredibly shrill and shattering their blissful afterglow. Sawyer slapped his hand down on top of the offensive machine to turn it off and looked at Royce.

"Rock, paper, scissors to see who has to start the coffee?" Sawyer asked.

Royce leaned over and kissed him. "I'll start the coffee. You fire up the shower."

Sawyer lay there admiring Royce's ass until his fiancé disappeared out of sight. Then he reluctantly threw back the covers and swung his legs over the side of the bed. He'd started the shower and was midway through brushing his teeth when Royce joined him in the bathroom.

"Bones said you didn't feed him," he said as he squeezed a line of toothpaste on his brush. "He's starving. Probably won't make it another ten minutes."

Sawyer rinsed his mouth and his toothbrush. "Lies."

They showered, dressed, and made breakfast together like they did whenever their schedules permitted. As they tucked into their fluffy scrambled eggs and turkey sausage, Sawyer decided to come clean about his run-in with Josiah Wheeler.

Royce's face tensed, and he halted midchew, remaining immobile as Sawyer relayed the conversation he'd had with Courtney afterward.

"I know. I know," Sawyer rushed to add. "I should've told you about this last night, but we were at Court's, and I didn't want to upset her. When we got home, I got wrapped up in your case updates. Then we settled into bed for some television and speaking his name in our sacred place just felt wrong."

Royce chewed slowly, and Sawyer thought he might be searching for the right words to express his reaction. He swallowed and snarled, "Fuck."

Sawyer waited for Royce to expand on his curse, but he ate another bite of food. "Are you mad at me?" he asked.

Silence was Royce's only reply, and he continued to eat while assessing Sawyer. His mercurial gray eyes seemed cold and flinty. Sawyer had only seen him aim that unyielding look at other people, never him. Well, not since the early days of their partnership. Sawyer searched for the right words to say to make this better. He could tell Royce wanted him to express remorse, but what would he apologize for? He didn't regret helping Courtney out or standing up to Wheeler, but he was sorry for not telling Royce right away. Before he could say anything, Royce's gaze softened.

"Hey," he said gently. "I'm not mad at you. I'm concerned about the additional stress your new friendship with Courtney is introducing into your life." Royce reached across the table and settled his hand over Sawyer's. "Stop that."

"Stop what?"

"You're twisting your engagement ring again. For a minute, I was afraid you were taking it off," Royce replied.

"Not even when a gun is pressed to my head."

Royce narrowed his eyes. "That makes two boneheaded moves you've made in a week, and it's only Tuesday morning. First the stunt with the ring, then you confront Wheeler on the front porch of his lover's house."

"The robbery happened on Saturday, so technically it was last week," Sawyer said. "And Wheeler is her ex-lover."

"So she says."

Sawyer didn't lose his temper often, but the maelstrom of emotions swirling inside him was the perfect storm to raise his ire. Heat suffused his cheeks even as the rest of him felt cold as if all his blood had rushed to his head. "You think she's lying?"

Royce held up his hand. "I didn't say that, baby."

Sawyer's temper was picking up steam. "You implied it. You don't even know Courtney."

"And neither do you," Royce said calmly. He cupped Sawyer's face, and despite his anger, Sawyer leaned into his caress. There'd never come a day when he turned away from Royce's touch. "You are drawn to wounded things like a moth to a flame." Sawyer wanted to contradict his assertion, but he couldn't, so he kept his mouth shut. "Not an insult, baby. It's one of the traits I cherish most about you. There is no one I love and respect more than you. Surely you know that." Sawyer inhaled deeply and nodded. "Please hear me out."

Sawyer turned his head and kissed Royce's palm, feeling foolish for his flare-up. "Always."

Royce brushed his thumb over Sawyer's mouth before lowering his hand. "Courtney has been under a ton of duress lately and is the textbook definition of an emotionally wounded person. First, there was the unexpected pregnancy and the fallout at CCSD. I think it's safe to assume Charlie wasn't exaggerating about that." Sawyer nodded but didn't speak. "Then she runs into you at the hardware store, and the two of you get caught up in a traumatic event. She hails you as this amazing hero to the press and everyone who will listen. According to your recounting, Courtney has known Wheeler for decades. What's the likelihood she didn't know how much Wheeler hates you?" Royce raised his hand to wave him off before Sawyer could respond. "Not fucking likely is the only answer, GB. Hell, for all we know, she whispered awful things about you in Wheeler's ear as some sort of foreplay."

"Okay," Sawyer said. "You scored that point. There's no need to beat it to damn death."

Royce smiled smugly and marked a point in the air. "So, if she knew about Wheeler's hatred, she'd know that praising you would really crank his gears. And it worked because look who showed up at her house with a bouquet."

"Courtney said—"

Royce waved him off. "You gotta give me that point too."

"Fine," Sawyer growled. "Two points, Royce. Sawyer none."

"Baby, I know what Courtney said, and I think she wants to believe it. She seems like a great gal, and I do like her."

"But?" Sawyer prompted.

"Her mom will go back to work, your attention will return to your investigations, and Courtney is going to have a lot of time on her hands to reflect. She'll either steel her resolve to move past her mistakes, or she'll fall right back into them. That isn't a decision you or I or even her mom can make for her. If Wheeler can use Courtney and Aiden to hurt you, he'll do it in a heartbeat and damn the consequences. Just be cautious. Proceed with your blinders down and your shields up a little. That's all I ask."

Sawyer mulled it over and knew Royce was right. "Okay. I'll lead with my brain and not my heart."

"Thank you." Royce leaned forward and kissed him. "Three points for me."

Sawyer laughed. "You're an insufferable dickhead."

"Yeah, but you're crazy about me." Royce collected their dirty plates and carried them to the dishwasher while Sawyer topped off their travel mugs and slipped Bones the piece of toast he'd pinched off for him.

"I saw that," Royce said, though his back was turned to them. "You can't use me as a scapegoat during his next checkup."

Sawyer handed Royce his mug. "I wouldn't dream of it."

"Uh-huh." Royce sipped his coffee. "What's on tap for you today?"

"I'm recording with the *Sinister in Savannah* crew," Sawyer replied.

"An update about Jessie Walters or a new missing persons case?"

Sawyer sipped his coffee and ignored the pang in his chest at hearing Jessie's name. "A new spotlight today, but we're recording the update with Jessie's parents on Thursday. Detective Santiago from Chicago PD got approval to participate and will join us on Zoom."

Royce studied him closely. "When's Jessie's funeral?"

"A week from today."

Royce took out his phone and asked, "What time?"

"Graveside service is at ten. Alice and Jack have asked us to gather at their home with friends and family afterward."

Royce entered the information into his phone, then glanced up. "And so we will."

Beverly Dodd looked thinner and weaker than she had when Sawyer had met with her ten days ago, but the determination in her eyes hadn't diminished. She adjusted her white headwrap with pink ribbons and smiled wanly at him. She'd put on a light amount of makeup and her lips shined from the pale pink gloss she'd applied.

"Am I camera ready?" she asked.

"Absolutely," Sawyer replied.

Bev nodded. "It's a good day to find my girl."

Everything inside Sawyer wanted to urge Bev to be cautious, to guard against unreasonable expectations. She must've sensed his hesitancy because she reached across the table and covered both his hands.

"I know what you must be thinking after receiving the awful news about Jessie Walters, but I know my Andrea is different. She's alive. I can feel it."

Rocky, Jonah, and Felix entered the studio before he could reply. Each of them shook Bev's hand and welcomed her warmly, then they took a few minutes to mic up and test the equipment to make sure everything was working properly.

Felix was the reporter and the natural one to lead Beverly through the interview portion. It never failed to surprise Sawyer just how charming his smartass friend could be when he put his mind to it. After he finished, Rocky took the figurative baton and went through a series of questions to help him narrow down his search. Sawyer supplied additional answers with places the police searched when the missing persons report was filed in 1987. There weren't many, so it didn't take him long, then Sawyer walked Beverly through the things going on in Andrea's life before she disappeared.

Beverly briefly closed her eyes and took a deep breath. Her pale eyes glistened with tears when she met Sawyer's gaze. "I've thought about this so much over the past thirty-five years, but even more since I started watching these segments." She glanced over at Rocky. "I remember the child psychologist you interviewed who said children are more often running from something than they are running toward something. That resonated with me and changed how I viewed those last months with Andrea. I realized there was a telling pattern I'd missed."

"How so?" Jonah asked.

"My Andrea was a calm, even-keeled young lady. Some teenage girls struggle with hormones, but she never did. Andrea was always polite, respectful, and very studious. About six months before she disappeared, my daughter's personality shifted drastically. Andrea started skipping school. She was failing her classes and had quit her extracurricular activities. She'd played sports year-round and even doubled up some seasons. Suddenly, she didn't want to participate anymore. Then she started losing weight and acting out at home. The night before she left…" Bev's voice broke, and her lips quivered.

Rocky reached over and patted her hand. "I know this is hard, and we'd spare you if we could. We need to know everything if we're going to find out what happened to Andrea. Take your time, Bev."

The older woman nodded and sucked in a gulping breath as tears cascaded down her face. She scrubbed at them with a tissue before taking a sip of water.

"Do you need to take a break to collect yourself?" Sawyer asked.

"No," Bev said, shaking her head. "I'm okay." After another deep breath and long drink, she continued. "The night before Andrea left, we got into a big fight. I'd asked if she was taking drugs, and she smacked me across the face and called me awful names. I didn't know who I was looking at. I'd raised Andrea by myself, and it had always been the two of us against the world. That night, I was looking into the eyes of a stranger. My sweet baby girl told me she hated me and hoped I died." Bev broke off and cried some more. "I sent Andrea to her room, knowing we'd work it out in the morning. I'd make her favorite breakfast, and we'd talk through whatever was bothering her. I made her banana nut pancakes and waited. Her alarm never went off, so I went to wake her up. That's when I found out she was gone. She'd packed a duffle bag with some clothes and taken all the money she'd saved from birthdays and Christmases. I never saw her or heard from her again."

"I'm so sorry, Bev," Felix said. "I can't imagine what you've gone through over the past thirty-five years. I hope like hell we can find some answers for you."

Sawyer wanted to think positively, but Jessie Walters's reality weighed heavily on his mind. He sensed there was more to Bev's story, but showing her well-intentioned platitudes wouldn't help them find Andrea. "Looking back at the situation, what do you think happened to cause the shift in Andrea's personality."

Beverly squared her shoulders and looked him dead in the eye. "I think someone hurt my baby. My time on this earth and the chance to make them pay is coming to an end."

"You don't think Andrea would've told you if someone had hurt her?" Felix asked gently.

Beverly's lips quivered, but she kept it together. "They might've convinced Andrea I wouldn't have believed her. Isn't that what abusers do?"

"It is," Jonah said. "If you could speak to Andrea today, what would you tell her?"

Tears slid down Beverly's face. "I want her to know I would've believed her. She was my entire world. Still is. I love her more than anything or anyone. Every heartbeat and every breath has been for her." Bev adjusted her head wrap once more. "And I want her to get tested for the BRCA gene mutation. My mother died from breast cancer in the seventies. I don't know if they did genetic testing back then, but if so, no one recommended it to me. I have the mutation and could've passed it along to my daughter. Andrea, if you're listening, get tested and do whatever it takes to prevent breast cancer." She cried a little harder. "And please call me. I just want to hear your voice one more time. I've wondered what you would sound like all grown up. You can tell me you still hate me. I just want to know you're okay."

They gave her a few moments to recover, then pivoted the interview to Jonah's section.

"I can't tell you what she sounds like, but I can give you an idea of what Andrea might look like today," he said. "Are you ready?"

Beverly nodded and whispered, "Yes, please."

Jonah removed the photo from the folder and slid it to her. To the audience, he said, "We'll post this image along with several others on our website, which we'll link below."

Beverly picked up the photo and covered her mouth with a trembling hand. She stared at the image as silent tears streaked down her face. After a few moments, she lowered the hand from her mouth and whispered, "This looks so much like my mother. I always said Andrea favored her, but this is crazy. How did your computer do this?"

"Remember those family photos you provided?" Jonah asked. Bev nodded. "I scanned those into the software along with Andrea's last known image. My software doesn't just progressively age Andrea's photo. It factors in the similarities in her bone structure and appearance to those of her family members at the age she'd be now to give me a more accurate profile."

"Wow," Beverly said without looking away. "May I keep this?"

"That's your copy," Jonah replied.

Beverly hugged the photo to her chest and smiled appreciatively at him. "Thank you."

"It's my pleasure. I hope this helps us find some answers."

They brought Cassandra from GeneMatch into the studio, and she swabbed the inside of Bev's mouth to get her DNA profile. She hugged Beverly afterward and promised to put a rush on the results.

Felix did a warm wrap-up and asked their followers and subscribers to please get in touch with any information on Andrea's whereabouts. He turned off the recording equipment, then they each took a turn hugging Beverly. Sawyer fist-bumped his friends and walked Beverly to her car where she hugged him again.

"This is going to work," she said. "I just know it."

He stood in the parking lot long after she drove away, trying to get his bearings after such an emotional interview. The urge to drive to the nearest donut shop or fast-food joint was strong, but Sawyer called on the discipline he'd developed as a chubby teenager who'd hated his body and sometimes himself. Lately, he'd eaten sweets when he was stressed out and had even skipped a few workouts. It sounded like no big deal, but it was too easy to slip back into bad habits. He recalled Royce's concern that Courtney might do the same thing with Wheeler and couldn't deny he'd made excellent points.

"Control what you can and let the rest go," Sawyer urged himself.

The familiar mantra used to help center him, especially when he decided to leave the sheriff's department. But now, that decision felt more like he'd run away from his problem, which had only come home to roost. His nemesis saw him as a weak and unworthy adversary. Sawyer could either confirm Wheeler's notion, or he could use the man's arrogance to reel him in and strike when he least expected it. One of those options was much more palatable to Sawyer, but was it because he needed the ego boost or because it was his true desire?

A hero complex? Was that what this was? Was his idea to run for sheriff about serving and protecting the people of Chatham County, or was it about gaining the upper hand on Wheeler? Was his operation to find Savannah's missing about the potential victims and their families, or was it a salve on self-inflicted wounds? By finding them he saved himself?

An altruistic vein ran through all law enforcement officers, soldiers, doctors, and firemen. They answered to a higher calling and were driven to serve and protect, to defend, to heal, and to rescue. There was no denying that some lost their way and the initial call to serve became a god complex. Their missions became self-aggrandizing and egocentric, living for the fame and glory and not caring about the cost or who absorbed the toll.

He stopped and stared at his reflection in the driver's side window just like Wheeler had the day before but not because he cared about his hair or appearance. Sawyer was vain as fuck and knew it, but this time, he wanted to know if he liked the person beneath the veneer. The spring sunshine bounced off the diamonds in his engagement ring, reflecting a riotous rainbow on the glass. Sawyer forced his gaze back up to his face and silently asked if this was the same man Royce Locke had sacrificed everything to be with.

The answer couldn't be yes. They'd been through too much together to remain the same. So, no, he might not be the same man Royce had fallen in love with, but he was the man Royce was going to marry. And Sawyer would ensure he never regretted it.

Maybe the real challenge wasn't a showdown with Wheeler but merely Sawyer accepting he'd made the best decision he could for himself at the time. Revenge wasn't always a dish best served cold. Sometimes the ultimate fuck you was to move on and be happy. Sawyer had accomplished one of those things. He passionately and irrevocably loved the life he'd built with Royce, but a piece of him was still clinging to the precipice of misguided principle. That was his true adversary.

His phone rang, and he smiled when he saw the name on the caller ID. *What perfect timing.* Sawyer accepted the call and said, "Is it in?"

A warm masculine laugh filled his ears. "Yes, Sergeant Key. When would you like to swing by to pick it up?"

"Right now."

"We'll see you soon," the man said.

Sawyer disconnected the call and grabbed his earbuds from his glovebox. His destination was only a few blocks away, and it was perfect weather for a brisk walk while listening to an audiobook. He pressed Play and set off, wondering what Royce would think about moving to a country village in England for retirement. Surely they could use a hardware store and a handyman.

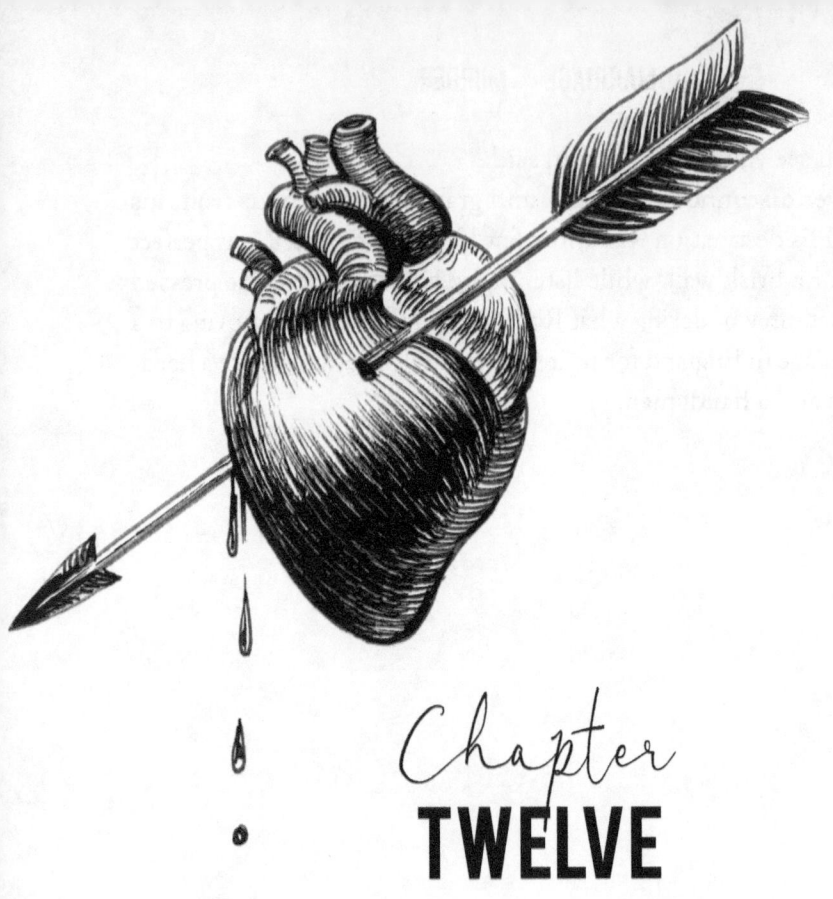

## Chapter
# TWELVE

"**W**HOA," TARA SAID.

Royce looked up from Leo's phone records and found Tara grinning like she'd scored front row tickets for her favorite band. "Well, at least one of us has found something." He'd hoped to find an interesting pattern or anomaly in Leo's cell phone activity—either from his usage or the tower pings to note his location. But nothing.

"There's a hit on the SoleMate database for the print we submitted," Tara said, then she did a chair shimmy.

Royce didn't know who had created the site to help law enforcement identify shoe and boot prints at crime scenes, but Tara clearly wanted to kiss them on the mouth. "And?" he asked.

"Those prints belong to a pair of Zamberlan Men's Lynx GORE-TEX hunting boots."

Royce's excitement ebbed a little. "This is Georgia. There must be tens of thousands of hunting boots in this state."

Tara's canary-eating grin returned. "Not these." She turned her monitor so Royce could see an image of light brown leather boots with dark brown trim and brown camouflage soles. "Take a gander at how much a pair of these bad boys costs."

"Two hundred bucks?"

Tara snorted. "Try four hundred and forty-nine."

Royce stiffened. "Hey, now. The average Joe isn't walking into Walmart or the local sporting goods store to buy those."

"Nope," Tara agreed. "I'll start a search for retailers who might've sold them, but I suspect they ordered the boots online. Better yet, I'm going to reach out to a buddy of mine who owns a sporting goods store in Bryan County. He can tell me what he knows about those boots and possibly help me identify the manufacturer of the arrow."

Royce leaned back and steepled his hands together in front of his chest and began thinking through the case.

"You look like Mendoza," Tara quipped.

"Thanks."

His partner chuckled and kept working.

"Something is bothering me," Royce said a few minutes later, "and I can't quite put my finger on it."

Tara stilled and looked up. "Start at the beginning and work through it." The advice sounded too simple, but it usually worked when one hit a snag.

"We know Leo Fellows called Glen Bishop at eleven. The call only lasted for ten minutes. They didn't talk long enough to work through the sources of their contention. I mean, Leo had an affair with Nancy Bishop, and Glen ousted Leo from the company he helped build from scratch. The call was too short to fix any of that."

"Agreed," Tara said.

"Yet it was too long to just trade insults. How many times can you tell someone to kiss your ass or fuck off in ten minutes?"

"Tons," Tara said. "You think Leo arranged to meet with Glen at a later time?"

Royce pondered her question briefly. "Glen answers and curses Leo out. Leo offers a token apology to keep Glen from hanging up. Maybe even points out that they'd both wronged each other. Asks to meet."

"Why?" Tara asked.

"Glen Bishop would ask the same thing. His curiosity wouldn't allow him to hang up. So, what did Leo say for the remainder of the call?"

"They could've been throwing out dates and times," Tara said.

"Fair point, but if the conversation led to Leo's murder, those last few minutes must've been wrought with tension. Leo had to have said something to ignite a spark."

"Did he?" Tara probed. "I mean, Glen's temper could've been simmering the entire time. He thought getting Leo out of his face and away from Nancy would've been enough to soothe his wounded pride, but what if it ate at him bit by bit. And who's to say firing Leo ended the affair with Nancy? What if they continued to screw around? It might've made the prospect even more alluring to Leo. Maybe he rubbed it in Bishop's face."

"Why wouldn't Glen just divorce his wife?" Royce asked.

Tara pursed her lips for a few seconds. "Could be a few reasons." She held up a finger, drawing a smirk from Royce. "They might've gotten married before any wealth was involved, and there's no prenuptial agreement." She held up two fingers and Royce shook his head. "Nancy could be the source of their wealth. Perhaps she's a trust fund baby and was the source of Glen's portion of the startup money." Three fingers earned a laugh from Royce. "Maybe he just freaking loves her and doesn't want a divorce. Maybe he convinced himself they could rekindle their marriage with Leo out of the way."

Royce nodded. "I think more than one of those things could be true."

"You still sound unconvinced," Tara said.

"Not about that. How did Glen know where to find Leo? Even if they'd decided to meet up to discuss their situation, Leo wouldn't have invited Glen to a venue where he was setting up a wedding reception."

Tara narrowed her eyes and stroked a finger over her lips. "True. There was no reason for Leo to tell Glen his location. He could've placed a tracker on Leo's car."

Royce rolled the idea over in his head, but it didn't feel right. "What if Glen phoned Cupid's Arrow and asked the personal assistant where Leo was?"

"Why would she give Leo's location to a random caller?" Tara asked. Then her eyes widened. "Glen might've pretended to be a vendor."

Royce pointed at her. "Bingo." He picked up his phone, called Cupid's Arrow, and asked for Stella.

Leo's former assistant came on the line within seconds and greeted him warmly. "How may I help you?"

"On the day Leo was murdered, did you happen to take a call from someone who was looking for Leo?"

She hummed. "I frequently fielded those types of calls. Do you mean did anyone ask for his specific location that day?"

"Yes, ma'am."

"Let me look through my contact notes for the morning. That was the Anders wedding." The clickety-clack of fingernails on a keyboard came through the phone. "Oh, here we go. I received a call from a vendor who said they'd written the address down wrong. I provided the correct one."

Royce sat up straighter in his chair as his adrenaline spiked. "This didn't strike you as odd at the time? You never mentioned the call during our interview."

Stella's breath hitched. "N-n-no. It happens all the time. Oh my god. Are you saying I'm the reason Leo is dead?"

"No, Stella. Whoever killed Leo is fully responsible for their actions. If not for you, they would've found Leo another way."

Sniffling came through the connection. "But I made it so easy for him."

"The caller was a man?" Royce asked.

More crying sounds filled the silence, followed by a deep breath. "Yes. But the caller didn't give a name. He was grumpy and surly and borderline belligerent, so I gave him the information he requested to get him off the phone. I killed Leo."

"You didn't," Royce replied, then worked to calm her down for a few minutes. "What about a call log? Does your company keep them?"

"Of course," she replied. "Why didn't I think of it?"

"Because I rattled you something fierce, and I'm very sorry for that."

Stella sniffled again, but it didn't drown out the sounds of her nails clacking away on her keyboard. "Let's see," she said. "It would've been late morning."

"Sometime after eleven," Royce told her.

"Aha! Here it is. Eleven twelve." Stella rattled off the number, and Royce wrote it down.

"Thank you," he said. "You might've cracked this case wide open."

"I hope so. I'll be more careful going forward."

"Don't blame yourself. Promise me," Royce said firmly.

Stella snorted. "I'll try."

"That's not a promise," Royce said.

"Then I won't be breaking one, will I?"

They said goodbye, and Royce disconnected. He hurriedly paged through Leo's phone records like a horny teen who'd pinched his older brother's *Playboy* magazine and was eager to lay eyes on the centerfold before someone banged on the bathroom door. He scanned the desired page, and the highlighted phone number was way sexier than Miss May 1998.

Royce lifted his head and smiled at his partner. "It's a match. Glen Bishop, or someone using his cell phone, called Cupid's Arrow and impersonated a vendor looking for Leo. They claimed to have written down the wrong address for delivery. Stella said the guy was surly and borderline belligerent, so she didn't ask questions."

"It must happen a lot," Tara said.

Royce nodded. "That's what Stella said."

Tara chuckled and shook her head.

"What?"

"If you belched right now, a yellow feather would come flying out of your mouth," she said.

"Gross." Though he couldn't deny he was damn pleased with his deductive reasoning. Look out, Sherlock. "Any luck with your sporting goods buddy?"

She held her hand up palm down and rocked it from side to side.

"He doubts anyone around here sells high-dollar boots like those. Maybe closer to Atlanta. He said our person most likely bought them through an online retailer. He was more helpful with the arrow."

"Yeah?" Royce asked.

"Custom made by Archery Pro. What I thought was a serial number was actually their logo. And my friend also noticed that the shaft was shorter than standard."

"It's not the size that counts," Royce said, outraged on behalf of shafts everywhere. "I mean, it clearly got the job done."

Tara rolled her eyes and sighed. "Remember when I suggested our killer might've been using a folding survival bow?" Royce nodded. "My buddy said those use shorter arrows."

"Nice work."

"But wait, there's more," Tara said. "While you were making Stella cry and swoon, I reached out to Archery Pro. They weren't going to help me until I explained someone had used one of their arrows in a homicide. I've emailed photos of the arrow shaft, and they will try to get back to us within a few hours." Tara mimed reeling in a big fish.

"That's terrific news for us, but terrible for Glen. Speaking of…" Royce checked his watch. "Glen is running out of time to contact us on his own."

"We'll keep running down every potential lead until then," Tara said.

As if Glen Bishop had heard Royce's invisible countdown clock, he called at nine forty-five.

"I'm available to meet at one o'clock at my office. Don't be late," the CFO said and promptly hung up without saying goodbye.

"He's totally the killer," Royce told Tara.

She snorted. "Because Bishop has bad phone etiquette?"

"It's a personality flaw," Royce said. "I don't think you should discount it."

Tara drummed her fingers on the desk. "How are we going to address the affair during the interview?"

"We don't," Royce said. "I don't want to do or say anything to tip off Glen that we spoke to Marcie or Rocky. I think today we should focus on getting a complete story from him. Then we can look for ways to punch holes in it."

"We have time to kill. What would you like to do?"

Royce lifted a thick stack of documents off his desk and let them fall with a thud, reminding him of Sawyer's early morning stunt. The memory was a moment of levity he embraced wholeheartedly.

Tara blew out a breath. "Are those Leo's financials?"

"Yep," Royce replied. "Credit cards, personal banking statements, and financials from Cupid's Arrow, but the business records only go back to when Leo took over as the controlling partner. Still waiting on his investment records and life insurance documents."

Some financial records required a forensic accountant, but Leo's seemed more straightforward. Other than the low six-figure severance payout from Abbot & Marsh and the purchase of Cupid's Arrow, Leo's dealings were pretty direct. It only took ninety minutes to paint a clear picture of his financial situation. Leo was drawing a healthy income from his new venture, but it was a fraction of what he'd made at Abbot & Marsh.

"I don't get it," Royce said. "I understand his joint accounts with Grace were frozen until his divorce was finalized, but it looks like Leo had a healthy balance in his new checking and savings accounts. He could've easily met his monthly obligation to Jennifer Ludwig. All his other bills were current. And why was his house so bare? Maybe you were right, and he'd just given up. Stopped caring."

"Or perhaps Leo truly expected a windfall soon and didn't want to pull the money from his savings account," Tara suggested. "We've been thinking about legal transactions, but what if Leo was expecting something off the books? Untraceable? Or maybe he just lived frugally." Tara tilted her head. "What if he was late on his payment to Jennifer because he'd decided the wedding planning business wasn't for him."

Royce picked up the contract Jennifer Ludwig's attorney had sent over. "He'd still be on the hook for all the money he owed her unless he found someone to buy his share."

"Why not sell it to some eager schmuck like Jennifer had done with him?" Tara asked.

Royce picked up the contract Sally Collins had emailed him soon after he'd arrived at the precinct. The subject of her correspondence had read: In Good Faith. "Sally had a veto clause. Leo couldn't just sell it to anyone without her approval."

Tara scrunched up her nose. "Then what was the point of having controlling interest?"

"Their new contract is fifty-fifty," Royce said, then showed her the bank statement where he'd deposited fifty thousand dollars into his savings account. "That money had come from Sally Collins as part of their new contract."

Tara stood up, lifted her arms over her head, and stretched her back. "So the financials are a swing and a miss so far. Then again, we've shifted away from Sally Collins and Jennifer Ludwig as our prime suspects in favor of Glen. He had the means and the motive." She blew out a breath and cocked her head to the side. "We need to prove Glen knew about the tunnels."

"Everyone knows about them," Royce said.

Tara narrowed her eyes. "We know they exist, but we don't all know how to access them or how to do it safely. Many of them would probably be extremely dangerous."

"Rocky said Glen is involved with the historical society," Royce said.

"But we have to discover that for ourselves without throwing Rocky under the bus."

"You're the social media guru," Royce pointed out. "You tackle Facebook, Twitter, and Instagram. I'll do a general Google search to see if his name comes up in connection with any historical society events."

Tara only took a few seconds to discover Glen Bishop wasn't on any social media sites. Royce took a little longer, but he found an article touting Glen as a guest speaker at a historical event on pirates in the Atlantic. He clicked on the link and began to read, a smile spreading when he saw a photo of Glen Bishop dressed as a pirate.

"Come see this," Royce said.

Tara walked around and stood behind him. "Christ. Was it Long John Silver day at Abbot & Marsh?"

"So much better than that," Royce replied. "Our boy Glen was a guest lecturer at a historical society event on pirates."

"Scroll down and let's see what he had to say."

Royce craned his neck to look up at her. "You're going to read over my shoulder?"

Tara rolled her eyes and walked away. "Fine. Print it out for me, and I'll read it at my desk."

Royce hit the command, and the printer fired up across the room. Tara snagged the pages from the tray and returned to her chair.

"There's a video link halfway down," she said.

Royce scrolled down. "That's much better than reading this." He looked up when Tara didn't join him. "You're not going to watch with me?"

"You mean over your shoulder?" Tara asked.

Royce heaved a sigh. "I'm sure I deserve a smartass partner like you."

Tara laughed and walked around to him. "I'm sure you deserve worse."

Royce shrugged and hit the Play button on the video viewer, and there was Glen Bishop in all his pirate glory. The display at the bottom said the video was a hundred minutes long, and Royce worried they'd have to watch the whole thing. Luckily, it didn't take long for Bishop to mention how pirates shanghaied drunken men.

"You're all familiar with The Pirate's House, right?" Glen asked in the video. Several people murmured their assent, but a few said no. Glen launched into a detailed history of The Pirate's House before he got to the good stuff. "There's a secret tunnel off the rum room below the restaurant. It leads to the Savannah River where a small boat would be waiting to take the pirates and captives back to their ships."

Royce stopped the video and smiled up at Tara. "You know what this means?"

"We have a lot of circumstantial evidence pointing toward Glen Bishop," she replied.

"True, but we now have time for a good lunch before we meet with Glen. How do you feel about lobster rolls?"

"Big fan," Tara said. She pocketed her keys and phone. "My treat."

Royce stood up and pushed in his chair. "Even better."

Once ensconced in Glen Bishop's office, they recited his rights, informing him that anything said could and would be used against him. The older man had gotten flustered until Tara explained it was nothing more than procedure.

Royce turned on his recorder and rattled off the date, time, and names of those present. Then he pretended to cling to every word the CFO uttered while discreetly counting the number of stuffed animal heads mounted on the wall or the taxidermy birds on display.

"Leo called me to bury the hatchet," Glen told them from behind his massive desk. His lawyer, Robert Atherton, had pulled up a chair beside him and was taking notes. They could fit two more lawyers and a paralegal back there. Who'd this guy think he was? The president?

Royce returned to his animal count. Two deer, two turkeys, a wild boar, a black bear, and two mallard ducks—one male, one female. Eight mounts in total.

"I told Leo it wasn't a good time and asked if we could chat later. I never intended to do so. There was nothing left for us to say," Glen added.

Royce didn't have anything against hunting in general, but the need to hang the kill up like a trophy bothered him a lot, and eight pairs of glass eyes boring into him disturbed Royce even more. He settled his unease by imagining him attaching Glen Bishop's nuts to a plaque and hanging it on a wall.

"Well, Leo must've guessed my intention because he kept me on the line a little longer, as the phone records indicate," the CFO said.

Glen's shrine to hunting didn't stop with the stuffed critters. One entire wall was filled with various hunting photos. Some of Bishop hunting in fields or by large bodies of water and others of him posing with his kill.

Royce sharpened his focus on Glen and said, "How?"

The older man tilted his head. "How what?"

"How did Leo keep you on the phone? What did he say?"

Glen puffed out his cheeks and exhaled slowly. "It's so inconsequential that I can't remember."

"Try," Tara said firmly.

"Watch your tone, or I'll call your superior officer, Detective," Atherton said without looking away from his notes. What was he really doing over there? The blowhard to his right hadn't uttered a single significant word. Royce guessed he was doodling. "Mr. Bishop," the lawyer said, "is only entertaining this interview out of respect for the police department."

Royce turned to look at Tara. "Go ahead and give him the number for your supervisor."

Tara rattled off a number for Atherton, who harrumphed and dialed. A second later, Royce's phone rang in his pocket, and he retrieved it. The lawyer scowled and disconnected.

"I'm her superior officer," Royce said tersely. "And if you want to complain to my boss, you'll need to call the precinct and ask for Chief Mendoza." Royce spelled out the chief's last name, then said, "And do not intimate again that Glen Bishop is doing us a favor. He was the last person to speak to Leo Fellows before he was killed, and they have a contentious history. Any idiot would insist on speaking to him, and I assure you, Mr. Atherton, neither of us"—he gestured to Tara and himself—"are idiots. Now, if you don't mind, I'd like Mr. Bishop to answer Detective South's question."

The lawyer narrowed his eyes but gestured for Bishop to continue.

The CFO chuckled nervously. "I'm afraid I don't recall the question now." Then he held up his hand as Tara began to speak. "I remember. You wanted me to try to remember what Leo and I discussed. Well, he tried reminding me of the good times by bringing up how we met in college and recalling the night Leo, Bart, and I decided to go into business for ourselves."

It took every ounce of willpower for Royce not to lift his hand and mime jacking off. Instead, he leveled a steely gaze at Glen and said, "I need you to recount your whereabouts from eleven in the morning to one in the afternoon on Saturday."

"Me?" Glen asked. "Why?"

Tara's phone vibrated, and she removed it from her pocket. She made her apologies and stepped outside Glen's office.

"For an alibi, sir."

"You don't have to answer him," Atherton said. "If he had something solid on you, he would've arrested you already."

"You can answer me now on your turf, or I'll take you downtown, and you can answer on mine. You choose."

Bishop looked to his lawyer for help, but Atherton was too busy staring at Royce to notice. Before either of them blinked, Tara stepped back inside the office. Her shit-eating grin spelled big trouble for the men behind the desk. She returned to her chair and passed her phone to Royce. It was an Archery Pro purchase order, and the buyer was none other than Glen Bishop. He'd custom ordered ten arrows and a folding survival bow in January. She scrolled down to show a picture of the items they shipped to Glen Bishop. Royce handed back her phone and smiled.

"What is it?" Bishop asked.

Atherton snorted. "Calm down, Glen. They haven't brought out the handcuffs yet."

"What we have is proof your client purchased the weapon that killed Leo Fellows," Tara said.

"That's impossible," Bishop said.

Royce stared at the older man in disbelief. "You haven't even asked how Leo died."

"It doesn't matter," Bishop replied. "I didn't have anything to do with it."

Tara turned the phone around so Bishop could see what was on the screen. All the color leeched from the man's face. "And this is where the cuffs come out," she said as she rose to her feet. "Glen Bishop, you're under arrest for the murder of Leo Fellows."

"What?" he said, trying to jerk his hands away when she rounded the desk to cuff him.

"Glen," Atherton said softly, "don't resist arrest. I'll get you out of this." Royce noticed the attorney had lost some of his bluster and arrogance. "Don't say a damn word to them. Don't eat or drink anything they give you."

"You think they'll poison me?"

"No, but they'll swab anything you've touched for DNA. Don't make their jobs easier for them. I'll be there when they question you."

"Okay," Glen said, sounding and looking fifteen years older than when Royce and Tara had arrived.

Tara continued mirandizing him. Once she finished, Atherton asked if they could use the executive elevators and exits to avoid humiliating Bishop in front of his employees and clients. Royce didn't fight the request, and he waited with Bishop by the doorway while Tara brought the Charger around. Since Bishop had been instructed not to talk, Royce killed time by humming a jaunty tune. Bishop scowled but didn't say a word and maintained his silence through transport and booking.

Royce decided to let Glen stew in a cell for a bit before they took their first crack at him.

"We should have a signed search warrant any minute now," Tara said.

Royce chuckled. "We just got back to the station."

"Dude, I started the process as soon as I got confirmation Glen purchased our murder weapon."

"You are the champ," Royce said.

Tara laughed. "Damn skippy."

They'd decided to bring four officers with them to help search Glen's home in case Nancy Bishop was home and available for an interview. A woman who looked remarkably like Grace Huxley opened the door.

"Mrs. Bishop?" Royce asked.

"Nancy," she corrected. "Mrs. Bishop was my mother-in-law."

Royce handed her the search warrant. She accepted the document and unfolded it.

Nancy had platinum blonde hair, crystalline blue eyes, and fair, unwrinkled skin. She wore wide-leg ivory pants, a flowy cheetah-print top, and lots of gold—in her ears, around her neck, stacked bracelets on one wrist, a diamond bedazzled watch on the other, and low-heeled sandals on her pedicured feet.

Nancy looked up with cold eyes. "What's this all about?"

"You mean you haven't heard?" Tara asked.

Nancy turned her gaze on Tara, and it grew even icier. "Obviously, I haven't if I'm asking. I think I should call my lawyer."

"You could do that, but he's a little tied up with your husband right now," Tara said.

"With Glen? What for?"

"We arrested your husband for the murder of Leo Fellows," Royce said.

Nancy's mouth gaped, and her eyes widened in shock. Staggering back a few steps, Nancy clutched the warrant to her chest. "I don't believe it. I won't."

"Which part?" Royce prodded. "That your husband killed Leo or that he made a mistake and got caught?"

She blinked as tears filled her eyes. "All of it." She continued to stare off into space as if she'd forgotten they were there.

"Ma'am," Royce said to regain her attention.

She shook her head and stood aside. "Should I leave or what?"

"Stay," Tara said. "We'd like to ask you a few questions."

Royce had already instructed the search team on what they were looking for, so he and Tara followed Nancy into a sitting room at the back of the house. One entire wall was windows overlooking the spacious backyard. The others were painted a pale lavender. The furniture was covered in a floral print he thought was called chintz.

"Please sit down," Nancy said. "Can I get you something to drink?"

Royce offered a smile. "No, ma'am, but thank you."

Nancy scowled slightly. "Ma'am is almost as bad as Mrs. Bishop."

She took a deep breath and said, "I suppose you'll find out some other way, so you might as well hear it from me." She paused for a moment before continuing. "I had an affair with Leo Fellows."

"For how long?" Tara asked.

"A little over a year."

Royce tilted his head. "Sounds like more than an affair."

Nancy briefly closed her eyes, then nodded. "I loved him." Her composure crumbled, and she began to cry.

"Did your affair precipitate Leo's termination?" Tara asked.

Nancy sniffled. "Yes."

"And what happened after his termination?" Royce pressed.

"Between Leo and me, you mean?"

Royce nodded.

Nancy heaved a deep sigh. "Leo asked me to leave Glen and start over with him someplace new. Glen had asked me to stay so we could work on our marriage. I was deeply divided and overwhelmed, and I asked Leo for time to think. He saw it as rejection and disappeared from my life. Poof! What do the kids call it these days? Haunting?"

Royce bit back a chuckle. "Ghosting."

"That's exactly what Leo did. He refused to take my calls or respond to my messages." Her chin wobbled, and her lip trembled. "I would've chosen him." A single tear streaked down her pretty face.

"Detectives," Officer Elizabeth Bates said from the doorway. "We found something you need to see."

Royce and Tara excused themselves and stepped outside the sitting room where Officer Laney Branwell held up a pair of Zamberlan boots with a gloved hand.

"I'll be damned," Royce said. "Flip it over and let me look at the tread."

Branwell did and Tara held a photo of the boot print next to it.

"Looks like a perfect match. Nice work."

Bates held an oversized evidence bag, and Branwell placed the boots inside and sealed it.

"That's not all we found," Branwell said. "Come with us."

Tara ducked her head into the sitting room and told Nancy they'd be right back, then they followed the officers to the garage. A series of closets lined one wall. All the doors stood open to reveal enough hunting clothes and gear to start a sporting goods store.

Officer Devon Hughes held up a brown camo backpack in one hand and a folding bow in the other. "The arrows are in the bag along with a crudely drawn map of the tunnel under the restaurant," he said. "We found the backpack and the boots hidden behind some coveralls and pants."

Tara snapped on a pair of gloves and inspected the arrows. "Exact match to the ones Glen ordered. And there are only nine in here. We both know where number ten ended up."

"Nice work, everyone," Royce said. "Let's see what else Nancy has to say."

When they reached the sitting room, she was talking to someone on her cell phone. Every ounce of emotion was gone from her face, and her arctic gaze shot shards of ice at them.

"They're back. I'll call you later." Nancy hung up and said, "That was Mr. Atherton. I won't be answering any more questions until he's available to be with me. And since you've dumped my husband in a cell and left him there while you search, I don't see that happening anytime soon."

"Have it your way, ma'am," Royce said. They had what they needed from her.

Once they returned to the station, Royce and Tara decided not to keep Glen Bishop or his attorney waiting any longer. Bishop was led to an interrogation room, and Atherton followed shortly after.

"You have some nerve keeping me waiting like I don't have someplace to be," Atherton snarled. "I had to shift my entire—"

Tara raised her hand to cut him off. "Save your energy for your client. He's going to need it."

Atherton shoved past her and opened the door. Tara and Royce exchanged a fist bump before following behind him. Royce flipped on the recorder and reminded Glen of his rights on record. Then he named everyone present in the room and the date and time of the interview.

Glen kept his eyes averted to the table in front of him, but Royce figured that wouldn't last long. He wasn't in the mood to dance around and play games.

"Nancy told us about the affair she had with Leo Fellows," Royce said.

Glen snapped his head up and glowered at Royce.

"Not a damn word, Glen," Atherton warned.

"Fine by me," Royce said. "I like the sound of my own voice. But you're going to want to pay close attention because I'm going to give you one chance to help yourself. Just one."

Glen said nothing but kept his gaze on Royce as he walked through Saturday's timeline, starting with Leo Fellows's phone call and ending with an arrow through Leo's heart a short while later. "We have the motive, the means, and we can place you at the crime scene with the murder weapon."

"When do you get to the part where you offer my client a chance to help himself?" Atherton asked.

"Right now," Royce said. "The last thing you want is for our DA to think Leo's murder was premeditated. One could argue that Leo took the first shot when he called you on Saturday morning. It would be in your best interest to tell us what Leo said to provoke the call to Cupid's Arrow to find his location, followed by a drive across town, and a walk through dank, dangerous tunnels to kill him."

Glen stared at him with cold, emotionless eyes. "I've got nothing to say to you."

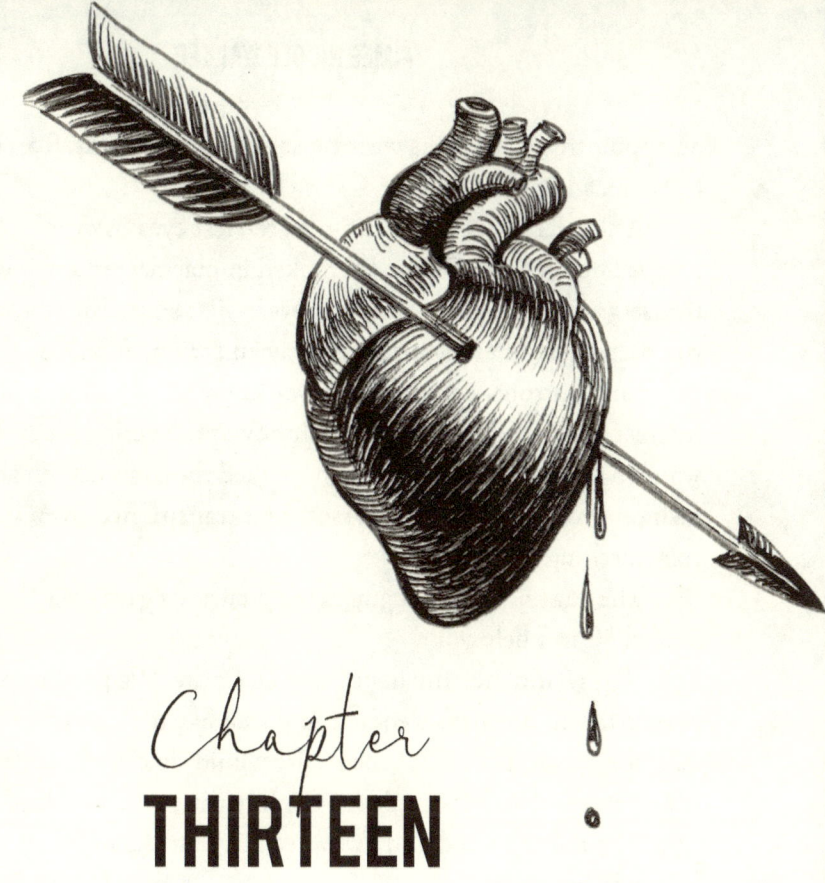

# Chapter
# THIRTEEN

BELLS JINGLED OVERHEAD WHEN SAWYER STEPPED INSIDE THE tailor's shop. Rows and racks of suits in every style and color met his wandering gaze. He didn't see the tailor or his fiancé. Royce had sworn up and down he'd be on time to pick up his suit for Jace's wedding and choose what they'd wear to their own.

*Their wedding.*

The reality of their pending nuptials hadn't fully hit Sawyer yet. Picking up Royce's ring from the jeweler and knowing he'd pick a suit from one of the hundreds in the store helped, but it still felt like an exceptional dream.

"Be right with you," a man called out.

Sawyer strolled through the suits and contemplated calling or texting Royce. He and Tara had made a significant arrest in their investigation, and it would be easy to get caught up in the aftermath and forget an appointment. But this wasn't just any appointment. Royce said he'd be there, and he would be.

A slender brunet guy with the greenest eyes Sawyer had ever seen stepped out of a back room. He looked immaculate in a pair of charcoal trousers and a pale gray corset vest over a lilac shirt. The vest was a chevron pattern in different shades of gray and trimmed in lilac thread with matching buttons. And now Sawyer knew what had spurned Royce's interest in corset vests. He'd thought it was the period piece they'd been watching on Masterpiece that had sparked the conversation about men's fashion evolution and how corsets had transitioned from vanity wear to something much sexier.

The snazzily dressed guy raked a curious gaze over Sawyer, then smiled. "Can I help you?"

"I'm waiting for my fiancé, Royce Locke. We need to pick up his tuxedo for his brother's wedding, and we'd like to talk to someone about suits for our own." Perhaps the reality would sink in a little deeper every time Sawyer thought or said it. "On July thirtieth," he added.

The tailor smiled and extended his hand. "I'm Julian, and I'd be happy to assist you."

Sawyer introduced himself and looked around the room. "There are so many options to choose from."

"I promise I'll make the selection easy and fun," Julian said. "Would you like to get started now, or would you like to wait for Royce?"

Sawyer glanced down at his watch and noticed his man was ten minutes late and debated again if he should check in with him. If he was too busy, Sawyer could just take his tuxedo home for Royce to try on. "Might as well make the most of our time," Sawyer said.

"Let's start with color. Do the two of you plan to wear matching suits, or do you each want to do your own thing?"

"No matching," Sawyer said. "And I have a pretty good idea what color I'd like to wear. I'm just not sure of the cut."

"You're leaps and bounds ahead of most men when they come in. Even the ones with marching orders stumble with choosing the right shade of black, gray, blue, or even white."

Sawyer knew the exact shade he wanted and headed toward the

section of gray suits in the store. He stopped at the one that most closely resembled the tempest in Royce's eyes when they made love. "This is the color," Sawyer said.

Julian walked around him and checked the details on the hanger tag, which allowed Sawyer to see the back of his corset vest. The fabric wrapped snuggly around Julian's body and met in the center of his back. Thin, crisscrossing ropes of gray and lilac thread connected the two pieces of fabric, leaving an inch gap between them.

"Beautiful choice," Julian said.

"Your corset vest is beautiful. Where did you find it?"

Julian turned and beamed up at him. "Thank you. I made it myself."

Sawyer stared at the fine embroidery details. "Wow. Do you make them for other people?"

Julian nodded. "It's my side hustle."

"I'm truly impressed." He was about to ask him the name of his business, but the door opened, and Royce rushed in.

"So sorry," he said, placing a quick kiss on Sawyer's lips. Then he greeted Julian with a warm smile and a handshake. "Wow. This vest is extra dapper."

Julian beamed with pride. "Thank you. Your fiancé was just admiring it too."

Royce looked at Sawyer and quirked a brow. "Was he now?"

The phone rang, and Julian headed to the counter to answer it, calling out, "Royce, your tuxedo is hanging in dressing room two. Try it on so I can make sure it fits perfectly."

Royce headed toward the dressing rooms, and Sawyer followed. He stopped outside door number two and smiled.

"Planning to come in and help me?" Royce asked.

Sawyer smiled wickedly. "Something like that."

Inside the small space, Sawyer crossed his arms over his chest instead of reaching for Royce's clothes. The two of them tended to get into big trouble in confined spaces, but it wasn't the reason he'd followed Royce into the room.

"Tara and I got so caught up in tying up loose ends that both of us nearly forgot important appointments. She'd promised to help her nieces pick out a new kitty at the animal shelter." His man could shimmy out of his clothes faster than anyone, and Sawyer enjoyed the sight of Royce wearing nothing but a pair of briefs and socks. "Thank goodness Tara's sister called to remind her, or I would've forgotten to meet you here." Royce put one leg in the trousers and cringed. "That sounded really bad. You do know how important our wedding is to me, right?"

"I do. I also know where your fascination with corsets and corset vests came from." He nodded toward the dressing room door.

Royce tugged his tuxedo pants up to his waist but left them open. "You're reading the situation wrong."

"Am I?"

Royce slid one arm into the dress shirt, then the other. He quickly worked the buttons with deft fingers. "So wrong."

Sawyer relaxed his arms and stepped forward. He took his sweet time tucking Royce's shirt into his pants. The back of his hand brushed over Royce's cock, and he fought the urge to tug the pants and underwear back down. Sawyer leaned forward until his lips were nearly touching Royce's. "Tell me how it is."

"You're right about my fascination with corset vests, but it's *you* wearing them in my fantasies, not Julian."

Sawyer's breath caught in his throat. "Me?"

Royce swallowed hard and pulled Sawyer's hands out of his pants. "Don't start something we shouldn't finish," he admonished lightly before reaching for the tie. "And, yes, you. It would frame your perfect ass so beautifully, and I think about running my fingers over the laces while I fuck you hard. Maybe even twisting them to pull the fabric tighter."

The air in the tiny room grew thick and heavy with desire.

Royce flipped his collar down over his tie and reached for the jacket. "I can't believe you were jealous."

"I'm human, aren't I?"

"Yeah, but you don't usually waste energy on useless emotions. I'm the one who gets worked up after reading the thirsty comments people make about you on the YouTube episodes." Royce narrowed his eyes, hooked his finger in Sawyer's belt loop, and tugged him closer. "Everyone wants my man."

Sawyer pressed a quick kiss against his lips. "They can't have me."

"Hell no, they can't."

Sawyer had been debating how and when to give Royce his ring. He'd opened the box more times than he wanted to admit and had slipped it into his pocket, knowing he'd be meeting Royce at the tailor's. Was the dressing room the right place? Was this the right time? Only one way to find out.

"I have something for you," Sawyer whispered.

Royce's grin was dirty and delicious. "Yeah? Here?"

Sawyer leaned forward and kissed Royce's neck just above the collar. "Right here." He placed another kiss on his jawline. "Right now." Sawyer removed Royce's ring from his pocket.

Royce stared at it for a long time, and Sawyer thought he might've miscalculated. Then Royce met Sawyer's gaze. A slow smile spread across his face, and joyous laughter rumbled from his perfect lips. He held up his left hand, and Sawyer slid the ring onto his finger. The dark tungsten looked good on his hand, and the meteorite inlay looked like shattered glass.

"I've never seen anything like this before," Royce said as he stroked it. "What's the metal?"

"Tungsten and the strip in the middle is made from meteorite. It's rock that's fallen from space. Probably an asteroid chunk that landed on earth. I thought it suited you well."

Royce waggled his brows. "Because I take you to heaven?"

"Well, yes," Sawyer said, "but that wasn't my main reason. You crashed into my universe like an asteroid and wreaked so much beautiful havoc. I'm so damn grateful for it."

Royce cupped Sawyer's face and kissed him hard. When he pulled back, he stared down at his hand and smiled. "Fits perfectly, and I love it."

"I'll be the judge of that," Julian said from the other side of the dressing room door. "Shall I come back in ten minutes?"

Sawyer and Royce laughed as they broke apart. He checked to make sure Royce hadn't sprung wood during their kiss. Sawyer didn't want Julian anywhere near Royce's dick, especially not while on his knees. He gave Royce a thumbs-up and opened the door.

"It's not what you think," Sawyer told Julian.

Julian laughed. "It never is, honey."

The tailor was flirty in tone but professional in deed. He deftly checked the fit of Royce's suit and gave his stamp of approval.

"I know you need to get back, so leave your suit in the dressing room," Sawyer said. "I'll take it home after I finish picking out my wedding attire with Julian."

Royce redressed in record time and stepped out of the dressing room. He pressed a quick kiss on Sawyer's lips and smiled at Julian. "I'll be back soon to pick out the suit for our wedding."

"Looking forward to it," the tailor called after him.

Royce disappeared through the door, and Julian turned to smile at Sawyer. "Let's finish picking out your suit, and I'll get some measurements."

"I'd like for you to take some extra measurements if you have time for a special project."

Julian cocked a brow. "Sounds interesting, and I'm all ears."

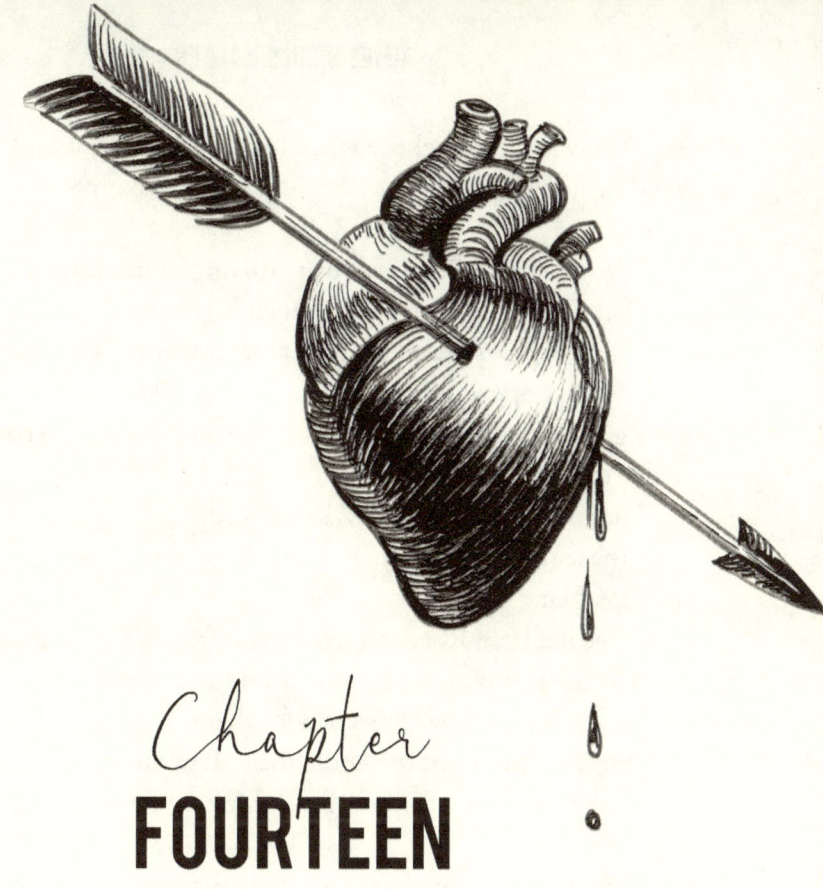

## Chapter
# FOURTEEN

**R**OYCE HAD NEVER BEEN AS AWARE OF ANYTHING AS HE WAS OF the ring on his left finger. And since he never expected to wear a wedding band or even get engaged, Royce figured the weight would feel foreign to him and would require an adjustment period. He was wrong. Nothing had ever felt so right in his entire life, but he could say that about all his milestones with Sawyer, from their first kiss to the moment Sawyer had slid the band on his finger.

He sat in his SUV for several moments staring at the band, tilting his hand this way and that to see how the sun reflected on the metal. "Tungsten and meteorite. So damn extra," he said. And though Royce disagreed with Sawyer's refusal to surrender his platinum and diamond ring to the gunman, he better understood why he'd made the decision.

Royce's phone rang, yanking him out of his daydream. He accepted the call and said, "I'm on my way back to the station."

"You will never believe what I just found," Tara said, her voice sounding urgent.

"What?"

"You'd better pull over if you're driving," Tara warned.

"I'm parked. Tell me what the hell is going on."

"Larry Fellows's cats are at the animal shelter," Tara said in a rush. "They were dropped off last night. The guy told the volunteer he was moving to a new location that didn't permit pets, and he couldn't find anyone to take them."

"Get the fuck out of here," Royce said.

"Those three cats are unique, and there's no mistaking them. I took a picture. Hang tight."

A second later, Royce received a text from Tara. He opened it and stared at the photo of the three cats huddled together in a cage. They looked terrified, and he felt so bad for them.

"How do you want to handle this?" Tara asked.

"I want to rescue the cats, but I think Bones would kill me in my sleep."

Tara snorted. "My nieces are taking the cats, so that's sorted. Why would Larry move anywhere he couldn't take his cats? Would you do that to Bones?"

"Never," Royce said vehemently. "And why didn't he tell us he was moving? Something is off. Let's have another chat with Larry. How soon will you be finished at the shelter?"

Tara hummed. "They're filling out the paperwork now. Give me ten or twenty minutes."

"I'm only a few blocks away from Grace Huxley's office," Royce said. "I'm going to see if I can catch her. I want to find out what her reaction is to Bishop's arrest. I'll probe a little deeper and see what I can learn about Leo and Larry's relationship." Royce blew out a breath. "We can't be thinking what we're thinking."

"I'm not exactly sure what we're thinking other than something isn't adding up," Tara replied. "Meet you at the station soon."

They disconnected and Royce headed to Grace's office. If she wasn't there, he'd try her at home. Royce momentarily berated himself for treating the case like an episode of a crime drama or *Dateline*. Investigations were always twisty and complicated in books, movies, documentaries, and television shows, but the reality was far different. Still, he'd do his due diligence because his conscience demanded it.

Grace Huxley was exiting her building when he pulled into the parking lot. She didn't see him, so he called out to her before she could get in her car. Grace spun around, clutching her chest.

"Sorry about that," Royce said as he approached. "I'm usually a bit more tactful in my approach."

"I'm just extra jumpy, I guess," she said.

Royce quirked a brow. "Because of Leo's murder?"

Grace nodded. "Yes. I've been looking over my shoulder since the day you arrived at my home, even though I don't have a reason to think someone is coming after me." She briefly closed her eyes and shook her head. "Congratulations on your arrest, by the way."

"Were you shocked?" Royce asked.

"You could've knocked me over with a feather when the news broke," Grace said. "Glen and Leo had always been so close. I knew there was new tension between them because Leo's termination came out of the blue or so it seemed to me." She took a deep breath and sighed. "I cannot imagine what pushed Glen so far."

"Can't you?" Royce asked gently. Had she really not known?

Grace's gaze sharpened, and she stood a little taller. "Are you saying Leo and Nancy…" Her words trailed off as if she couldn't complete the thought. Royce noted again how much the two women looked alike. "No," she said, shaking her head.

"I'm afraid so. Nancy admitted as much to us."

"How long?" Grace asked tersely.

"Nancy said they'd had an affair for a year before Glen found out. From what I can tell, Leo was fired a few days after that."

"I wonder why Glen didn't tell me." She tilted her head slightly to the right. "How'd he find out?"

"Nancy changed her mind about speaking to us without her lawyer present before I could delve too deeply. I'm sorry to be the bearer of bad news again."

Grace took a deep breath and said, "Actually, it makes things a little easier for me. I appreciate your honesty." She turned back toward her car, then reconsidered. "Larry called me this morning, and he expressed his frustration again that the medical examiner hasn't released Leo for burial yet. Without the death certificates, he can't take steps to settle Leo's estate."

"Homicides take longer," Royce said. "I'll check to see what's holding the ME up and give Larry a call."

Grace smiled warmly. "You're a prince. Thank you."

"No problem," Royce replied. "I'll get Larry's new address while I'm at it, so I know where to send Leo's possessions once they're released."

Grace frowned. "He's moving? Since when?"

Royce shrugged. "I don't know when he made the decision. He took his cats to the animal shelter because he couldn't take them where he's going."

"No way," Grace said. "Someone has given you false information. Larry loves those cats more than he ever loved his brother. Leo was highly allergic to cats and couldn't even step foot in Larry's house. Leo told his brother it was him or the cats, and Larry chose the cats."

Alarm bells were clanging, and he hoped his mask of neutrality hadn't slipped. Royce recalled the cats' agitation as they'd crawled all over Larry. He'd assumed their behavior was them sensing his distress. And Larry's red, watery eyes and sniffling? He appeared to be mourning the loss of his brother, but what if it was allergies instead? A ringing interrupted his thoughts, and he automatically reached for his cell phone.

"It's mine," Grace said. She checked the screen and grimaced. "I really must take this, Sergeant. Can we talk another time?"

"I have everything I need right now," he said. "Take care."

"Sergeant," she called out. "I notice you're wearing new hardware on your ring finger. If you ever need my services."

Royce smiled. "I assure you I won't."

"That's what they all say," she said before answering her phone.

Royce didn't linger on her parting shot because his mind was too busy turning the unimaginable into something tangible. He called Tara as soon as he got into his SUV. She listened without interruption while he repeated his conversation with Grace Huxley.

"No fucking way," she said once he'd finished.

In the background, a little girl said, "Auntie Tara said a bad word, Mom."

"Hang on," Tara said. Footsteps echoed on a hard surface followed by a door opening. "No fucking way," Tara repeated. This time her voice was firmer and full of disbelief. "Do you mean to tell me you think Larry Fellows is the one in our morgue, and Leo is pretending to be his brother?"

"Crazy, huh?" Royce asked.

Tara was silent for a moment. "Maybe, but it's not impossible."

"We need to talk to Larry again."

"And quickly," Tara added.

"Meet me at the station, and we'll ride over to his house."

"Be there in five," Tara told him.

Larry looked shocked to find them on his doorstep. His eyes were still red and swollen, but getting rid of the cats wouldn't eliminate the dander already in the house. Could this really be Leo?

"Detectives, what a surprise. I didn't expect to see you again since you wrapped up your investigation. Thank you, by the way."

"Can we come in?" Tara asked.

Larry frowned and glanced over his shoulder. "Um, yeah," he finally said and stepped aside. "The place is a little messy."

Even after hearing Larry planned to move, Royce was still shocked by the number of boxes stacked in towers in the dining room. He must've been working around the clock since they'd first arrived at his house on Sunday. Larry walked over to a box on the table and resumed packing newspaper-wrapped items inside it. The hutch was open, and the china was missing, so Royce assumed that's what Larry was carefully packing away.

"Where are the cats?" Royce asked.

Larry had his back to them, but Royce saw the way the man stiffened. He continued working and didn't face the detectives when he said, "Oh, I shut them in the bedroom. They were making a nuisance of themselves. The last thing I wanted to do was accidentally box them up too. You mentioned you had some questions for me," Larry prompted.

They hadn't said that, but Royce wasn't going to pass up the opportunity.

"Did you know your brother was carrying on a torrid affair with Glen Bishop's wife, Nancy?"

Tara shot him a questioning glance, but Royce just winked as if to say *I got this.*

Larry stopped packing and turned to face them with a glower. "Torrid affair?" he asked in a snide voice. "Do you often editorialize in such a manner?"

"When it's necessary." Rattling Larry's chain was essential. "Were you aware of their relationship?"

"Yes," Larry said, then resumed packing once more. "I asked Leo why in the world Glen and Bart had forced him out of the company he'd helped build. Leo confessed his indiscretion."

"They were screwing around for over a year," Royce said coarsely, hoping to get under his skin even more. "Hardly seems like a single indiscretion."

Up to that point, Larry had been using his left hand to fill the box, but it wouldn't require much skill from someone looking to fake their dominant hand temporarily. More complex tasks like writing would need more practice and training. If Royce could throw him off-balance, Larry might slip up.

"I didn't say that. You're putting words into my mouth," Larry said. "And I don't appreciate your crude remarks about Leo and Nancy."

"My apologies," Royce said. "Do you know Nancy?"

"No," Larry said, but both his voice and body language were defensive. Why?

Larry gently placed another dish in the box, then turned to face them. "Now that you've found my brother's killer, how soon will his body be released? I want to give him a proper burial before we leave."

"We?" Royce asked.

Larry smiled. "Me and the cats. We're moving permanently to my St. Simons property. I retired last year and two houses are too much for me to keep up with."

"Of course."

"It shouldn't be too much longer," Tara said to Larry. "We can call the medical examiner if you'd like."

"That's very kind of you."

"I'll call," Royce said. "You find out what Larry's new address will be so we can send Leo's personal effects once the trial is over."

Tara approached the table with her portfolio while Royce dialed. He'd hoped she would give him the pen so Royce could see which hand he used, but she jotted down whatever Larry said.

Sawyer answered on the third ring. "Hey, baby. Will you be home for dinner?"

"This is Sergeant Locke calling for Dr. Fawkes," Royce said.

"Do you want me to drive across town and hand her the phone?" Sawyer asked.

"Yes, I'll hold."

Sawyer chuckled. "Fine. I'll play along." After a pause, he said, "This is Dr. Fawkes," in a falsetto voice.

"Dr. Fawkes, it's Sergeant Locke. How are you?"

"Horny as hell. My man got me excited but didn't follow through," Sawyer said in a husky voice. Royce realized Sawyer would take advantage of his inability to talk freely to wind him up good.

"I'm fine too," Royce said. "I was wondering when you might be finished with Leo Fellows's autopsy. His family is eager to plan his funeral."

Across the room, Tara held the box closed while Larry taped it in place.

"Tell you what," Sawyer said gruffly, "You drive over here and get on your knees, beg for it real pretty like, and I'll see what I can do."

Royce nearly choked on his saliva. He might've given himself away, but Larry looked around the table for something, and Tara held up a

Sharpie for him. The man smiled at her, pulled the lid off, and wrote DINING ROOM in big, bold letters with his right hand while chatting with Tara. Larry Fellows was left-handed. His partner glanced at Royce, but her expression gave nothing away.

"You've been very helpful," Royce said. "Thank you for your time, ma'am." Larry turned around once Royce disconnected and looked at him curiously. "Dr. Fawkes plans to release Leo to the funeral home tomorrow, Thursday at the latest. She apologized for the holdup. I'm sure you heard about the multivehicle pile-up on the interstate that resulted in several cars catching fire. There were numerous casualties, and the identification process was difficult under the circumstances. She asked me to extend her apologies and her condolences for your loss."

"I had heard about the tragic accident," Larry said. "What a shame for the families. Thank you so much for helping me out."

"No problem," Royce said.

"Was there anything else? If not, I have a lot of packing to do."

"We just wanted to make sure you knew about Glen Bishop's arrest," Royce replied. "We'll let you get back to packing."

Once outside, Tara whispered, "Who'd you call?"

"Sawyer." Royce shook his head and smiled. "Smartass had a lot of fun at my expense." He took out his phone and tapped out a quick message. *No, I won't be home for dinner. This case just took a weird twist.*

"That's not Larry Fellows inside the house, is it?" Tara asked once they were in Royce's SUV.

"Nope. Now we just have to prove it."

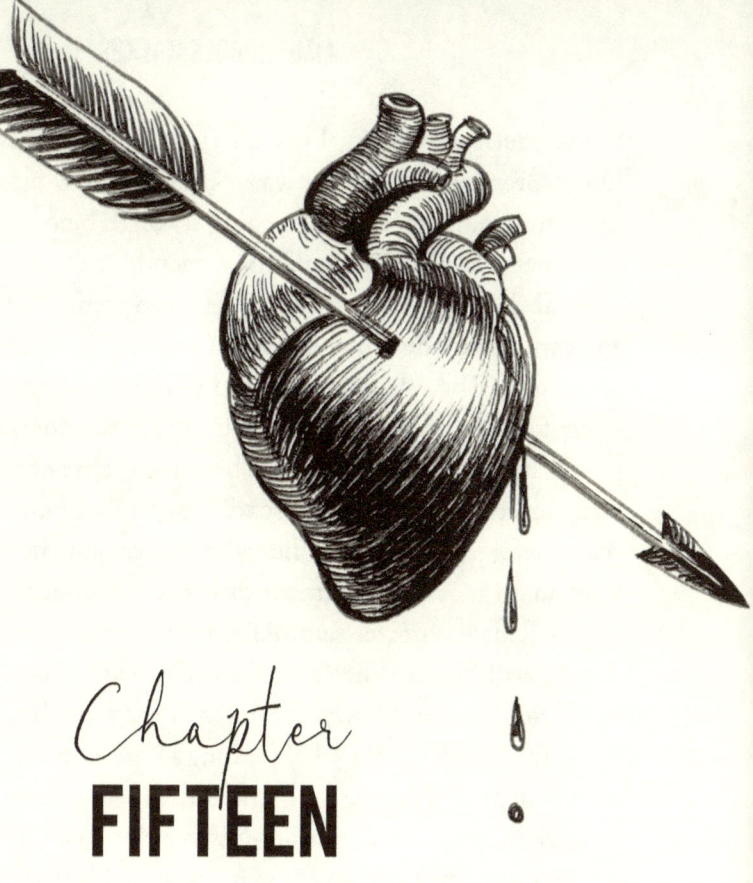

*Chapter*
# FIFTEEN

SAWYER WAS STILL SHAKING HIS HEAD OVER THE CONVERSATION he'd had with Royce long after they'd hung up. His face hurt from smiling so much. Oh, what he wouldn't give to know exactly what his man had been thinking and feeling when Sawyer had suggested Royce could get down on his knees and beg for it. And where had the boldness come from? Sawyer blamed Julian and the corset vest he'd commissioned for their wedding. He couldn't wait to surprise Royce with it on their big day and live out Royce's fantasy with him after the official festivities ended.

He'd checked in with Courtney to make sure she was doing okay. She'd told him she was doing as well as could be expected with a newborn. There'd been a note of defeat in her voice that said she was anything but good. Courtney said her mom had made a big pot of soup, then had gone to work for a little bit. Something about a work emergency she couldn't ignore. Courtney had sounded so disappointed, and

Sawyer decided to swing by to check on her. He'd never seen postpartum depression but knew it was common in new moms. Throw in everything Courtney had been going through before delivering Aiden, and Sawyer figured she could use a friend.

He decided to swing by Love Bytes to grab a chef salad for himself and some premade sandwiches for Courtney to nosh on whenever she got hungry. The café was quiet, and Levi had already left for the day. It didn't take long for Micah to put his order together, and he didn't linger to chat like he usually would because a sense of urgency was prodding him to get back on the road. Sawyer was half a block down the street before he turned on the radio and caught the tail end of a news bulletin on a local station that nearly made him sideswipe a parked car.

A female reporter said, "Allegations are coming in tonight, Tom, that Sheriff Josiah Wheeler had an affair with a female deputy."

"No! No! No!" Sawyer shouted at the radio but to no avail.

"The sheriff is accused of creating a hostile environment after learning the deputy was pregnant," she added.

"Similar to the allegations Sawyer Key made against Wheeler in his lawsuit a few years ago," a man, presumably Tom, said.

"As you recall, the lawsuit was dropped when the county and then deputy Key reached an undisclosed settlement. I've contacted SPD where Sawyer Key is now the sergeant in charge of the Cold Case Unit, but he wasn't available for comment."

"Bullshit," Sawyer snarled. He had no missed calls or voicemails, and no one from SPD had alerted him that a reporter was looking for him, not that he would've spoken to her.

"Have you learned the identity of the woman?" Tom asked.

"Not yet," she said, "but I can confidently say I'm getting closer to confirming my suspicion. I'll keep you informed as I learn more."

"Looking forward to it. Thanks, Gail," Tom said before pivoting to sports.

"Fuck! Fuck! Fuck!" Sawyer roared.

He called Courtney, but his call went straight to voicemail as if she'd turned off her phone or the battery was dead. Luckily, he'd been just a few blocks away from her house when the news broke. With any luck, he'd have her and Aiden moved someplace safe and secure before the vultures showed up. Sawyer's chest tightened as he neared Courtney's house, and he held his breath when he turned onto her street.

"No reporters." Yet.

He nailed the pothole again and cursed a blue streak. Then he killed the engine, grabbed the food he brought for Courtney, and jogged up to the front door. It swung open to reveal a sobbing Courtney.

"D-d-did you do this to m-m-me?" she asked between broken sobs.

"No, of course not." Sawyer reached for Courtney, but she stepped back and wrapped her arms around her chest.

"I'd turned on the radio, hoping the music would soothe me, and heard the news break. I want to believe you so badly, but I don't know who to trust anymore, including myself."

"Can I please come in?" he asked gently.

She paused for a moment, then nodded.

Sawyer stepped inside the house and looked around him. The once neat room looked as if a bomb had gone off. Her mother's luggage was still in the living room. One suitcase was open, and someone had rifled through the clothes, tossing various pieces onto the surrounding furniture. Several baby bottles in different stages of consumption littered the table, as well as a stack of disposable diapers, a large tub of wipes, and butt cream. A half-eaten bowl of soup sat on the end table next to an empty bottle of water.

Aiden was crying, and Courtney took a staggering step toward the hallway. She still wore the same clothes she'd had on when Sawyer had brought her home from the hospital. Her hair hung lank around her face, and he could pack his entire wardrobe in the dark bags beneath her eyes. This woman needed his help whether she wanted it or not.

"Hey, hey," Sawyer said gently. "You sit down. I'll bring him to you."

She flopped down in the chair as if she hadn't just delivered a tiny human, then winced. "Everything has gone to hell. Aiden suddenly hates my boobs, and the formula pisses him off. And now this shit with Josiah. And my workaholic mom thought her work emergency was more important. I love her so much, but I feel so alone and useless right now. I just wish I could come first in someone's life. Just once." Courtney started sobbing again, and Aiden did his best to match her.

Sawyer set the bag of sandwiches on the coffee table, squatted down, and took her hands. "You're not useless, and you're not alone. I'm going to get Aiden and bring him to you. Maybe he's struggling to eat because you're ten kinds of wound up right now. Let's work on calming you down first and then we'll see if he relaxes to eat."

"What if that doesn't work?"

Sawyer squeezed her hands. "I'll call in reinforcements who have a lot more experience with babies than I do." As the words left his mouth, he realized he'd have to do that anyway. Courtney and Aiden couldn't stay here. "I know how scary it is to trust people, but I promise you *can* trust me."

Courtney searched his eyes for several seconds before nodding. Sawyer made to stand, but she tightened her grip to keep him there. "You probably shouldn't trust me, considering my track record with Josiah, but you can. I won't betray you."

Royce's warning echoed in Sawyer's mind. It wasn't that he'd dismissed Royce's concerns outright; more like he tabled them. Sawyer could not leave Courtney to the wolves, especially not in her present condition. His decision had nothing to do with a hero complex or getting even with Wheeler. Even if his kindness backfired later, he had to do the right thing now. That's the man Royce Locke had fallen in love with.

"I trust you," Sawyer said.

Courtney released his hands and relaxed back against the chair, and Sawyer quickly made his way down the hallway to get Aiden. The newborn lay on his back, kicking his legs and waving his tiny fists at the world. It looked like Aiden had inherited his fit-throwing skills from his mom and grandma.

"Now, now there, little guy," Sawyer said. "What's all the fuss about?"

Aiden stopped crying, and his sweet little bow mouth trembled.

Sawyer stroked his finger over his downy cheek and wiped away his tears. "As bad as that, is it?"

The reprieve from Aiden's tirade didn't last long, but it wasn't as intense. Sawyer had babysat his nieces and nephews enough times to know the routine. He first checked Aiden's diaper and discovered nothing was wrong with his pooper. The stuff was like black tar, but Sawyer eventually got him clean. Just as Sawyer slid a new diaper under his butt, the baby boy released an impressive arc of urine that would be the envy of anyone looking to enter a pissing contest.

Sawyer quickly covered the stream with the diaper to absorb the pee, then gingerly checked to see if the coast was clear a few seconds later. He deftly replaced the diaper with a clean one and managed to powder and redress the little guy without further incident. Sawyer grabbed a receiving blanket off the stack by the bassinette and swaddled the tiny pissed-off human as best he could.

"Freshly changed and ready to eat," Sawyer said when he reentered the living room and placed Aiden in Courtney's arms. "Do you want to try breastfeeding?"

Courtney swallowed hard. "I can't take the failure right now. I have some bottles ready in the warmer."

"I bought one of those for my friend who'd recently had a baby. They make some cool gadgets these days," Sawyer said as he grabbed the sandwiches off the table and headed to the kitchen. He tucked the food away in the refrigerator and grabbed a bottle from the warmer.

When he returned to the living room, Courtney was gently swaying side to side and whispering something to Aiden. Sawyer felt like an intruder, but he recalled the reporters talking about her situation. He strode across the room and extended the bottle to Courtney. She started to accept it, but she pulled her hand back.

"I think you're right about me not being calm enough. Will you try?" she asked.

"Of course."

Sawyer set the bottle on the coffee table, eased Aiden from her arms, and sat down. The baby attacked the nipple when Sawyer held it to his lips.

"Easy there, little guy. You'll get an upset tummy," Sawyer said.

"I think he hates me," Courtney said and began to cry.

Sawyer pinned her with an incredulous look. "Not possible, but I think tonight's breaking news is making you dislike yourself."

Courtney snorted. "It was just the straw that broke the camel's back."

"As soon as Aiden finishes his bottle, we need to pack some things for the two of you and get you out of here before the press shows up."

Courtney groaned. "And go where? This is my home. I don't have the extra money for a hotel or short-term rental. I'll just have to hunker down and ignore the press until they go away."

"That could be days or even weeks," Sawyer said. "I have a solution, and it won't cost you a dime."

Courtney arched a brow. "Surely, you're not going to suggest I stay with you? Can you imagine the field day the press would have with that? Won't they be camped outside your house too?"

Sawyer shook his head. "They know SPD will run them off. They'll just harangue me at the station. But I have someplace else in mind for you to stay until the buzz dies down."

Narrowing her eyes, she said, "Where?"

"I need to make a phone call first, then I'll tell you."

Aiden fell asleep halfway through his bottle, so Sawyer handed him over to Courtney to burp while he stepped into the kitchen and dialed his personal superhero. She answered on the second ring.

"Mom, I need your help."

"Name it," came Evangeline's immediate reply.

Thirty minutes later, Sawyer, Courtney, and Aiden were in his car headed to his parents' house on the Isle of Hope. He'd planned to make the trip in silence, but Courtney switched on the radio. Another breaking news bulletin was in progress, this time involving a sound bite of Wheeler responding to the allegations. Sawyer moved to change the channel, but Courtney stopped him.

"We can't afford to bury our heads in the sand," she said. "Information is knowledge, and we need to know what Wheeler is thinking. That smug bastard won't be able to keep his mouth shut. He'll project his every move. He'd be horrible at chess."

Sawyer glanced over and noticed her fighting spirit had improved her color.

On the radio, Wheeler said, "My attorney advised me not to comment, but I don't have anything to lose."

"See?" Courtney said wryly. "Idiot."

Sawyer bit his lip to keep from laughing because nothing about the situation was funny, but having Courtney in the trenches with him made it a little better. As supportive as his loved ones and friends were, they couldn't understand the demoralizing circumstances of workplace abuse because they'd never experienced it firsthand. Sawyer wanted to believe he and Courtney would make it through to the other side with their sanity and budding friendship intact.

"I am not now nor have I ever engaged in an extramarital affair," Wheeler said firmly. "The idea that I've fathered an illegitimate child is preposterous slander, and I will do whatever it takes to protect my reputation."

"Such as?" a female reporter asked.

"A lawsuit is one option, and the other is exposing my enemy for the liar he is," Wheeler replied.

"Sounds like you know who started these rumors, Sheriff," a man said.

"I was speaking generally," Wheeler replied. "I am going to prove this story is nothing more than a vicious, cheap attack from a political rival."

"What political rival?" a second man asked. "You're running unopposed."

"For now," Wheeler replied. "I've heard rumblings that someone is thinking about taking a run at me. I'd rather the coward do it man to man rather than this underhanded crap, but that's his MO."

"Are you referring to Sawyer Key," a different woman asked.

"No comment," Wheeler said. "That's all I have to say right now."

"An attack can be vicious and cheap but still be true," a man yelled, but Wheeler didn't comment further.

"What a mess," Courtney said.

"I promise you I didn't leak your situation to the press."

She sighed. "I know. I am sorry for the way I acted when you arrived. I'm a hot mess."

"I think anyone in your shoes would've reacted the same way," Sawyer said.

"Every person who worked for the sheriff's department knew about our disastrous affair," Courtney said. "I could have dozens of witnesses to back up the heinous way he treated me, but none of them will stand up to him." Sawyer felt her eyes on him but kept his gaze trained out the windshield. "You're the only one who has dared to take him on."

Sawyer shook his head. "I gave in too easily. I was deeply depressed after losing Vic, and I just didn't have the fight in me to see it through. The arbitrators proposed a deal I thought I could live with. It turns out I was wrong."

"Are you going to run for sheriff? You're who he keeps referring to, right?" Before Sawyer could answer, Courtney added, "Never mind. Don't tell me. I need to earn your trust first."

"The truth is, I don't know. I won't deny I want a shot to take him down, but I'm not sure public office is the answer." Sawyer glanced over at her. "At least not right now. I'm getting married in a few months, and we want to start a family soon."

"You'll make wonderful fathers," Courtney said.

Sawyer thought of the way Royce had looked while cradling Aiden in his arms. "I think so too."

He pulled up to his parents' house a few minutes later and saw his mother waiting for them on the porch.

"Wait. Evangeline O'Neal is your mom?" Courtney asked. "How did I not know that?"

Sawyer laughed. "People think she's too flawless for kids, but they couldn't be more wrong. Besides, the woman doesn't age. She credits her skincare regimen for her smooth skin, but I'm pretty sure she made a deal with a crossroads demon."

Courtney looked down at herself. "I can't stay here. I'm a mess."

"You'll feel differently once you're in my mom's warm orbit," Sawyer promised.

His friend inhaled deeply and nodded. "Okay. Let's do this."

They removed their seatbelts and opened the doors. Evangeline stepped off the porch and quickly crossed the driveway to reach them. She ignored Sawyer and went straight for Courtney, opening her arms and offering her a hug. Courtney only hesitated for a second. Once enfolded in Evangeline's embrace, she burst into body-racking sobs.

Evangeline met Sawyer's gaze over Courtney's shoulder and gave him a thumbs-up to say *I've got this.*

Once Courtney settled down, she pulled back and scrubbed at her face. "Lord, I'm a mess."

"As every mother is at some point in her life. Show yourself some grace and turn yourself over to me. I'll make this all better."

Courtney's chin wobbled, and Evangeline cupped her jaw. "Deep breath in and slowly blow it out. Everything will be fine."

Sawyer walked around and unbuckled Aiden's car seat, and Evangeline grabbed the luggage they'd hastily packed.

"I hope I remembered everything," Courtney said as she followed Evangeline and Sawyer inside.

"It's not a problem if you didn't," Sawyer said. "I can run to the store and grab whatever you need."

"As can your father," Evangeline called over her shoulder. Once inside, she put the bags in the foyer and faced Courtney. "Honey, does your mom know where you are?"

She nodded. "I called her before we left."

"She's more than welcome to stay here too," Evangeline said. "Once the police figure out your identity, they'll look for you at her house when they realize you've left your own."

Courtney stiffened and said, "I won't risk them following her here and bringing trouble to your front door."

"Please don't worry about that," Evangeline said.

Sawyer sensed Courtney's hesitation to have her mom join them went much deeper than this one incident, so he caught Evangeline's eye and gave her a subtle shake of his head.

"The offer stands if you change your mind," Evangeline said to Courtney. "You're in the driver's seat, honey. I'm just providing the getaway car. Let's get you both settled, then we can see if you have everything you need."

Evangeline led them to one of the guest bedrooms that just happened to be his old room. On the other side was the nursery Evangeline had set up once she started having grandchildren. The look and theme of the space had changed over the years, but she would keep the crib up until all her babies finished having babies.

Sawyer unbuckled Aiden, gently placed him in the crib, and swaddled him once more. "Snug as a bug," he pronounced.

Courtney joined him at the crib and sighed. "You've got the touch."

"He's had a lot of practice. You'll get the hang of it," Evangeline said. "Let's leave the little angel to sleep while we unpack your bags next door." She switched on a monitor attached to the crib. "You'll be able to hear him when he wakes up."

Courtney laughed. "I won't need the monitor for that."

"Kid has some pipes," Sawyer agreed.

He followed the two women out of the room. Evangeline asked if Aiden was breastfed or took a bottle. Courtney said she'd prefer to breastfeed, but Aiden didn't seem interested.

"There could be many reasons for that, and none of them are anything you should feel shame over," Evangeline said. "We'll try to sort him out."

"Sounds like I'm leaving you in good hands," Sawyer said.

"Leaving already?" Evangeline asked. "Seems like I hardly see you anymore."

Sawyer kissed her cheek. "I'll be back soon." He hugged Courtney next and made her promise to call if she needed anything.

"I'm just going to walk Sawyer out," Evangeline told Courtney, then hooked her elbow through Sawyer's arm and led him from his old room. "Spill it, son."

"Spill what?"

"The scalding hot tea," Evangeline replied. "What's going on? I heard what the dickbag said to the press."

"Nothing is going on," Sawyer replied.

Evangeline stopped and gaped at him. "You think you can fool me? Ha! Try again. You're acting like your ass is on fire. Where are you going?"

"To talk to Charlie," Sawyer said. "Someone is running their mouth, and I want to shut them up."

"Is that the right approach?" Evangeline asked, looking worried.

Sawyer pondered for a moment. "Look, if I ever decide to run for sheriff, it will be because I think I'm the best person to represent the people of Chatham County in the position. I'm not there yet, Mom." As he spoke, his convictions grew stronger. "I want to marry Royce and start a family. I want to continue investigating cold cases and finding answers for people who've given up hope. That's how I choose to make a difference for the community at this time. I'm sorry if my lack of ambition disappoints you."

She glared menacingly, and Sawyer knew he'd gone too far. "Disappointed? Don't be silly. Happiness is all I've ever wanted for you. I only offered to assist with the exploratory committee because it seemed like something you were considering."

"I was," Sawyer admitted, "but not for the right reasons. The sheriff needs to get up each day and strive to serve the people, not himself."

Evangeline smiled proudly. "That can be your slogan when you decide to run."

"*If*, Mom." He leaned forward and kissed her cheek again. "Thank you again for helping Courtney and Aiden."

"It's my pleasure," Evangeline said. "But what's the situation with Courtney and her mom?"

Sawyer told Evangeline about the condition he'd found Courtney in and how Kathy had gone into work and left her with the baby.

"I'll withhold judgment about the situation for now," Evangeline said coolly. "I promise to take good care of them."

"I know you will."

"And Sawyer," Evangeline called out after he'd taken a few steps toward his car. "Give Charlie my love, but tell him he'll find me on his doorstep if he doesn't knock this shit off."

Sawyer laughed. "Yes, ma'am."

When he reached his car, Evangeline had already disappeared back inside the house. Sawyer removed his phone and typed out a quick text to Charlie. *We need to talk.*

Charlie's reply came fast. *Figured I'd hear from you. At Ethan's ball game. Should be done by seven.*

Sawyer wasn't going to crash his kid's game. He'd take the time to eat his chef's salad and prepare what he wanted to say to Charlie. Sawyer typed, *I'll be over at seven thirty.*

Charlie returned a thumbs-up emoji, and Sawyer sent him the middle finger.

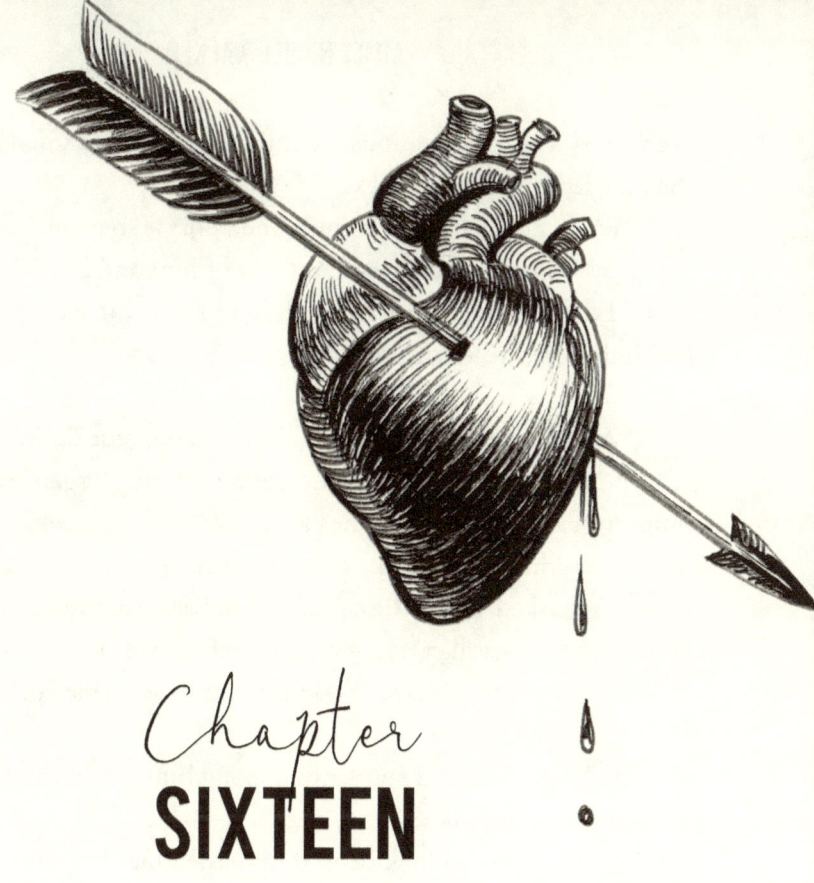

# Chapter
# SIXTEEN

D R. Fawkes had been out in the field when Royce and Tara had called on her, but one of her assistants promised to have the ME phone them when she returned. Royce had stressed it was urgent, and the exhausted woman said, "It always is."

"We have some free time on our hands and need to figure out if we're looking at one crime or two," Royce said. "If Larry is the dead Fellows brother in the morgue, does that mean Leo killed him and framed Glen?"

"Or," Tara said, "Did Glen kill the wrong Fellows brother and the surviving one assumed the other's identity?"

"There could be a third alternative," Royce said. "Larry and Glen could've conspired together to kill Leo. Larry plans to flee the country and can't take the cats with him."

"Maybe," Tara said, "but I think the first two options are strongest."

"Let's put ourselves in Leo's shoes. If he wants to lure his twin brother to The Pirate's House to kill him and frame Glen Bishop for the murder. How does he do it?"

"Accessing Glen's bow, arrows, and boots is step one," Tara replied.

Royce steepled his hands in front of him and leaned back in his chair. "Leo and Nancy carried on an affair for a year. Rocky told us Leo let himself in through a side door on their garage, right?"

"Yes."

"We have one of those digital locks on our side door," Royce said. "Maybe she'd given the code to Leo, and he used it to gain access to the hunting gear Glen keeps in the garage."

"Wouldn't the Bishops have changed the locks if that were the case?" Tara asked. Before he could respond, she continued. "Maybe Leo and Nancy were still carrying on their relationship."

Royce stroked his jaw. "It's possible, but she seemed genuinely hurt about Leo ghosting her."

"Whoa!" Tara said suddenly, making him jolt in the chair. "How am I just noticing that?"

Royce turned to look behind him, then met her gaze once more. "Noticed what?"

"Your engagement ring," Tara said. She narrowed her eyes. "Or did the two of you sneak off for a quickie wedding at the courthouse?"

"No quickie of any kind today," Royce replied. "My engagement ring arrived, and Sawyer was eager to give it to me."

Of course, Candy chose that exact minute to breeze into the bullpen with the kids and overheard the last part of his remark. She smirked at Royce and said, "I just bet he was."

Royce lifted his hand. "My ring, you dirty perv."

"What's a dirty perv?" Daniel asked.

Candy glared at Royce. "Never mind, sweetheart."

"Unca Ro!" Bailey squealed and ran to him with her arms in the air.

Royce swooped her up into his arms and kissed her little face until her excited shrieks threatened to deafen him. Bailey settled on his lap and cuddled against his chest, and Royce stuck out his tongue at Tara and mouthed. "Still my girl."

Daniel had brought one of his dinosaurs and went on a Godzilla-worthy rampage on Tara's desk.

"Oh no," Candy said. "Maybe I shouldn't have caved and let him eat one of your cookies."

"Cookies?" Tara and Royce asked at the same time.

"I baked today." Candy reached into her ginormous tote bag and removed a plastic container. She lifted the lid and revealed several types of cookies. "I baked a lot."

Royce reached out to snag a cookie, but Bailey beat him to it.

"Bite," he pleaded with her. Bailey held the cookie to his mouth, and he imitated the Cookie Monster as he chomped into it. Bailey giggled and took a much smaller bite than his. Royce watched Candy extend the container to Tara, who seemed too spellbound by Candy's dazzling smile to be interested in food. "What are you nervous about?" Royce asked.

Candy turned to look at him, and her grin faded as if someone had slid her dimmer switch down a notch. "What are you talking about?"

Royce knew her habits all too well. Candy baked when she was nervous. Before her wedding to Marcus, she baked six dozen cookies, two pies, and three cakes. Royce had talked her off the ledge then, and he wanted to do it now but wasn't sure how to proceed since they had an audience.

"Who wants to go see the new classrooms where Uncle Ro and I will be teaching in a few months?"

Three little voices shouted, "Me!"

Bailey scampered down from Royce's lap. Instead of being annoyed, he was grateful for his partner's perception. Tara stopped next to Candy, slid an arm around her waist, and kissed her cheek.

Once they were alone, Candy slumped into Tara's vacant chair. She folded her arms on Tara's desk and buried her head in the space. "I'm in a bad way." Candy's muffled voice sounded dazed, not upset. She suddenly bolted upright and stared at him with wide eyes. "What was I thinking to let her go off with the kids by herself. Those hellions will scare her off."

Royce watched her theatrics with a smile on his face. "I assure you, that's not going to happen."

Candy narrowed her eyes and assessed him. "Why? What has she said about me—um, us?"

Royce shook his head. "Nope. Not going to betray what my partner has said in confidence. I'm just going to tell you to relax and enjoy what you've found with Tara."

Candy closed her eyes and inhaled slowly, and after she expelled the breath, Candy smiled and nodded. "She's amazing, Ro. I'm terrified of ruining it."

"So talk to her. I promise you won't regret it."

Candy smiled. "Yeah?"

"I love you more than life itself, Candy Cane. Would I steer you wrong?"

She scrunched up her face and shook her head.

"Then relax."

Tara and the kids returned a few minutes later. The kids were chattering excitedly as she patiently answered all their questions. She shot a questioning glance between Candy and Royce. "Everything okay?"

Candy smiled and stood up. "Perfect. I better get these heathens out of here before they break something."

"Mom, we just got here," Marc complained.

"Walk us out?" Candy asked Tara.

Royce leaned forward and snagged the container of cookies off Tara's desk. "I'll guard these." The kids took turns hugging him goodbye. Bailey clung to his neck and gave him a sloppy kiss. "Love you guys," Royce said as they followed Candy and Tara, who were holding hands as they headed out of the bullpen. Three precious voices returned his affection and Candy blew him a kiss.

Royce devoured a half dozen cookies and rolled their investigation around in his mind while waiting for Tara to return. His partner looked a little dazed when she strode into the bullpen and nearly missed her chair when she sat down. It must've been some goodbye kiss Candy had planted on her. Tara leaned forward to snag a cookie and said, "Where were we?"

"We think we know how Leo would've gotten his hands on Glen's hunting gear. We should be able to confirm whether the locks or codes were changed." Royce's desk phone rang, and he snagged the receiver. His eyebrows rose when the desk sergeant informed him that a man was at his desk claiming to have important information on the Leo Fellows investigation.

"We'll be right there," Royce said. He hung up the phone and shook his head.

"What?"

Royce told Tara about their visitor. "Maybe this guy can fill in some of the blanks for us."

"Here's hoping," Tara said as she stood up. "This is the longest Tuesday to ever Tuesday."

A tall, lean man with salt-and-pepper hair and bloodshot eyes was waiting for them when they reached the front desk. His clothes were wrinkled and hung from his frame. The bags under his eyes said he probably hadn't slept in days.

Royce made quick introductions and learned the man's name was Paul Jarvis.

"Let's go someplace private so we can chat," Tara said. "Can I get you something to drink, Mr. Jarvis?"

"Paul, please, and no thank you."

Royce led them to an interview room, and Paul started talking before he could close the door.

"The man claiming to be Larry Fellows is not Larry Fellows," Paul said, his voice firm and resolute.

"How can you be so certain?" Royce asked.

"Because Larry was my lover for two years," Paul said, retrieving his phone.

He showed Royce and Tara a photo of Paul and one of the Fellows brothers gazing into each other's eyes over a candlelit dinner. Royce couldn't tell which brother it was, but he recognized love when he saw it.

Paul set his phone down. "That man who answered his door looks like Larry and even smells like him, but he's not Larry. He treated me like I was nothing more than Larry's neighbor on St. Simons Island because that's all Leo knew me as. Larry wasn't out to anyone, not even his twin, and Larry planned to keep his sexuality a secret until his father passed away." He closed his eyes and took a shaky breath. "If Leo is masquerading as his twin, that would mean my Larry is the one who was killed."

Royce had so many questions firing in his exhausted brain that they became a jumbled ball. He struggled to pull a single one of them from the melee.

Paul's lips quivered and he briefly covered them with his hand. "You think I'm crazy, don't you?"

"No, sir," Royce said. He wasn't sure what the hell was going on, but he recognized genuine grief when he saw it.

Paul relaxed his shoulders slightly, then tensed right back up again. "I have proof!" He pulled a sandwich bag containing a folded piece of paper out of his pants pocket. "I wore cleaning gloves when I retrieved it. I know a sandwich baggie isn't the best thing to preserve evidence, but it's the best I could do on the fly."

Tara pulled a pair of gloves from someplace and accepted the baggie from him. She eased the paper from inside and unfolded it. Royce heard a slight hitch in her breath and leaned over to examine the document.

Son of a bitch. Someone had practiced Larry Fellows's signature no less than thirty times.

"Where'd you get this?" Royce asked.

"From Larry's trash can."

God, Royce had so many questions. He took a calming breath to settle his mind. "I think we need you to start from the beginning."

"Gladly," Paul said.

He started with Friday evening when Larry called him to say he wouldn't be coming down to St. Simons until he tracked Leo down and got his signature to move their father. He explained that the next payment was due in two weeks, and Larry wanted everything settled so they weren't paying that exorbitant price ever again.

"Wait," Royce said. "I thought Leo was the one who wanted to move their dad."

"No. It was Larry," Paul replied.

"You know what," Tara said. "When we first met the guy claiming to be Larry, he said 'my brother' wanted to move their father. He didn't use Leo's name specifically."

"You're right," Royce said. "Please continue, Paul."

He told them Larry never showed up on Saturday, and he didn't answer any of Paul's phone calls or texts until Sunday. "Knowing he'd be around family, I didn't send anything risqué in my texts. Just simple inquiries on when he'd be back. A few said I was worried about him. He finally replied saying Leo had been murdered, and he wouldn't be back until he handled his affairs. I asked how long that would be, and he replied 'however long it takes.'" Paul took another deep breath and swallowed. "The tone was all wrong, even for someone who'd suddenly lost their brother. I offered to come to Savannah to help, and he coldly shut me down. Three words. 'That's not necessary.' Then complete radio silence. I knew in my heart those texts weren't from Larry, but I tried to convince myself I was being ridiculous. The alternative was unimaginable to me. I held out until today.

"I haven't eaten or slept much since Saturday, but I didn't imagine Leo's stunned reaction when he opened the door and found me on the porch. Leo's surprise turned to anger, and he demanded to know what I was doing there. His eyes were so cold and cruel. Larry never looked at me so hatefully. A small part of me still held out hope, and I asked if I could come in. I explained I only wanted to assure myself that he was really okay. Leo softened a little and stepped aside. The house was a mess and moving boxes were everywhere. Larry was a neat freak. He would've been tidier and arranged the stacks against the wall instead of leaving them haphazardly all over the place. But Larry has a habit of running his hands through his hair when he's tired or frustrated, so when Leo did the same thing, I was just so relieved that I hugged him without thinking my actions through."

"How'd he act?" Tara asked.

"He went stiff as a board in my embrace, and every nagging doubt screamed louder. So, I said, 'I've missed you, baby.'"

"And?" Royce asked.

Paul's lips trembled again, and he said, "Leo flinched from my embrace and stared up at me in utter shock. It only lasted a minute, but there was no missing it."

"What did he say?" Tara asked.

"Nothing," Paul replied. "His phone rang, and he checked the caller ID. He said it was Sam calling, which I knew was Larry's nephew. Leo excused himself to take the call and left me alone in the kitchen. One part of my brain screamed at me to get out of there and go to the police, but the other said I was acting insane. I went to the trash can to throw out my gum and saw that." He nodded to the paper on the table. "I found a pair of cleaning gloves and a box of sandwich bags and collected it. There are more pages in the trash. I only took one so he wouldn't miss it. Again, my instincts told me to bolt, but I knew it would look suspicious. I forced myself to wait for him to finish his call and apologized for showing up after he'd asked me not to come. Then I left."

"Why didn't Larry want his father to know about your relationship?" Royce asked.

"He would've cut Larry out of the trust and given everything to Leo." Paul sighed. "God, that sounds mercenary, and maybe it was, but I also understand why he felt that way. Larry loved their father, but he was also very bitter and resentful at times."

"Does Larry have any unique identifiers on his body that Leo wouldn't?" Royce asked.

Paul brightened. "Larry has an appendectomy scar on his abdomen and another scar on his leg from a compound fracture when he fell off the treehouse ladder as a kid." He picked his phone up once more and scrolled through it, finally landing on a picture of Larry sprawled out on a beach towel. He was smiling at the photographer who stood above him. The scars Paul told them about were evident in the picture. Paul's chin quivered and Royce's heart went out to him. "We took a trip to the Bahamas for our anniversary."

"Could you text that photo to me?" Tara asked softly.

"Of course. What's your number?"

Royce waited for Tara to receive the image before he spoke again. "I can't say much about an ongoing investigation, but when I can—"

Paul waved him off. His lips trembled and tears rolled down his cheeks. "I already know my Larry is gone." He sniffled and rubbed his face. "What about Larry's cats? I didn't see any signs of them at the house."

Royce and Tara exchanged a glance, both wondering how much they should share.

"They're living in a house with three little girls," Tara said. "I promise they're in good hands."

"Well, I'll take comfort in that much." Paul shook both their hands and let himself out of the interrogation room."

Royce and Tara looked at one another once the door shut behind him. "Holy shit," they said at the same time. There was no joy in their voices.

"Well, at least we have solid information to give Dr. Fawkes instead of wild speculation when she returns my call," Royce said. "We know from Grace that Leo has a dental implant and learned from Paul that Larry has distinct scars. We'll be able to resolve one thing tonight."

"But we still aren't any closer to figuring out if Leo killed Larry and framed Glen or if he happened to take advantage of Larry being in the wrong place at the wrong time."

Royce's cell phone vibrated with an incoming message from Dru.

*Will you and Sawyer still be able to help us move this weekend?*

Absolutely, he replied. *We'll even supply the pizza.*

*You're the best. Love you, Ro.*

Her affection was the shot of energy his exhausted brain and body needed. *Love you too, Dru.*

"What now?" Tara asked. "This feels impossible."

"Not at all," Royce replied. "Until we find proof that says otherwise, we have to pursue the charges against Glen for killing one of the Fellows twins. If we get confirmation that Larry Fellows is the one in the morgue, we arrest Leo for impersonating his brother and go from there. At this point, it's not likely he's accepted any money or other gains meant for Larry. If he comes clean now, he probably won't do any time."

Royce's cell phone rang, and he smiled when he looked at his screen. He put the call on speaker and said, "What's up, Doc?"

"You tell me. You're the one with an emergency."

"I don't want you to think I've lost my mind," Royce said.

Dr. Fawkes snorted. "Too late. Just spit it out, Locke. It's been a very long day."

So he did. The medical examiner hummed a few times but didn't interrupt him.

"The Mr. Fellows in my morgue doesn't have fingerprints on record, but I have scanned the body from head to toe and completed a full autopsy. My guest doesn't have a dental implant. I did note the appendectomy and prior femur break in my report. I'm going to request Leo Fellows's dental records just to err on the side of caution. That should clear everything up."

"Thank you, ma'am," Royce said. "How long will that take?"

"Usually a day or two, but I will stress the urgency," Dr. Fawkes said. "Dental offices are usually good about prioritizing the requests. I'll be in touch as soon as I have answers."

When he disconnected the call, Royce expected Tara to be ready for a high five or fist bump, but she was scowling down at her phone.

"What's wrong?" he asked.

Tara turned her phone around, and he saw a breaking news banner about Sheriff Wheeler.

"Fuck," Royce growled. He dialed Sawyer and stepped outside the bullpen.

"I'm fine," Sawyer said instead of his usual greeting. Then he told him about moving Courtney and Aiden to his parents' house. "I couldn't leave them to face that shitstorm alone."

"I know, baby. I just wish you would've told me."

"I'm sorry," Sawyer said. "I had to act fast before the press showed up outside Courtney's house."

"Is she okay?"

"No," Sawyer replied. "Her mom went back to work for some emergency. Courtney's had no sleep, and she's struggling to get Aiden to eat. She was on the verge of falling apart when I arrived."

"Your mom will make it better for Courtney and Aiden, but what about you?"

"I'm fine. I'm thinking more clearly now than I have in a long time," Sawyer said. "How's your night going?"

"This is the most bizarre case I've ever worked."

"I thought you were just tying up loose ends," Sawyer said.

"Yeah, that's what we thought until everything unraveled. I'll explain when I get home. Are you sure you're okay?"

"I promise I'm fine. I'm heading over to Charlie's house to hash things out once and for all."

"That sounds ominous," Royce said. "With any luck, I should be home soon. I love you."

"Love you most."

They said goodbye and disconnected. When Royce walked into the bullpen, Tara glanced up from her computer with a determined look on her face.

"Everything okay?"

"Yeah," Royce said. God, he was ready to go home, but they weren't quite done yet. "Guess we better start putting the warrants together. That way we're ready to submit them to a judge as soon as Fawkes confirms the guy in her morgue isn't Leo Fellows."

"Already on it."

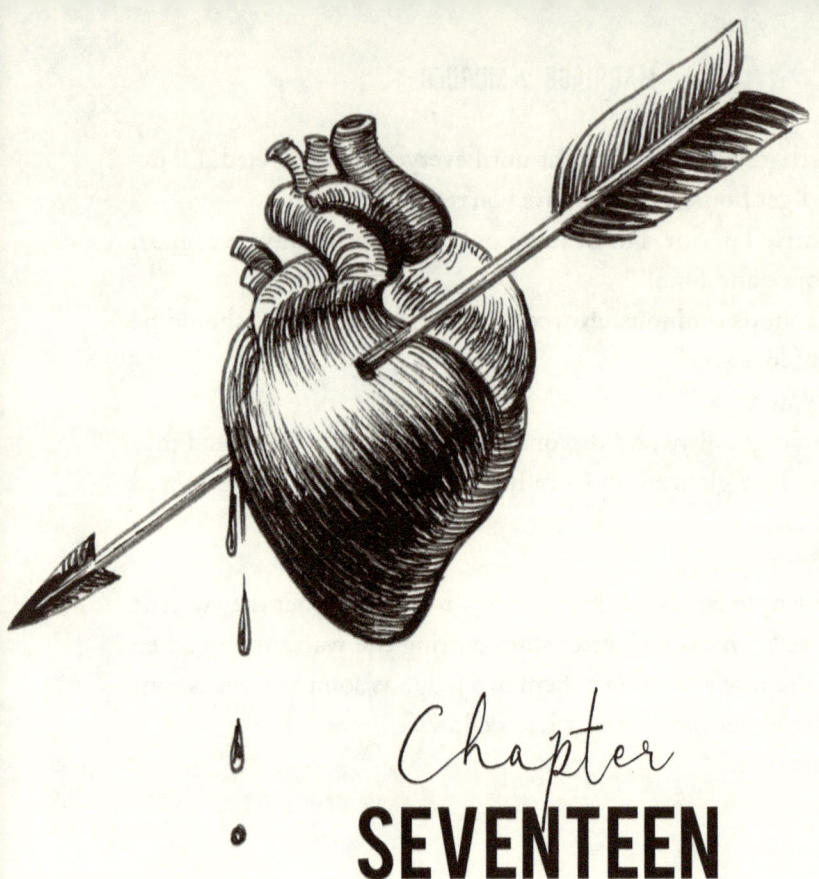

*Chapter*
# SEVENTEEN

**G**EMMA PRICE ANSWERED SAWYER'S KNOCK WITH A HUGE GRIN and bear hug. "It's been too long," she said. "We've missed you so much."

She pulled back and smiled up at him. Her hair was as curly as ever, but he noticed some gray woven into the pitch black. Gemma's dark eyes radiated warmth and welcome.

"I've missed you too," Sawyer said.

Gemma stepped back and gestured for him to come in. "He's in his man cave. I'm sure you remember the way."

After Vic died, Sawyer had spent more time at the Prices' home than he had his own. They'd patiently and lovingly nursed him through a broken heart, which made his former partner's betrayal that much harder to comprehend. Sawyer had forgiven Charlie because he genuinely believed he'd had his best interests in mind, but he wouldn't forget it.

"Sure do."

Charlie and Gemma's three little rug rats swarmed him when he stepped inside the house. A lump of regret lodged in his throat and left an acrid aftertaste in his mouth. How many birthdays and big moments had he lost with them? Curtis, Beau, and Natalie all started talking to him at once. Instead of heading straight to the man cave, Sawyer took the time to catch up with them, smiling as they regaled him with their latest adventures and hobbies.

"Okay, okay," Gemma said. "That's enough out of you. I know three chatterboxes who need to take showers and finish their homework if they hope to get any screen time before bed."

The three kids hugged Sawyer amid protests and grumbles before trudging up the stairs.

Gemma heaved a sigh of relief. "That should buy me a few minutes to enjoy a damn beer." She patted Sawyer on the arm and headed toward the kitchen.

He followed behind her but veered off toward the garage Charlie had converted into a man cave, complete with a sports-themed bar and pool table. His friend looked up just as he took his shot. The striped ball bounced off the corner and rolled back toward Charlie while the white ball fell into the pocket instead.

"Well, hell," Charlie said.

Sawyer collected the rack and the few balls Charlie had managed to sink, then set them up on the felt like old times. He retrieved a cue from the wall mount and smiled at his friend. "I would've thought you'd be better at shooting pool with all the practice you get."

Charlie scoffed and watched Sawyer set up the next game. "I don't play as much as I used to, and it shows."

"Aren't the other deputies allowed to come out and play?" Sawyer asked as he chalked his cue tip.

Charlie shrugged. "On occasion. They're just not the friends I wanted to hang with."

An apology was on the tip of Sawyer's tongue, but he swallowed it down. Charlie had been the one in the wrong, and Sawyer suspected he had resorted to his old tricks again, which was the reason he'd stopped by. He wasn't there to choke on nostalgia and regret.

"You want something to drink?" Charlie asked. "I've got beer, soda, and something harder."

"A beer sounds good."

Charlie headed to the refrigerator behind the bar. "Go ahead and break."

Sawyer removed the rack and leaned over the table. With his right hand on the bottom of the pool stick, Sawyer positioned the cue tip between the forefinger and middle finger on his left hand. Sawyer worked the stick back and forth between the fingers to test the feel and find the correct grip. He made a few tiny adjustments, and once pleased, Sawyer pulled his right hand back and prepared to strike.

He'd just thrust the cue forward when Charlie loudly said, "So, I reckon you're here to talk about Wheeler."

Sawyer's aim went left of center and sent the white ball sailing past the triangle of colored balls arranged in the middle of the table. The cue tip scraped against the green felt but thankfully didn't tear it.

Charlie set Sawyer's beer on the edge of the pool table and smirked at him. "I may be rusty, but I believe you were supposed to hit the balls."

Sawyer leaned his cue against the table and snatched up his beer. "You did that on purpose," he accused before tipping the bottle to his lips and taking a long drink.

Charlie shrugged, grabbed his stick, walked around to the opposite side of the table, and got into position. He looked up at Sawyer before taking a shot and said, "Had to create an advantage if I hoped to stand a chance of winning."

Sawyer set his bottle down and crossed his arms over his chest. "Is that why you went to Felix about Courtney?"

Charlie averted his gaze to the pool table and took his shot. It too went wide but managed to connect with the right side of the triangle, sending the green-striped ball toward the corner pocket near Sawyer. He reached down and snagged the fourteen ball before it could sink into the hole.

"Hey!" Charlie cried.

It was Sawyer's turn to shrug off the outrage. "Just creating my own advantage."

Charlie set his stick down, picked up his beer, and nodded toward the bar. "Come on. Let's hash this out so we can have a clean game."

"It's cute you think we'll still be talking to each other afterward."

Charlie's steps faltered, but he didn't stop until he reached a stool. He slid onto it and patted the one beside him, but Sawyer remained standing. He wasn't sure how long he was willing to stay. "It's not possible for you to be any colder to me than you have been for the past four years." He tilted his bottle toward Sawyer's left hand. "That's new since the last time I saw you. Congratulations."

Sawyer took another sip. "Thanks."

"Are you going to invite me to the wedding?" Charlie asked.

"Gemma? Yes. I'll wait to hear what you have to say for yourself before I decide if she can bring a plus one."

"Ouch."

"You deserve it," Sawyer replied.

Charlie bobbed his head from left to right as he considered Sawyer's accusation, then said, "Probably."

"Why, Charlie?"

His friend scratched a spot under his bottom lip. "Care to be more specific? Are you seeking answers to the mysteries of the universe or love? I'm not that great at science, and I can't explain human nature."

Sawyer wasn't swayed by the humor he heard in Charlie's voice. "Why did you throw Courtney under the bus?"

Charlie took a deep breath. "Why aren't you more concerned about yourself?"

Sawyer was relieved his friend wasn't going to deny his latest sneaky behavior. "I've been through this before, and I'm battle hardened. Courtney isn't. She just had a baby for fuck's sake. Did you think the vultures wouldn't put two and two together and come up with four? I can't believe you." Sawyer growled his frustration and paced away from the bar.

Charlie must've thought Sawyer was leaving because he called out, "Wait. Please hear me out."

Sawyer stopped, turned around, and headed back to the bar. This time he sat on the empty stool. "I'm listening."

"When I leaked the information to the press, Courtney hadn't gone into labor yet. It was days before the incident at the hardware store. The robbery, as well as other newsworthy events like the massive wreck, delayed the release of information until after Courtney's name was splashed all over the damn newspapers. She laid that hero stuff on thick, huh?"

Sawyer clenched his jaw to restrain the slew of curses he longed to release. "Let's pretend I believe the bit about the timing. Make me understand your motivation."

"I'd hoped Wheeler would resign over the controversy. It's worked with other politicians, so why not him?"

"And if he doesn't resign?" Sawyer asked.

Charlie averted his gaze to the label on the beer bottle he was peeling. Frown lines creased the corners of his mouth and the space between his eyes. Sawyer nudged Charlie's shin with his foot and his former partner snapped his head up to meet his gaze. "I thought the controversy would make excellent fodder for campaign ads for you or someone else who wanted to run against Wheeler."

Sawyer crossed his arms over his chest as simmering anger began to bubble and boil. "Another example of you creating an advantage?"

Charlie's heavy sigh and his hangdog expression was that of a defeated man. "I've been beating myself up enough for both of us, and I'm exhausted. Why don't you just leave now and spare us both the wasted energy? Walking away is what you do best, isn't it?"

Sawyer reared back as if Charlie had slapped him. He balled his hands into fists to return the invisible blow with a physical one. He inhaled slowly, drawing precious air into his lungs to settle his temper and loosen the tension gripping his chest. Charlie had been right. Sawyer had walked away from CCSD and their friendship, but he hadn't quite closed the door. His reasons for leaving it cracked open were very different but not so complicated in Charlie's case. Sawyer would never forget the nights he spent on Charlie and Gemma's couch when the idea of facing an empty house without Vic was just too much to bear. "Make me understand."

Charlie's handsome face morphed into an angry beast Sawyer didn't recognize. "You nearly died. You were my best friend, a brother really, and I watched your soul shrivel before my very eyes." He rubbed a hand over his face and blew out a breath. "And as bad as the abuse was for you, it was ten times worse for Courtney. You still had most of the deputies' respect, but Court…" Charlie took a deep breath, and Sawyer braced himself for the worst. "They all turned on her. If they weren't disgusted by her behavior, they were trying to get in on the action. Some assholes fell into both camps. I did my best to be a friend to Courtney, to let her know she had at least one ally in the whole damn world, but I wasn't always around."

Sawyer's heart sank and he almost stopped him from saying more, but he was the one who'd told Charlie to make him understand.

"When Gemma and I took the kids to Disney World during Thanksgiving break, Courtney responded to a sticky domestic situation. She'd requested backup when both of the armed homeowners shifted their anger to her. No one answered the call for help. Not a single fucking one. Courtney somehow deescalated the situation and arrested both spouses without incident. She could have died."

Sawyer thought of Courtney and sweet Aiden, and his heart hurt at the idea of never knowing them.

"And I had to do something," Charlie said. "Quitting and leaving the job would've left her even more vulnerable, so I resorted to my old tricks. I tried to influence things from the inside. I'm truly sorry you and Courtney are caught up in the shitstorm." He heaved a deep sigh. "And I regret the dig I made about you walking away. That was wrong."

Sawyer was on the verge of accepting his apology, but something occurred to him. "I didn't run," he said, his voice barely above a whisper. "I didn't run." The words were firmer and louder the second time around. Sawyer met Charlie's gaze head-on. "I had the nerve to square off against Wheeler, and I did, but I ended up choosing the best path for my mental health at the time." And for the first time since he made that fateful decision, Sawyer believed it.

The truth felt like an invisible fist reaching down into the pit of his soul and yanking up the weeds of discontent by their roots. The relief was immediate as if an enormous weight had been lifted off his chest.

"I've already won," Sawyer told Charlie, eradicating another fistful of weeds with another revelation.

His friend smiled and raised his beer in a toast. "I'll drink to that."

They both tipped back their bottles, then Sawyer said, "I have a suggestion if you've decided you aren't done avenging Courtney and me."

Charlie grimaced and took another sip of beer. "I'll bite. What is it?"

"Stop lurking in the shadows and take Wheeler on directly. You be the candidate to take him down at the ballot box, but do it fair and square."

"Sawyer, I can't do that," Charlie said. "If anyone finds out I was the one talking to reporters, I'll lose the respect of everyone in the department."

"So don't tell them. Everyone already thinks I'm the culprit, so let them think it. Felix would never betray you. Who are the other journalists?"

Charlie rattled off a few more names, but they were reporters with a lot of integrity.

"Take him down, Charlie."

"I wouldn't know where to begin," his friend said, looking and sounding shell-shocked.

"My mom would give you excellent advice."

"I'll think about it." Charlie cocked his head to the side. "Are you going to invite me to the wedding now?"

"Depends," Sawyer said

"On?"

"If you can beat me at pool without cheating."

"Best of three?" Charlie asked.

"You got it."

A few hours later, Charlie walked him out to his car. "We had a deal. I'll expect to see my invitation in the mail."

Sawyer chuckled and opened his car door. "We should do this again soon. Maybe you and the family can come over for a swim when the weather gets hot enough."

"Sounds great."

Sawyer felt lighter than he had in a long time when he drove away from Charlie's house. The euphoria persisted even when he pulled into the garage and noticed Royce still wasn't home. He apologized profusely to Bones for being out so late and compensated him with an extra half spoonful of ocean fish pâté in his dish.

"I don't know how in the hell you eat that stinky stuff," Sawyer said as he immediately helped himself to Royce's fake-ass cheese. This time, he didn't bother with crackers or pepperoni. Sawyer tipped his head back and squirted it into his mouth. Bones scowled at him in disgust. "Don't you dare judge me. It's been a day."

As if the universe had perceived Sawyer's remark as a challenge, the doorbell rang. Then his visitor pounded on his door.

"Who the fuck?" he asked, knowing the correct answer was *no one good.*

The visitor alternated between knocking and ringing the doorbell obnoxiously. When Sawyer was halfway to the entrance, he recognized the voice shouting his name on the other side of the door.

"Fuck me," Sawyer groaned.

He could tell by Josiah Wheeler's slurred words that he was drunk as hell. Sawyer eased over to a window and peeked outside to see if the sheriff was alone or if he'd brought a friend with him. He liked his odds one-on-one but wasn't looking to get ambushed at his own home. The oversized truck in his driveway was empty. Wheeler's backup might've been hiding off to the side to make a move when Sawyer opened the door, but he sounded too drunk to come up with a solid game plan.

"I know you're fucking in there, Key! Open this door right now before I kick it in."

Sawyer wasn't afraid for his life. For one thing, he was still wearing his service weapon. For another, Sawyer was stone-cold sober. Opening the door and confronting Wheeler was unavoidable, but he decided to phone in the disturbance and request a squad car. The dispatcher on duty was Kyra Hendrickson.

"Officers in route and should be there in just a few minutes," Kyra told him. "Do you want sirens off or on?"

"Off. I'd like to keep this as low-key as possible."

"Stay on the line with me, Sergeant."

"Okay," Sawyer replied, "but I'm going to put my phone in my pocket to free up both hands in case there's a confrontation."

Sawyer listened as the dispatcher updated the responding officers with his request.

"I'm back," Kyra said. "I'd prefer you didn't go outside until the backup unit arrives. ETA is less than two minutes."

A thundering crash echoed through the foyer as Wheeler slammed his body against the door. "Come out and fight me, you pussy. Take your ass beating like a man."

"Lord save us all from the ignorant," Kyra muttered.

"I'd like to spare my neighbors from as much of this as possible. I'm going out there."

Sawyer dropped his phone into his pocket, knowing their conversation would be recorded, and swung the door open so fast Wheeler nearly fell through it. The man staggered into Sawyer, then took a wild swing at him. Sawyer ducked, placed both hands in the center of his chest, and shoved the man hard enough to knock him on his ass. The sheriff did a backward somersault off the porch and landed in Royce's flowers. He slowly got to his hands and knees. Sawyer wanted to make a crack about the position, but he remembered the call would be recorded.

"Locke is going to kick your ass for that," Sawyer said.

Wheeler tried to get up, but only managed to rock back and forth on his hands and knees. "Fucking fairies don't scare me."

"So much for that sensitivity training," Sawyer challenged.

Wheeler turned his head to sneer at him. "I didn't go to that pussy class. Others need to toughen up."

Sawyer fought the urge to grin, knowing dispatch was recording Wheeler's confession. Instead, he feigned shock. "You're not in compliance with our agreement. Guess that means I don't have to abide by it either."

"You've already broken it by going to the press. I'm only breaking it after you broke it. So it doesn't count."

"I kept my mouth shut and walked away. Good luck proving otherwise," Sawyer said. "What are you even doing here?"

Wheeler tried to snort, but it turned into a grotesque belch. "You going to pretend you're not the one trying to ruin my life?"

"I don't have to pretend, Wheeler. I know damn well I haven't done anything to you."

Blue and red lights lit up his neighborhood as the squad car silently approached Sawyer's house.

Unaware of officers Brenna Pumphrey and Davis Rudnick approaching with their hands on their weapons, Wheeler looked up at Sawyer and sneered. "I'm going to fucking kill you."

"Are you now?" Sawyer asked.

"Yeah. Then I'm going to rip your head off and shit down your—"

"Kinky," Sawyer said.

"Sheriff Wheeler?" Brenna said firmly. "Put your hands up where we can see them."

Wheeler jolted and swiveled his head in their direction before glaring at Sawyer. "You called your cop buddies on me?" He staggered to his feet and made no move to comply with Brenna's demand.

"Hands in the air." Davis reached for his taser when Wheeler continued to hurl insults at Sawyer. "I'm not telling you again."

Wheeler turned around and glared at the officers. "You have no power over me. Do you know who I am?"

"Yeah," Brenna said. "You're the guy we're arresting for drunk and disorderly."

"Fuck you," he said, lunging for them.

Davis pulled the trigger on the taser, hitting Wheeler center mass in his chest. The sheriff stiffened when the charge hit him, and he toppled like a statue. He landed face-first in Royce's flowers again. "Looks like we're tacking on resisting arrest to your charges," Davis said.

"I pissed myself," the drunk man mumbled. "I'm going to sue."

Brenna leaned over his prone body to cuff him, then staggered back and gagged. "You shit yourself too." She looked up at Sawyer. "Do we have to put him in our car?"

He chuckled. "The asshole can't stay here."

Brenna slapped cuffs on the prone man and the two officers helped him to his feet. And that's when Royce pulled to a stop at the curb in front of their house. He got out of his SUV and hurried over.

"What the hell is going on here?" Royce asked when he reached them.

"Oh, look. It's the other fairy," Wheeler sneered, sounding even drunker after the voltage had run through his body.

Royce scrunched up his nose and fanned the stench away from his face. "Did you roll in pig shit before coming here? You reek, man."

"Come on," Brenna said, tugging on Wheeler's arm. "Let's get you booked in for the night."

"Can one of you move his pickup out of our driveway before you go?" Royce asked.

"Yeah," Davis said. "I'll do it once we get him in the cruiser."

"You have some serious explaining to do," Royce said, gesturing to the front door. Then he saw the condition of his flowers. "Are you kidding me right now? It looks like a damn elephant trampled my camellias." He leaned over and tried to straighten them out.

"Just a drunken sheriff," Sawyer said. "Sorry about Aunt Tipsy's flowers. Do you think they'll make it?"

"They survived that awful hailstorm a few weeks ago, so they'll survive that crazy fool too."

Royce looked over to where Davis was backing Wheeler's truck out of their driveway. The officer parked it at the curb, locked the vehicle, then joined his partner in the cruiser. With a two-finger salute, Davis dropped into the passenger seat and closed the door. He rolled his window down a second later, and the last thing they saw was his miserable grimace before Brenna drove away. Sawyer retrieved his phone from his pocket and said goodbye to Kyra before disconnecting.

Royce turned a stern look on Sawyer. "Start at the beginning and tell me what happened."

Once inside the house, Sawyer said, "I woke up horny and hard, so I knocked a book off the nightstand to wake you up."

Royce hooked his arm around Sawyer's neck and pulled him in for a quick kiss. "There's no way that was this morning."

"Yep."

"Huh-uh. Two weeks have surely passed."

"Nope," Sawyer said.

"Two days?"

Sawyer shook his head. "Not even one day. Barely twelve hours." He sighed heavily. "Possibly the longest twelve hours of my life."

"Tell me," Royce urged.

Sawyer pressed a lingering kiss to his lips. "This will require ice cream."

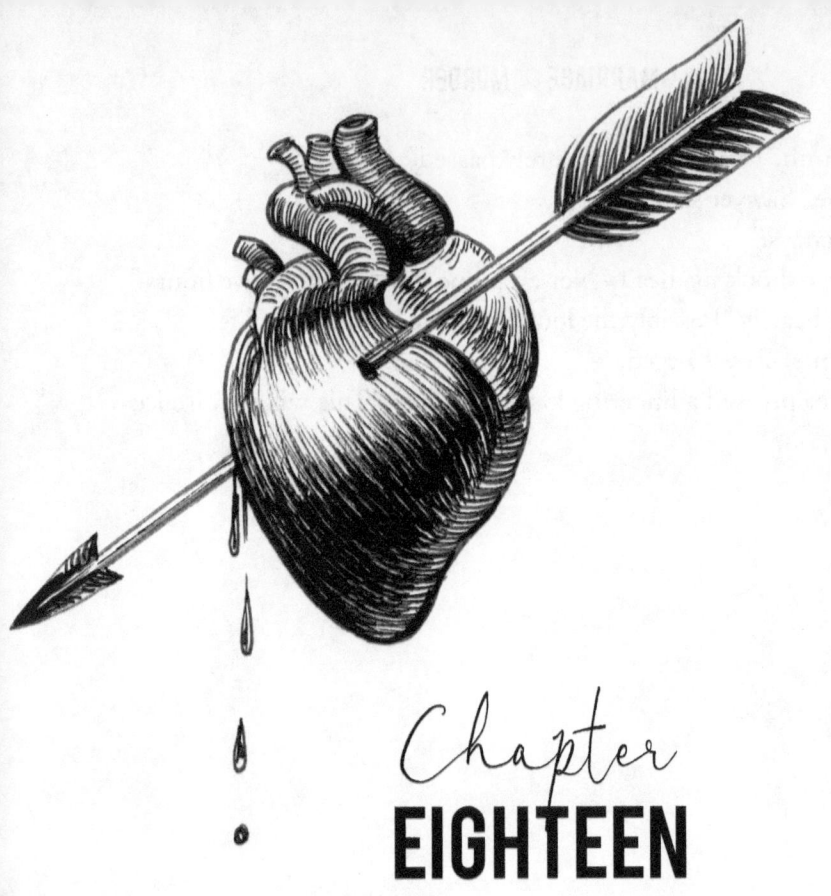

## Chapter
# EIGHTEEN

B ONES DESCENDED ON ROYCE, AND HE LEANED OVER, SCOOPING up the furry beast and cradling him against his chest. The sounds rumbling out of the feline were a mixture of happy purrs and annoyed growls. Bones was glad to see him but angry about their prolonged separation.

Royce kissed the top of his furry head and laughed when Bones rubbed the side of his face against Royce's scruffy jaw. "I missed you too." A forlorn meow met his sentimental words. "Oh, that bad, is it? Daddy didn't feed the beast?"

"I damn well did," Sawyer said. "Your cat is a liar."

Royce smiled wolfishly, even though Sawyer couldn't see his glee. "It's about time you admit he's mine."

"Lose the smirk," Sawyer said as they entered the kitchen. "The cat plays you like a cheap violin."

*Meow.*

Sawyer snorted. "Ease up, Bones. You'll break his strings. I even gave you extra food tonight, so stop begging for it."

Sawyer's remark about begging reminded Royce of a similar one Sawyer had made earlier in the evening. The result was a fist to his gut. The air froze in his lungs when he recalled Sawyer's husky voice telling him he could get down on his knees and beg for it. Bones must've sensed the shift in Royce's attention because he squirmed free and sprang to the floor with the elegance of a jungle cat. Sawyer stopped at the refrigerator and opened the freezer door. Royce reached out and slammed it shut before Sawyer could remove the ice cream.

Keeping his right hand pressed against the freezer, Royce snaked his left arm around Sawyer's waist. "I want your dick inside me." He stepped up behind Sawyer until their bodies were flush. Raking his nose along the back of Sawyer's neck, Royce whispered, "Please. I'll do anything."

Sawyer shivered hard and pressed back against him. "I'm not convinced," Sawyer said in a shaky voice.

Royce stepped back, and Sawyer turned to face him, a smug smile teasing his lips.

"Try harder," Sawyer encouraged.

Royce licked his bottom lip. "You want me on my knees?"

Sawyer's nostrils flared, and a hot flush colored his cheeks. "You know damn well I do."

"Say it," Royce urged him. "Just like you did on the phone today."

Sawyer's smile stretched. "Liked that, did you?"

"Repeat it and find out."

Sawyer reached up, cupped his jaw in a firm grip, and said, "Get on your knees. Beg for it real pretty like, and I'll see what I can do."

Royce grabbed his hand and tugged Sawyer through the house, not stopping until they reached their bathroom. Royce turned on the shower and shifted his entire energy to stripping Sawyer—then himself—naked while the water heated up.

Sawyer pushed him up against the shower wall as soon as they stepped inside. Royce hissed when his bare flesh connected with the cold tile. "I don't hear any begging," Sawyer said. "I'm not convinced you want my dick in any part of you."

Royce glanced down at his throbbing erection before meeting Sawyer's gaze. "The problem is, I want your dick everywhere inside me at the same time."

A new light, dirty and devious, sparked in Sawyer's chocolate brown eyes. "You want to feel stuffed at both ends at once?"

Royce closed his eyes and let his imagination run wild, picturing himself on his hands and knees between two Sawyers bracketing him like the sexiest bookends Royce had ever seen. One sentinel fed his dick to Royce's greedy ass while the other fucked his eager mouth. Royce's core spasmed with a spike of lust so strong he swayed. Sawyer caught his arms to steady him, and Royce snapped his eyes open. Sawyer's gaze was hotter than the sidewalk during a Savannah summer.

"I...uh..." Royce tried to voice his needs but couldn't. Besides, the dirty promise Sawyer offered wasn't something he could deliver unless he knew how to clone himself. But Royce couldn't get the image out of his mind. The impossibility only made the longing stronger.

Sawyer brushed a thumb over Royce's trembling lips. "Be right back." Sawyer stepped out of the shower and had reached the bathroom door before Royce regained his ability to think and speak.

"Hey!" Royce called out. "You're just going to leave me here like this?" Where the hell was he going? A horrific thought doused his lusty haze like a bucket of ice water. "You better not be phoning a friend."

Sawyer ducked his head back into the bathroom and glared at him. "As if I'd ever invite another man into our bed."

Royce opened his mouth to point out they weren't in bed, but Sawyer bit out a hasty, "Shut up," before disappearing again. He returned a moment later with his arms hidden behind his back.

"I've got something for you." Sawyer's voice was a cross between a promise and a warning.

Royce was too busy watching Sawyer's muscles bunch and shift beneath his skin. "I want whatever you've got," he heard himself say as he opened the shower door so Sawyer could step in.

"Prove it," Sawyer said, positioning his body to keep the surprise behind his back.

Royce dropped to his knees and kissed the crown of Sawyer's cock, collecting a pearl of precum. Sawyer inhaled sharply, and a tremor ran down his legs. Royce swelled with pride and set about shifting the power dynamic back to himself. He licked and sucked Sawyer's erection, then pulled back to tease his balls. He glanced up Sawyer's torso and noted the way his man had tipped his head back, watching the bob of his Adam's apple when he swallowed hard. Swirling his tongue around Sawyer's swollen cockhead, Royce forgot all about his wily plans to seize control and set about pleasing his man. Until Sawyer finally pulled his arms out from behind his back and revealed a dildo with a suction cup in one hand and a bottle of lube in the other.

Royce's mouth went slack, and Sawyer's dick slid free. "Whatcha got there?"

"You're going to fuck yourself on this," Sawyer said, hoisting the dildo, "while sucking me off. Full at both ends."

Sawyer leaned forward and savagely knocked the bottles of shampoo and body wash off the built-in ledge they used for storage and sex purposes. He'd lost count of the number of times one of them had bent forward and held on to it for purchase while the other—

Royce's thoughts were interrupted by a *thud* as Sawyer attached the dildo's suction cup to the tile.

"On your feet," Sawyer demanded. The sexy show of dominance made Royce dizzy as he eagerly obeyed. "Brace your hands on the wall so you won't touch yourself."

Royce knew damned well he'd still be tempted, but he did as instructed. The snick of the lube bottle opening echoed in the intimate space, and anticipation hummed through Royce when he felt the heat of Sawyer's body draw nearer.

Gripping his left ass cheek, Sawyer exposed Royce's pucker and teased it with a slick finger. Royce flexed and pushed back against the caress.

"Damn, baby," Sawyer whispered huskily, sliding the finger inside him and pegging the sweet spot that would make Royce agree to nearly anything. "You're in a really bad way."

Royce nodded. "Please."

Dark and delicious laughter rumbled from Sawyer's chest as he pressed the button again. "Not yet."

Sawyer took his sweet time stretching him with one finger, then two. He added more lube to the point Royce was sloppy wet but so horny he didn't care.

"Almost ready," Sawyer said. "The dildo is thicker than I am. I don't want you to hurt yourself."

Royce recognized manipulation when he saw it, or felt it in this case, and blurted the first protest that came to mind to spur Sawyer on. "We're going to run out of hot water."

Sawyer snapped off the water and said, "Takes care of one worry."

Goose bumps pebbled all over Royce's skin as the steam clouds from the shower floated like apparitions toward the cooler air in the bedroom. When Sawyer eased his fingers free of his ass, Royce's full attention fell to his aching pucker. Sawyer gripped Royce's hips and turned him around, capturing his mouth in a tongue-tangling kiss. Royce was so rattled when Sawyer broke off that he couldn't decide what to do next. Sawyer guided him by the hips until the tip of the dildo brushed against his hole.

Royce gasped out when the broad head pushed past the ring of muscles, and he tensed up. Even with the generous amount of lube, Royce didn't think he'd be able to take the dildo much deeper.

Sawyer pressed a quick kiss to his lips, then whispered, "Close your eyes and relax. Pretend you're sinking down on my cock." Sawyer reached between Royce's legs to firmly massage his balls. The pressure was perfect, and his breath rushed between parted lips. Royce sank farther onto the dildo, feeling stretched to his limits. "Fuck, you're so damn sexy," Sawyer said. "Take it. Take all of me." Sawyer reached a second hand down to stroke his cock while fondling his balls.

Royce threw his head back and cried out as he sank down until the back of his thighs pressed against the cold tile, and the dildo's silicone balls were tucked against his own. He looked up at Sawyer and said, "So full."

Sawyer cupped his chin and stroked a thumb over his bottom lip. "Not yet." He leaned forward and kissed Royce until he forgot his own name. Drawing back, he commanded, "Now ride it."

Royce braced one hand on the ledge next to his leg and the other on the wall beside him. Using his thighs, he rose a few inches and sank back down. Mouth gaping open on a silent cry of ecstasy, Royce repeated the motion, but this time he rose higher and fell faster, jarring the air from his lungs.

"That's it, baby," Sawyer said. "Do it again."

Royce rose and fell on the dildo over and over. His thigh muscles burned in protest, but he couldn't stop chasing his orgasm as if his life depended on it. Just when he thought it couldn't get any better, Sawyer released his cock and balls, propped a foot on the ledge, and fed Royce his dick, one slow inch at a time.

Royce's rhythm faltered, and he sat on the dildo, taking it to the root. Embracing the rapture of being filled from both ends, he moaned and watched as a mirroring euphoria vibrated through his lover's taut abdomen.

Sawyer cupped the back of Royce's head with one hand, braced the other on the wall, and rocked his hips forward to push his dick deeper inside Royce's mouth. "Suck me off like you mean it."

Royce's blood rushed in his ears, drowning out all sound but his beating heart. He shifted his grip from the tiled ledge to Sawyer's calf and used his core muscles to grind on the dildo while working Sawyer's cock in and out of his mouth. Each pass up and down both shafts earned him different rewards. Sawyer gifted him with more of his essence at one end, and the dildo rubbed against his prostate at the other. The pressure and pleasure were so intense Royce thought he might blow apart before he reached his climax. He tilted his head so he could catch a glimpse of Sawyer's face from the corner of his eye. With his head tilted back and his sexy lips parted to pant and moan, Sawyer looked like the embodiment of rapture.

Fingers tightened in Royce's hair, and the thick vein in Sawyer's cock throbbed against his tongue. Royce knew what was coming and hollowed out his cheeks, intensifying the pressure until Sawyer came in his mouth with a shout. Royce forgot all about the dildo in his ass in favor of taking care of his man, who fell to his knees afterward and captured Royce's mouth in a lusty, salty kiss.

Royce widened his legs to make room for him, and Sawyer slid down his body to take Royce's cock deep inside the wet heat of his mouth.

"Fuck! Fuck! Fuck!" Royce chanted, his hips like pistons working the dildo up and down with each curse. Sawyer cupped his sac and tugged just the way he liked.

Royce came so hard his vision dimmed, and black dots danced in front of his eyes until his hips stilled with the toy buried deep inside him. "That was…" Royce searched for the right word, but he couldn't think of an adjective worthy of the way he felt right then.

Sawyer chuckled and kissed his lips. "Yeah, it was." His man didn't need the words. They were in sync as always. Or so he thought until Sawyer scowled at him. "Phone a friend?"

"I couldn't imagine how you were going to be in two places at once without some help." Royce eased off the dildo and stood up. "I wasn't wrong." He extended his hands to Sawyer, who took them and pulled himself up.

"No, you weren't."

Sawyer stepped back and turned the faucet on without warning. Royce yelped when the cold water hit him square in the face and chest. Luckily, it didn't take long for the water to turn hot, and their kisses scalding, as they washed each other from head to toe. Afterward, Royce gestured to his still-limp dick.

"I think you broke it. Normally I'd be raring to go again."

"Maybe some ice cream and a nap will help," Sawyer suggested.

"For who? Me or him?"

"Both," Sawyer said.

They strolled buck-ass naked into the kitchen to choose their pints of ice cream. Sawyer had a low-fat sea salt caramel he wanted to try, and Royce went with peanut butter chip. Once they were under the covers,

Royce flipped on the television for background noise and asked Sawyer to tell him about his day. He'd already heard the highlights but wanted to hear the play-by-play like Sawyer was breaking down a World Series game for ESPN.

"I've never been so happy to be wrong," Royce said once Sawyer finished.

Sawyer quirked a brow. "About what?"

"Courtney," Royce said, spooning a bite of ice cream into his mouth. "She didn't deserve my doubt."

Sawyer's brown eyes melted like chocolate. "You were just looking out for my best interests."

"Always." Royce pointed his spoon toward Sawyer's pint. "How's your ice cream taste?"

Sawyer grimaced. "Like skunk piss."

Royce nearly choked on a chocolate chip. Once he righted himself, he said, "But you're still eating it?"

Sawyer spooned another bite into his mouth and shrugged. "It's growing on me."

Royce shook his head. "Skunk piss. That would make a perfect name for a craft beer."

Sawyer laughed. "Maybe we'll buy a hardware store *and* a brewery when we retire."

Royce tilted his head to consider it. "I'll turn in my papers tomorrow."

"Is this Cupid case the one to do in the great Royce Locke?" Sawyer asked.

"It's making me doubt my sanity."

Sawyer scowled in disbelief. "How so?"

Royce laid it all out for him. By the time he finished, both men were scraping the bottoms of their pints. "And now I sound like a raving lunatic with my wild theories."

"There's no one's judgment I trust more than yours," Sawyer said. He set his empty ice cream container on his nightstand, walked into the bathroom, and returned with his phone in hand.

Royce sat up straighter. "Who are you calling?"

Sawyer looked up and smiled. "Evangeline. When *Dateline* comes a calling after this case breaks, you're going to need an agent."

Royce snorted and fell back against the cushions. "She'll be too busy planning our wedding."

"She can juggle many things," Sawyer replied.

"Like a wedding and a campaign for sheriff?"

Sawyer shook his head. "No campaign. At least not now. You and our future kids will be all the challenge I'm going to need for the next decade or two. And besides, I didn't mean Evangeline would represent you, but she can put you in touch with her people."

"Hard pass. I've got all the excitement I can handle right here."

Sawyer returned to their bed with a devilish grin on his lips. "You think?"

Royce pulled him close and kissed him until nothing and no one existed except for his man. He broke away a few minutes later and said, "I know." Then he whipped the covers back like a magician to reveal his erection. "It's alive."

Royce whistled as he walked into the bullpen on Wednesday morning, a little later than usual thanks to a routine cleaning at the dentist. Oh, the irony.

Chen and Blue looked up from their conversation and were wearing matching smirks.

"What's gotten into you?" Chen asked.

Blue's big grin said he knew exactly what had gotten into Royce.

"It's going to be a wonderful day, Ky. I will wrap up this case in time for my vacation so I can shift my full attention to my best man duties for Jace." They'd stayed late and uncovered additional evidence to prove the man taking up residence in Larry Fellows's home was actually Leo, then found millions of motives for him doing so. They needed the dental records to nail the coffin shut and validate the warrants they had ready to go.

"Speak it into existence, boo," Blue said, holding up his fist for Royce to bump.

"And you can start in there," Ashcroft said after exiting Mendoza's office. Chen's partner looked as if the chief had ripped him another asshole. The armed robberies had started taking a toll on Mendoza. Royce could only imagine the pressure on their chief's shoulders. Ashcroft rubbed his ass for emphasis and hooked his thumb toward Mendoza's office. "Your turn, Locke."

"Time to face the music," Royce said. "With any luck, I can take the brunt of whatever is riding him and spare my partner."

Chen chuckled. "Tara pretty much said the same thing before being summoned in there. She faced the firing squad first. Damn early bird caught something far worse than a worm this morning."

Royce blew out a nervous breath and crossed the bullpen. *Best not to keep the chief waiting.* He rapped on the door and was commanded to enter. Royce took one look at Mendoza's face and knew some kind of devil had their chief by the short and curlies. He closed the door, crossed the room, and took a seat. "You wanted to see me, Chief?"

"Yes, I sure as hell did. Glen Bishop's lawyer has been blowing up my phone every twenty minutes with demands you free his client. I'd like to give him a valid argument why I won't do that, but I've discovered the lead detectives now question the identity of the man in the morgue and have prepped warrants in case the ME confirms their hunch."

"Not a hunch, Chief."

"Good," Mendoza said. "I'm dying to hear all about it."

Royce carefully recounted the revelations he and Tara had uncovered during their investigation. Mendoza stayed silent as usual with his hands steepled at his chest. His black eyes never wavered from Royce's face, and the furrow between his brows never eased.

"That's pretty much what South told me when she was in the hot seat," Mendoza said after Royce finished.

Even when Mendoza was in his best mood, Royce never would've asked the chief why he'd requested Royce repeat the story, but something in his expression must've given him away because Mendoza snorted, rested his arms on his desk, and leaned forward.

"Come on, Locke. Surely you can understand why the hell I wanted to hear this theory repeated. And it has nothing to do with believing you over South."

"Of course not, sir," Royce said. And he meant it.

Mendoza expelled a long breath. "For the record, I'd believe South over you."

Royce smiled. "Any sane person would."

Mendoza scowled and said, "Don't make me laugh. I'm not in the mood to be in a better mood."

Royce immediately wiped the grin off his face. "No, sir."

Mendoza's lips twitched at one corner, but he managed to hold on to his frown. "Tell me again."

So Royce did.

Mendoza didn't look any happier when Royce wrapped it up the second time. "What a cluster fuck."

"Yes, sir."

"I do not want our department to become a laughingstock. Call the DA's office and hold off on arraignment for as long as they can. We need the charges to be accurate. Ask them to shift the docket to buy you some more time." Mendoza's scowl grew darker. "We need those damn dental records today. Yesterday would've been better. Do we want to invite a media shitstorm?"

"No, sir."

Mendoza's phone rang, and he checked the screen. His lips quirked into some semblance of a smile, and Royce had a pretty damn good feeling he knew the caller's identity. "I gotta take this. Show yourself out."

Royce stood up. "Tell Sheriff Beecham I said hello."

Mendoza narrowed his eyes. He'd seen a similar look on Bones's face when a plus-sized dove landed on the windowsill. Bones had leaped from his tree to the window and pawed at the glass long after the bird flew away. Royce was seconds away from being reduced to nothing more than a pile of bones and feathers.

"You just can't help yourself, can you?" he whispered to himself as he headed for the door.

Royce kept his hand on the knob once he pulled the door shut, leaving a tiny crack so he could hear Mendoza's voice when he said, "Hey, babe" or "Hey, Abe." Royce couldn't say which and pressed his ear to the door. Mendoza's laughter sounded muffled, but Royce could tell the difference between the laughs he shared with the department and the ones he shared with the caller. Mendoza started speaking again. The timbre was low and husky. The man was definitely talking to someone he had an intimate relationship with.

A throat cleared behind him. Royce released the handle and whipped around to find Tara standing there. Her blonde brows crept toward her hairline, and Royce expected her to give him shit. Instead, she smiled and pulled a piece of paper from behind her back.

"Now look who's belching up yellow feathers," Royce said. "Is that what I think it is?"

"Signed, sealed, and delivered."

Leo answered the door wearing a confused expression. "Did you need something else from me?"

"May we please come in, Mr. Fellows?" Tara asked.

Leo frowned and made no move to grant them entrance. "I don't understand. Why do you need to come in?"

"There are some things we need to discuss with you," Royce said. "We can do this inside your house or in front of your neighbors." Royce nodded in the direction of the lady watching them from her side yard.

Leo huffed a sigh and stepped aside, waving them in. He led them into the kitchen but didn't offer anything to drink. Leo dropped down into a chair and they sat across the table from him. "Let's get this over with, Detectives."

"Are we interrupting something?" Royce asked.

"Would it matter if you were?"

"Depends," Tara said as she looked around the room. She removed a folded piece of paper from her portfolio, which now rocked colorful dinosaur stickers, and extended it to Leo.

"What's that?" the older man asked.

"Only one way to find out," Royce suggested.

Leo snatched the document from her hand and unfolded it. His brows snapped together in confusion as he read. "This is an arrest warrant for my deceased brother. I don't understand."

"No," Tara said calmly, "it's an arrest warrant for you, Leo."

Royce removed his recorder and flipped it on before stating the date, time, and parties present. Then he read Leo his rights. After he finished, "You not only have the right to remain silent, Leo, you really should. Listen to the evidence we've collected against you. When we're finished, I'm going to give you a single chance to help yourself. If you interrupt me or try to bullshit me, I'll just turn everything I have over to DA Babineaux and let the chips fall where they may."

Leo crossed his arms over his chest and leaned back in his chair, which Royce took as his cue to continue.

"Taking the cats to the shelter was your first mistake. They all have very distinguishable marks, but then again, who could've predicted Detective South taking her nieces to the shelter to pick out kitties?" Leo flicked his glance toward Tara but wisely kept his mouth shut. "During our second visit to your house, you were packing your belongings into boxes. You let your guard down and wrote with your right hand. Larry Fellows is left-handed." Royce had to hand it to Leo. Not even a flicker of emotion crossed his face. Then again, he was just getting started.

"I know what you're thinking," Royce said. "None of these things would hold up in court." He reached into his portfolio and pulled out the sheet of paper where Leo had practiced writing his brother's signature with his left hand. Leo swallowed hard but it was his only tell. His expression remained impassive and unimpressed. "Paul found this on top of the trash when he threw out his gum last night. Then again, we both know Paul recognized you weren't Larry before he found your practice sheet."

Leo opened his mouth to speak but Royce quickly silenced him.

"Don't do it," Royce said.

Leo snapped his mouth shut and gestured for Royce to continue. So he did.

"Right now, you're probably still thinking you'll be back in time for *Oprah* or *Ellen*, but I promise we're just getting started. According to dental records, Leo Fellows has a dental implant after a mishap. He looked at Tara and said, "Was it roller skating?"

"Kayaking," she said. "His son accidentally hit him in the face with a paddle."

"That's right. Kayaking." Royce met Leo's gaze again. "The man in the morgue doesn't have a dental implant where the dentist said he should. But wait, we've got more. Larry Fellows has two distinct scars—one on his abdomen from an appendectomy and one on his right thigh from a compound bone fracture when he fell off his treehouse ladder."

Tara pulled out a copy of a Polaroid they'd found in the thousands of images scanned onto the flash drives they'd confiscated from Leo's house. A teenage boy sat in a lawn chair holding a popsicle in his left hand and propping his right leg on an upside-down bucket. A thick, white plaster cast covered the limb from foot to hip. Someone had written the name Larry Fellows and the year 1975 on the white strip beneath the image. She followed that with the picture Paul had texted to her, pointing to the scars on Larry's body.

"Do you know who else has those same scars?" Tara asked, then raised her hand. "Don't answer that. It was a rhetorical question. The man in our morgue has those exact scars. We've told you how we know you're really Leo Fellows, and now we're going to tell you why you're better off making a deal with the DA than facing a jury of your peers."

"If Leo Fellows is presumed dead, you'd have a minimum of ten million reasons to assume Larry Fellows's identity," Royce said. "The remaining balance in your parents' trust would pay out to the surviving brother, and that doesn't include Leo's personal assets. Leo Fellows is either listed as the beneficiary or named the custodian on the accounts until his son turns twenty-five. There are no provisions on the accounts earmarked for Sam that would prevent *Larry* from withdrawing all the money and disappearing. Throw in the evidence of you practicing Larry's signature, and I can no longer chalk up your motives to merely being afraid for your own life."

"Some might even think you killed Larry and framed Glen," Tara said. "We considered it until our cyber unit unlocked your phone and computers. Your email and encrypted documents were eye opening." She removed six sets of documents from a bottomless portfolio Mary Poppins would covet and slid them across the table. Leo reached for the paperwork and the color drained from his face as he read it. "You knew something was off with the quarterly earnings Glen had presented to the board, and maybe you even started to suspect the unimaginable and started asking questions."

"Glen Bishop was embezzling money from the company you'd built together and had altered the quarterly reports to hide his treachery," Royce said. "We found original data for three quarters that showed an astounding profit and the doctored statements for the same quarters that showed a staggering loss." Royce couldn't say how Leo had gotten his hands on the original reports, but he suspected Marcie had played a role in it. "Glen needed to find a way to shut you up and discovering the affair with his wife was the perfect excuse to get Bart and the board members to turn on you. Once you got your hands on proof of Glen's crimes, you used it to blackmail him. That's why you called him on Saturday morning. His time to pay was up, and you wanted your money. You never stopped to consider that Glen would try to kill you, and you never intended for your brother to get caught in the middle of your fight with Bishop. I truly believe that part." Royce paused to let his words sink in and to let Tara takeover.

"And I'm not sure if this will make the bitter pill easier to swallow," she said, "but our DA is turning over the embezzlement evidence to the FBI. He won't get away with killing Larry or stealing from the company. You're just not going to personally profit from it."

"This is the part where you can help yourself, Leo," Royce said. "Up to this moment, you haven't committed any heinous acts. You've clearly thought about committing them. DA Babineaux will work with you if you drop this nonsense and confess."

Leo held his gaze for a few moments, and Royce thought Leo might come clean. Instead, the older man shook his head and said, "I'll take my chances."

Royce instructed him to stand up and place his hands behind his back. Leo docilely did as he was told, and Royce rounded the table and snapped the handcuffs on his wrists. Then Tara perp-marched Leo down the driveway while the neighbors watched. The lady who'd been out earlier was still there, and her jaw nearly hit the ground when they put Leo in the back of Royce's vehicle.

"And she thinks she's shocked now," Royce said.

Tara snorted. "Right?"

"Just drive," Leo snarled from the backseat.

And Royce did…extra slow so the neighbors could gawk, film, and take photos of the arrest.

At the station, Royce turned in his seat and looked at Leo. "Last chance."

"I want my lawyer."

Tara took Leo to booking while Royce found a quiet corner and called Paul Jarvis. The man had said he already knew the truth, but Royce thought there might still be a little pearl of doubt. He knew first-hand that those pearls could turn into massive, all-consuming boulders, and he wanted better for Paul. Mostly, Royce just wanted to apologize for the man's loss. Their conversation was brief and mostly one-sided, but Paul tearfully thanked Royce for his thoughtfulness at the end of the call. He wanted to call Grace Huxley, but it could wait a little while.

Once Leo finished with booking, Royce took him down to the holding area and placed him in a cell next to Glen. "Welcome to the C-suite," he said jovially. "This should be fun, yeah?"

Glen stood up and walked over to the bars. "What's Larry doing here?"

"This is Leo," Royce replied.

Glen shook his head as if he were trying to clear the cobwebs. "Then why am I here?"

"Because you killed the wrong brother, asshat." Royce stood back and surveyed the men. Leo was madder than a wet cat, and Glen looked as pale as a ghost. "Maybe the two of you can ride the same bus to your arraignments. It will be like old times, yeah? We enjoyed the photos of the boys' trip out west for spring break. What year was that?"

Leo silently glared, but Glen whispered, "1981."

"If you truly care about your son," Royce said to Leo, "you'll do the right thing and confess. The longer this drags out, the more media attention it will garner. The teenage years are hard enough without your dad pulling a stunt like this. He'll be going to college soon. Don't rob him of epic road trips."

"I. Want. My. Lawyer."

"I'll get right on that," Royce called out as he walked away.

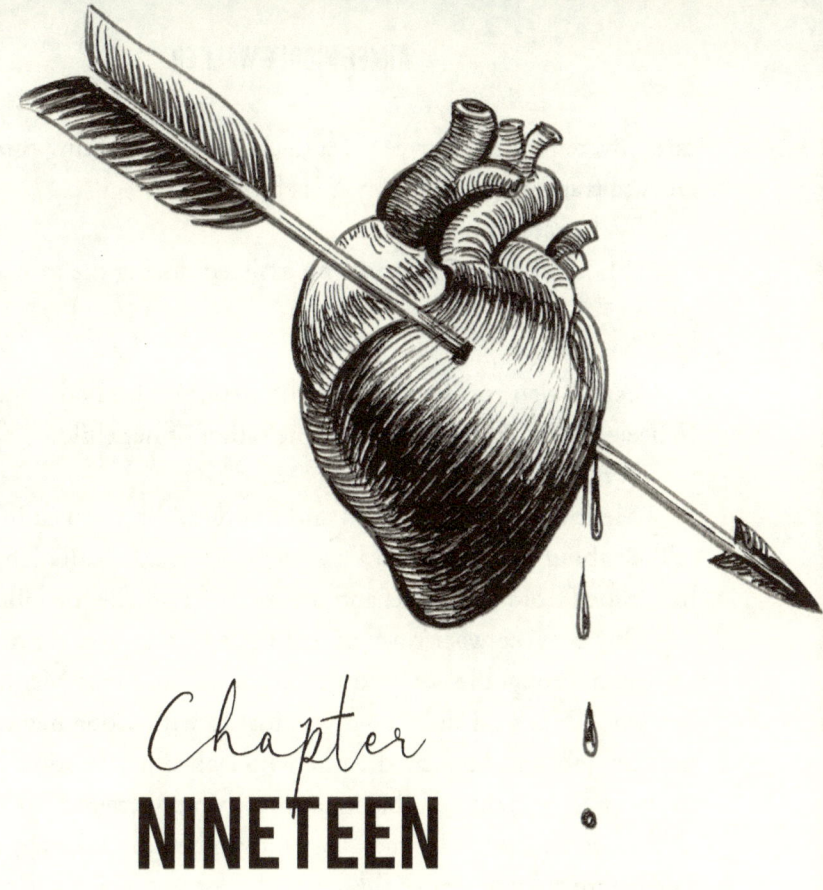

# Chapter
# NINETEEN

A KNOCK ON HIS DOORFRAME PULLED SAWYER'S ATTENTION FROM Holly's latest report to find Chief Mendoza standing in the doorway.

"Hello, Chief. To what do I owe the pleasure?"

Mendoza's right brow winged up. "Pleasure, huh?" A wry smile teased his lips as he strolled into the room and shut the door. He gestured to the empty chair in silent question, and Sawyer nodded. Since when did Mendoza seek someone out? He beckoned, and they responded. "Apparently, no one else in the precinct warned you I was on a tear earlier this morning."

"Uh, no. This is the first I've heard about it."

Mendoza steepled his fingers and stared at Sawyer, who fought the urge to squirm. Was he in trouble for something? If so, what?

"Courtney Capshaw," Mendoza said, enunciating slowly and

carefully, reminding Sawyer of a sleek predator stalking through high grass to track its clueless prey. Was he the prey?

"What about her?"

"She's the sheriff deputy you assisted during the armed robbery, correct?"

"Yes, sir."

"Am I also to assume she's the deputy who had an affair with Wheeler, who is presumed to be the father of her child."

"Yes, sir."

Mendoza pursed his lips and nodded. "And you didn't think to tell me about any of this?" His voice had turned deadly. The predator had leaped from the weeds and was poised to make the killing strike.

But Sawyer wasn't a helpless little bunny, and he hadn't done anything wrong. He squared his shoulders and met Mendoza's gaze head-on. "No, sir, I didn't. My friendship with Courtney doesn't impact my job, and I wasn't the one who leaked her relationship details to the press and invited this madness. I simply offered her my friendship when she needed it most and moved her and the baby someplace safe before the vultures could descend. None of which had anything to do with my duties."

Mendoza's nostrils flared, and he lowered his hands to grip the armrests. "What about the impact on your personal safety? Am I allowed to be concerned about that? Should I have minded my own business when I learned the sheriff of Chatham County arrived at your home last night and threatened you?"

"I called for backup, and everything was fine. Wheeler was just drunk and blowing off steam. He resisted arrest and got tasered. The only things injured were Wheeler's pride, his pants, and Royce's beloved camellias."

Sawyer's attempts to downplay the incident weren't working. Mendoza's jaw worked from side to side. "Wheeler made bail early this morning. Once he passed a sobriety test, I drove him to your neighborhood to retrieve his truck. It allowed me to have a private word to ensure he didn't retaliate against my two best sergeants."

"We appreciate both your diligence and the compliment."

"I told that weak-ass bastard I'd make him disappear if he ever so much as looked in your direction again."

A lump formed in Sawyer's throat, and he swallowed it down. The chief continued talking before Sawyer could express his gratitude further.

"He plans to resign as sheriff later today and will enter rehab for his addiction."

The enormity of the announcement rocked Sawyer. "Sex or alcohol?" he asked.

Mendoza smiled for the first time since entering Sawyer's office. "Probably both." He tilted his head slightly. "Were you planning to run for sheriff?"

"For about five minutes," Sawyer replied. "My motives for doing so weren't good enough, and I enjoy working for you, sir. It might be something I decide to do down the road, but I promise you'll hear it directly from me if the time comes."

"Thank you," Mendoza said and rose to his feet. "For what it's worth, I think you'll make a damn fine sheriff someday." He made the inevitability sound more like *when* than *if*. "Times are changing, and people don't get so hung up on guys like us anymore. Have a good day, Sergeant." Then he was gone leaving Sawyer to stare into space.

*Guys like us?* What was he trying to say? Sawyer's eyes widened as the significance hit him. "Damn it." He'd have to tell Royce he was at minimum half right. It was possible the *vibe* Royce had picked up on was unrequited love.

Sawyer's phone rang, jarring him back to reality, and he answered without checking the caller ID.

"Sergeant, it's Cassandra with GeneMatch."

Sawyer started to brace himself for bad news, but he realized she sounded peppier than the last time she'd called. No funeral voice. He straightened in his chair. "You have another positive match, don't you?" *Please let it be for Andrea Dodd, and please let her be alive.*

"I do," Cassandra said. "This time we matched your sample with someone in our genealogy search database."

"So they're alive?" Sawyer asked hopefully.

"They were at the time they uploaded their DNA. The rest will be up to you."

Sawyer's pulse hammered in his throat, adding a slight quiver to his voice when he said, "Who is it?"

"Sophia Gifford," Cassandra said.

Sawyer searched his brain and came up empty, but that only amplified his excitement. "An assumed name or a relative?"

"You would know her as Andrea Dodd."

"Holy shit. Beverly was right. Her daughter is still alive. Where does she live?"

"Washington," Cassandra said.

"State or DC?"

"State," Cassandra replied. "Which means she got about as far away from her family as she could in the US. I'm going to share her contact information with you, but I'd like you to keep that in mind when speaking to her. We all feel awful for what Beverly has gone through—is—going through, but I suddenly feel very protective of this lady, and I don't know why."

Some of Sawyer's excitement dissipated as Cassandra's warning sank in. She was absolutely right. Andrea had cut ties with her family and moved across the country. She'd assumed a new identity. She wouldn't have done so on a whim. All these years without a single attempt to contact her family? But she'd submitted her DNA profile to a genealogy site. That had to mean something, right?

"I'm not looking to scrape the scabs off this woman's old wounds and make her bleed." Sawyer thought of Beverly and the battle she was losing with cancer. "But I also can't pretend this call didn't happen. I will handle the situation with extreme care. You have my word."

"That's good enough for me." Cassandra passed along the contact information for Sophia Gifford, which included her physical address, a cell phone number, and an email address.

Sawyer dialed the phone number before he lost his nerve, then remembered the time difference. He'd decided to hang up and call back a few hours later, but a woman answered before he could disconnect the call. Her voice was crisp and clear without lingering sleepiness. She was either an early riser or hadn't gone to bed yet. Sawyer was suddenly struck with a rare wave of self-doubt. Who the hell was he to disrupt this woman's life? He should've at least planned out what he wanted to say first.

"Hello," she said again, snapping Sawyer out of his musings.

"Miss Gifford?"

"Speaking. Who's calling please?"

"My name is Sawyer Key. I'm a cold case detective with the Savannah Police Department." The woman sucked in a sharp breath, and Sawyer feared she was going to disconnect the call. "Please don't hang up. I don't want to cause you any trouble, and I promise I will not share your contact information with anyone without your permission."

"I'm listening," she said slowly.

Sawyer told her about the joint missing persons initiative with *Sinister in Savannah*. "We recently featured the case of a young lady who disappeared in 1987. We uploaded her mother's DNA profile into a genealogy site and matched her to you." Sawyer's Poirot moment was met with silence. "Andrea, are you still there?" Too late, he realized he'd addressed her by the wrong name.

"Andrea," she whispered. "It's been so long since someone called me by that name. It feels like rediscovering an old favorite sweater in the back of the closet, but it no longer fits. Andrea," she repeated. "Still too snug for comfort. Let's stick with Miss Gifford, shall we?"

"Yes, of course. I'm truly sorry. My intentions are good, I assure you."

Miss Gifford chuckled dryly. "Good intentions. I'm sure that's what my mother-in-law had in mind when she bought those dumb heritage kits for the entire family for Christmas. If I'd refused, she would've wondered why." Miss Gifford sighed heavily. "They say the road to hell is paved with them. Good intentions, that is. I heard the expression in church enough times to gag a horse. I had my reasons for leaving Savannah, and I bet an astute person such as yourself can guess why."

"I have my suspicions."

"My fire and brimstone, Bible-thumping uncle had a penchant for teenage girls, even ones that were related to him," Miss Gifford said. "I'd like to believe my mother didn't know what her younger brother was like when she let him move in with us after losing his job. But Uncle Ben could do no wrong in her eyes. It was always someone else's fault when things went against him—arguments with friends and family or lost jobs. Uncle Ben was too smart for his own good or people just didn't understand him. The sick fucker dared me to tell my mother what he was doing to me. Said she'd choose him over me. I believed him then, and I believe him now."

Sawyer felt like the worst kind of asshole for triggering her. "Miss Gifford, I am truly sorry."

"Thank you," she replied. "Is this where you say I owe it to my mother to hear her out?"

The man who'd sat with Beverly Dodd on a few occasions and had seen her rapid decline wanted to say yes. He wanted to tell this woman her mother was dying and the only thing she longed for in the world was to hear her daughter's voice once more. Beverly wanted to apologize for failing her. Sawyer couldn't add to Andrea's hurt, though. She was the victim, and he would not manipulate her. Letting Beverly die without knowing her daughter was alive felt like the worst act of cruelty he could enforce on a person. Sawyer was well and truly stuck between a rock and a hard place, and he suddenly found it hard to breathe.

"No," he finally said. "I won't ask you to do that. I've inflicted enough trauma. Do I have your permission to at least offer Beverly the comfort of knowing you're alive and well? I can tell her you do not want to speak to her. I promised I wouldn't share your contact information, and I meant it."

Andrea blew out a breath. "I don't know. I need to think about it. What's this *Sinister in Savannah* thing you mentioned?"

Sawyer told her about the podcast and some of the significant investigations that had earned them worldwide attention.

"And they're doing a piece on me?" Andrea asked in disbelief. "Please tell me they used good photos."

Sawyer chuckled. "They were mostly candid family photos. A few were from your cheer squad. None of the official school pictures everyone loathes."

"Thank goodness," Andrea said. "So what all goes into these episodes? Did you say they're on YouTube?"

"Yes," Sawyer replied, then walked her through the agenda they followed.

"Age progression images?" she asked. "Those things are generally awful and make everyone look like a serial killer."

"Normally, I'd agree with you, but I think Jonah's program is a few steps above the ones we're used to seeing."

"I'm curious, but I'm also afraid," Andrea said. "What did my mother say about me in her interview?"

"I'm not going to be the person who manipulates you into doing something you don't want to do," Sawyer said.

"That's a nonanswer if ever I heard one," she said. "I get the impression you're trying to tell me something without actually telling me."

"I'm not trying to be coy or play mind games," Sawyer replied. "The answers you want are in the episode. I can send you a link or you can google the podcast, or even your name, and find it." Channeling the most incredible mother to ever live, Sawyer said, "You're in the driver's seat. Let me know what direction you want to go."

Andrea sighed heavily. "I will. Thank you."

Sawyer sat in silence for a long time after they disconnected. He felt no better after talking to her than he had before dialing her number. His phone vibrated with an incoming text from Felix.

*Wheeler's arrest at your residence is about to hit the wires. Wow! That mug shot. Care to comment?*

*Fuck off,* Sawyer replied. He debated telling his friend about the phone call with Andrea, but he decided to wait until he heard back from her.

Felix sent a laughing emoji, followed by another text. *Know anything about the press conference he's got scheduled this afternoon?*

*Fuck all the way off,* Sawyer replied.

Felix sent a kissy face emoji. *Aww. Love you too, man.*

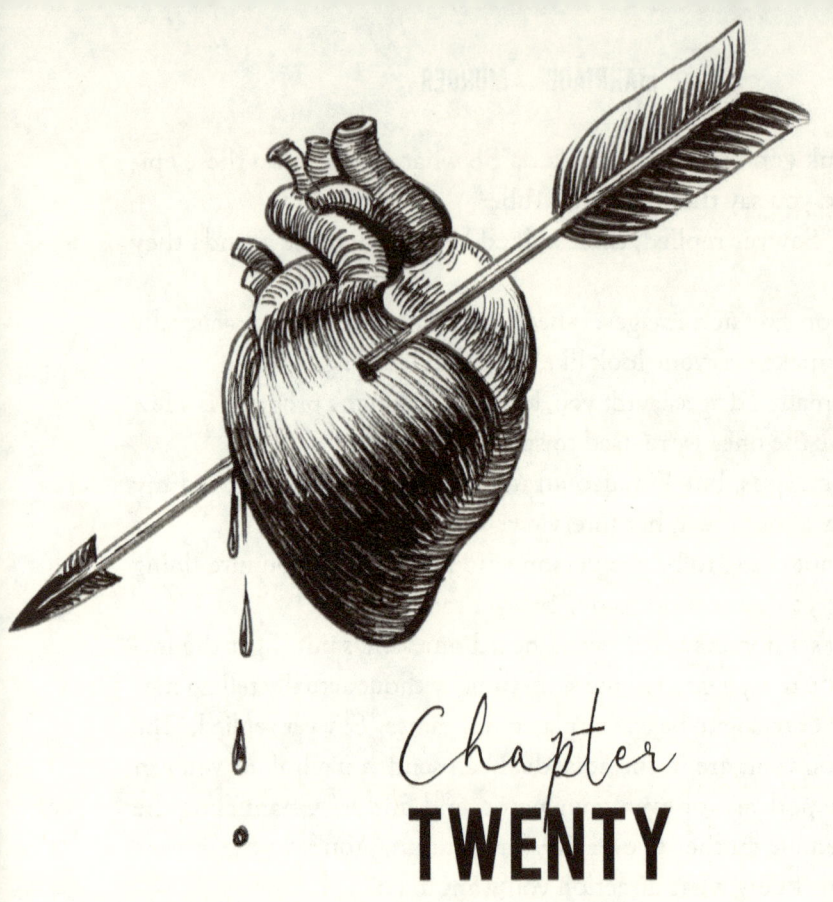

## Chapter
# TWENTY

"**S**HERIFF WHEELER, DOES YOUR RESIGNATION MEAN THERE
will be a special election in Chatham County?" a female
reporter shouted.

"That isn't my decision to make," Wheeler said. "I know the county
will be in excellent hands with Brian Houser at the helm. He's served
and protected the people of Chatham County for three decades and
has been invaluable as my undersheriff."

"Sheriff Wheeler," a man called out, "would you consider another
run at a later date?"

"Also not my decision to make," the sheriff replied. "At least not on
my own. As I stated, I'm stepping down to focus on my family and my
health. They deserve a better version of me. Please respect our privacy."

A chorus of reporters shouted his name, vying for his attention.

"I have no further comments at this time."

Royce switched off the radio and looked at Sawyer sitting in his passenger seat. They'd carved out some time between reports and other administrative duties to eat at the Hummingbird Café before meeting with Sherry about cake options. Royce had just pulled up to the bakery when Wheeler's press conference had started.

Sawyer turned his head and met his gaze. His facial expression and body language were neutral, giving nothing of his thoughts away. "We going to eat cake or what?"

"In a minute," Royce said. "How are you feeling?"

Sawyer narrowed his eyes. "Worried I'll eat my emotions in cupcakes and gain a bunch of weight before the wedding?"

Royce snorted. "No. Are you worried about that?"

Sawyer smiled. "Maybe a little." He bit his lip and tilted his head. "A celebration cupcake does sound pretty good."

"Eating it naked in bed with you would make it better."

"Yeah, but you'll be busy typing the reports for the department and the DA," Sawyer said.

Royce leaned forward and pressed a quick kiss to his lips. "Delayed gratification on all counts."

"At least we'll have cake samples to tide us over." Sawyer returned Royce's gesture, but he lingered longer and teased him with the barest hint of tongue.

"Maybe I could extend my break a little longer," Royce offered.

Sawyer chuckled and pushed open his door. "Come on. We don't want to keep Sherry waiting."

Royce scrambled out of the SUV and caught up to Sawyer before reaching for the door. "What's Houser like?"

"He's an okay guy," Sawyer said. "I just think it's going to be impossible for him to climb out from under Wheeler's shadow. New leadership is still best." He smiled over at Royce. "No, I haven't changed my mind. Maybe someday, when I have different priorities, but right now—"

"Cake!" Royce cheered.

Grinning, Sawyer shook his head. "Among other things."

Royce held open the door for his love, then followed him inside the bakery. Royce smiled when he recognized the young lady behind the counter. It had taken him a few moments because she looked so different from the girl who'd sobbed in his arms because he'd shown her a little bit of kindness. Though he hadn't seen Abby since that evening, Royce thought of her and baby Noah often. Jason kept him updated, but talking to teenagers was like pulling teeth. The kid had a one-word answer for everything. To him, Abby and Noah were fine or good. And that was that.

Abby's cheeks no longer looked hollow, and her skin and hair were both vibrant, so he could see Jason had been right. Abby was indeed doing fine.

Royce smiled as he approached the counter. "It's so good to see you. I didn't know you were working here."

"Hi, Royce," Abby said. "Um, this is just my second week at the bakery." She smiled and blushed, shifting her gaze between Royce and Sawyer.

"This is my fiancé, Sawyer Key," Royce said. "Sawyer, this is Abby."

Sawyer extended his hand, and Abby shook it, staring up at him with an awed expression Royce couldn't begrudge. "It's nice to meet you. I've heard all about you from Jason and Royce."

*All about you?* Did Jason give Sawyer more than one-word answers? He loved the idea of them bonding but wasn't sure how he felt about Sawyer sweeping in and becoming everyone's favorite uncle.

Sherry Rigby breezed out of the kitchen and greeted them with warm hugs and a smile. "I'm so honored you want me to design a wedding cake for you." She worried her bottom lip with her teeth for a few seconds. "But are you sure? I don't make the fancy cakes you see on shows and in magazines."

"We're not looking for fancy," Sawyer told her. "We have something a little less traditional in mind."

Sherry gestured to a door with a sign that read Consultations. "I'm intrigued."

Royce fell in behind Sherry and Sawyer but paused at the threshold. He half turned so he could look at Abby. "You going to be around a little longer? I'd like to catch up."

The young lady nodded. "Until the bakery closes at seven."

Royce winked and headed inside the bubble gum pink room with Sawyer and Sherry.

"Welcome to my broom closet," Sherry teased. "Maybe I should've opted for a slightly bigger space."

"This is fine," Royce assured her as he took a seat beside Sawyer. The chairs were so close their knees knocked against each other as they tucked in under the table. He looked at the framed posters of cakes and pastries on the walls and started to salivate.

Sherry opened a notebook and pulled a pen out of her apron pocket. "So, what do you have in mind?"

Sawyer leaned into Royce, bumping their shoulders together. "Tiers of cupcakes and pastries."

Sherry pulled a binder off the shelf and opened it to the middle. "Something like this for the cupcakes?" she asked, showing them the image of a multitiered display. Beautifully decorated cupcakes lined the four bottom tiers, and a small cake sat on the top. "You have some options with this. You can cut the grooms' cake at the reception or freeze it and save it for your first anniversary. Cupcakes are for the guests, but you could feed them to each other if you want to save the cake."

Royce and Sawyer grinned at each other.

"This is exactly what we're looking for. It's simple and elegant," Sawyer said.

"And you'll make it exceptionally tasty too," Royce added.

Sherry smiled happily, then jotted a note in her book. "You could pick a variety of cupcake flavors and either alternate the layers or mix and match throughout the tiers. The grooms' cake can be one of the cupcake flavors, or a combination of them, or something completely special just for the two of you. And I'll do smaller displays with the pastries and tuck fresh cut flowers among the tiers to dress it up and tie everything together."

"Sounds amazing," Sawyer said.

Royce rubbed his hands together. "When do we get to the tasting part?"

Sherry laughed and stood up. "I'll go get a variety of cupcakes and pastries for you to sample so we can narrow down the flavor profile for your desserts."

Once alone, Royce reached up and carded his fingers through Sawyer's hair. "This is happening."

Sawyer leaned in for a quick kiss. "Damn right it is."

Sherry returned with a heaping tray of desserts. "I don't expect you to sample everything now. You can take this stuff home and try it over the next few days."

Royce snorted. "I can hoover that up in a few hours." He snagged a bear claw off the plate and sank his teeth into it. He toasted Sherry with the pastry and raised the thumb on his free hand."

"Bear claws were a given," Sherry said, but she smiled and added the note.

They sampled pastries and cupcakes until they almost made themselves sick. They narrowed the flavors to red velvet, lemon chiffon, banana pudding, coconut, chocolate, and vanilla.

"What about the grooms' cake?" Sherry asked.

Royce looked at Sawyer and knew his expression was just as indecisive as his fiancé's.

"I can't," Sawyer said. "I love them all."

Royce looked at Sherry. "Baker's choice. Surprise us."

With an arched brow, she said, "Are you sure? I don't need a decision today."

"We're sure," Royce and Sawyer both said.

They pivoted to colors and the number of guests they anticipated.

"We don't have a headcount yet," Sawyer said, "but my mom is working on the invitations. We're planning an intimate gathering with our family, closest friends, and colleagues."

"Color doesn't matter to me, except I'd prefer to stay away from blush pink since that's a color in my brother's upcoming wedding," Royce said.

"No blush pink," Sherry said, making a note. "Why not keep it classic? We can do ivory roses. Perhaps a pop of gold sheen here or there to elevate it."

"Perfect," Royce and Sawyer said.

Sherry laughed. "You guys are too adorable for words. I'm so honored to be part of your special day."

Sawyer's phone rang. Since they were sitting so close, Royce saw Number One Mom pop up on the screen.

"You better answer," Royce said.

"Probably wants to chat about the press conference." Royce could tell by Sawyer's droll tone that he was ready to move past anything to do with Josiah Wheeler. "I'll just step outside and take this."

Once Sawyer left, Royce removed a folded piece of paper from his pocket and slid it to Sherry.

"What's this?" she asked.

Royce suddenly found it hard to speak. Too many emotions were swirling inside him, and they all seemed lodged in his throat. He swallowed hard and blew out a short breath. "It's a copy of my mom's chocolate cake recipe. I don't share it with anyone, and I only bake this cake for special occasions. I can't think of a single event more special than our wedding. I'd like…no, I'd *love* it if you could use this recipe for our grooms' cake. It'll be a lovely surprise for Sawyer, and I love the idea of honoring my mom on our big day."

Sherry's eyes filled with tears. She reached across the table and clasped his hands. "I'd be honored to make this cake for you. I promise I won't share the recipe with anyone or recreate it."

"I trust you."

Sherry released his hands and stood up. "I'll go box these up."

"Wait," Royce said, then snagged another pastry before she could leave. "I have room for one more."

He bit into the pastry and sighed with contentment as he tried to mentally process all that had transpired. He'd learned just before dinner that both Leo and Glen had been arraigned. They'd entered not guilty pleas and the judge had denied them bail. He'd also heard through the grapevine that the two men had squabbled to and from the courthouse, and the imagery helped lesson his dread for the hours of report writing to come. He'd gotten a jumpstart before dinner and stopped because they read like a screenplay instead of incident reports, but the sooner he finished, the sooner he'd get home to the sexy man who strolled into the room.

Sawyer dropped into his vacated chair. He shook his head and reached over to wipe the corner of Royce's mouth with his thumb. "I'm going to head over to my parents' house after you drop me off at my car."

"Everything okay with your folks?" Royce asked.

"Yeah," Sawyer said. "She wants to finalize the guest list and get the invitations out in the mail this weekend. She says she's not disappointed I decided not to run for sheriff, but—"

"Are you kidding me?" Royce asked. "Your reason for not running is because you want to become a father. You think she'd choose politics over more grandkids?"

Sawyer laughed. "Yeah, you're right. She's quite smitten with Aiden and dropping not-so-subtle hints about us giving her more babies to spoil."

Royce cupped Sawyer's face and kissed him. "See? You have nothing to worry about. Besides, you couldn't disappoint Evangeline if you tried."

"And I have no desire to test your theory," Sawyer said.

Sherry returned with a pink bakery box. "Here you go. Just give me a call about the pastries you want me to make."

"We will," Royce said, accepting the box. They each hugged her before stepping into the main part of the bakery. Royce handed the box to Sawyer and said, "Get Evangeline and Courtney's opinions. Do you mind if I chat with Abby for a few minutes?"

"Of course not." Sawyer's phone rang again. "It's Felix. He probably just wants my reaction to the Wheeler news. I'll distract him with an update on the Andrea Dodd case. I'm going to step outside again."

Royce walked over to the counter and propped an elbow on the display case. "How's it going, kiddo?"

"Much better than last time," she said. "Noah sleeps through the night now, and that's helped a lot."

"I bet he's growing like a weed. Got any pictures with you?"

Abby pulled her phone out of her apron pocket, tapped the screen a few times, and handed it to Royce. She pulled up an album titled Noah. There were hundreds of pictures of the little guy cataloging his first months of life. The last picture on the roll included the last people Royce expected to see. Benji McKay cradled Noah, and his parents sat on either side of him, smiling down at the sleeping infant.

Royce handed the phone back to her. "He's adorable, Abby."

Her smile was luminous. "I love him so much. Thank you, Royce."

"For what?" he asked.

"Everything, but especially talking me out of making rash decisions. I wasn't in the right state of mind to decide what to wear, let alone decide Noah's future." She reached up and tucked her hair behind her ear. "I'm sure you didn't miss the picture of Noah with the McKays."

"I saw it. How's that going?"

"Really good," Abby said. "Um, Benji and I aren't dating or anything, but finding out Ian had killed Rachel threw Benji for a loop. He grew up fast. He came to see me and said he'd changed his mind about giving Noah up. By then, I had changed my mind too. We formed a truce, and he introduced us to his parents."

"How'd that go?" Royce asked.

"They were as shocked as you can imagine, but one look at Noah and he had them wrapped around his little finger. Mrs. McKay watches Noah when I work. She also helped me enroll in summer classes at the college. Sometimes our personalities clash, but she just wants what's best for Noah. I keep that in mind, even when I'm standing my ground on an issue."

"Such as?"

"Preschool. Mrs. McKay already wants to enroll him because the waiting list to get in is so long."

"Wow," Royce said, suddenly feeling nervous about the parenting thing.

"Right? I told her I don't want to send Noah to some stuffy preschool that will make me feel like a loser because I don't drive a Mercedes."

"What did she say?" Royce asked.

Abby snickered and rolled her eyes. "She asked me what color I wanted. I told her no way, but we compromised."

"On the school?" Royce asked.

Abby nodded. "And on a more reliable car for me. I refused to drive a new luxury car, so she bought me a used Subaru."

"Highest safety ratings," Royce said.

"Exactly. And I do love it."

"What about Benji's dad?"

"Noah has Mr. McKay smitten too," Abby said. "Benji said he didn't know his dad even knew how to smile. Mrs. McKay waved that off, but even she seemed stunned."

"And how are your parents handling the situation?" Royce recalled Jason saying they were prideful and stubborn.

"Better. I think the McKays' generosity stings their pride a little, but they suck it up for Noah and me."

The bells over the door jingled, and a group of teenagers walked in. They all greeted Abby, and she waved at them.

"I won't keep you." Royce backed away so the new customers could step up. "Don't be a stranger, okay?"

Abby smiled and nodded before shifting her attention to the people at the counter. When Royce reached the door, he heard one of them asking to see the latest pictures of Noah.

Sawyer was leaning against the SUV and talking on his phone. Both his posture and expression were relaxed as he chatted with Felix. Sawyer looked up as he drew near and smiled.

"I gotta go," Sawyer said as he got into the vehicle. "I'll keep you posted if I hear back from Andrea." He listened for a second and said, "Later, man."

Royce climbed behind the steering wheel and shut the door. "You didn't have to hang up on my account."

Sawyer waggled his brows. "I have other things I want to use my mouth for right now."

"Yeah?" Royce asked hopefully.

"Not while you're driving."

Royce fired up the engine and drove Sawyer to the Hummingbird Café. Once in the parking lot, they made out like teenagers, and Sawyer promised more delights when he got home later. He wasn't sure which was harder—his dick or watching Sawyer drive away knowing it would be hours before he got home. Royce decided he would break a world record for speed writing the reports, but then he glanced over at an intersection and saw Eddie's Harley parked outside one of his favorite haunts. When the light changed, Royce turned instead of going straight and pulled up behind the motorcycle.

What he was about to do was dangerous and foolish, but he didn't care. Eddie might be the only person who could talk some sense into Benton, and Royce had to try. He felt every pair of eyes on him as he walked through the seedy bar. The stench of stale beer and cigarettes soured his stomach. Smoking had been banned for a long time, but the odor still lingered on everything. He found his old man seated in the back with a scantily clad biker chick in his lap. His dad had one meaty hand on her thigh and the other on a large breast.

"Well, well, well," Eddie said, squeezing the woman's flesh. "If it ain't the prodigal son returning to his roots."

Royce stopped a few feet from the tableau. "I'm not your son, prodigal or otherwise."

Eddie turned his head and spat tobacco onto the floor. "What the hell do you want?" Eddie's brusque tone caught the attention of the people around them, and a few of the guys ambled closer. Royce kept them in his periphery, adjusting his angle to make sure none of them came up on his blind side.

"To talk about Benton. Step outside with me."

"Why can't we talk here?" Eddie asked as he slid his hand down the woman's torso to toy with the button on her cutoff jeans. "Does this place offend your delicate sensibilities?"

"You're not going to goad me into a fight, Eddie. If you give a flying fuck about the only one of your kids willing to speak to you, you'll follow me outside."

Royce pivoted, nodded at Eddie's buddies, and headed outside. He gratefully sucked fresh air into his lungs, vowing to give his dad no more than five minutes to follow him. Surprisingly, it only took Eddie three minutes to pry himself away from Biker Barbie and lumber out the door.

"What's this about?" Eddie demanded.

"Benton is part of the crew responsible for the recent armed robberies."

If Royce hadn't been watching Eddie closely, he would've missed the slight tightening around his mouth and eyes. "I don't know what you're talking about."

"Shut the fuck up and listen. This only ends one of two ways, Eddie. They either get arrested or die in a shootout with the police or a trigger-happy citizen. There is no blaze of glory here, just dead people and shattered lives. Benton needs to turn himself in before it's too late. They'll go easier on him if he does."

"Bullshit. The cops will want to make Benton their snitch. He'll be dead either way. Is that all you want? My lady is waiting on me."

"Wow," Royce said dryly. "And I thought you couldn't possibly sink any lower."

Eddie advanced on him with his index finger pointing at Royce's face. "This isn't on me. I told him to stay away from those—" Eddie stopped suddenly when he realized he'd nearly slipped up and told Royce who Benton was running with. "I tried to talk some sense into him, but he wasn't interested in what I had to say. Just like the rest of you. Jace didn't even invite me to his wedding. Dru and the boys are moving out."

"Maybe you should think about why that is," Royce said.

Eddie narrowed his eyes. "Why are your lips swollen? Were you sucking cock before you arrived?"

Unwilling to let Eddie ruin his good mood, Royce shook his head and headed to his SUV. "Don't knock it until you try it."

Then he used Sawyer's dirty promises as motivation to get his work done so he could go home and live them out.

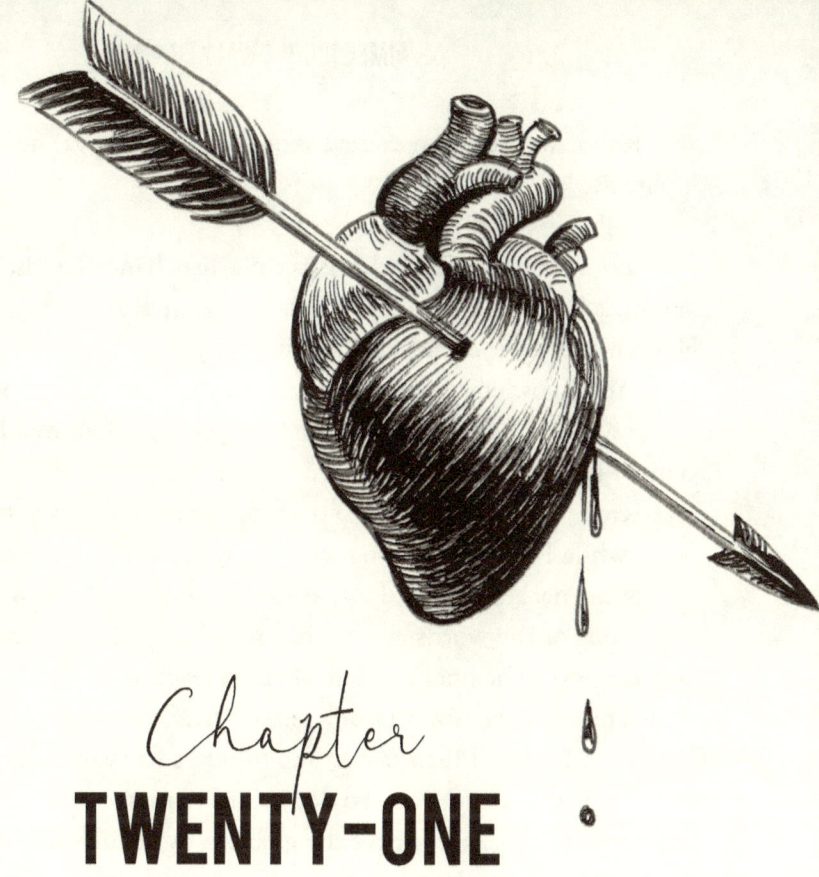

*Chapter*
# TWENTY-ONE

**S**AWYER PUT THE FINAL PLATE IN THE DISHWASHER AND STARTED it. He lifted his wineglass and said, "Here's to the end of a successful week. You and Tara solved a complicated murder investigation with a twist, and I, along with our friends, helped to reunite a family."

Sawyer had been buzzing on an energy high for hours after Beverly had called to let him know Andrea had reached out and was flying in to see her on Sunday. Andrea's husband couldn't get away yet, so he and their children were arriving midweek. Beverly had wept and thanked him profusely. Sawyer was humbled by her praise and hoped the team had more positive outcomes in the future.

Royce smiled and clinked his beer bottle to the glass. "And here's to the start of my vacation week where we will help Dru and the boys move into their new place, and I will assume my official duties as best man."

"So maybe take off your service weapon and stay a while."

Royce had been too excited about the feast Sawyer made to make it past the kitchen.

"I'll drink to that," Royce said.

Just as they started to drink, the playlist changed to the next song, and Elvis Presley's "Suspicious Minds" came on. Royce snagged Sawyer's glass and set their drinks on the counter.

"You know what this means," Royce said, extending his hand.

Sawyer slid his fingers through Royce's and followed him to the center of the kitchen. "We dance."

Royce pulled Sawyer into his arms, and they slowly swayed in a circle while Royce sang along with the lyrics. Sawyer pressed his lips to Royce's neck and kissed a sensuous path up to his jaw, feeling the vibrations of the words against his mouth. He didn't want Royce to stop singing, so he hooked a left when he reached his stubbled jaw and trailed his affection toward a different target. Sawyer sank his teeth into Royce's earlobe. His man gasped and missed a few words but continued singing. Royce's hands roamed downward to rest on the upper swell of Sawyer's ass cheeks. He gave the globes a tight squeeze and kept his hands there for the duration of the song. An eighties power ballad came on next, and they continued to dance, but Royce put his lips to better use, kissing Sawyer until he was dizzy with need.

"What do you say we record *Dateline* and take this to the bedroom?" Royce asked.

"Hell yes." Sawyer started to lead Royce to the bedroom but saw Bones watching them from his perch. There was a particularly wicked gleam in the beast's eyes, and Sawyer knew he was up to something, but what? Then Sawyer recalled what he'd prepared for dinner and the detritus left in the trash can. He halted suddenly and leaned closer to Royce. "Our cat is planning to raid the trash for chicken bones the moment we're distracted."

Royce followed his gaze and chuckled. "I can't blame him, but he'll be disappointed. I licked them clean, not a morsel left. That was absolutely the best chicken I've ever eaten." Royce narrowed his eyes. "But there will be hell to pay if you ever tell Evangeline I said so."

Sawyer mimed zipping his lips before heading to the trash can to spoil his feline's diabolical plans. After he tied off the bag and pulled it free, Sawyer said, "I'll meet you in the bedroom." He started to reach for his earbuds on the counter, but Royce stopped him.

"Huh-uh," he said. "If you fire up the next chapter in your audio-book, you'll lose interest in me."

Sawyer snorted. "Name a time that's ever happened."

"There's a first time for everything."

"Never going to happen," Sawyer called out over his shoulder on his way to the door.

Even though they'd gotten a late start on dinner, Sawyer was some-how surprised to see darkness had descended on their quiet neighbor-hood. He chuckled at his thoughts, thinking he was starting to sound like a Keith Morrison sound bite. Nah, Sawyer would need to embel-lish it a lot more than that. Various adjectives cycled through his brain as he lifted the lid on the trash bin, but he dismissed them as too or-dinary. He'd managed to compare the damp air to a saturated sponge and the darkness to an ominous blanket when the hair on the back of his neck stood up. Sawyer wanted to blame the reaction on his overac-tive imagination, but dismissing one's instincts was how a person often ended up the subject of a Keith Morrison report.

So why did he ignore his instinct to run back inside when his sen-tience grew stronger?

Because he was done running.

Adrenaline pumped through his veins, threatening to dull his senses. Sawyer took a calming breath to remain in control. Who was it? Wheeler again? Benton? Sawyer closed the trash can lid and decided to face the ambush head-on, but the scuffling of soles on concrete nearby told him he might be too late. He'd managed to turn enough to see a figure clad in dark clothes lunging at him. Moonlight glinted off a metal object as it swung toward his head. Sawyer ducked in the nick of time and felt the whoosh of the thing as it sailed past him. The blunt object smashed into the brick over his head with a tremendous crack, and an explosion of jagged clay shards cut the side of Sawyer's face.

The neighbor's dog, a lab named Katie, barked loudly and fero-ciously, and the other neighborhood dogs joined her. The noise wasn't enough to drown out his attacker as he roared and reared back to take another swing. Sawyer bull-rushed in his direction, plowing his shoulder into his assailant's chest and driving him to the ground. The blunt object, an aluminum bat based on the clanging sound it made when it hit the concrete, slipped from his attacker's grasp. The man was too small and wiry to be Wheeler, and he reeked of sweat and body odor. Sawyer knew he was grappling with Royce's younger brother, but the thought of going easy on him didn't even cross Sawyer's mind. He only cared about surviving.

Benton drove his knee up and nailed Sawyer's nuts. Black dots exploded in Sawyer's vision, and he momentarily lost his breath. Benton took advantage and rolled Sawyer onto his back, climbed up his body, and pinned Sawyer's arms down with his knees. Benton might've been slender, but he was strong. Narcotics and rage would make him lethal if Sawyer didn't use his best weapon—his brain. Sawyer's stomach cramped, and bile rocketed up his throat, warning him he was close to losing his dinner. He didn't want to choke to death on his own vomit. Benton's added weight on his chest made it hard to breathe, but he continued to fight.

Sawyer bucked, trying to knock Benton off-balance and free his arms, but to no avail. The tweaker only doubled down, wrapping his hands around Sawyer's neck and squeezing. Benton leaned close and laughed. Sawyer refused to believe his was the last face he'd see before death or his foul breath the final smell.

"Dad said Royce had a message for me," Benton said. "And now I have one for him." Benton squeezed harder and dots danced in front of Sawyer's eyes. He was running out of time to act. Sawyer jerked his head forward and rammed his forehead into Benton's nose. The crack sounded as loud as the bat hitting the brick wall. Benton screamed as blood spurted from his nose and sprayed Sawyer's face and neck, but at least he'd released Sawyer.

Bucking with all his might, Sawyer managed to dislodge Benton from his chest just as the floodlights came on and Royce burst out of the house with his gun drawn. He drove his knee into Benton's lower back, pinning him to the ground, and jammed the gun into the back of his brother's head.

"How does it feel to have a gun to your head, little brother?" Royce pushed even harder. "I should do everyone a favor and pull the trigger."

"No," Sawyer pleaded, his weak, scratchy voice drowned out by Katie's continuous barking. Where the hell were her owners? He tried to get up to help Royce, but the world spun sickeningly fast. He vomited onto the concrete and collapsed again. His lungs still felt like someone was sitting on them, and he realized he was having an anxiety attack.

Royce must've sensed his struggle because he holstered his gun and removed his cuffs instead. He quickly secured Benton's wrists and left him to check on Sawyer. Before he could say anything, their neighbor yelled over to see what was going on. *Finally.*

"Call 911, Bill," Royce yelled. "Tell them an officer is down." Royce's phone was still on the counter where he'd placed it when he'd started the mood music for dinner. "Don't you dare die on me, asshole. You owe me more dances, and a wedding, and babies. And *Dateline* looks especially intriguing tonight." Sawyer would've laughed if he could have. "You promised me forever, Sawyer. I'm holding you to it. Please don't leave me."

Sawyer realized Royce had seen his bloody face and the aluminum bat nearby and jumped to the wrong conclusion. Sawyer still struggled to draw a full breath into his lungs, but he managed to say, "Not my blood" before passing out.

"Are you sure he doesn't need to go to the hospital?" Royce asked in the back of the ambulance parked in their driveway. "He fainted from his injuries."

"I didn't faint," Sawyer grumbled. "I blacked out and only for a few seconds."

Royce looked away from Beth, the EMT, and scowled at Sawyer. "What's the difference?"

"Fainting is for gentle ladies upon seeing a naked man for the first time." Sawyer waggled his brows, hoping to ease the frown lines marring Royce's handsome face. "I've seen plenty of naked men."

Royce rolled his eyes and returned his attention to Beth. "He's clearly suffering from head trauma or lack of oxygen to his brain if he's attempting to make jokes at a time like this."

She shook her head. "You washed his face, and we both inspected his head for signs of injury. He just has minor abrasions on one cheek. His pupils look good, and he's coherent. No labored breathing. Pretty sure Sergeant Key got his bell rung at the other end."

Sawyer's hand automatically moved to shield his aching balls. Royce's menacing scowl turned into a sympathetic wince, but the pardon didn't last long.

"I've been at this for a long time," Beth said. "A bag of frozen peas for his boys, and he'll be right as rain in no time." She smiled over at Sawyer and patted his shoulder. "Maybe work on the timing of your jokes, doll."

Sawyer slowly eased off the gurney. "Yeah, I'll try." His nuts felt like they weighed ten pounds each, and he might've faceplanted on the concrete if not for Royce's help getting down. Sawyer gingerly walked toward their house, knowing he looked as bowlegged as a cowboy after a week on the range.

Once alone in the house, Royce pulled Sawyer into his arms, buried his head in Sawyer's neck, and burst into tears. Sawyer was at a loss for words, at least the right ones, and simply stroked Royce's hair.

"I'm okay, baby. You heard Beth. My boys will be back in fighting shape in no time."

Royce laughed through his tears and pulled back to look into Sawyer's eyes. "I wondered what was taking you so long. I started to think one of your thirsty new fans nabbed you or something."

"You really need to stop reading those comments."

"But it was so much worse," Royce said. "I saw you on the ground with blood all over your face. And the bat…" Royce groaned. "Benton told me he came to kill you. He was watching us through the windows, biding his time. You took out the trash and he…he…"

"Got his nose broken for his effort," Sawyer said, leaning his forehead against Royce's. "I won't pretend there weren't some scary seconds, but Benton was the only thing standing between me and the future I want with you. There was no way he was going to win."

Royce took some shaky breaths. "Don't expect me to turn you loose anytime soon."

Sawyer pressed a tender kiss to his trembling lips. "Fine by me. Let's grab some ice cream, cuddle, and watch our show."

True to his word, Royce kept his hold on Sawyer while they retrieved two pints of ice cream and a bag of frozen peas.

"Guess this puts a damper on our bedroom shenanigans for a few days," Sawyer said.

Royce snorted. "Your hands aren't injured."

Sawyer threw his head back and laughed. "There's my guy."

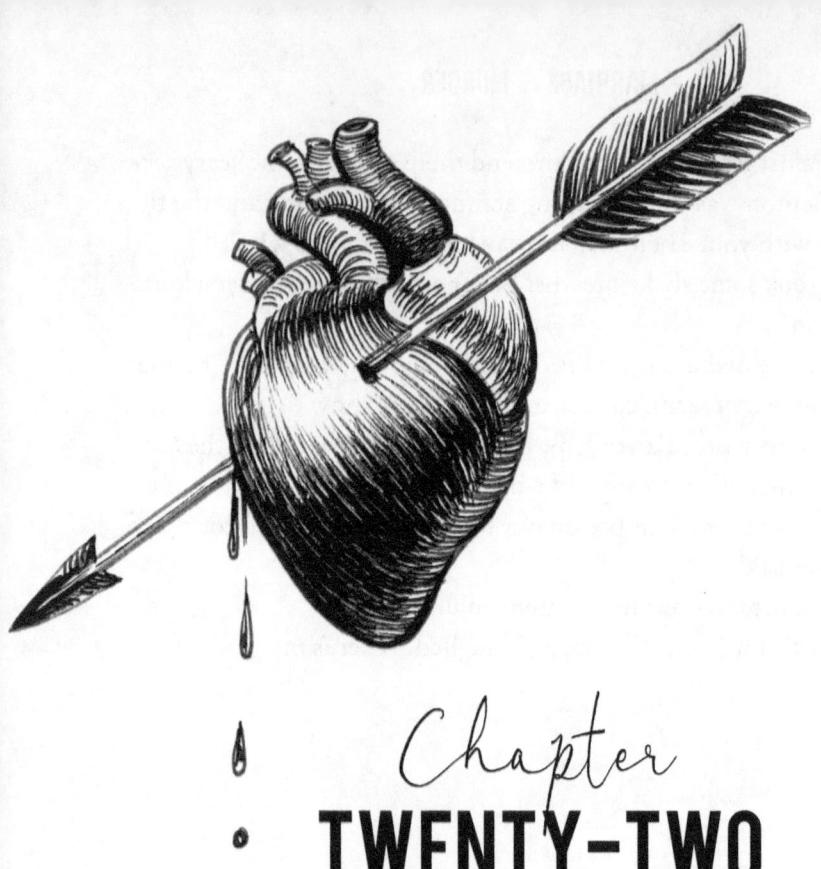

*Chapter*

# TWENTY-TWO

B Y SUNDAY, ROYCE STILL HADN'T RECOVERED FROM HIS ROLLER-coaster week. He'd woken feeling battered and raw until Sawyer rolled him to his back and made him feel well-loved and thoroughly used in the best possible way. A lazy brunch in bed with his tousled and sated man had given him the energy boost required to help Dru, Jared, and Jason move into their new townhouse. Their energy was palpable and kept his drive going through multiple trips up and down steps and back and forth from his SUV to his father's house.

Holly and Jace had met them at Eddie's. Royce took one look at their desolate expressions and whipped-puppy body language and knew they'd also visited Benton. Royce had gone Saturday afternoon when the worst of Benton's withdrawals had eased. Royce hadn't recognized the lifeless husk sitting across the table from him. His skin had been an unhealthy gray and his eyes were sunken and hollow. Royce had hoped Benton would be willing to listen to reason, but he couldn't tell if he'd even comprehended a single word. His younger brother had kept his gaze averted and refused to speak to him.

Holly kissed Royce's cheek and headed inside to lend a hand, and Jace crossed his arms over his chest and leaned against the side of Royce's SUV.

"Don't just stand there," he said, pointing to all the boxes on the overgrown lawn.

Jace sighed and retrieved a stack of three boxes. He dropped them unceremoniously in the SUV, earning a scowl from Royce until he saw just how heartbroken Jace was.

"You go to see Benton?"

"Last night," Jace replied.

Royce patted his brother's shoulder. "You guys didn't have better luck?"

Jace shook his head. "He wouldn't say a word to us. I don't know what it will take for him to see he has no choice but to cooperate with the police."

Royce sighed. "We can't make him do the right thing. We tried our best, J. That's what we've always done." The truth of his words lanced deep, severing the chains that tied him to a past he hadn't asked for or wanted.

Jace hooked an arm around Royce and leaned into him. "I know. It just sucks when your best isn't good enough."

"But is that really on us?"

The familiar rumble of an approaching Harley Davidson drowned out Jace's reply.

"Just fucking great," Jace said when Eddie killed the motorcycle engine, swung his leg over, and swaggered over like his balls weighed ten pounds each. Jace took two steps forward but stopped when their father put both hands up in surrender.

"I'm not here to cause any trouble," Eddie said.

Royce shouldered past Jace and didn't stop until he was nearly in his father's face.

"Did you send Benton to our home to kill Sawyer?"

"God no," Eddie said. "I don't understand your attraction, and I still think it's unnatural, but I didn't send Benton over there to hurt your man."

"His name is Sawyer," Royce said tersely.

"Okay, then. I didn't want him to hurt Sawyer. I only did what you asked me to. I told Benton he needed to turn himself in and work with the police. Benton freaked out and stormed out of the bar. I had no idea he was heading over to your house." Eddie dropped his hands to his sides. "Look, I just came from talking to Benton. He's agreed to cooperate with the police. I waited with him until the detectives arrived. An Asian guy and a stocky older white guy that looked like a detective on *NYPD Blue*."

Royce knew a thank-you was in order, but he'd rather choke on the words first.

"Look," Eddie said. "I'm man enough to admit this entire situation is my fault. I know I wasn't the daddy you needed growing up, and I'll never be the kind of man my children respect." He nodded to Dru's toolbox with a pink bow affixed on top. "I did teach you some valuable lessons." He grinned slyly and added, "Even if most of them were things *not* to do. Then again, maybe that's why you boys are better men than I'll ever be. I don't suppose I'll be hearing a thank-you anytime soon."

Royce and Jace spoke simultaneously. The former telling Eddie not to hold his breath and the latter uttered a terse "Hell no."

Movement in his periphery made Royce turn his head. Sawyer walked down the steps carrying two large boxes. He glanced in Eddie's direction but kept his attention on Royce, trying to gauge his emotions. Sawyer placed the boxes in the back of the SUV and faced the standoff.

"Everything okay?"

Eddie stepped forward with his hand extended to Sawyer. "We've never met, but I'm Eddie Locke."

Sawyer shook his hand. "Sawyer Key."

"I'll get out of everyone's hair," Eddie said, stepping back. "Tell Dru to leave the keys in the mailbox. I'll get them later."

Royce should've told him to go in the house and tell her himself, but he was still too stunned to speak. Eddie climbed onto his Harley, gave them a two-fingered salute, then fired up his beast and drove off.

"What the fuck just happened here?" Jace asked once the loud re-verberations quieted.

"I'm pretty sure Eddie apologized for being a shitty parent and praised us for being good men," Royce said.

He and Jace stared at each other for a few heartbeats. Mirroring wry smiles pulled at their lips.

"Nah," they both said at the same time.

Holly came to the front door and called Jace into the house to help her with something, leaving Royce and Sawyer alone.

"I know your dad is a douche, but—"

"Don't say it," Royce said.

"He's really fucking hot."

"Oh god, you said it," Royce moaned. "I recognize that gleam in your eye, but I'm terrified to even consider what it might mean."

Sawyer leaned closer. "Just hear me out. You in your riding leathers, me with a well-lubed ass leaning over the sexy Harley currently parked in our garage. What do you say?"

Royce snagged him by the belt loop and tugged him closer for a quick kiss. "It's about damn time I get you on that bike."

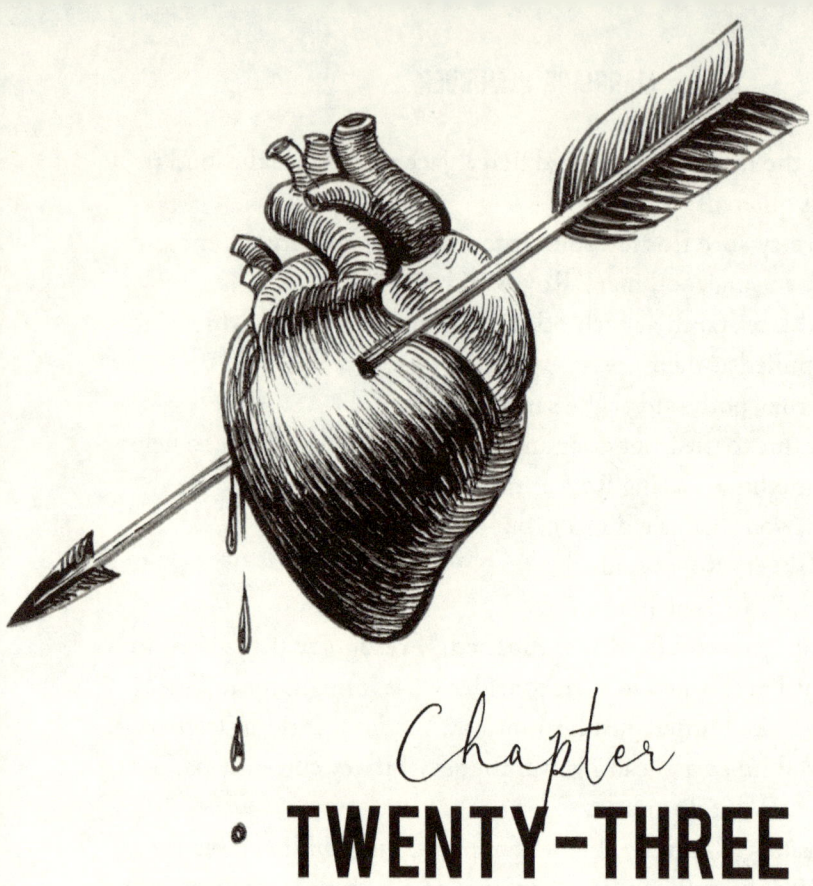

*Chapter*
# TWENTY-THREE

ROYCE STOOD OUTSIDE THE DOOR TO THE GROOM'S SUITE AT THE Ships of the Sea Maritime Museum and wiped his eyes. "Pull yourself together," he whispered. Royce blew out a shaky breath and opened the door. Jace, who'd been checking his appearance in the mirror for the umpteenth time, caught Royce's reflection and spun around. A look of pure panic seized his big brother's features.

"Oh god. Did Holly change her mind? Please tell me my girl is here."

Royce wrapped his arms around his brother and hugged him tightly. "You're a fucking idiot."

Jace pulled back and stared at him. "Yeah, but am I a fucking idiot about to get stood up at the altar?"

"These tears aren't about you," Royce said. "I've just come from seeing my best friend on her wedding day, and I'm all up in my feelings."

Jace smiled. "Bet she's the most beautiful bride you've ever seen."

"Without a doubt," Royce said.

He didn't know what type of dress she wore, but it was ivory lace with pearls and sparkly things strategically placed. She'd pulled her dark hair back from her face and left her curls cascading down her back. Sawyer and Royce had bought her a pair of pearl and diamond earrings for her special day, and Royce had loved seeing them on her. He'd burst into tears, and Holly had first made sure Jace hadn't run away, then she'd laughed at Royce's emotional outburst.

"You guys don't need all the fairy lights in the garden trees or in the reception pavilion. Holly is glowing bright enough to illuminate the city."

"I can't wait to see her," Jace said.

"Glad you feel that way because it's showtime, big brother."

Royce turned and headed for the door, but Jace called his name. Royce turned around, and Jace plowed into him, hugging Royce tightly.

"Thank you for being my best man and the best brother a guy could ask for."

Royce cupped his brother's face and grinned. "No place I'd rather be today than beside my hero."

"Shit," Jace hissed. "Here come the waterworks."

"Wait until you see Holly, bro." Royce clapped him on the shoulder. "Come on. Let's go get you hitched."

The two of them took one last glance in the mirror before exiting the room and heading out to the grounds. They went out a side entrance and walked around to the venue. A hush fell over the guests when they appeared from the side of the garden and joined the minister. Moments later, the opening strains of classical music began, and the first bridesmaid appeared on the terrace at the back of the lush garden. She carefully made her way down the steps and followed the pathway toward the altar. When she was midway down the walk, the next bridesmaid appeared. Finally, Candy, the maid of honor, stepped out onto the terrace looking stunning in her blush pink dress. Royce couldn't help but glance over at Tara and smiled at the gobsmacked expression on her face.

Candy waited at the bottom of the steps because Daniel and Bailey were the ring bearer and flower girl, and she wanted to make sure they didn't stumble. Candy leaned over and kissed them both before she headed toward the altar. The kids waited a few minutes as they'd rehearsed the previous night, then slowly followed their mom. Bailey was nearly out of flowers before she even reached the seated section, but she hammed it up for her audience when they started down the aisle. Daniel came to stand with Royce, and Bailey ran to her mom, handing the last flower in the basket to her.

The music changed to the bridal chorus and Holly appeared at the terrace door with her dad.

"Oh my god," Jace whispered.

"Indeed," the minister said.

Royce glanced over at Jace in time to catch the first tears spill down his face. Royce reached inside his suit jacket, removed a handkerchief, and handed it to Jace. Too bad he hadn't packed one for himself. Sawyer leaned forward from the front row and gave him one, and Royce winked to thank him.

It seemed like it took forever for Holly to reach Jace, and his brother was a bundle of nerves when Holly placed her hands in his and they faced each other.

"Ladies and gentleman," the minister said in a warm voice, "we are gathered here today to witness the marriage between Holly Rebecca Stein and Jason Michael Locke."

The ceremony itself was sweet and simple. The reverend had a great sense of humor and timing and didn't drag it out like some did. Royce was charmed when Jace's voice cracked while reciting his vows. Holly cupped his face and wiped his tears with her thumb. Jace leaned into her touch, took a deep breath, and continued. When the reverend pronounced them married and instructed Jace to kiss his bride, Jace dipped Holly low and planted one on her amid the cheers and clapping of their guests.

The pavilion was decked out with white bunting and thousands of fairy lights. Royce was seated with the wedding party while Sawyer sat at a nearby table with Royce's uncle Jerry and aunt Sheila, Drusilla, Jason, and Jared. Dru was leaning her head against Sawyer's shoulder, laughing at something he said, and Royce gave her a playful glare to warn her off. Dru held both hands up in the air and straightened in her chair.

The food was delicious, but Royce didn't eat much because he was nervous about giving his speech. He knew everyone would expect him to get up there and crack jokes, and maybe he would have if he hadn't fallen in love with Sawyer and understood what this night meant to Holly and Jace. When someone clanked their fork against their champagne glass, Royce took a deep breath and rose to his feet. The emcee handed him a microphone and Royce greeted the crowd.

"I rewrote this speech a billion times this week, trying to find the right words to honor Jace and Holly. And I want to start by thanking you both. Jace, thank you for showing me what courage and character look like. I'm honored to call you my brother and stand beside you on your wedding day." Jace's lips trembled, and Royce pointed at him. "Don't you start. Let me get through this, bro." Jace laughed and wiped his eyes. "And Holly," Royce managed before she burst into tears. Jace wrapped his arm around his wife and kissed her temple, whispering something in her ear that was just for them. "You are the personification of patience and loyalty and unyielding love. You've always been the sister of my heart, and now you are my sister in name." Royce held up his glass of champagne. "I wish you a lifetime of joy, laughter, good health, and immeasurable love. To Jace and Holly!"

"To Jace and Holly!" the guests repeated.

Candy stood up and wowed everyone with a beautiful poem she'd written. Royce bit back a chuckle watching Tara's enamored expression.

After the speeches, the emcee called the bride and groom out onto the dance floor. Royce couldn't even say what song they danced to, but it didn't matter. The bride and groom appeared to be floating on air as everyone watched in awe. When the song ended, Holly danced with her father, and Aunt Sheila filled in for their mother, dancing with Jace. Royce wondered what their mom would think, but he didn't have to ponder for long. She'd be over the moon for Holly and Jace. Royce didn't often think about eternity and the afterlife, but if there was a heaven, he was confident his mother and Aunt Tipsy had excellent seats for the wedding.

Jace hugged Aunt Sheila when the song ended, and they headed off the dance floor.

The emcee announced it was time to get the party started and played a bass-thumping song that got most of the partygoers out on the dance floor. Royce didn't consider himself a great dancer, but he sure as hell loved any excuse to be close to his man. He rose from the wedding party table and walked over to Sawyer. After hugging his family, Royce extended a hand to Sawyer.

"Dance with me?" he asked.

"Always."

They hit the floor and stayed there for hours, dancing, laughing, and singing along to the songs they knew. When the next slow song came on, Royce pulled Sawyer into his arms and pressed a long kiss to his lips.

"You know, I realized something recently," Royce said.

"What's that?"

Royce scanned the pavilion and smiled as he watched the people he loved celebrating and having fun. "My family is pretty awesome."

Sawyer smiled. "I agree. I can't wait to claim them as my own."

Royce rubbed his nose against Sawyer's. "I've spent the past few years thinking I need to rid myself of the Locke curse, but there's no such thing. A few bad apples haven't spoiled the bunch. There's nothing I need to rid myself of."

"Maybe your suit when we get home," Sawyer said.

"That's a given."

"Hey, you two," Holly said as she and Jace danced up beside them. "Maybe dial it down a little bit. You're showing us up at our own wedding." The twinkle in her eyes said she loved every minute of seeing them so happy.

"We'll get even at your wedding, you know," Jace teased as he spun Holly around and danced her in the other direction.

"Two more months until you're officially mine," Royce said.

"Baby, you had me at first glare."

To be continued in *Killer Honeymoon*…

Want to be the first to know about my book releases and have access to extra content? You can sign up for my newsletter here: eepurl.com/dlhPYj

My favorite place to hang out and chat with my readers is my Facebook group. Would you like to be a member of Aimee's Dye Hards? We'd love to have you! Go here: www.facebook.com/groups/AimeesDyeHards

*Other Books by*
# AIMEE NICOLE WALKER

**Curl Up and Dye Mysteries**
*Dyeing to be Loved*
*Something to Dye For*
*Dyed and Gone to Heaven*
*I Do, or Dye Trying*
*A Dye Hard Holiday*
*Ride or Dye*

**Road to Blissville Series**
*Unscripted Love*
*Someone to Call My Own*
*Nobody's Prince Charming*
*This Time Around*
*Smoke in the Mirror*
*Inside Out*
*Prescription for Love*

**Welcome to Blissville Collection (Both M/M Blissville series)**
*Volume One*
*Volume Two*

**The Lady is Mine Series**
*The Lady is a Thief*
*The Lady Stole My Heart*

## Queen City Rogue Series
*Broken Halos*
*Wicked Games*
*Beautiful Trauma*

## Zero Hour Series
*Ground Zero*
*Devil's Hour*
*Zero Divergence*
*Zero Hour Box Set*

## Sawyer and Royce: Matrimony and Mayhem
*The Magnolia Murders*

## Sinister in Savannah Series
*Ride the Lightning*
*Mr. Perfect*
*Pretty Poison*

## Savannah Universe Standalone Books
*Invisible Strings*
*Bad at Love*

## Standalone Novels
*Second Wind*

## Fated Hearts Series
*Chasing Mr. Wright*
*Rhythm of Us*

## Coauthored with Nicholas Bella
*Undisputed*
*Circle of Darkness (Genesis Circle, Book 1)*
*Circle of Trust (Genesis Circle, Book 2)*

# ACKNOWLEDGMENTS

Many, many thanks to Susie Selva for her incredibly thorough edits and to Lori Parks for her keen eye during proofreading. These ladies are consummate professionals and are an absolute joy to work with. And much love to Jay Aheer and Wander Aguiar for this gorgeous cover and to Stacey Ryan Blake for her stunning interior designs. All of you make my books sparkle and shine so beautifully—inside and out. I thank my lucky stars that I get to work with such wonderfully talented people.

Many, many hugs to Melinda James Rueter and Racheal Yunk for bravely reading my rough drafts and providing priceless feedback. Love you, ladies!


xoxo
Aimee

*About*

# AIMEE NICOLE WALKER

Ever since she was a little girl, Aimee Nicole Walker entertained herself with stories that popped into her head. Now she gets paid to tell those stories to other people. She wears many titles—wife, mom, and animal lover are just a few of them. Her absolute favorite title is champion of the happily ever after. Love inspires everything she does, music keeps her sane, and coffee is the magic elixir that fuels her day.

She'd love to hear from you.

Want to connect? All her links are in one nifty location. Click here:
linktr.ee/AimeeNicoleWalker